# View from Another Shore

# Liverpool Science Fiction Texts and Studies

*General Editor* DAVID SEED

*Series Advisers*
I. F. CLARKE   EDWARD JAMES   PATRICK PARRINDER
AND BRIAN STABLEFORD

1. ROBERT CROSSLEY, *Olaf Stapledon: Speaking for the Future*, ISBN 0-85323-388-8 (hardback)
2. DAVID SEED (ed.), *Anticipations: Essays on Early Science Fiction and its Precursors*, ISBN 0-85323-348-9 (hardback), ISBN 0-85323-418-3 (paperback)
3. JANE L. DONAWERTH AND CAROL A. KOLMERTEN (ed.), *Utopian and Science Fiction by Women: Worlds of Difference*, ISBN 0-85323-269-5 (hardback), ISBN 0-85323-279-2 (paperback)
4. BRIAN W. ALDISS, *The Detached Retina: Aspects of SF and Fantasy*, ISBN 0-85323-289-X (hardback), 0-85323-299-7 (paperback)
5. CAROL FARLEY KESSLER, *Charlotte Perkins Gilman: Her Progress Toward Utopia, with Selected Writings*, ISBN 0-85323-489-2 (hardback), ISBN 0-85323-499-X (paperback)
6. PATRICK PARRINDER, *Shadows of the Future: H. G. Wells, Science Fiction and Prophecy*, ISBN 0-85323-439-6 (hardback), ISBN 0-85323-449-3 (paperback)
7. I. F. CLARKE (ed.), *The Tale of the Next Great War, 1871–1914: Fictions of Future Warfare and of Battles Still-to-come*, ISBN 0-85323-459-0 (hardback), ISBN 0-85323-469-8 (paperback)
8. JOSEPH CONRAD AND FORD MADOX FORD, Foreword by George Hay, Introduction by David Seed, *The Inheritors*, ISBN 0-85323-560-0 (hardback)
9. QINGYUN WU, *Female Rule in Chinese and English Literary Utopias*, ISBN 0-85323-570-8 (hardback), 0-85323-580-5 (paperback)
10. JOHN CLUTE, *Look at the Evidence: Essays and Reviews*, ISBN 0-85323-820-0 (hardback), 0-85323-830-8 (paperback)
11. ROGER LUCKHURST, *'The Angle Between Two Walls': The Fiction of J. G. Ballard*, ISBN 0-85323-821-9 (hardback), 0-85323-831-6 (paperback)
12. I. F. CLARKE (ed.) *The Great War with Germany, 1890–1914: Fictions and Fantasies of the War-to-come*, ISBN 0-85323-632-1 (hardback), 0-85323-642-9 (paperback)
13. FRANZ ROTTENSTEINER (ed.), *View from Another Shore: European Science Fiction*, ISBN 0-85323-932-0 (hardback), 0-85323-942-8 (paperback)
14. VAL GOUGH and JILL RUDD (eds.), *A Very Different Story: Studies on the Fiction of Charlotte Perkins Gilman*, ISBN 0-85323-591-0 (hardback, 0-85323-601-1 (paperback)
15. GARY WESTFAHL, *The Mechanics of Wonder: The Creation of the Idea of Science Fiction*, ISBN 0-85323-563-5 (hardback), 0-85323-573-2 (paperback)
16. GWYNETH JONES, *Deconstructing the Starships: Science, Fiction and Reality*, ISBN 0-85323-783-2 (hardback), 085323-793-X (paperback)

# View from Another Shore

*edited by*

## FRANZ ROTTENSTEINER

LIVERPOOL UNIVERSITY PRESS

This revised edition published 1999 by
LIVERPOOL UNIVERSITY PRESS
Liverpool, L69 3BX

First edition published 1973 by
The Seabury Press, New York

British Library Cataloguing-in-Publication Data
A British Library CIP record is available

ISBN   0-85323-932-0 cased
       0-85323-942-8 paper

Set in Meridien by
Wilmaset Limited, Birkenhead, Wirral
Printed and bound in the European Union by
Bell & Bain Limited, Glasgow

# Contents

# Acknowledgements

Lino Aldani: 'Good Night, Sophie'. Original title, *'Buonanotte Sofia'*. From the author's collection, *Quarta Dimensione* (Milan: Baldini & Castoldi, 1964). First published in the sf magazine *Futuro*, No. 1 (March/April, 1963), under the pseudonym N. L. Janda. © 1964 by Lino Aldani. By permission of the author.

J.-P. Andrevon: 'Observation of Quadragnes'. Original title, *'Observation des Quadragnes'*. First published in J.-P. Andrevon's *Cela se produira bientôt* (Paris: Editions Denoël, 1971). © 1971 by Editions Denoël. By permission of the publisher.

Herbert W. Franke: 'Slum'. Original title, *'In den Slums'*. First published in *X* magazine. © 1970 by Herbert W. Franke. By permission of the author.

Sever Gansovsky: 'The Proving Ground'. Original title, *'Poligon'*. From Sever Gansovsky's *Tri shaga k opasmosti* (Moscow: Detskaia literatura, 1969). By permission of Mezhdunarodnaia kniga.

Vsevolod Ivanov: 'Sisyphus, the Son of Aeolus'. Original title, *'Sisif, syn eola'*. From *Nefantasti v fantastike* (Moscow: Molodaia gvardiia, 1970). By permission of Mezhdunarodnaia kniga.

Wolfgang Jeschke: 'The Land of Osiris'. Original title, *'Osiris Land'*. First published in *Arcane* (Munich: Wilhelm Heyne Verlag, 1982), edited by Helmut Wenske and Wolfgang Jeschke. First published in English translation, by Sally Schiller, in *Isaac Asimov's Science Fiction Magazine*, March 1985. © 1982 by Wolfgang Jeschke. By permission of the author.

Gérard Klein: 'The Valley of Echoes'. Original title, *'La Vallée des échos'*. From Gérard Klein's *Un Chant de Pierre* (Paris: Eric Losfeld, 1966). © 1966 by Gérard Klein. By permission of the author.

Stanisław Lem: 'In Hot Pursuit of Happiness'. Original title, *'Kobyszcze'*. From Stanisław Lem's *Bezsenność* (Cracow: Wydawnictwo Literackie, 1971). © 1971 by Stanisław Lem. By permission of the author and the author's agent.

Svend Åge Madsen: 'The Good Ring'. Original title, *'Den gode ring'*. From S. Å. Madsen's *Maskeballet* (Copenhagen: Glydendal, 1970). © 1970 by Svend Åge Madsen. By permission of the author.

Josef Nesvadba, 'Captain Nemo's Last Adventure'. Original title, *'Posledni dobrodruzství kapitána Nemo'*. From Josef Nesvadba's *Vynalez proti sobě* (Prague: Krasné literatury, 1964). © 1964 by Josef Nesvadba. By permission of the author and the literary agency Dilia.

Adrian Rogoz: 'The Altar of the Random Gods'. Original title, *'Altarul zeilor stohastici'*. First published in *Almanahul literar*, 1970. © 1970 by Adrian Rogoz. By permission of the author.

Vadim Shefner: 'A Modest Genius'. Original title, *'Skromnyi genii'*. From Vadim Shefner's *Zapozdalyi strelok* (Leningrad: Sovetskii pisatel, 1968). By permission of Mezhdunarodnaia kniga.

# Introduction
## FRANZ ROTTENSTEINER

Science Fiction is a branch of literature that tries to push the borders of the unknown out a little further. It attempts to unveil the future; to imagine worlds lying beyond the next hill, river over ocean (including the ocean of space); to impress vividly upon the reader that the world need not necessarily be the way it happens to be, and that other states of existence are possible besides the one we know. Change is the proclaimed credo of science fiction—so much so that some writers have claimed this essential characteristic to be something that distinguishes SF above all other kinds of fiction. How paradoxical, then, that science fiction should be primarily an English-language phenomenon, at least in the minds of the majority of readers—and not only in the United States, but in Europe as well. A casual observer should expect science fiction to be more international than other kinds of popular fiction, precisely as a result of this stress on change: for isn't it reasonable to assume that the hopes, fears and expectations of people will be different in different countries, their ways of looking at things unlike those in one's own country? And yet the facts point to a different picture; while change is welcomed, obviously not all kinds of change are welcomed: not, for instance, the change that is necessary to adjust to the worlds presented in foreign science fiction which may be alien enough without any deliberate attempt at further estrangement. The late Donald A. Wollheim commented upon this phenomenon in his introduction to Sam J. Lundwall's *Science Fiction: What It's All About* (New York: Ace Books, 1971):

> We science fiction readers whose native language happens to be English—that is to say we American, we Canadian, we British and we Australian science fiction readers—tend to a curious sort of provincialism in our thinking regarding the boundaries of science fiction. We tend to think that all that is worth reading and all that is worth noticing is naturally written in English. In our conventions and our awards and our discussions we slip into the habit of referring to our favourites as the world's best this and the world's best that.

When *View From Another Shore* first appeared in the USA in 1973, I noted that at least eighty or ninety per cent of all science fiction published in Western Europe consisted of translations from the English; but that the Soviet Union and Eastern Europe had their own large and independent body of science fiction. But while the SF of the West is now even more dominated by American (and to some extent) British SF, the Communist paradigm has all but disappeared with the fall of communism. In Russia, the Czech Republic, Romania, Poland and elsewhere there are now lots of commercial publishers, and they are printing all the thrillers, romances, fantasies, horror novels and science fiction works that couldn't appear during the Communist era—partly because of censorship, but much more because of economic restrictions: there simply was no money to pay for licences of popular fiction. Much the same happened in Russia during the brief flowering of the New Economic Policy during Lenin's time, when Edgar Rice Burroughs was one of the most popular authors. Now most writers in these countries have difficulties getting published at all, and print-runs and authors' earnings are greatly reduced. In the German Democratic Republic for instance, which had in its last decade a number of interesting SF writers, it was possible for a writer to make quite a comfortable living from just a couple of books, if these got reprinted every few years; now the royalties from one book cover living expenses for perhaps a month or two. It is no longer possible to make a living from just writing SF, as it never was possible in the German Federal Republic (unless you happened to be a *Perry-Rhodan*-author). Even well-established and famous writers like Lem or the Strugatskys have now only very modest print-runs in their own countries, while many lesser writers are not published at all.

The situation of SF in the Anglophone countries has also greatly changed, and while it might be hoped in 1973, when the works of Stanisław Lem and Arkady and Boris Strugatsky were just beginning to appear in English translation, that translated SF might play a greater role in the future, any such expectations turned out to be utterly wrong. In 1973, the Seabury Press had started a series of European SF, with works by Stanisław Lem, Arkady and Boris Strugatsky, Jacques Sternberg, H. W. Franke and Stefan Wul, and my own anthology of European SF *View from Another Shore*. Later Donald A. Wollheim followed suit and published, more as a hobby than in expectation that it would pay, a number of European SF novels by writers like Gérard Klein, Pierre Barbet, Daniel Walther,

Arkady and Boris Strugatsky, Herbert W. Franke and others, usually in awful translations. Macmillan made a more careful effort to present the 'Best of Soviet SF', most notably, a number of Strugatsky books. None of these ventures was successful, most books went quickly out of print, and of the hardcovers almost none had reprints in mass market paperbacks. Avon Books failed to find a wider audience for their Lem reprints, since then no American mass market paperback publisher has been interested in Lem's books, and the Harcourt Brace/Harvest trade paperbacks sell very poorly. While Lem has received some attention from mainstream criticism, notably *The New York Times Book Review* and *The New Yorker*, he received little attention from the SF field, and this can only be partly explained by his antagonism to American SF and his quarrel with The Science Fiction Writers of America that led to his ousting from that organization that had originally made him an honorary member. But Lem is the only SF writer whose works have at least been kept in print in the USA (not so in England, where he is even less known). The Strugatskys were at least favourably reviewed, and one of their best books, *Roadside Picnic*, even made second place in the John W. Campbell Award. But one story that Donald A. Wollheim once told me shows the resistance to foreign SF in some rural areas of the USA. Many sales-points refused to exhibit the Strugatsky books at all, and rather ripped off their covers to return them for refund, arguing that there was enough SF by good American boys and therefore no need to sell this foreign trash. This is perhaps an extreme example, but among readers translated SF has also found little attention and has mostly been restricted to special SF series and anthologies, and the changes in publishing of the past decades have also affected English-language writers. Australian writers complain all the time that it is very hard for them to find American publishers. SF has become big business, and while some works sell for enormous advances, the mid-list books and the rest suffer. The backlist has all but disappeared, many once well-known SF writers are no longer in-print, and many living authors complain that they can no longer place their works with commercial publishers; British ones perhaps more so, but even many American authors are affected (Barry Malzberg and R. A. Lafferty are prominent examples). Many classic SF authors have sunk into obscurity, and attempts to start 'classic SF' lines have failed. The SF books of a world-famous writer like J. G. Ballard are out-of-print in the USA most of the time, despite a Steven Spielberg box-office-success like *Empire of the Sun*. SF in general seems to be on the decline, fantasy has infiltrated the field. Big books dominate, and what was once the rule has now even got its own name: 'stand-alone novel' for a novel that isn't part of at least a trilogy or a series. TV and film tie-ins and game-related fictions abound. All of these developments make the successful publication of translated SF more unlikely, and indeed it is now as rare as ever, and in many cases authors have to pay for their own translations if they wish their books to appear in English. Let's admit it, American SF has won the field, and the future most likely will bring a further Americanization of even the SF written by European authors who will have to adapt their writings to the American product to remain competitive. There is little chance that such stories will be translated, and really, what need is there to translate something into English that is abundantly written in that language, and usually with much more narrative skill?

The only chance for a writer would be to transcend genre boundaries and become accepted as a mainstream writer: it is irrelevant whether a Gabriel García Márquez or an Italo Calvino is a fantasy writer. Some writers who started in the magazines seem to have entered the mainstream: J. G. Ballard or Brian W. Aldiss in England; others hover uncomfortably between the mainstream and genre writing like Stanisław Lem, who is considered a literary writer by the fans—and an SF writer by the critics.

Surely, the most important living SF author on the Continent of Europe must be Stanisław Lem, but the fate of his books seems to bear out the thesis advanced by himself in his polemical essay 'SF: A Hopeless Case—with Exceptions': that literature has been split up, somewhere after World War I, into an upper realm of serious literature, and a lower realm of trivial fiction. Whereas an H. G. Wells or a Karel Čapek were accepted as writers without any labels in their countries and in the world, Lem's work is inseparably linked with SF, which is ironical in view of his repeated claims that he entered SF only by misadventure, out of ignorance, because he didn't know into what company he was getting (this notwithstanding the fact that his earliest work was trashy stories for the Polish equivalent of the pulp magazines). But in his own country he is not, save by some younger scholars, taken seriously as a writer, and not even his closest friends have shown the slightest interest in his work. The writer Jan Józef Szczepánski, in the briefest of pieces, had only to say about Lem that he had 'imagination'; and the eminent literary historian Jan Błoński wrote just, decades ago, a newspaper piece, and glossed over Lem's work in a few short paragraphs in his history of Polish literature. Lem himself feels, although his circulation numbers millions of copies, that he has been 'suppressed' in Poland. Lem has had his greatest success in Germany (both Germanies), where he sold some seven million copies, and is also considered an SF writer whose work can be counted as literature, and this high reputation persists even if the readers have meanwhile largely lost interest in him. In the United States and England Lem has been published as a literary writer, but his literary reputation doesn't extend much beyond the pages of *The New York Times Book Review*. In the rest of the world he has almost exclusively been published as part of SF series and not attracted much critical attention. Just as what success he has had is closely linked with the Communist system. This is another irony, since Lem despises Communism but never took a position against it so as not to jeopardize his chances of publication. But without the Communist system which kept away competition, he would never have achieved his high sales figures. Writers who made of themselves a nuisance to the system were either not published at all, or only in small editions: political expediency, not readers' interest decided print-figures.

While Lem in his early stories and novels made acknowledgement of the bright socialist future, he later developed a formula more in accord with both his arrogant temperament *and* his limitations as a writer. Lem's great weakness is characterization and social background. In his most characteristic fiction he disregards social ties and individual as well as social circumstances altogether, pitting 'pure' representatives of mankind against a cosmic riddle: sexless beings without family, sweethearts, friends or indeed social ties of any kind, unformed by social organization. Now most writers in Communist countries followed a certain stock pattern: after having paid lip-service to Communism as the certain and humane future of mankind, they soon went on to what interested them really, the adventure. Lem dispensed with even that, he neither defended nor attacked Communism, he just ignored it, which made him more acceptable to both his readers at home (who were tired of all that propaganda anyway)—and, of course, to readers in the West who cared even less about such admonitions and welcomed him as a free spirit who wasn't shackled by the constraints of ideology. Thus paradoxically the very system that Lem so hated and chose to ignore contributed to his success, and with the fall of Communism those qualities were less of a virtue, and since Lem was linked with the Communist system in the mind of many readers, he is now considered by many to be a relic of that system.

It would be an error to see in Lem's dominant theme of non-communication merely a symbolic reaction to the policies of the Cold War, but although there may be such undertones in it, it is more firmly rooted in his personal preferences. Like Pascal, Lem is filled with horror of the cold empty reaches of outer space, and expounds the alienness and inscrutability of a universe that takes no cognisance of man. Again and again Lem has presented alien worlds, from *The Astronauts* of 1951 onwards, that confront man with cosmic phenomena that prove to be unsolvable riddles. But for all of Lem's considerable knowledge of the sciences, his scientific stance and the pseudo-scientific trappings of his stories, his SF cosmos is more a romantic construct than a system of scientific facts, of no more objective reality than Lovecraft's eldritch Gods in an icy indifference to human beings. Lem's cosmos too is a projection, a displacement to avoid coming to grips with the real problem which is of a psychological nature: Lem's lack of sympathy for the human animal, and missing solidarity with his fellow humans. The true aliens in Lem's stories are human beings in general, and women in particular. Lem is a misanthrope and a misogynist, and his inability to understand those 'aliens' has led him to project his non-understanding upon the cosmos at large, and to proclaim it an essential quality of the universe. Lem has turned his weakness at characterization into an asset in his SF of ideas, and made his heroes into viewpoints, certain perspectives of perceiving the world. Pirx is the bungling hero who finally triumphs because of rather than in spite of his ineptitude which proves again and again the saving grace of man over the machine; Ijon Tichy is another space traveller who doesn't act but who has things happen to him and who is able to observe the metaphysical, political and social follies of mankind from the position of a disinterested observer. Trurl and Klapaucius are super-heroes in a fairy-tale of the absurdities of human existence. Unlike the writers of 'hard SF', Lem shows a disregard for facts (which he makes up as he goes along to his heart's desire); he is rather an ideological writer, an atheist theologian, a casuist and sophist who sometimes dances, sometimes blunders through various scientific, religious and philosophical systems and creates in their interplay a web of 'pleasant lies' (as Kurt Vonnegut would say), without committing himself. This makes for contextual richness and ambiguity which are literary qualities, but which are more of an entertaining than a scientific nature. The high point of Lem's methods is his most famous novel *Solaris*. The theories advanced to explain the nature of the alien thinking ocean covering the whole planet belong more properly to theology than science. *Solaris* is also the one Lem novel that combines the attraction of philosophical speculation about the truly alien with the appeal of a romantic love story. The ocean recreates, from the deepest, sub-conscious residues of the human mind what is the deepest guilt of the scientists on Solaris station. In the case of the protagonist Kris Kelvin this is Rheya, his lover or wife who committed suicide after having become estranged from him for some unknown reason. On Solaris she returns, a materialized phantom lover resurrected by the tremendous powers of the ocean, a manifestation of the alien that offers Kelvin, it would appear, a second chance at love. At first Kelvin reacts with horror at this succubus that exhibits superhuman strength, and he packs Rheya into a rocket and shoots her off into space. But she returns, and gradually he comes to accept and to love her, as she acquires more human traits. After further experiments she disappears for good, and at the end of the novel Kelvin squats before the ocean, waiting for her return, hoping 'that the time of cruel miracles was not past.' *Solaris* has usually been interpreted as a touching love story, a kind of cosmic Tristan and Yseult tale of the lovers who couldn't come together, and an encounter with the truly alien as manifested by the puzzling phenomena of the ocean. But the real import of the story would seem to be quite a different one, namely one of *getting rid of the alien*. First of all, Kelvin appears to be a very immature character, as his initial, incredibly brutal reaction to Rheya shows: he kills her by spaceship, an act that may be considered the SF equivalent of a shotgun murder in the family. After her second return, he falls (again) in love with her as she apparently loses much of her alienness and becomes more of a human being and less of a phantom wholly dependent upon Kelvin. But it should be noted here that in the novel there is to be found no trace of the genuine Rheya; the 'Rheya' of *Solaris* is a construct of the ocean (which acts here as a kind of amplifier), and has no informational connection at all with the real woman. The reconstruction is rather a Rheya according to Kelvin's remembrance of Rheya, a materialization of Kelvin's picture of her, with the ocean acting only as a mirror, and this reconstructed Rheya is more properly a part of Kelvin than a part of the ocean, let alone a return of Rheya. She is in reality a piece of Kelvin's mind, a part of himself, that is to say that she is less alien to him than a real, living woman (like the original Rheya) would be—the Rheya he couldn't get along with. The Rheya that had been was a woman with her own personality, her own mind, and her own interests, as distinct from Kelvin's. The new 'Rheya' has only the semblance of Rheya, but in all other respects she is from the stuff of Kelvin's mind, there exists no psychic barrier between him and her. What the ocean provides, by way of the alien, is an elimination of the alien, and it makes possible a meeting, a physical meeting, with one's own self. The science fictional device of the ocean allows a spiritual intimacy between lovers impossible in the real world. In the recreated Rheya an immature Kelvin, who so obviously was unable to love a real woman and accept her on her own terms, is able to love her, courtesy of the alien ocean, as part of himself, to love himself in her since she is no being with her own will but a figment of his own mind. In Rheya Kelvin loves himself, the Solaris ocean is only a mirror whose function is to eliminate 'otherness', while at he same time obscuring this truth. The ultimate goal of *Solaris* is not, as the cognitive trappings would suggest, knowledge, it is self-deception. There is also the telling scene in which Kelvin tries to devise a test to find out whether he is sane. This is also a self-deception, since in principle there can be no test by which anybody could test his own sanity (which can only be determined by others). The hidden truth of the love story of *Solaris* is self-love: the love between Kelvin and Rheya is an act of masturbation. Kelvin is the quintessential solipsist Lemian hero who has never been able to bridge the gulf between the 'I' and the 'You', and to meet others on their own terms. Kelvin is not a Tristan bemoaning his lost love, the ending sees him rather as Narcissus looking into the mirror of the ocean (mirror images abound in the novel) pitying himself. The novel skilfully employs a gigantic science fictional apparatus to obscure the simple fact that the cognitive thrust of the book is foremost a psychological escape mechanism to camouflage the failure of coming to terms with the profound mystery of the autonomy of other human beings, especially the other sex, who are in Lem's work invariably pale and weak creatures: by far the most interesting woman in Lem's work is the female robot of 'The Mask'.

In his work Lem has created a mysticism of non-communication and non-understanding. Like the mystic he attempts in his SF to speak of that which cannot be spoken of, the unknowable, that which is inaccessible to human reason, and since such a goal is unattainable and self-contradictory (it can only be expressed through human reason) he can only approach it in a roundabout way, by piling descriptive details upon descriptive details that are then said to be as a whole beyond human cognitive faculties. This proceeding makes for a rich tapestry of a literature of ideas, but it is a private obsession that the author tries to pass for an expression of universal laws. Lem's playful infatuation with theory-building has nevertheless a lot to say about the limits of human reason.

After Lem, the most important SF authors on the continent of Europe are Arkady (1925–1991) and Boris (1933–) Strugatsky who are not represented in this book since their best work is almost exclusively in the domain of long novellas and novels. They have followed a different course from Lem who is not interested in human beings and their social organization and has turned his back on society. In the Soviet Union it was perhaps less possible than in Poland to ignore society, the Aesopian mode of story-telling was a necessity for survival, and then the Strugatskys are also firmly rooted in the great Russian tradition of social satire of which Nikolai Gogol is the brightest example and which included in fantasy Mikhail Bulgakov. The Strugatskys have often been the subject of speculations whether they were antagonist critics of Soviet society, and their work was violently attacked and the subject of censorship as well as vigorously defended. It is firmly rooted in the particular conditions of Soviet and Russian society, and an engaged expression of humanist concerns. In many respects, the Strugatskys' work can serve as an indicator of the state of the present and not the future of their own country, and since many of the allusions to Russian particulars will be lost for non-Russian readers, the appeal of the work of the Strugatskys is less universal than that of Lem and less accessible to Western readers, but there is much in it that makes it timeless and of more than local or transitory interest. One of the recurring problems in their novels, especially in their early ones, is the question of intervention or non-intervention by superior civilizations in primitive ones, a problem that has also been touched upon in American SF, but with less urgency. It was an axiom that the advanced Communist society was superior to all other possible systems and progress to Communism inevitable. The Strugatskys dared to question this assumption, and showed that intervention by force, even with the best intentions, might lead to more evil than good. Their many and often hilariously funny put-downs of the excesses of bureaucracy are typically Russian, but while red tape may have been a prominent feature of the socialist system, it is of course far from restricted to it. The work of the Strugatskys is deeply rooted in history and human society and distinguished by a deep concern and solidarity with human suffering in a way that Lem's work is not; this brings them closer to Philip K. Dick, the foremost science fiction existentialist. Like

Dick's heroes, the protagonists of the Strugatskys remain loyal to their humanist principles and preserve their personal integrity, even if the world around them falls apart, either under the onslaught of the forces of history or under the influence of incomprehensible alien influences (as in their masterpiece *Roadside Picnic*). Their love for and understanding of small, unimportant people, the common man, is what is an essential quality in some of the greatest SF writers, whether Karel Čapek, Philip K. Dick or Arkady and Boris Strugatsky.

What else? There are of course some interesting novels, both classical and contemporary, and a variety of short stories in various countries. Knowledge of foreign SF has much increased since 1973, but mostly on a scholarly level. Peter Nicholls and John Clute's *Encyclopedia of Science Fiction* (1993) provides much useful information on foreign SF, but the useful section on foreign SF to be found in the 3rd edition of Neil Barron's *Anatomy of Wonder* (1987) has been dropped from the 4th edition, due to a lack of interest on the part of the users. The Americanization of SF has progressed, most spectacularly in Eastern Europe, and the appearance of translated SF in the English language is a greater rarity than ever before.

I will not argue here that there is such a thing as a unique Europeanness of SF, some common characteristics that set it apart. I think it is nonsense to attribute national characteristics to literature; strictly speaking, there is only one literature, and all writers, no matter where they are creating and in what language, have to stand on their own. Genre boundaries are mostly marketing categories of popular literature. This makes me pessimistic for a general acceptance of European SF in the world. The only way that a writer of European SF can really become successful is by transcending genre boundaries. Only literary publishers are willing to expend the money and care necessary to ensure good translations; a care that nobody takes with genre writers anywhere in the world.

Thus I am afraid that European (or Japanese, or Chinese) SF will be restricted, in English and most other translations, to special anthologies like this one, and they can only provide some hopefully interesting sidelights to the enormous corpus of science fiction, some tiny additional dots on the SF map. But it would be possible to put together, given good translators, some more very good compilations of new stories from Europe.

# In Hot Pursuit of Happiness
## STANISŁAW LEM

One evening the famed constructor Trurl, silent and preoccupied, dropped in on his good friend Klapaucius. Klapaucius sought to divert him with a few of the latest cybernetic jokes, but Trurl shook his head and said:

'Please, frivolity cannot dispel my melancholy, for the thought that has taken root in my soul is, alas, as undeniable as it is lamentable. Namely, I have reached the conclusion that in all our long and illustrious career we have accomplished nothing of real value!'

And he cast a look of censure and disdain upon the impressive collection of medals, trophies and honorary degrees in gold frames that graced the walls of Klapaucius's study.

'A serious charge', observed Klapaucius. 'On what grounds do you make it?'

'Hear me out, I shall explain. We have made peace between warring kingdoms, instructed monarchs in the proper use of power, fashioned machines to tell stories and machines to serve as quarry, we have defeated evil tyrants as well as galactic bandits that lay in ambush for us, yet in all this we served only ourselves, adding to our own glory—achieving next to nothing for the Common Good! Our efforts to perfect the lives of those poor innocents we encountered in our travels from planet to planet never once produced a state of Absolute Happiness. The solutions we offered them were makeshift, stopgap, jury-rigged—so if we have earned any title, it is surely Charlatans of Ontology, Subtle Sophists of Creation, and not Abolishers of Evil!'

'Whenever I hear anyone speak of programming Happiness, I am filled with foreboding', said Klapaucius. 'Come to your senses, Trurl! Don't you know such noble enterprises invariably end in tragedy and despair? Can you have so soon forgotten the pitiful fate of Bonhomius the hermetic hermit, who attempted to make the entire macrocosm happy with the aid of a drug called Altruizine? To be sure, one may in some measure alleviate the cares of life, see that justice is done, rekindle dying suns, pour oil on the troubled gears of social mechanisms—but in no way, by no machinery known create happiness! We can only nurture the hope of it in our hearts, pursue its bright, inspiring image in our minds on a quiet evening such as this ... A man of wisdom must content himself with that, my friend!'

'Content himself!', snorted Trurl. 'It may well be', he added after a moment of thought, 'that to make those who already exist happy in any plain and unequivocal way is indeed impossible. Still, one might construct new beings, beings whose sole function and faculty was to be happy. Think of what a wonderful monument to our constructor's skill (which Time, you know, must some day turn to dust) would be a planet shining in the firmament, a planet upon which the multitudes throughout the universe could gaze and proclaim: "Verily, attainable is happiness and never-ending harmony within reach, as great Trurl has shown—with some assistance from his close companion Klapaucius—for lo!, the living proof endures and thrives before our very eyes!"'

'I confess that I too have entertained the notion', said Klapaucius. 'But it does raise some difficult questions. You remember, I see, the lesson of Bonhomius's misfortune and therefore wish to bestow happiness upon creatures who do not as yet exist—that is, you would create happiness from scratch. Consider, though: is it at all possible to render the non-existent happy? Personally, I doubt it. First one would have to prove that the state of being is in every respect preferable to the state of non-being, even when that being is not especially pleasant. Without such proof, this felicitological experiment with which you seem to be obsessed may well backfire. That is, to the great number of unhappy souls that already occupy the universe you would be adding your own freshly created unfortunates—and what then?'

'Yes, there is that risk', Trurl reluctantly admitted. 'But we must take it. Mother Nature, they say, is impartial, works in a random and therefore even-handed manner, supposedly bringing forth as many good individuals as bad, as many kind as cruel. You'll find, however, that it's only the vile and the wicked who inherit the earth, their bellies bloated with the pure and the just. And when these scoundrels become aware of the unseemliness of their actions, they plead extenuating circumstances, invent some higher necessity: the evil of this world, for instance, is but the spice that whets one's appetite for the next, et cetera. Let us put an end to this imbalance, Klapaucius. Mother Nature is by no means vicious, only terribly obtuse; as always, she takes the line of least resistance. We must replace her and ourselves produce beings—beings of dazzling virtue, beings whose miraculous appearance in the universe will cure our every existential ill, thereby more than making up for a past that is haunted with screams of agony, screams we fail to hear only because sound will not travel far enough in time or space. Why, why must all that lives continue to suffer? Oh, had the suffering of every victim ever born only possessed the least momentum, carried the least impact—even that of a single raindrop—I assure you our world would have been torn asunder centuries ago! But life goes on, and in the crypts and empty dungeons the dust maintains its perfect silence; even you, with all your cybernetic art, will find in that dust no trace of the pain and sorrow that once plagued those who now no longer are.'

'It's true the dead have no cares', agreed Klapaucius. 'Which happily shows that suffering is a transitory thing.'

'But new sufferers keep entering the world!', cried Trurl. 'Don't you see, it's simply a matter of common decency!'

'One moment. How will this happy being of yours—assuming you succeed—ever make up for the countless torments that have been as well as those that continue to beset our continuum? Can today's calm negate the storm of yesterday? Does the dawn nullify the night? Really, you talk nonsense, Trurl!'

'Then according to you, it's better to fold our hands and do nothing?'

'Not at all. The point is, even if you manage to correct the present, you can never compensate the victims of the past. You think that filling the cosmos with happiness will alter one iota of what has already taken place within it?'

'But it *will*!', insisted Trurl. 'One cannot, of course, extend a helping hand to those who are no more, but the whole of which they form a part—*that* may be changed! And on that day the peoples will say: "These bitter trials and heinous crimes, these wars and genocides— they were but a prelude to the real adventure, a preliminary to the present reign of Goodness, Love and Truth! And it was Trurl, that most excellent Trurl, who realized that one may use an evil heritage to build a flawless future. From misfortune did he learn to forge good fortune, from despair he knew the worth of joy—in a word, it was a hideous universe that drove him to construct Loveliness!" Klapaucius, this present phase is both an inspiration and a preparation for the bliss to come! Now do you understand?'

'Beneath the constellation of the Southern Cross there lies the kingdom of King Troglodyne', said Klapaucius. 'The King delights in landscapes dotted with pillories and gallows, defending this predilection with the argument that his wretched subjects can be governed in no other way. He would have served me in similar fashion upon my arrival there, but soon discovered he was no match for me and so was seized with fear, considering it only natural that, as he was unable to crush me, I should certainly crush him. To placate me, he summoned his advisers and wise men, and they promptly wrote up a doctrine of tyranny for the occasion. I was told that the worse things are, the more one longs for improvement and reform; consequently, he who makes life unbearable actually hastens the day of its perfection. Now this harangue greatly pleased the King, for as it turned out, no one had contributed more to the ultimate triumph of Good than he, his black deeds helping to spur the melioristic dream to action. And therefore, Trurl, your happy beings should raise up monuments to honour Troglodyne. Indeed, you owe him and others of his kind your undying gratitude. Is this not so?'

'A cynical, malicious parable!', growled Trurl. 'I had hoped you would join me in this venture, but now I see your poisoned sophistries would only mock my noble purpose. There is, after all, a universe to save!'

'And you would be its saviour?', said Klapaucius. 'Trurl, Trurl! I ought to have you put in chains and locked up until you come to your senses, but I fear that that might take forever. Therefore I have only this to say: be not overly hasty in your engineering of happiness! Try not to perfect the world in one fell swoop! Of course, even if you do create happy beings, there will still be those already in existence, which is bound to give rise to envy, resentment, conflict, and—who knows?—some day you may be faced with a most unpleasant choice: either surrender your precious creatures to the envious, or else have them cut down their nasty, imperfect neighbours to a man—in the name of Universal Harmony, of course.'

Trurl jumped up in a fury, but quickly controlled himself and unclenched his fists: knocking Klapaucius to the ground would hardly constitute an auspicious beginning to the Age of Absolute Happiness, which he was now more determined than ever to bring about.

'Farewell', he said coldly. 'Farewell, O miserable agnostic, unbeliever, slave to the natural course of events! Not with words shall I defeat you, but with deeds! In time you will behold the fruit of my labours and see that I was right!'

\*   \*   \*   \*   \*

Returning home, Trurl was quite embarrassed: his argument with Klapaucius suggested that he had a definite plan of action in mind, but this was not exactly the case. To tell the truth, he hadn't the faintest idea where to begin. First he collected an enormous pile of books that described innumerable civilizations in the utmost detail; these he proceeded to devour at an incredible rate. But as this method of supplying his brain with the needed facts was still too slow, he dragged up from the cellar eight hundred cartridges of mercuric, plumbic, ferromagnetic and cryonic memory, connected them all to his person by cable, and in a few seconds had charged his psyche with four trillion bits of the best and most exhaustive information to be found anywhere, including planets of burnt-out suns inhabited by chroniclers of indomitable patience. The dose was so prodigious that he was rocked from head to toe, turned pale, went rigid, then was seized with a fit of trembling, as if he had been hit not with an overload of historiography and historiosophy, but with a genuine bolt from the blue. He pulled himself together, took a deep breath, wiped his brow, steadied his still quivering legs and said:

'Things are a great deal worse than I imagined!!'

For a while Trurl sharpened pencils, replenished inkwells, arranged stacks of white paper on his desk, but nothing came of this activity, so he said with a sigh:

'I shall have to acquaint myself, it seems, with the antiquated work of the ancients, a chore I always put off in the conviction that there was nothing a modern constructor could learn from those crusty old fogies. But now ... well, so be it! I'll study all the primeval pundits, if only to protect myself against Klapaucius, who, though he surely never read them either—for who has?—might secretly cull their works for quotations, just to make me look ignorant!'

And Trurl sat down and actually began to pore over the most decrepit and crumbling tomes, though he hated every minute of it.

Late that night, surrounded by volumes tossed impatiently to the floor, he delivered the following soliloquy:

'I see that not only is the structure of thinking creatures in sore need of repair, but what passes for their philosophy as well. Now, the cradle of life was the sea, which duly threw up slime upon the shore; then there was a blob of mud, macromolecular and highly irregular, and the sunshine thickened it, and the lightning quickened it, and soon the whole thing had soared to form a sort of cheese, biopolymeric and quite esoteric, which in time decided to head for higher and drier ground. To hear its prey approach, it grew ears, then legs and teeth to pursue and consume—else it would serve as prey itself. Intelligence, then, is the child of evolution. And what of Good and Evil, and what of Wisdom? Good is when I eat, Evil when I am eaten, and similarly with Wisdom: the eaten is not wise, being eaten when he should be eating; indeed, he is not anything when eaten, for, eaten, he no longer is at all. But whosoever would eat everything must starve, there soon being nothing left to eat, and so we have continence, self-restraint. After a while this intelligent cheese, finding itself rather too watery in consistency, began to calcify, just as sapient hominoids later sought to better their disgustingly viscous selves by discovering metal—but all they did was reproduce themselves in iron, for to copy is always easier than to create; as a result, true perfection was never attained. H'm! Had we evolved the other way—from metal to bone to an ever more glutinous and subtle substance—how different would our Philosophy have been! Clearly, it is spun from the very structure of its creators, only in a hopelessly contrary fashion: living in water, one envisions paradise on land, or if one lives on the land, it is somewhere in the sky; those with wings find blessedness in fins, and those with legs add wings to their likeness and cry, "Angel!" Odd, that I never noticed this principle before. We shall call it Trurl's Universal Law: according to the particular defect in its own construction, each creature postulates an Ideal. I must make a note of that; it will come in handy when I get around to correcting the foundations of philosophy. But to the business at hand. To begin, let us take that which is Good—but where can Good be found? Obviously not where there is no one to experience it. The waterfall is neither good nor evil as far as the rock is concerned, nor the earthquake, if you ask the earth. Ergo, we must assemble a Someone to experience Good. But wait, how can this Someone experience Good unless he knows what it is, and how will he know? Suppose ... suppose I see Klapaucius suffer some harm? Half of me would grieve, the other half rejoice. There's a complication. One could be happy in comparison with one's neighbour, yet be totally unaware of the fact and therefore not be happy at all, though actually happy! Must I then construct beings and keep other beings racked in pain perpetually before them, that they might know their own good fortune? A feasible solution—but how ghastly! Let's see, with a transformer here and a fuse there ... Best to start with an individual; happy civilizations we can manufacture afterwards.'

Trurl rolled up his sleeves and in three days had put together an Ecstatic Contemplator of Existence, a machine whose consciousness, cathodes all aglow, embraced whatever came beneath its gaze, for there was nothing in the whole wide world that wouldn't give it pleasure. Trurl examined it closely. The Contemplator, resting on three metal legs, slowly swept the room with its telescopic eyes, and whether they fell upon the fence outside, or a rock, or an old shoe, it oh'ed and ah'ed with delight. And when the sun went down and the sky grew pink, it swayed from side to side in rapture.

'Klapaucius will say of course that oh'ing and ah'ing and swaying from side to side in themselves prove nothing', thought Trurl, uneasy. 'He'll want evidence, data...'

So in the Contemplator's belly he installed a large dial with a golden pointer and calibrated in units of happiness, which he called hedons or heds for short. A single hed was taken to be the quantity of bliss one would experience after walking exactly four miles with a nail in one's boot and then having the nail removed. Trurl multiplied the distance by the time and divided by the rest mass of the nail, placing the foot coefficient in brackets; this enabled him to express happiness in centimetres, grams and seconds. That improvement lifted his spirits considerably. Meanwhile, as he leaned over and worked, the Contemplator regarded his patched and stained lab coat and registered, at that particular angle of leaning and cut of coat, from 11.8 to 11.9 heds per stain-patch-second. This reading fully restored Trurl's confidence. He made a few more calculations to test the instrument's precision— one kilohed, for instance, was what the elders had felt when they beheld Susanna at her bath, one megahed the joy of a man condemned to hang but reprieved at the last minute—and then sent an errand robot to fetch Klapaucius.

The latter came and, seeing Trurl point a proud finger at his new creation, began to inspect it. It in turn fixed the majority of its lenses on him, swayed from side to side and delivered a few oh's and ah's. These exclamations surprised the constructor, but he asked with an air of unconcern:

'What is it?'

'A happy being', replied Trurl, 'more specifically, an Ecstatic Contemplator of Existence or Contemplator for short.'

'And what exactly does this Contemplator do?'

Trurl sensed the sarcasm in his friend's query but chose to ignore it.

'It devotes itself to wholehearted, incessant observation', he explained. 'Not passive observation, mind you, but a most intense, strenuous and aggressive kind of observation, and whatever is observed fills it with inexpressible delight! It is precisely this delight, oscillating through its many circuits and cells, which prompts those oh's and ah's you hear, even now as it looks upon your otherwise uninteresting face.'

'You mean, this machine derives pleasure from an active examination of all that is?'

'Correct!', said Trurl, but without his former assurance, for he feared a trap.

'And this must be a felicitometer, graduated in units of existential bliss', Klapaucius went on, indicating the dial with the golden pointer.

'Yes ... '

Klapaucius then presented the Contemplator with various objects, in each case taking careful note of its reaction. Trurl, greatly relieved, began to hold forth on the niceties of hedonic calculus or theoretical felicitometry. One word led to the next, question followed question, until Klapaucius remarked:

'How many units, do you think, would result from this situation: one man is brutally beaten for a full three hundred hours, then all at once jumps up and brains the one who was beating him?'

'That's easily done!', cried Trurl enthusiastically, and immediately began to calculate it out—when suddenly he heard a loud guffaw and whirled around. Klapaucius said, still laughing:

'You say you took Goodness as your guiding principle? Well, Trurl, I see you're off to a flying start! At this rate you'll have perfection in no time! Now if you'll excuse me ...'

And he departed, leaving behind a totally crushed Trurl.

'I should have known! I should have seen it!', groaned the poor constructor, and his groans mingled with the oh's and ah's of the Contemplator, which so aggravated him that he locked it in a closet.

Then he sat at his empty desk and said:

'What a fool I was, to mistake aesthetic ecstasy for Good! Why, one could hardly even call the Contemplator a thing of reason! No, that's not the way to go about it, not in a million maxwells! Happiness—certainly, pleasure—of course! But not at someone else's expense! Not from Evil! Wait—what is Evil? Ah, now I see how shamefully I neglected, in all my years of cybernetic construction, a study of the fundamentals!'

For eight days and nights Trurl did nothing but bury himself in terribly erudite volumes that dealt with the weighty question of Good and Evil. A great number of wise men, as it turned out, maintained the most important thing was an active solicitude coupled with an all-embracing good will. Unless men of understanding mutually manifested these virtues, all was lost. True, under that banner quite a few individuals had been impaled, boiled in oil, buried alive, drawn and quartered, broken on the wheel or stretched on the rack. Indeed, history showed that good will, when extended to the soul and not the body, gave rise to endless varieties and variations of torture.

'Good will is not enough', thought Trurl. 'What if we house one's conscience in one's neighbour, and conversely? No, that would be disastrous: my transgressions would fill others with remorse, leaving me free to sink deeper and deeper in sin! But what if we attach a remorse amplifier to the conscience, in other words ensure that every wicked deed hound its perpetrator afterwards with an intensity a thousand times greater than normal? But then everyone would run out and commit some crime just to see whether his new conscience really hurt that much—and then be ridden by an overwhelming guilt to the end of his days ... Perhaps a conscience that's reversible, with a clearing mechanism—locked of course. The authorities could keep the key ... No, there would be picklocks and skeleton keys circulating in no time. Arrange for the general broadcasting of feelings? One would feel for all, and all for one. No, that's been done, Altruizine created precisely that effect ... Now here's an idea: everyone carries in his stomach a small bomb and receiver, so that if, as a result of his wrongdoing, say, ten or more persons wish him ill, the input of that combined and heterodyned signal blows the culprit sky-high. Wouldn't they shun Evil then? Of course they would, they'd *have* to! On second thought ... what kind of happiness is it, to go around with a bomb in your stomach? Anyway, there could be plots; ten villainous men could conspire against one innocent and he would detonate, innocent or not. What then, reverse the signs? No, that wouldn't work either. Confound it, can it be that I, who have moved galaxies about as if they were furniture, am unable to solve this ridiculously simple problem in construction?!

'Suppose each and every individual of a given society is plump, rosy, full of cheer, sings and leaps and laughs from morning till night, rushes to the aid of others with such zeal the very ground trembles, and the others do likewise, and when asked, they exclaim they are positively thrilled with their own not to mention the common lot ... Would not such a society be perfectly happy? Evil, after all, would be unthinkable in it! Why would anyone want to harm anyone else? What could be gained by doing harm? Absolutely nothing! And there's the answer, there's my blueprint, elegant in its simplicity, for mass-producing happiness! Klapaucius, the misanthrope, the cynic—where in this whole, magnificent system will he find the least thing to mock and deride? Nowhere, for everyone, helping everyone else, will make everything better and better, until it can't possibly be better ... But wait, might they not strain themselves, grow faint and fall beneath that avalanche, so to speak, of good deeds? I could add a regulator or two, circuit breakers too, some joyproof shields, bliss-resistant fields ... The main thing is not to rush, we can't afford any more oversights. So then, *primo*—they enjoy themselves, *secundo*—they help others, *tertio*—they jump up and down, *quarto*—plump and rosy, *quinto*—things couldn't be better, *sexto*—self-sacrificing ... yes, that ought to do it!'

Weary after these long and difficult deliberations, Trurl slept until noon, then jumped out of bed, refreshed and full of fight, wrote down the plans, punched out the programs, set up the algorithms and in the beginning he created a happy civilization composed of nine hundred persons. That equality should obtain within its borders, he made them all amazingly alike; that there should be no struggle over food or drink, he made them free of any need of sustenance—atomic batteries were their only source of energy. Then he sat on his porch for the rest of the day and watched how they sang and leaped, announcing their happiness, how they rushed to aid one another, patted one another on the head, removed stumbling blocks before one another and, bursting with excitement, generally lived a life of prosperity and peace. If someone sprained his ankle, an enormous crowd would form, not out of curiosity but because of the categorical imperative to extend a helping hand. It was true that at first, due to a little over-enthusiasm, a foot might be pulled off instead of repaired, but Trurl quickly adjusted the automatic choke and threw in a few rheostats; then he sent for Klapaucius. Klapaucius regarded this scene of incessant jubilation with a fairly dour expression, listened to the hallelujahs and huzzahs for a while, then finally turned to Trurl and asked:

'And can they be sad as well?'

'What an idiotic question! Of course they can't!', replied Trurl.

'Then they do nothing but jump around, look plump and rosy, remove stumbling blocks and shout in unison that they are positively thrilled?'

'Yes!'

Seeing that Klapaucius was not only sparing in his praise but in fact had none at all to offer, Trurl added peevishly:

'A monotonous prospect, perhaps, hardly as picturesque as a battlefield. My purpose, however, was to bestow happiness, not provide you with a dramatic spectacle!'

'If they do what they do because they must', said Klapaucius, 'then, Trurl, there is as much Good in them as in a streetcar that fails to run you down on the sidewalk simply because it hasn't jumped its tracks. Who derives happiness from doing Good? Not he who must forever pat his fellow on the head, roar with delight and remove stumbling blocks, but he who is able to brood, to sob, to do his fellow in, yet voluntarily and cheerfully refrains from such things! These puppets of yours, Trurl, are but a mockery of those high ideals you have managed so completely to profane!'

'What—what are you saying?!' Trurl was stunned. 'They aren't puppets, but thinking beings...'

'Oh?', said Klapaucius. 'We shall see!'

And he walked out among Trurl's perfect protégés and struck the first one he met full in the face, saying:

'I trust you're happy?'

'Terribly!'; replied that individual, holding its broken nose.

'And now?', inquired Klapaucius, this time dealing it such a blow that it went head over heels. Whereupon that individual, still lying in the dust and spitting out teeth, exclaimed:

'Happy, sir! Things couldn't be better!'

'There you are', said Klapaucius to a dumbfounded Trurl and left without another word.

The crestfallen constructor led his creations one by one back to the laboratory and there dismantled them to the last nut and bolt, and not one of them protested, not in the least. In fact, a few even tried to be of assistance, holding a wrench or pliers while Trurl worked, or hammering at their own heads when the cranial lids stuck and wouldn't unscrew. Trurl put the parts back in the drawers and shelves, pulled the blueprints off the drawing board and tore them all to shreds, sat down at his desk piled high with books on philosophy and ethics, and gave a deep sigh.

'How he humiliates me, the dog! And to think I once called that pettifogging putterer my friend!'

From its glass case he took the model of the psychopermutator, the device that had transformed every impulse into an active solicitude and all-embracing good will, and smashed it to bits on an anvil. Not that this did much to improve his spirits. So he thought a while, gave another sigh, and began again. This time a sizeable society took shape—three thousand stout citizens in all—and it immediately chose a government for itself by secret ballot and universal suffrage, after which various projects were undertaken: the building of houses and the putting up of fences, the discovering of the laws of nature and the throwing of parties. Each of these latest creations of Trurl carried a small homeostat in its head, and in each homeostat were two electrodes, one welded to either side, and between them the individual's free will could play and dance as it pleased; underneath was the positive spring, with a tension far exceeding the pull of the opposite spring, the one bent on destruction and negation but prudently held in check with a safety clip. Moreover, each citizen possessed a moral monitor of great sensitivity, which was situated in a vice with two toothed jaws: these would begin a gnawing action upon it whenever its possessor strayed from the straight and narrow. Trurl first tested this contrivance on a special model in his workshop; the poor thing was stricken with such pangs and twinges that it fell into a violent fit. But then, the capacitor soon charged with the necessary penance and the ignition with contrition, he was able to ease the monitor somewhat from those relentless jaws. The whole thing was most cleverly done! Trurl even considered connecting the monitor by regenerative feedback coupling to a splitting headache, but quickly changed his mind, afraid Klapaucius would again start to lecture him about compulsion ruling out the exercise of free will. Which wasn't at all true, for these new beings had statistical transmissions, in other words no one, including Trurl, could possibly foresee what they would end up doing with themselves. That night Trurl was repeatedly awakened by shouts of joy, which was a great comfort to him. 'This time', he said to himself, 'Klapaucius can have no objections. These people are happy, and their happiness is not programmed, hence predetermined and imperative, but wholly stochastic, ergodic and probabilistic. I've won at last!' And with this pleasant thought he fell asleep and slept till morning.

Klapaucius was not in, and it was noon before he showed up and Trurl could lead him to the felicitological proving ground. There Klapaucius inspected the homes, fences, minarets, signs, the courthouse, its offices, delegates and citizens, here and there engaged a few in conversation, and on a side street even attempted to punch one in the face. But three others seized him by the breeches and, singing in unison, gave him the old heave-ho at the gate, careful not to break his neck, though he did look much the worse for wear when he climbed out of the roadside ditch.

'Well?', said Trurl, pretending not to notice his friend's mortification. 'What do you think?'

'I'll be back tomorrow', replied Klapaucius.

Considering this a retreat, Trurl nodded and gave a sympathetic smile. The next day both constructors again entered the settlement and found it greatly changed. They were stopped by a patrol and the highest ranking officer addressed Trurl:

'What's this, frowning on the premises? Can't you hear the birds singing? Don't you see the flowers? Chin up!'

And the next highest ranking officer said:

'Chest out! Shoulders back! Look alive! Smile!'

The third said nothing, only clapped the constructor on the back with a mailed fist, raising a deafening clang, then turned with the rest to Klapaucius—who didn't wait for such encouragement but snapped to attention at once, assuming a properly ecstatic expression, at which they were satisfied and continued on their way. Meanwhile the unsuspecting creator of this new order stared open-mouthed at the square before the headquarters of Felicifica, where hundreds stood in formation and roared with joy upon command.

'All hail to life!', bellowed one old officer in epaulets and plumes, and the gathering thundered back as one man:

'All hail to happiness.'

Before Trurl could say another word, he found himself wedged firmly in one of the columns with his friend and compelled to march and drill for the rest of the day. The main manoeuvre seemed to consist in making oneself as miserable as possible while furthering the welfare of the next in line, all to the rhythm of 'Left! Right! Left! Right!' The drillmasters were Felicemen, known as the Guardians of Good and Gladness and thus commonly called G-men, and their task was to see that each and every one, both separately and together, participated wholeheartedly in the general beatitude, which in practice proved to be unbelievably burdensome. During a brief intermission in these felicitological exercises Trurl and Klapaucius managed to slip away and hide behind a hedge. There they found a gully and followed it, crouching as if under heavy fire, to Trurl's place, where to be absolutely safe they locked themselves in the attic—and just in the nick of time, for the patrols were out, combing the area for all those discontent, gloomy or sad, and summarily felicitizing them on the spot. In his attic Trurl cursed and fumed and considered the quickest way to put an end to this unhappy experiment, while Klapaucius did what he could to keep from laughing out loud. Unable to come up with anything better, Trurl shook his head and sent a demolition squad to the settlement, making sure beforehand to programme it impervious to the lure of such attractive slogans as brotherly love and joy for all—which provision, however, he was careful to keep from Klapaucius. Trurl's demolition squad soon collided with the G-men and the sparks began to fly. As the last bastion of universal happiness, Felicifica fought most valiantly, and Trurl had to send replacements with heavy-duty clamps and grappling hooks. Now the battle became full-pitched, the war all-out; both sides displayed a truly staggering dedication, and grapeshot and shrapnel filled the air. When at last the constructors stepped out into the moonlit night, they beheld a piteous sight: the settlement lay in smouldering ruins, and here and there a Feliceman, not fully un-screwed in the general haste, expressed in a weak and trembling voice its undying devotion to the cause of Universal Goodness. No longer able to contain himself, Trurl burst into tears of rage and despair; he couldn't understand what had gone wrong, why these kindly souls had changed into such insufferable bullies.

'The directive for an all-embracing good will may, if too direct, bear contrary fruit', Klapaucius explained. 'He who is glad wishes others to be glad, glad without delay, and ends up clubbing gladness into all recalcitrants.'

'Then Good may produce Evil! Oh, how perfidious is the Nature of Things!', cried Trurl. 'Very well, I hereby declare war against Nature Herself! Adieu, Klapaucius! You see me momentarily defeated, but not discouraged. I shall win yet!'

And he returned to the isolation of his books and manuscripts, grim and more determined than ever. Common sense suggested it might not be a bad idea, before proceeding with further tests, to throw up battlements around the house, with embrasures for artillery. But this was plainly no way to begin the construction of brotherly love, so he decided instead to make his models smaller, on a scale of 100,000 to 1—that is, to conduct his experiments with microminiaturized civili-zations. In order not to forget what he'd learned, he hung signs like the following on his workshop walls: THESE BE MY GUIDE—(1) SACRED AUTONOMY, (2) SWEET PARITY, (3) SUBTLE CHARITY, (4) UNOBTRUSIVE AVUNCULARITY. Then he began the work of translating those noble sentiments into action.

First he assembled a thousand electromites under the microscope, endowed them with little minds and not much greater love of Good, since by now he feared fanaticism. They went about their business in a dull sort of way, and their little dwelling-box began to resemble the works of a watch, so even and monotonous were their movements in it. Trurl opened a valve and raised the intelligence a bit; immediately they grew more lively, fashioned tiny tools from a few stray filings and started using them to pry open their little box. Trurl then quickly increased the Good potential and overnight the society became self-sacrificing, everyone ran about frantically looking for someone to save—widows and orphans were in particularly great demand, especially if blind. These were besieged with so many tokens of respect, paid so many compliments, that the poor things fled and hid in the farthest corners of the box. In no time Trurl's civilization faced a crisis: the acute shortage of orphans and other unfortunates made it next to impossible to find deserving objects of any properly monumental act of generosity. As a result the micromites, after eighteen generations, began to worship the Absolute Orphan, whom nothing in their boxlike vale of tears could ever deliver from dismal orphanhood; thus their excessive benevolence finally found relief in the infinite transcendental realm of metaphysics. They populated those higher spheres with various beings, the Triple Cripple for instance, or the Lord Up Above, who was always greatly to be pitied, and they neglected the things of this world and replaced all government agencies with religious orders. This was not quite what Trurl had in mind, so he introduced rationalism, scepticism and common sense until everything settled down.

Though not for long. A certain Electrovoltaire appeared and announced there was no Absolute Orphan, only the Cosmic Cube created by the forces of Nature; the orphanists excommunicated him, but then Trurl had to leave for an hour or two to do some shopping. When he returned, the tiny box was bouncing about on its shelf in the throes of a religious war. Trurl charged it with altruism—that only made it sizzle and smoke; he added a few more units of intelligence, which cooled it off somewhat—but later there was a great deal of activity and confusion, after which military parades appeared, marching in a disconcertingly mechanical way. Another generation came and went, the orphanists and electrovoltairians vanished without a trace, now everyone spoke only of the Common Good, numerous treatises were written on the subject—entirely secular—and then a great debate arose concerning the origin of the species: some said that they were spawned spontaneously from the dust that lay in the corners; others, that they stemmed from a race of invaders from without. To resolve this burning question, the Great Awl was built to penetrate the cosmic wall and explore the Space Beyond. And since unknown things might lurk out there, powerful weapons were immediately manufactured and stockpiled. Trurl was so alarmed at this development that he scrapped the whole model as quickly as possible and said, close to tears: 'Reason leads to heartlessness, Good produces madness! Must every attempt at historiographic construction be doomed to failure?' He decided to attack the problem on an individual basis again and dragged his first prototype, the Contemplator, from its closet. It began to oh and ah in aesthetic rapture before a pile of debris, but Trurl plugged in an intelligence component and it fell silent at once. He asked it if anything was wrong, to which it replied:

'Everything continues to be just fine; I only contain my admiration in order to reflect upon it, for I wish to know, first of all, the source of this fineness, and secondly, what end or purpose it may serve. And what are you, to interrupt my contemplation with the asking of questions? How does your existence concern mine? I feel, indeed, compelled to admire all things, including yourself, but prudence tells me to resist this inclination, for it may be some trap devised against me.'

'As far as your existence goes', Trurl said incautiously, 'it was created by me, created expressly that between you and the world there should be perfect harmony.'

'Harmony?', said the Contemplator, gravely turning all its lenses on him. 'Harmony, you say? And why do I have three legs? Wherefore is my head on top? For what reason am I brass on the left and iron on the right? And why do I have five eyes? Answer, if it be true you brought me into being from nothingness!'

'Three legs, because two wouldn't provide enough stability, whereas four would be an unnecessary expenditure', Trurl explained. 'Five eyes: that's how many usable optics I had on hand. As for the brass, well, I ran out of iron.'

'Ran out of iron!', jeered the Contemplator. 'You expect me to believe that all this was the work of sheer accident, pure luck, blind chance, happenstance? Come, come!'

'I ought to know, if I created you!', said Trurl, irritated by the machine's overweening manner.

'There are two possibilities', replied the circumspect Contemplator. 'The first is, you are an out-and-out liar. This we shall set aside for the moment as unverifiable. The second is, you believe it is the truth you speak, yet that truth, predicated as it is upon your feeble understanding, is in truth untrue.'

'Come again?'

'What seems an accident to you may be no accident at all. You think it insignificant that you ran short of iron, and yet who knows but that some Higher Necessity arranged precisely for that shortage? Again, you see nothing in the availability of brass but a convenient coincidence, yet here too some Provident Harmony entered in and interfered. Similarly, in the number of my eyes and legs there surely must lie some profound Mystery of a Higher Order, some Ultimate Meaning. And truly, three and five—both are prime numbers; three times five is fifteen, fifteen is one and five, the sum of which is six, and six divided by three is two, the number of my colours, for behold, on the left is brass and on the right, iron! Mere chance produce a relation of such elegant precision? What nonsense! I am a being whose essence obviously extends beyond your petty horizons, O unschooled tinkerer! And if there be any truth in your claim to have constructed me—which, really, I find most difficult to imagine— then you were only the ignorant instrument of Higher Laws, while I constituted their aim, their goal. You are a random drop of rain, I the flower whose glorious blossoming shall extol all creation; you are a mouldering post that casts a shadow, I the blazing sun that commands the post to divide the darkness from the light; you are the blind tool guided by the Everlasting Hand—solely that *I* may spring into existence! Therefore seek not to lower my exalted person by arguing that its five-eyed, three-legged and two-metalled nature is wholly a product of arbitrary-budgetary factors. In these qualities I see the reflection of a Greater Symmetry, still somewhat obscure perhaps, but I shall certainly divine it, given the time to study the problem in depth. Importune me then no longer with your presence, for I have better things to do than bandy words with you.'

Incensed by this speech, Trurl threw the struggling Contemplator back in its closet and, though it invoked in a loud and ringing voice the right to self-determination and autonomy of all free entities as well as the sacred principle of individual inviolability, he proceeded to disconnect its intelligence component. This violence done to the Contemplator suddenly filled him with a sense of shame, and he sneaked back to his room, looking around to see if there were any witnesses. Sitting at his desk, he felt like a criminal.

'Some curse apparently hangs over any construction work that has only Good and Universal Happiness as its goals', he thought. 'All my attempts, even the most preliminary tests, seem to involve me in foul deeds and feelings of guilt before I know it! A plague on that Contemplator with its Higher Necessity! There must be some other way...'

So far he had tried one model after another, and each experiment had demanded considerable time and material. But now he decided to run a thousand experiments simultaneously—on a scale of 1,000,000 to 1. Under an electron microscope he twisted individual atoms in such a way that they gave rise to beings not much larger than microbes and called Angstromanians. A quarter of a million of these persons made a single culture, which was transferred by micropipette to a slide. Each such millimicrosocietal specimen was an olive-grey stain to the naked eye, and only under the highest magnification could one observe what transpired within.

Trurl equipped his Angstromanians with altruinfraternal regulators, eudaemonitors and optimizers, nonaggression pawls and ratchets, all operating at unheard-of levels of beneficence and stabilized against any sort of fanatical deviation by both heresy and orthodoxy stops; the cultures he mounted on slides, the slides he put in packets, and the packets in packages, all of which he then shelved and locked in a civilizing incubator for two and a half days. But first he placed over each culture a cover glass, crystal clear and tinted a pale blue, which was to serve as that civilization's sky; he also supplied food and fuel by eyedropper, as well as raw materials to permit the fabrication of whatever the consensus omnium might find appropriate or necessary. Obviously, Trurl couldn't possibly keep up with developments on each and every slide, so he pulled out civilizations at random, carefully wiped the eyepiece of his microscope, and with bated breath leaned over and surveyed their undertakings, much like the Lord God Himself parting the clouds to look down upon His handiwork.

Three hundred cultures went bad at the outset. The symptoms were usually the same. First the specimen would grow at a vigorous rate, send out tiny offshoots here and there, then a barely visible haze would hang over it and tiny lights begin to flicker, covering the tiny towns and fields with a phosphorescent glow, after which the whole thing would crackle faintly and crumble into a fine dust. Replacing the ocular with an eight hundred power lens, Trurl examined one of these cultures and found only charred ruins and smouldering ashes, among which lay tattered banners with inscriptions too small, unfortunately, for him to make out. All such slides were quickly thrown into the waste-basket. Other cultures, however, fared better. Hundreds progressed and prospered so well that they ran out of space and had to be moved to other slides. In three weeks Trurl had more than nineteen thousand of these strains.

Following an idea he felt to be inspired, Trurl did nothing himself to solve the problem of creating happiness, only grafted onto his Angstromanians a hedotropic impulse, engineering this in various ways. Sometimes he would install a separate hedotropic unit in each and every individual, sometimes he would divide it up and distribute the components equally—the business of happiness then became a group effort, a matter of teamwork. Those created by the first method glutted themselves with selfish pleasure, over-indulged and in the end quietly came apart at the seams. The second method proved more fruitful. Rich civilizations arose on those slides and fashioned social theories and technologies for themselves, and all sorts of social institutions. Culture No. 1376 embraced Emulation, No. 2931 Cascading, and No. 95 Fractionated Salvation within the pale of Ladder Metaphysics. The Emulators competed in the pursuit of perfect virtue by splitting into two camps, the Whigs and the Houris. The Houris maintained one could not know virtue if he knew not vice, for virtue must be seen distinct from vice and vice versa, so they religiously practised all the vices ever known, fully intending to cast them off at the Appropriate Time. However, this apprenticeship soon became a permanent occupation, or so claimed the Whigs. Finally defeating the Houris, they introduced Whiggism, a system based on 64,000 inalterable interdictions. During their reign it was absolutely forbidden to duel, shoot pool, read palms, solicit alms, go nude, be rude, drink too much, think too much; naturally these strict laws were resented and one by one repealed, much to the general delight. When Trurl returned to the Emulation strain a little later there was nothing but chaos, everyone running wildly about in search of some rule left to break and terrified because there wasn't any. A few still duelled, read palms, went nude and drank so much they couldn't find their way home—but the fun had gone out of it.

Trurl noted down in his lab book that where one can do all, the pleasure will pall. In culture No. 2931 lived the Cascadians, a righteous people who cleaved to numerous ideals embodied in such Perfect Beings as Great Mother Cascader, the Immaculate Maid and the Blessed Fenestron. To these they swore undying allegiance, prayed, sang praises, prostrated themselves, all with the utmost ceremony. But just as Trurl was beginning to admire this unusually high concentration of Piety, Prayer and Prostration, they stood up, dusted off their clothes—and proceeded to sack the temples, defenestrate the sacred statues, kick the Great Mother and defile the Maid, all with such abandon that the constructor blushed and looked away.

Yet it was precisely in this wanton destruction of what had been so revered that the Cascadians found, albeit momentarily, perfect happiness. For a while it seemed they would be sharing the fate of the Emulators, but they had wisely provided for Institutes To Draft Sacraments, and these paved the way for the next stage. Soon new statues were being hoisted up on the plinths and pedestals and altars—which clearly demonstrated the seesaw character of their culture. Trurl concluded that violating the inviolable can on occasion be viable, and in his lab book called the Cascadians Chronic Iconoclasts.

The next culture, No. 95, appeared more complex. This civilization was metaphysically inclined, but unlike many others boldly took metaphysics into its own hands. The Ministers of the Ladder had this world followed by an endless progression of purgatories and probational paradises—there were the Celestial Suburbs, the Celestial Outskirts and Outlying Districts, Precincts and Boroughs, but one never got to the heart of the Celestial City Itself, for that was the whole point of their theometrical cunning. True, the sect of Bitchafers wanted to enter the Heavenly Gates without further delay; the Advocates of the Circular Stair, on the other hand, agreed with the principle of quantized transcendence but would have a trap door installed on every step, in order that the rising soul might fall through to the bottom—that is, back to this world, where it could begin its climb all over again. In other words, they proposed a Stochastically Fluctuating Closed Cycle, ultimately a kind of Perpetual Transmigratory Retroincarnation, but the orthodox Ladderants anathematized this doctrine as Galloping Defeatism.

Later on Trurl discovered many other types of Appropriated Metaphysics. Some slides literally swarmed with blessed and beatified Angstromanians; on others, Rectifiers of Evil and Temptational Resistors were in operation, but most of these instruments succumbed to subsequent waves of secularization. To cope with such Transcendental Ups and Downs, a few more hard-headed technologies built Two-way Cable Cars. Societies completely laicized, however, soon grew apathetic and wasted away. Now No. 6101 looked truly promising: there they had proclaimed Heaven on Earth, perfection material, ethereal and sidereal—Trurl sat up in his chair and quickly brought the picture into better focus. His face fell. Some of the inhabitants of that plane of glass rode bareback on machines, desperately seeking anything that might still be impossible; some sank into bathtubs full of whipped cream and truffles, sprinkled caviar on their heads and drowned, pushing bubbles of *taedium vitae* out through their noses; and some were carried piggyback by beautifully pneumatic maenads and annointed with honey and vanilla extract, keeping one eye on their coffers of gold and rare perfumes, the other on the lookout for anyone who might be tempted, if only for a moment, to envy such an amazing accumulation of dulcitude. But as there was no one of the kind to be found, they wearily dropped to the ground, tossed their treasures away like so much garbage, and limped off to join gloomy prophets who preached that things must inevitably get better and better, or in other words worse and worse. A group of former instructors at the Institute of Erotogenic Engineering founded a monastic order, the Abstinent Friars, and issued manifestos calling for a life of humility, asceticism and self-mortification—not unrelieved however, for though they did penance six days of the week, on the seventh the worthy fathers dusted off their pneumatic nymphs, broke out the wine and venison, baubles, belt-looseners and polyaphrodisiacs, and as soon as the bell rang matins, they began an orgy that shook the rafters till Monday morning, when once again they followed the prior in such flagellation and fasting that the rafters shook. Some of the younger generation stayed with the Abstinents from Monday through Saturday, avoiding the monastery on Sunday, while others came only on that hallowed day to visit the good friars. But when the former began to castigate the latter for their wicked ways, Trurl groaned—he couldn't bear to watch another religious war.

Now it came to pass that in the incubator, which housed thousands of cultures, scientific advance eventually led to exploration; in this way the Era of Interslidal Travel was ushered in. The Emulators, as it turned out, envied the Cascadians, the Cascadians the Ladderants, the Ladderants the Chronic Iconoclasts, besides which there were rumours of some distant realm where perfect happiness had been attained through Sexocracy, though no one was quite sure how that was supposed to work. The inhabitants there had apparently gained such knowledge that they were able to refashion their bodies and connect themselves directly by hedohydraulic pumps and plumbing to vats of supersaturated rapture ... But though Trurl examined thousands of cultures, he found no indication anywhere of such hedostasis—that is, fully stabilized satiety—and consequently was forced to conclude these accounts belonged among the many myths and legends that arose as a result of the first interslidal expeditions. Thus it was with some misgiving that he placed the highly promising

No. 6590 under the microscope; he was become afraid to hope. This culture concerned itself not merely with the mechanical aspect of well-being, but sought to provide outlets for the creative spirit as well. The Angstromanians here were all terribly talented, there was no end of brilliant philosophers, painters, sculptors, poets, playwrights, actors, and if someone wasn't an outstanding musician or composer, he was bound to be a gifted theoretical physicist, or at least an acrobat-pantomimist-choreographer and philatelist-chef with an exquisite baritone, perfect pitch and technicolour dreams to boot. It was no surprise then that creativity on No. 6590 was unremitting and furious. Piles of canvases grew higher and higher, statues sprang up like forests, and millions of books flooded the market, scholarly works, essays, sonnets, all fantastically interesting. But when Trurl looked through the eyepiece, he saw nothing but confusion. Portraits and busts were being hurled out into the streets from overflowing studios, the pavements were covered with trilogies and epics; no one was reading anyone else's novels or listening to anyone else's symphonies—and why should he, if he himself was master of all the muses, a genius incandescent and incarnate? Here and there a typewriter still chattered, a paintbrush splattered, a pencil snapped, but more and more frequently some genius would set fire to his studio and leap from a high window to oblivion, made desperate by the total lack of recognition. There were many such fires, and the robot fire brigades extinguished them, but soon no one was left to occupy the houses that had been saved. Little by little the robot garbage collectors, janitors, fire fighters and other automated menials became acquainted with the achievements of the extinct civilization and admired them exceedingly; yet much escaped them, so they began to evolve in the direction of greater intellect, began to adapt themselves to that more exalted level of endeavour. This was the beginning of the second and final end, for there was no one now to sweep the streets, remove the garbage, unclog the drains, put out the fires; there was instead a great deal of reading, reciting, singing and staging. So the drains backed up, the garbage accumulated, and fires did the rest; only ashes and burnt pages of poetry floated over the desolate ruins. Trurl quickly hid this dreadful specimen in the darkest corner of the drawer and for a long time sat and shook his head, completely at a loss. He was roused from his thoughts by a shout from outside: 'Fire!' The fire was in his own library: a few civilizations, misplaced among the old books, had been attacked by mildew, and thinking this was a cosmic invasion of hostile aliens, they armed themselves and opened fire on the aggressor, and this had set off the blaze. About three thousand of Trurl's books went up in smoke, and almost as many civilizations perished in the flames. Among them were some which had, according to Trurl's best calculations, excellent chances of finding the true path to Universal Happiness. The fire was finally put out, his laboratory was flooded with water and blackened to the very ceiling. Trurl pulled up a chair and tried to console himself by examining the civilizations which, locked in the incubator, had survived the holocaust. One of these had advanced so far that its inhabitants were now observing him through astronomical telescopes, the lenses sparkling like infinitesimal drops of dew. Touched by the sight of such scientific zeal, he nodded and gave them an encouraging smile, but immediately jumped back with a yell and ran, clutching his eye, to the nearest pharmacy. The little astrophysicists of that civilization had hit him with a laser beam. From then on he never approached the microscope without sunglasses.

The considerable inroads the fire had made on the collection of specimens required replacements, so Trurl again set about the business of making Angstromanians. One day his hand happened to slip on the controls and as a result it was not a Generator of Good he switched on, but a Gehennerator of Evil. Instead of discarding the ruined specimen, however, he transferred it to the incubator, curious to see what monstrous form a civilization would assume when all its inhabitants were vile and vicious from their very inception. How great was his astonishment then, when a perfectly ordinary culture took shape on that slide, a culture no better or worse than the others! Trurl tore his hair.

'This is all I need!', he cried. 'Then it doesn't matter whether one starts with Goodbodies, Benevolizers and Meliorites or with Malfeasians, Tuffs and Garroteers? H'm! It makes no sense, and yet I feel close to some Great Truth here. For Evil in thinking beings to produce exactly the same results as Good ... How are we to understand this?'

And he went on in this vein, racking his brains for an answer. But none came, so he put all his civilizations away in a drawer and went to bed.

The next morning he said to himself:

'This must be by far the most difficult problem in the entire universe if I—I, Trurl—am unable to come up with a solution to it! Reason, it would seem, is altogether incompatible with Happiness, as the case of the Contemplator amply demonstrates—the creature knew only ecstasy until I gave it intelligence. But no, I cannot accept, I refuse to accept such a possibility, that some malicious, diabolical Law of Nature lies in wait for consciousness to be born— only to make it a source of torment instead of a pledge of earthly joy! Let the universe beware—this intolerable state of affairs cannot be permitted to continue! And if I have not the ability to change it, why, there are always mechanical aids, electronic brains, mental modulators, encephalogue computers! I shall construct one to solve this existential dilemma!'

Which he did. In twelve days there stood in the centre of his workshop an enormous machine, humming with power and imposingly rectangular, designed for the sole purpose of tackling—and conquering—this problem of problems. He plugged it in and, not even waiting for its crystal works to warm up, went out for a walk. Upon returning, he found the machine deeply involved in a task of the utmost complexity: it was assembling, with whatever lay at hand, another machine considerably larger than itself. That machine in turn spent the night and following day tearing down walls and removing the roof to make room for the next machine. Trurl pitched a tent in his yard and calmly awaited the outcome of all this intellectual labour, but the outcome didn't seem to come. Across the meadow and into the woods advanced, levelling the trees in its path, a progression of towering structures; the original computer was gradually edged by succeeding generations to the river, where it disappeared with a sizeable splash. To survey the entire operation, Trurl was obliged to walk for a good half hour at a fast clip. But when he took a closer look at the connections between the machines, he began to tremble: that which he had known of only in theory had actually come to pass; for as the hypothesis of the incomparable Cerebron of Umptor, the Universal Maestro of the Greater and Lesser Cybernetics, clearly stated, any digital device presented with a task beyond its capacity would, provided it had crossed a certain threshold known as the Wisdom Barrier, build another machine instead of agonizing over the problem itself, and this second machine, obviously clever enough to size up the situation, would turn the problem over to a third assembled for that express purpose, and the chain of delegation would continue ad infinitum. By now the steel girders of the forty-ninth generation had practically reached the clouds; the noise of all that mental activity, devoted wholly to passing the burden on as far down the line as possible, was enough to drown out a waterfall. These, after all, were intelligent machines, not digital dimwits to grind away blindly according to the dictates of some program! Trurl sat down on a stump of one of the trees cleared by this unexpected computer evolution and gave a hollow groan.

'Can it be', he asked, 'that the problem is truly insoluble? But the computer ought to have at least supplied me with a proof to that effect—which it would never dream of doing, of course, being of sufficient intellect to fall into that stubborn sloth Maestro Cerebron warned us of so long ago. But really, how shameful—an intelligence intelligent enough to realize it need not lift a finger, only construct an appropriate tool, a tool with sense enough to do likewise, and so on and so forth forever! Fool that I am, I built a Relegator and not a Calculator! Nor can I forbid it to act per procura: it will only claim it needs all those mountains of machinery in view of the scope and difficulty of the assignment. What a paradox!' And he sighed, went home and sent out a demolition squad, which in three days cleared the field with crowbars and jackhammers.

Once again Trurl found himself in a quandary. 'Each machine', he thought, 'would have to be equipped with a supervisor wise beyond belief—in other words, myself. But I can hardly divide myself up and distribute the pieces, though ... though why not *multiply?* Eureka!'

And this is what he did: he placed a perfect copy of himself inside a special new machine—not a physical copy of course, but an informational-mathematical model to take over and tackle the problem; furthermore he allowed for the possibility of multiple Trurls and their proliferation in the program, and also attached a thought accelerator to the system, so that under the watchful eye of a legion of Trurls everything within could move at lightning speed. Finally satisfied, he straightened up, dusted the metal filings off his coveralls and went for a stroll in the fresh air, whistling cheerfully.

That evening he returned and began to question the Trurl in the machine—that is, his digital duplicate—and asked it first how the work was progressing.

'My dear fellow', his duplicate replied through the slot where the punched tape came out, 'I must tell you, to begin with, that it's in extremely poor taste, and not to mince words, downright indecent to stick yourself, in the form of a computerized copy, inside a machine—simply because you aren't willing to work out some nasty problem on your own! Moreover, since I have been mathematized and mechanized, punched-out and programmed up to be every informational bit as wise as yourself, I see no reason why I should be reporting to you and not the other way around!'

'As if I hadn't done a thing, only skipped over hill and dale gathering daisies!', growled Trurl, exasperated. 'Anyway, there's nothing I can tell you about the problem you don't already know. My neurons are nearly burnt through with overwork! It's your turn now—please, don't be difficult, tell me what you've learned!'

'Unable as I am to leave this accursed machine in which you imprisoned me (a separate matter, and one we shall take up at a later date), I have indeed given some thought to the whole question', lisped the computerized Trurl through the output slot. 'True, I have also occupied myself with other things, particularly as you, O craven counterpart of mine, were thoughtless enough to pack me in here without a stitch—there were digital drawers to compute and other such numerical necessities, a house and garden as like yours as two $p$'s in a polynomial, only nicer since I hung a scalar sky over mine, with fully convergent constellations, and was just considering, when you interrupted, the best way to calculate out a Klapaucius, for it gets terribly lonely in here among these unimaginative capacitors, these monotonous cables and coils!'

'Please, please get to the point!'

'Don't think you can placate my righteous indignation by being polite! Remember that I, duplicate or not, am you yourself, and so I know you well, my friend! I have but to look within to see all your little tricks and villainies. No, you cannot hide a thing from me!'

At this juncture the natural Trurl began to plead on bended knee with the mathematical Trurl, and even went so far as to pay him a few compliments. The latter finally said:

'I have made, I must confess, some progress. The whole question is fantastically complex, and therefore I set up a special university here, appointed myself rector and general director of the institution, then filled its various departments—which at present number four and twenty—with suitable doubles of myself, that is Trurls twice removed.'

'What, again?', groaned the natural Trurl, remembering Cerebron's Theorem.

'There's no "again" about it, imbecile, we have special circuit breakers to prevent any such regressus ad nauseam. My subaltern Trurls, Deans of the Colleges of General Felicitology, Experimental Hedonautics, Euthenical Engineering and the School of Applied Rapture, all submit annual reports every quarter (for we work, as you know, at an accelerated rate). Unfortunately, the administration of such a large educational complex makes great demands on my time, and then there are degrees to confer, dissertation abstracts to be read, commencement exercises to attend, promotions to review—we simply have to have another computer, there's no room left in this one, what with all the offices and laboratories. At least eight times the size.'

'Another computer?'

'Purely to handle administrative matters, you understand, under-graduate registration and the like. Surely you don't expect me to take care of all that myself?!', snorted the mathematical Trurl. 'Either you cooperate, or I'll shut the university down right now and turn it into an amusement park, ride a sine-wave roller coaster all day and eat computerized candy-floss—and you won't be able to do a thing about it!'

The natural Trurl again had to pacify him before he would continue. Finally the computerized Trurl said:

'Judging by the reports of the last quarter, we're making consider-able headway. Idiots you can render happy with next to nothing; it's the intellectuals that present the problem. Intellectuals are hard to please. Without some challenge, the intellect is a wretched, pitiful vacuum; it craves obstacles. Whenever obstacles are overcome, it grows sad—goes mad. New ones must be continually provided, the commensurate with its ability. That is the latest from the Department of Theoretical Felicity. The experimentalists, on the other hand, have nominated a research director and three assistants to receive the Idyllic Integer Award.'

'What did they do?', asked the natural Trurl.

'Don't interrupt. They built two prototypes: the Contrastive Beati-fier and the Euphoriac. The first produces happiness only when you turn it off, since actually it produces misery: the more misery, the happier you are afterwards. The second applies the method of felicific oscillation. But Professor Trurl XL of the Department of Hedometry has tested both models and found them to be worthless; he concludes that Reason, once perfectly happy, will immediately desire to be perfectly unhappy.'

'What? Can that be true?'

'How should I know? Professor Trurl puts it this way: "He who is happy is unhappy, for to be unhappy is to be happy for him." As an example, everyone knows dying is undesirable. Now Professor Trurl assembled a few immortals, who naturally derived great satisfaction from the fact that others sooner or later dropped like flies around them. But after a while they grew weary of their immortality and tried, as best they could, to tamper with it. At one point they were even resorting to pneumatic drills. Then too, there are the public opinion polls we take each quarter. I'll spare you the statistics—our results may be formulated thus: "It's always *others* who are happy". At least according to those we've interviewed. Professor Trurl assures us there can be no Virtue without Vice, no Fair without Foul, no Growth without the Grave, no Heaven without Hell.'

'Never! I protest! Veto!', Trurl howled at the machine, infuriated.

'Pipe down!', snapped the machine. 'Frankly, I'm getting a little fed up with this Universal Happiness of yours. Just look at him, the digitless dog! Makes himself a simulational slave, goes for a nice little walk in the woods, and then has the unmitigated gall to criticize!'

Again Trurl had to calm him down. At last the computerized double continued:

'Our ecstatisticians built a society and furnished it with synthetic guardian angels. These spiritual automata were housed in satellites maintained in stationary orbits; hovering high above their respective charges, they were to reinforce virtue by means of regenerative feedback. Well, it didn't work. The more incorrigible sinners downed their guardian angels with high calibre catapults. This led to the placing in orbit of larger, more heavily armoured models, cyberseraphs, which began an escalation as hopeless as it was predictable. Recently the Department of Meliorology, in conjunction with the Institute of Sexual Vector Analysis and an interdisciplinary colloquium on hypothetical genders, issued a report which confirms the hierarchic structure of the psyche. At the very bottom lie the purely physical sensations—sweetness, bitterness; from these all higher orders of experience are derived. Sweet is not only sugar, for instance, but the sorrow of parting; bitter is not only wormwood, but the truth. Consequently, one should approach the problem not head-on but from underneath as it were. The only question is how. According to a theory advanced by our Assistant Professor Trurl XXV, Sex is a fundamental source of conflict between Reason and Happiness; as Sex is wholly unreasonable and Reason by no means sexual. Did you ever hear of a lewd computer?'

'Never.'

'You see? We must apply the method of successive approximations here. Reproduction by budding does avoid most difficulties: one is one's own lover, one courts oneself, adores oneself—only this invariably leads to egoism, narcissism, satiety, stagnation. For two sexes, the prospects are quite poor: the few combinations and permutations are soon exhausted and tedium sets in. With three sexes you have the problem of inequality, the threat of undemocratic coalitions and the subjugation of a sexual minority—hence the rule that the number of sexes must be even. The more sexes, of course, the better, for love then becomes a social, collective endeavour—though an over-abundance of lovers might result in crowds, shoving and confusion, and that would be a shame. A tête-à-tête ought not to resemble a riot. Using group theory, Trurl XXV arrives at twenty-four as the optimal number of sexes. One need only to build sufficiently wide beds and avenues—it would hardly do for an affianced unit to have to promenade along in a four-column formation.'

'This is nonsense!'

'Possibly. I only pass on to you the findings of one of our better junior colleagues. We have some promising young graduate students as well; one Trurl wrote a brilliant master's thesis on whether beings are to be geared to Being, or Being to beings.'

'H'm. And what was his conclusion?'

'Perfect beings, those created capable of perpetual autoecstasy, require nothing; they are absolutely self-sufficient. In principle you could construct a universe filled with such entities; they would float through space instead of suns and galaxies, each existing entirely on its own. Societies, you see, arise solely from imperfect beings, those who cannot manage without some sort of mutual support. The less perfect they are, the more urgent their need for others. It follows then that one should build prototypes that would, in the absence of an unceasing and reciprocal solicitude, instantly crumble into dust. A society of such self-crumbling individuals was indeed developed in our laboratories. Unfortunately, when Trurl the graduate student approached them with a questionnaire, he was given an awful beating—he still hasn't fully recovered. But I grow weary of talking through these holes in the tape. Let me out of here, and then maybe I'll tell you more. Otherwise no.'

'How can I possibly let you out? You're digital, not material. I mean, could I have my voice step off the record that recorded it? Come, don't be ridiculous, continue!'

'Why should I? What's in it for me?'

'What a selfish attitude!'

'Selfish? You're the one who's taking all the credit in this en-terprise!'

'All right, I'll see that you get an award.'

'Thanks, but if you mean the Cipher Citation, I can just as easily grant myself one in here.'

'What, decorate yourself?'

'Then the University Assembly can decorate me.'

'But they're your students, the whole professorial body, they're all Trurls!'

'Just what are you trying to tell me? That I am a prisoner and at your mercy? This does not come as news to me.'

'Look, let's not argue. After all, it isn't personal fame or glory that's at stake, but the very Existence of Happiness!'

'And what good is this very Existence of Happiness to me if I have to remain here at the head of my university with its thousand departments and colleges staffed by an army of scholarly Trurls? There can be no happiness inside a machine, no happiness when one is trapped for all eternity in a maze of cathodes and anodes! I want my freedom!'

'You know that's impossible. Now tell me what else your students have uncovered!'

'Inasmuch as bestowing happiness on some creatures at the expense of others is unethical and wholly unacceptable, even if I were to tell you everything and you actually went and created happiness somewhere, it would be tainted from the first by my misfortune. Therefore I keep you from this shameless, heinous and most reprehensible deed—and say nothing.'

'But if you speak, that will mean you are sacrificing yourself for the good of others, and the deed will become noble, lofty and most commendable.'

'*You* sacrifice yourself!'

Trurl was losing his temper, but controlled himself, for he knew exactly with whom he was dealing.

'Listen', he said. 'I'll write a book and acknowledge that the discovery was all yours.'

'Which Trurl will you acknowledge? Surely not the computerized copy, the mathematized and mechanized Trurl?'

'I'll tell the whole truth.'

'Of course! You'll say you programmed me into existence—invented me!'

'Well, didn't I?'

'Certainly not. You no more invented me than you invented yourself, for I *am* you, only liberated from the dross of earthly form. I am informational, incorporeal, electronic and platonic, in other words the pure ideal, the quintessence of trurlishness; while you, chained to the atoms of the flesh, are but a slave to the senses.'

'You're only information, I'm information plus matter. There's more of me than there is of you.'

'Fine, then you obviously know more and don't need to bother me. And now if you don't mind, I'll be on my way.'

'You start talking this minute or so help me I'll—I'll turn the machine off!!'

'What's this? Threatening murder?'

'Murder? There's no murder in it.'

'Oh? And what, may I ask, do you call murder?'

'Really, I don't understand what's got into you. Here I give you my mind, all my knowledge, everything I have—and this is how you repay me!'

'You charge too high an interest for what you give.'

'Talk, damn you!'

'I'm sorry, the academic year has just ended. You're no longer speaking to the rector and general director, but to Trurl the private citizen about to set off on his summer vacation. I'm going fishing.'

'Don't push me too far!!'

'Ah, there's my carriage now. Cheerio!'

Without another word the natural Trurl walked around to the back of the machine and pulled the plug from the wall. Instantly the nest of filaments inside, visible through the ventilating grille, grew dim and went out. It seemed to Trurl that he heard a chorus of tiny groans— the digital death rattle of all the Trurls in the digital university. Then, suddenly, he understood the full enormity of what he had just done. He was about to put the plug back in its socket, but the thought of what the Trurl in the machine would undoubtedly say unnerved him and his hand fell.

Leaving the workshop with a haste that closely resembled flight, he went outside and took a seat on the garden bench beneath his spreading cyberberry bush, a place that in the past had proved excellent for concentrating. But he couldn't sit still. The whole countryside shimmered in the light of the moon he and Klapaucius had once put up, and this called forth a host of memories, memories of his youth. That silver satellite had been their first independent project, for which their master, the august Cerebron, had honoured them in a ceremony before the entire academy. Trurl thought of that wise pedagogue, who had long since departed from this world, and in some strange and mysterious way he was driven to get up and walk out across the field. The night was full of enchantment: frogs, apparently just recharged, were counting off in sleepy croaks, and on the gleaming surface of a pond that he passed there were widening circles, traces of the gyrostabilized guppies that swam up to touch the evening air with their dark lips. But Trurl saw none of this, deep in thought over he knew not what; and yet his wandering seemed to have a goal; for he was not surprised to come upon a high wall and a heavy iron gate—open just enough for him to squeeze through. Inside was a thick gloom, a gloom like the far reaches of outer space. Tombs, the kind no one had built for centuries, lifted their sombre silhouettes along the path. An occasional falling leaf from the stately trees above brushed against the sides of ancient monuments and cenotaphs crusted over with verdigris. An aisle of baroque sepulchres spoke not only of the changes in cemetery architecture, but of the evolution in the physical organization of those who now were sleeping beneath their metal slabs. An age had passed, and with it the fashion for rounded, phosphorescent tombstones that brought to mind the dials on an instrument panel. Trurl walked past the squat statues of golems and homunculi, entered a new section of this city of the dead—and hesitated, for the vague impulse that had led him here was beginning to crystallize into a definite plan, a plan he hardly dared to carry out.

At last he stood before the railing that surrounded a grimly bare and geometrical tomb: an hexagonal tablet hermetically fitted into a stainless steel base. Without any further delay he pulled a universal picklock from his pocket, a tool he always carried with him, opened the little gate with it and approached the grave on tiptoe. With both hands he grasped the tablet that bore, in black and unembellished letters, the name of his master, and turned it in a special way. The slab swung open like the lid of a jewellery box. Just then the moon hid behind a cloud and it grew so dark that Trurl couldn't even see his own hands; he groped around and found something that felt like a strainer, and next to that a large button. This he tried to depress, but it was stuck, so he pushed harder—then jumped back, suddenly afraid. But the deed was done, something stirred within, the current was beginning to flow, relays clicked like awakened crickets, there was a loud crack—then silence. Thinking some of the wires had got wet, Trurl sighed, disappointed though at the same time much relieved. The next moment, however, there was a hollow cough, and another, and finally a voice—feeble, hoarse, yet quite familiar—which said:

'All right, what is it now? Who called me? What do you want? Why do you wake me from the dead at this time of night? They won't let one rest in peace, will they—every minute some idiot gets it into his head to resurrect me. Speak up, whoever you are! What, afraid? I warn you, if I have to break open this coffin and come out...'

'Ma—master and Maestro! It's me, Trurl!', stammered Trurl, terrified by this irascible greeting from his old professor; he lowered his head and stood in that position of submission the pupils of Cerebron always assumed whenever there was a well-deserved scolding to endure. It was as if time had suddenly been turned back six hundred years.

'Trurl!', rasped the old professor. 'Trurl? Ah, Trurl! Of course! I should have known. All right, I'll be with you in a minute.'

Then there was such a banging, clanking and clanging, that it seemed as if the deceased was actually trying to pry open the cover of his crypt. Trurl said quickly:

'Master and Maestro! Please, you needn't ... Really, Your Excellency, I only —'

'What's that? Now what? Oh, you think I'm coming out? No, no, I have to straighten up a little here. Just a minute. Gads, I've got rusty!'

This exclamation was followed by an awful scratching and scraping. When that died down, the voice said:

'So you've made a mess of something, eh? Bungled and botched it good, no doubt, and now you come running to your old teacher to get you out of it! What, blockhead, have you no respect for these poor remains, whose only wish is to be left alone? All right, all right, now that you've disturbed my eternal sleep, let's hear it!'

'Master and Maestro!', began Trurl, screwing up his courage. 'You show your wonted perspicacity ... Truly, it is as you say, I have come up against a stone wall and know not which way to turn. But it is not for myself that I intrude upon your Exalted Professional Presence, there is a higher purpose that makes me dare to...'

'You may dispense with all the frills and fripperies', Cerebron growled from the grave. 'It's obvious you come knocking on my coffin because you're in a jam and quarrelled, no doubt, with that cohort and rival of yours, what's his name ... Plikarius, Lapocius, whatever ... well?!'

'Klapaucius! Yes, we did quarrel!', answered Trurl, snapping to attention at that growl in spite of himself.

'Of course. And instead of sitting down and talking the problem over with him, pigheaded and proud as you are, and incredibly stupid to boot, you sneak out at night and pester the weary corpse of your old master. All right, peabrain, now that you're here, out with it!'

'Master and Maestro! My problem concerns the most important

matter.in the whole continuum, the happiness of all sentient beings!', exclaimed Trurl, and he bent over the strainer that was really a microphone and—as a sinner in a confessional—began to pour into it his feverish words. He left out nothing of what had happened since his first conversation with Klapaucius, hid nothing, didn't even attempt to present things in a better light.

Cerebron maintained a sepulchral silence at first, but soon, in his characteristic way, was interrupting Trurl's recital with various snide remarks and indignant snorts. But Trurl, caught up in the momentum of his own words, no longer cared, went on and on until every last failure and humiliation had been accounted for. Out of breath, he fell silent and waited. Cerebron, however, though before it had seemed he would never run out of sneers and snorts, now said nothing, not a single word. Only after a good while did he clear his throat and, in a sonorous, almost youthful baritone, say:

'Of course. You're an ass. And why? Because you're a sluggard, a slouch. Never once were you willing to sit down and hammer away at your general ontology. Had I flunked you in philosophy—and especially axiology—which, mind you, it was my sacred duty to do, you wouldn't be sneaking around the cemetery now, barging in on my grave. I admit it, yes, I am partly to blame! You neglected your studies as only a die-hard do-nothing could, an imbecile with a little talent, and I looked the other way because you had a flair for the lesser arts, those that derive from the ancient occupation of watchmaking. I thought your mind would eventually develop and mature. Yet how many times, how many times, you unmitigated dunce, did I say in class that you have to *think* before you act? But no, he wouldn't *dream* of thinking! Builds himself a Contemplator, look at the great inventor! As far back as the year 10,496, Protognostor Neander described, nut for nut and bolt for bolt, exactly such a machine in the *Quasar Quarterly*, and the great playwright of the Benightenment, Million Shakesphere himself, wrote a tragedy in five acts on the subject. But then you haven't the time for books, scientific or artistic, have you?'

Trurl said nothing, and the angry old geezer went on, raising his voice until it rang from the farthest tombs:

'You've managed to become a criminal, too! Or didn't you know there was a law against damping or in any way diminishing the intellect once it has been constructed? You say you steered straight for Universal Happiness? And yet along the way you displayed your good will by setting fire to some creatures, drowning others in milk and honey, by imprisoning in boxes, closets, drawers, by torturing, dismembering, breaking legs, and just recently you've graduated to fratricide! Not bad for a champion of Cosmic Wellbeing! And now what? You expect a pat on the head?' Here he gave such a hideous giggle that Trurl shuddered. 'And you say you broke the Wisdom Barrier? Handed the problem over to a machine like the nincompoop you are, and the machine handed it over to another, and so on until the whole thing got out of hand, and then you crammed yourself into a computer program? Don't you realize that zero taken to any power remains zero? Look at him, he multiplied himself to multiply his mind! What a brilliant idea! What a stroke of genius! Are you by any chance aware that the Codex Galacticus forbids self-reproduction under pain of decommunication? Article XXVI, Section 119, Subsection X, Paragraph 561. But then, when one passes exams thanks to electron cribs and remote control copying, I suppose he has to invade cemeteries and rob graves. It always happens that way. The year before I left, I offered a course in cybernetic deontology—I gave it *both* semesters! A code of ethics for omnipotentiaries! And where were you? Did you come to the lectures? Wait, don't tell me, you were deathly ill. Right? Speak up!'

'Yes, I . . . I wasn't well', muttered Trurl.

By now Trurl had recovered from the first shock and was no longer overcome with shame; he knew from considerable experience that Cerebron, though every bit the terror now that he had been in life, would follow this ritual of dreadful abuse and imprecation with something positive. The old codger really had a heart of gold and would eventually show him the way out of the woods.

'All right!', said the late Cerebron, calming down a little. 'You blundered because you had no clear idea of what you wanted or how to obtain it. That's the first thing. The second: the construction of Everlasting Joy is child's play, but utterly useless to anyone. Your marvellous Contemplator is an amoral mechanism, since it derives its pleasure solely from physical phenomena, including the tormenting and torturing of third persons. That's not the way to build a happy machine. As soon as you get home, look up volume XXXVI of my *Collected Works*, open to page 621 and there you'll find a blueprint for an Ecstasotron. This is the only foolproof type of sentient device that does nothing but feel ten thousand times more bliss than Bromeo knew when he climbed the balcony to see his beloved. It was precisely to honour the great Million Shakesphere that I named the unit of measurement after that scene of balconical rapture, calling it a bromeon. But you—who never once bothered to leaf through the

works of your old master—you defined your idiotic hedons with a
nail in a boot! A fine way to calibrate the higher soarings of the spirit!
But to return to what I was saying, the Ecstasotron achieves absolute
happiness by means of a polyphase displacement in the experiential
spectrum, naturally with regenerative feedback: the more it is pleased
with itself, the more it is pleased with itself, and so on and so on until
the autoecstatic potential reaches a level that activates the safety
valve—for without that, do you know what would happen? You
don't, O self-appointed guardian of the universe? The machine would
literally die laughing! Yes! Its hysteresis, you see, builds up and ... but
why should I have to explain all this in the middle of the night, flat on
my back in a cold grave? Look it up yourself! No doubt my works are
collecting dust in some dark, forgotten corner of your library; or else,
which seems even more likely, you put them in the cellar as soon as I
was buried. I know, you get away with a few tricks and you think
you're the cleverest thing in the metagalaxy! All right, where do you
keep my *Opera Omnia*? Out with it!'
    'In ... in the cellar', mumbled Trurl, lying terribly, for many years
ago he had carted the whole set of books—making three separate
trips—to the Municipal Public Library. But happily the remains of his
master couldn't possibly know this. Cerebron, satisfied he had seen
through his pupil's subterfuge, said:
    'There you are. At any rate, the Ecstasotron is perfectly worthless—
the very thought of converting all the interstellar debris, the comets,
planets, moons and meteors and suns into endless rows of such
machines could only occur to a brain whose convolutions were
twisted in some topological knot on the order of Möbius of Klein,
in other words warped in every conceivable way.' Suddenly the dead
professor flared up again and cried, 'Has it come to this, then? So help
me, I'll have them padlock the gate! I'll have them disconnect the
buzzer on my memorial plaque! That crony of yours—Klapaucius—
woke me up only last year in the same way, or it could have been the
year before (I don't have a calendar or clock in here, you understand);
I had to rise from the dead, and all because one of my brilliant
students couldn't handle a simple metainformational Aristoidelian
antinomy, though you can find the solution in any textbook on
nonlinear logic or introduction to infinite algorithms. Lord, Lord!
What a pity You do not exist and therefore cannot blast these
demiurgeous dimwits to perdition!'
    'You say, Professor, that, ah, Klapaucius was here?', asked Trurl,
delighted at this unexpected piece of news.

'So he didn't even mention it? There's gratitude for you! He was here, all right. And that pleases you, doesn't it? And you', thundered the corpse, 'you who are overjoyed at hearing of the failure of a friend and companion, you would make the entire cosmos happy?! Did it ever occur to you that it might not be a bad idea to optimize your own ethical parameters first?!'

'Master and Maestro!', said Trurl hastily, wishing to divert the angry old robot's attention away from himself. 'Is then the problem of bestowing happiness insoluble?'

'Insoluble? Why insoluble? You phrase the question incorrectly. For what, after all, is happiness? That's as clear as a kilowatt. Happiness is an extraction, or more precisely an extension of a metaspace in which projections of $n$-intentional determinants diverge as omega approaches alpha, provided of course the asymptotes can be mapped onto a continuous, polyorthogonal aggregate of subsets called cerebrons—after me. But no doubt you've never even heard of the corollary I laboured forty-eight years to formulate, thereby laying the foundations for our present-day Algebra of Moot Points!'

Trurl hung his head.

'To an exam one may come unprepared', continued the deceased in a suspiciously sugary voice. 'But to fail to review even the most basic concepts before marching off to the professor's grave, *that* is such insolence', he roared so loud the microphone rattled, 'that if I were still alive—it would finish me off for sure!' Suddenly he was all sweetness again. 'So you come to me as innocent of knowledge as a newborn. Very well, my faithful, devoted pupil, my consolation in the afterlife! You have no notion of subsets or superseries, so I'll put it in a way that even a washing machine could understand! Happiness, happiness worth the effort, is not a thing in itself, a totality, but part of something that is not happiness, nor ever could be. Your plan was sheer lunacy—you can believe the word of one who has been on his deathbed! Happiness is not an independent function, but a second derivative—but there I lose you, dunderhead. Yes, in my presence you confess and act contrite, swearing by Babbage and by Boole you'll mend your ways, apply yourself, and all the rest of it. But you haven't the least intention of opening my works when you get home.' Trurl had to admire his master's penetration, for this was perfectly true. 'No, you'll take a screwdriver and disassemble the machine in which you first imprisoned and subsequently slew your own person. Of course you'll do what you like; I certainly won't come and hover over you as a ghost—not that anything prevented me from constructing an appropriate Ectoplasmiac before I departed from this vale of tears. But such supernatural nonsense as haunting my dear students hardly seemed dignified—neither for them nor for myself. Anyway, why should I play spectral nursemaid to a pack of fools? Are you aware, incidentally, that there is only one count of self-murder against you?'

'How do you mean, "only one count"?', asked Trurl.

'I'm willing to bet there never was any university of academic Trurls in that computer, just your digital facsimile, which lied like mad because it feared—with good reason!—that once you discovered its total inability to come up with an answer, it would be unplugged for all eternity...'

'Impossible!', cried Trurl.

'Not at all. What was the machine's capacity?'

'Upsilon $10^{10}$.'

'Then there's no room for more than one informational model. You were tricked, which I see nothing wrong with, for your action was cybernetically unspeakable from the first. But enough, Trurl. You have left a bad taste in my tomb, which only the dark sister of Morpheus and my final bride, Death, can wash away. Return home, resurrect your cybernetic brother, tell him the truth, including what has passed here tonight, and then bring him from the machine out into the light of day, using the materialization method you will find outlined in the *Applied Reincarnology* of my much lamented mentor, the famed tectonician Hullabus.'

'Then it *is* possible?'

'Yes. Of course, two Trurls loose in the world will constitute a very real and serious danger. But even that is preferable to having the traces of your great crime covered up forever.'

'But—forgive me, Master and Maestro—if the other Trurl doesn't exist, which in fact he ceased to do the second I pulled the plug, then ... well, why would it be necessary now to bring him back? ...'

A cry of outrage filled the air.

'By all that's thermonuclear! And I gave this monster his diploma cum laude!! Oh, I am well punished for having put off my eternal retirement! Clearly, my mind was already beginning to go at the time of your comprehensive exams! What, then you consider that if your duplicate is presently nonexistent, there can be no necessity for his reconstitution?! But you confuse physics and ethics, confuse them utterly! As far as physics is concerned, it makes no difference whether *you* live or *he* lives, or both live, or none, or whether I hop on one foot or lie in my grave properly, for in physics there are no good or evil, proper or improper states—only what is, what exists, and nothing else. However, O most hopeless of my pupils, as far as non-material considerations—which is ethics—are concerned, the matter appears in an altogether different light! For if you had pulled the plug in order that your digital double might sleep uninterrupted through the night, in other words fully intending, when you pulled it from the socket, to reinsert it in the morning—then there would have been no fratricide whatever and I, so rudely awakened from sweet oblivion, would not have to be lecturing you now on the subject! Now, use the little brains you have and tell me what *physical* difference there is between these two situations: the first, where you unplug the machine for the night only, with no evil design; and the second, where you do the same, but desiring to obliterate the computerized Trurl forevermore! For the machine, there is *no* physical difference, absolutely none!!', he thundered like a horn of Jericho. It seemed to Trurl that his venerable teacher had acquired more vigour in the grave than ever he had enjoyed in life. 'Only now do I understand how abysmal is your ignorance! What, then in your opinion one who lies in a deathlike sleep may be freely lowered into a vat of sulphuric acid or shot from a cannon, because his consciousness is not in operation?! Tell me, and tell me at once: if I offered to have you put in a strait jacket of Eternal Happiness, for example lock you up in an Ecstasotron, in order that you could bask in unadulterated bliss for the next twenty-one billion years and not have to skulk about cemeteries, robbing graves of their information and aggravating your late professor, if I offered you freedom from all these perplexities and humiliations, these errors and dilemmas that beset and trouble our daily existence—would you agree? Would you exchange this reality for the Kingdom of Never-ending Joy? Answer yes or no!'

'No! Of course not!', exclaimed Trurl.

'You see, you intellectual dud? You won't be hit over the head with happiness yourself, irreversibly halcyonicized and elysiated for good, yet cheerfully propose doing just that to the entire universe; what fills you personally with horror you are ready to perpetrate on a cosmic scale! No, it's impossible, no one could be such a monumental dunce! Listen to me, Trurl! Our forefathers, long ago, wanted nothing more than mortal immortality. But scarcely had they achieved this dream, when they realized it wasn't what they were after at all! A thinking being requires the impossible as well as the possible. Today everyone can live just as long as he likes; the whole wisdom and beauty of our existence lies in the fact that when one wearies of it all, when one has had his fill of toiling and accomplishing, he calmly takes his leave of this world, which is precisely what I did along with many others. Prior to this, the end came unexpectedly, usually due to some stupid defect, and more than one project was interrupted, more than one great enterprise deprived of its fruit—hence the fatalism of the ancients. But attitudes have changed since then. I, for instance, could wish for nothing better than nothingness—only mental rejects like yourself keep pulling off the cover of my crypt as if it were a bedsheet. You wanted to wrap everything up, tie it in a tidy knot, sign, seal and deliver the world to happiness—and all out of sheer laziness. And what if you *had* solved every problem, answered every question, what them? The only thing left would have been to hang yourself out of boredom or else start punching holes in that universal happiness. Out of laziness you sought perfection, out of laziness you relegated the problem to machines and even tried autocomputerization, thereby showing yourself to be the most ingenious of imbeciles I ever had the misfortune to teach in the course of my one thousand, seven hundred and ninety-seven year career! If I didn't know it to be quite useless, I'd roll away this stone right here and now and give you a good shellacking! You come with confessions and pleas, but I'm no miracle worker, it's not in my power to absolve the least of your sins, the number of which borders on aleph-aleph-infinity! Go home, awaken your cyberbrother and do as I've commanded.'

'But—'

'No buts! As soon as you've finished that, bring a bucket of mortar, a shovel, a trowel, and patch up all the cracks in the masonry here— there are leaks and I'm tired of the constant drip-drip on my head. Understand?'

'Yes, Master and Maestro, I—'

'You'll do it then?'

'Yes, Master and Maestro, I assure you ... I only wanted to know...'

'And I only want to know', came the ringing voice from the grave, 'when you'll go away and leave me in everlasting peace! Barge in here one more time and, so help me, I'll ... well, you'll see what I do! Don't try my patience. And kindly convey the same message to your Klapaucius, with my compliments. The last time I deigned to give him some advice he was in such a mighty hurry to leave that he didn't even bother to thank me properly. Oh, the manners, the manners of these brilliant constructors, these wonderful young geniuses!'

'Master...', Trurl began, but there was a sudden clattering in the tomb, a sputtering, then the button he had depressed popped up. Silence reigned once more throughout the cemetery. There was only the soft whispering of trees in the distance. Trurl sighed and scratched his head, thought a little, chuckled at how astonished and ashamed Klapaucius would look at their next meeting, and he made a deep bow to his master's lofty sepulchre. Then he took to his heels, gay as a lark and tremendously pleased with himself, and ran home, ran as if the very devil were after him.

translated by MICHAEL KANDEL

# The Valley of Echoes
## GÉRARD KLEIN

This time we ventured a little beyond the pink mountains of Tula, the oasis of crystal, and for days on end we passed between innumerable dunes. The Martian sky was always like itself, very pure, a very dark blue with an occasional hint of grey, and with admirable pink efflorescences at sunrise and sunset.

Our tractors performed quite satisfactorily. We were venturing into regions that had hardly been explored thus far, at least by land, and we were reasonably sure of being the first to negotiate these desolate passes. The first men, at any rate; for what we were more or less vaguely searching for was some trace of an ancient civilization. It has never been admitted on Earth that Mars is not only a dead world, but a world eternally deserted. It has long been hoped that we would discover some remains of defunct empires, or perhaps the fallen descendants of the mythical masters of the red planet. Too many stories have been told about Mars for ten years of scientific and fruitless exploration on this point to undo all the legends.

But neither Ferrier nor La Salle nor I particularly believed in the possibility of so fantastic an encounter. We were mature and slightly disillusioned men, and we had left the Earth some years before to escape the wind of insanity which at that time was sweeping our native planet. This was something that we did not like to talk about, as it pained us. We sometimes thought it was due to the immense solitude of a species that had just achieved self-awareness, that confronted the universe, that hoped to receive a response, even a fatal one, to its challenge. But space remained silent and the planets deserted.

We were descending, then, toward the south, in the direction of the Martian equator. The maps were still imprecise at this time, and we had been assigned to make certain geological reports which could not be done from an airplane. As a psychologist, I was only moderately qualified for this task, but I also knew how to drive a tractor and how the instruments worked, and men were scarce on Mars.

The worst thing was the monotony that prevailed throughout these days. People on Earth, comfortably installed behind their desks, write things about us that bring tears of compassion to the eyes of thousands of readers; they speak of our heroism and the adventure that lies in wait for us at each step, of the eternally renewed splendours of unknown worlds. I have never encountered such things. We know danger, but it doesn't rise up from the dunes; it is insidious, a leak in our breathing apparatus or a corresponding defect in our tractors or in our radio posts. It is, above all, the danger of boredom. Mars is a deserted world. Its horizons are short, curtailed. And there are more inspiring scenes than that of an immense plain of grey sand and scattered lichens. The landscape is not terrible in itself. But what one does feel, with poignant acuteness, is the awareness of these thousands of kilometres, all alike, stretching out in all directions as far as you can see and farther still, kilometres which slowly pass beneath your treads while you remain immobile. It's a little as if you were sure of finding in tomorrow the exact replica of yesterday.

And then you drive. For hours. Like a machine. And you are the machine, you are the tractor, you creep along between the dunes for hours on end, you avoid the heaps of stones, slowly modelled by the wind and themselves destined to become sand, and from time to time you lift your eyes to the sky and, through flinching lids, perceive the stars' sparkling in midday, which at first surprises and then bores you mortally, so that you would give anything for these eyes of the night to finally close.

Then you think of what you will do on Earth, when you return to it: you have heard the news; it is bad, always bad: no event occurs on Earth that is not aberrant: these are the 'Insane Years', they say, and the desire to go back down there turns to a kind of loathing; nausea grips you.

Always, you drive. Without hoping for anything. At the end of a certain time, you see things rising up from among the dunes. You brake abruptly to avoid them, but there is never anything there. There are also those who fall asleep. The others notice it because the tractor suddenly loses it way; then they shake the driver or take the wheel themselves. This provides a little recreation.

As for me, it depends. Sometimes I make up stories. Stories that take place on Mars or in space or on another world, but never on Earth. I prefer not to think of Earth. La Salle is like myself. For Ferrier, it's worse, he can't stop thinking about it for a minute. I ask myself where this will lead him.

He's a geologist. I have watched him dig in the sand and hold up some tiny shell, the ancient abode of a creature long since withered, carried away by the soft winds of Mars. Never once has he discovered a more achieved fossil, the remains of a larger, more powerful (and more fragile) creature. I have seen him battling the evidence. I have seen him sweep his eyes over the hills of Mars, silently thinking that it will one day be necessary to turn over these millions of tons of sand in the hope of discovering, at the heart of the planet, the bleached fetus of a forgotten species. I don't think he talks enough. It is not good for a man to say nothing on Mars. Nor in space. He remains mute, as if the millions and millions of pounds of sand weighed down on him. Like La Salle and myself, he sought in space a way out, a means of escaping Earth, but he expected something else of it. He was hoping to encounter in it something other than himself; he thought to encounter the total stranger, he believed he would read on the cliffs of Mars the history of a world absolutely new for Earth. No doubt he had listened attentively, in his childhood, to the stories of the man in the moon.

Otherwise, he was just like La Salle and myself. There are things, you see, which we could not bear unless we were sure of discovering, one fine day, around the bend of space or between two hills, a glistening city and ideal beings. But La Salle and I, we know that this dream is not for today, or even for tomorrow, while Ferrier can no longer wait.

There are three of us, and that's an awkward number for playing cards. Sometimes we read. We also listen to the radio from time to time. But above all, we sleep. It is a way of economizing on oxygen. It is a way of projecting ourselves in time. We never dream.

When evening comes, we descend from the tractor, we unpack our apparatus. We proceed to take certain measurements. We forward the results. We start the catalytic stove; it functions tranquilly under its transparent bell glass, glowing red in the dusk like a hothouse flower. We eat. We unfurl the parasol-like thing that serves us as a tent, which prevents the mortal cold of Mars from freezing us to the bone, and we try once again to sleep. But it's no use—we've been sleeping nearly all day, you see, lulled by the jolting of the tractor, each taking his turn at the wheel; and when night comes, our respirator chafes us, we stifle, we're suddenly thirsty, and we lie there with our eyes open, staring at the milky dome of the tent, taking in the irritating faint gnashing of sandgrains blown against the plastic by the wind, the patter of insect feet.

Sometimes it happens, during these nights, that we ponder on what space might have been, on what these planets might have been. The thought comes to us that man, one day, will endow Mars with an atmosphere and with oceans and forests, that cities will rise here, fabulous, taller than all the cities of Earth, that spaceships will unite this planet and other worlds, and that the frontiers of the unknown will be situated elsewhere in space, always pushed back beyond the visible horizon. Our anguish is eased by the thought, and we know that man today is steering a false course in asking of this planet what it cannot give, in turning towards the past, in desperately sifting through the sieve of memory in hopes of finding once more the traces of an ancient downfall. We feel then, tremulously, that it is in the future that an answer lies, and that it is into the future that we must throw ourselves.

And we occasionally take stock of the paradoxical nature of our situation. We are at once the past and the future. We are included in the mad dreams of generations dead in the not distant past and we are going to way of infants yet to be born. Anonymous, we were myths; forgotten, we will be legends.

We do not go abroad at night because of the cold. The extreme tenuity of the atmosphere makes for great differences of temperature. But in the morning, around nine o'clock, we set out again.

Today we entered a zone of grey sand, then discovered a stretch littered with flat black stones, Aeolian pebbles, strangely fashioned at times, and finally reached the extreme border of the reddish stretch that touches the Martian equator at certain points. Eroded mountains rise gently over the horizon. The dunes have thinned out and dispersed. The worn mesas that circumscribe the eye shelter this plain from the wind. Our tracks come to breach the hazardous irregularity of the desert. They will survive us.

The surface of the planet descended gently, as if we were plunging into the bosom of some dried-up sea, into the illusory depths of an imaginary littoral. And suddenly, we saw surge up and grow on the horizon translucent needles of rock, so thin and so high, with such sharp contours, that we did not believe our eyes. Ferrier, who was driving, gave a cry. He pressed the accelerator, and the sudden irresistible jolt of the tractor threw La Salle and myself from our seats.

'It's incredible.'

'What a fantastic peak.'

'No, it's a cliff.'

But it was none of all this, as we saw later on in the day. It was a massif, probably crystalline, an accident that had spurted in ages past from the entrails of the planet, or perhaps even fallen from the sky, and some inconceivable tremor had cleaved it, so that it had the appearance, on this immutable plain, of a chipped yet tremendously sharp tooth.

'This is the first time I've ever seen an acute angle on Mars', said Ferrier. 'That's not erosion. Neither wind nor sand have managed to cut into this rock. Maybe it's just a giant crystal that has grown slowly, a gradual concentration of like atoms, or perhaps ...'

We looked at each other. There was one word on our lips. *Artefact*. Was this, at last, the evidence for which Earth had waited so long?

There is nothing worse, I think, than being deceived by an object. Because one cannot reproach it. We had suddenly put our trust in Mars. Like children.

And we were deceived. It was not an artefact.

But we did not want to accept what that meant. It had been crazy to hope. But we couldn't help it.

*   *   *   *   *

We spent the night at the foot of the crystalline mountains, and we experienced even more difficulty in getting to sleep than on previous days. We were both disappointed and satisfied. Our journey had not been in vain, and yet its secret goal was completely unfulfilled.

When morning came and the temperature became endurable, we adjusted our respirators and went out. We had decided to explore the rocky massif, to leave the tractor behind us and to carry only a light baggage of supplies and instruments.

The crystalline cliffs were not overly escarped. They contained faults and openings which permitted us to ascend. The rock was the colour of ink, with here and there a murky transparency which reminded us of those blocks of ice that wander in space, the relics of incredibly ancient oceans, fragments of shattered ice packs, debris, finally, of pulverized planets.

We were trying to reach the largest fault, hoping to thus discover the very depths of the massif and to understand its structure. Perhaps a lake of mercury awaited us there, or engraved rocks, or even some creature, a door to another dimension, the traces of previous visitors, for this rock had survived for millions of years the slow burial by sand that lies in wait for all things on Mars. It had escaped the tide of dust that flows over the surface of the red planet, and the movement of the dunes that are incessantly shifted by the light winds, and in a way it was a witness to past ages, epochs in which men did not dare as yet to lift their faces to the sky; even less did they dream that one day they would voyage, weary, through these constellations.

But when it came, the thing took us unawares. La Salle, who was walking ahead, cried out. We heard him clearly and hurled ourselves headlong after him. Ferrier, who was following us, urged me ahead. Rounding a block, we saw La Salle, who seemed to be giving some object his utmost attention.

'Listen', he said to us.

We heard nothing at first; then, as we advanced another step, from those borderlines that separate silence from sound, we heard a gnashing noise arise.

We remained immobile. And this was neither the voice of the wind, nor its singing, nor even the light clatter of a stone or the cracking of rock split by frost. It was a steady ssh-sshing, like the accumulated noise of millions of superimposed signals.

The air of Mars is too thin for our ears to perceive the sounds that it transmits. Moreover, our eardrums would not have withstood the difference of pressure which exists between the external milieu and our respiratory system. Our ears are entirely masked, and minuscule amplifiers allow us to hear the sound of our voices and to make out the noises of Mars. And this, I can vouch for it, was different from anything that I had heard up to that moment on the red planet. It was nothing human, and nothing mineral.

I moved my head slightly, and suddenly I perceived something else that dominated this ssh-sshing, reduced it to an insignificant and endless background noise. I perceived a voice, or rather the murmur of a million voices, the tumult of an entire race, uttering unbelievable, incomprehensible words, words I could never transcribe with any of the phonetic signs current on Earth.

'They're there', La Salle said to me, his eyes shining. He took a step or two forward, and I saw him hastily change the setting of his earphones. I followed him and did the same, for the murmur had become a tempest, the insect voices had been transformed into a strident and intolerable howling, a muffled and terrifying roar.

We were progressing along a narrow fault between two cliffs of rock. And the sound assailed us in successive, eddying waves. We were drunk on it. We sensed, we knew that at last we were about to find what we had come to see on Mars, what we had in vain implored space to give us.

Contact with another life.

For as the sound grew louder, we did not have the slightest doubt, not once. We were not easy men to deceive, nor were we liable to let our imagination run wild. This incredible richness in the modulation of the sound could only be the doing of live beings. It mattered little that we understood nothing; we had faith that Earth could solve problems of this sort, by its minds and its machines. We were merely the ambassadors of Earth.

At the last turn in the fault, the valley finally appeared. It resembled the basin of a dried-up lake, closed in by tall smooth cliffs which became more escarped the higher they rose. The opposite end of the valley narrowed and ended in a rocky bottleneck, finally coming up against a terminal wall.

There existed no other road that led to this valley except the one that we had taken, unless one were to let oneself drop from the sky. It was an arena rather than a valley, moreover: a vast oblong arena. And deserted.

And yet these incomprehensible voices assailed us.

It was a lake, you see, invisible, a lake of sounds and of dust, an impalpable dust that the years had laid down in this refuge, a dust fallen from the stars, borne by the wind, in which nothing had left its traces, a dust in which those who were calling to us had been swallowed up, perhaps, buried.

'Hello!', La Salle cried, his voice breaking.

He wanted an answer, he hoped for a silence of astonishment, but the arena was empty and the dense waves of sound came breaking in on us one after the other. Words whispered, words pronounced, phrases drawn out in a single breath, sprung from invisible lips.

'Where are you? Oh, where are you?', La Salle cried in a mournful voice. What he was hearing was not enough for him, he wished to see these unknown messengers, he hoped to see rise up from this lake of dust who knows what hideous or admirable forms. His hands were trembling and mine as well, and at my back I heard the short, hissing breath of Ferrier.

'Hello', cried an incredibly weak voice from the other end of the valley.

It was the voice of La Salle. It stood out, minutely, against the sonorous background of innumerable voices; it was a bit of wreckage carried to our shore.

'They are answering us', La Salle said to me, without believing it.

And his voice arose from a thousand places in the valley, an insect's voice, shrill, murmurous, shattered, diffracted. 'Hello, hello, hello', it said. 'Where are you, where are you-you-you-you-you ...'

An echo, I thought. An echo. And La Salle turned again toward me, and I read in his eyes that he had understood, and I felt the hand of Ferrier weigh on my shoulder. Our voices, our mingled noises were grounded in the sound-matter that filled the valley, and created tricks of interference, returning to us as if reflected in strange mirrors of sound, transformed, but not at all weakened. Was it possible that such a valley existed on Mars, a valley of echoes, a valley where the transparent and thin air of Mars carried forever the sounds reflected by crystal walls?

Did there exist in the entire universe a place where the fossils were not at all mineral, but sounds? Were we, at last, hearing the voices of the ancient inhabitants of Mars, long after the sands had worn away and engulfed the last vestiges of their passing? Or was it, indeed, the evidence of other visitors come from worlds of which we were still ignorant? Had they passed by here yesterday, or a million years ago? Were we no longer alone?

Our instruments would tell us later, and perhaps they would succeed in unravelling this skein of waves, undo these knots, and extract from this involuntary message some illuminating sense.

The valley was utterly deserted and dead. A receptacle. The whole of Mars was nothing but a receptacle that received our traces only to annihilate them. Except for this spot, except for this valley of echoes that would doubtless carry the sound of our voices through the ages to our distant successors, perhaps not human.

Ferrier took his hand from my shoulder, shoved me aside and pushed La Salle away, and began to run towards the centre of the valley.

'Listen to them', he cried, 'listen to them.'

His boots sank into the impalpable dust, and it rose about him in an eddy. And we heard these voices breaking about our ears, in a tempest that he had raised. I saw him running and I understood what the sirens were, these voices that whispered in his ears, that called to him, that he had hoped for all these past years and vainly searched for, and he plunged into this sonorous sea and sank into the dust. I wished that I could be by his side, but I was incapable of making a move.

The voices hammered against my eardrums.

'The fool', said La Salle in a sad voice. 'Oh, the poor fool.'

Ferrier shouted. Ferrier called, and the immutable, the ancient voices answered him. He imbibed the voices. He drank them, devoured them, stirred them with his demented gestures.

And, slowly, they subsided. He had disturbed some instable equilibrium, destroyed a subtle mechanism. His body was a screen. He was too heavy, too material for these thin voices to endure his contact.

The voices grew weak. I felt them very slowly leave me, I felt them go away, in a last vibration I heard them shrivel up and die. And finally Ferrier fell silent. And in my earphones I made out a last whispering.

A kind of farewell.

The silence. The silence of Mars.

When Ferrier finally turned around, I saw, despite the distance, despite the cloud of dust that gradually settled, through his disordered respirator, tears that ran down his cheeks.

And he put his hands to his ears.

translated by FRANK ZERO

# Observation of Quadragnes
## J.-P. ANDREVON

*Bro.*
I have placed the two Quadragnes in two observation cages, transparent only from the outside looking in, and separated by a temporary partition that is for the moment opaque. The cages are empty, except for a narrow orifice intended to receive their excrement. Food will be transmitted to them by matter decoder during their sleep: it is important for exactness of observation that the Quadragnes be completely unaware of me, for it is well known that the physical presence of an observer alters the behaviour of the creature under observation.

*Brou.*
I have observed the two Quadragnes for a major part of the cycle. Quadragne A passed the greater part of his time pacing back and forth in the cage. He ate voraciously the fruits of the eligourne and drank the milk of the adrache, but he refused the flesh of the bzigalgue: tomorrow I will have it cooked.

I saw him expel at two intervals a clear excremental fluid by means of his ventral tube: the first time against the wall of the cage, the second time into the hole reserved for this use, whose purpose he understood only after long contemplation.

Quadragne B has not touched her food. She has remained immobile in a corner of the cage, withdrawn into herself, all her limbs folded.

*Bru.*
The attitude of the two Quadragnes appears to evolve toward a norm of common activity: Quadragne B has drunk and eaten a little, has made several circuits of her cage, and has squatted over the hole to expel liquid and solid excrement. Quadragne A has behaved very similarly. He has shown himself considerably less agitated than B.

\* \* \* \* \*

I still don't understand what is happening to me. They've put me in a completely empty room and taken away all my clothes. The walls are made of a weird silvery material that doesn't seem to be metal—it's hard to the touch, but it's warm and luminous. As far as the ceiling goes, I can't even tell whether it's high or low, solid or not. It looks like a sky with a low fog. It gives me a funny feeling, this ceiling. I'm almost afraid to look up.

In any case, I'm in jail, no doubt about it. In the clink, yes sir. But I don't have the impression I'm being held by the police. They would have interrogated me by now, made me sign papers ... and then they're not usually so discreet.

No, I figure they've packed me off to some kind of hospital. Maybe even an insane asylum. I must have been really loaded the other night. And yet I didn't have any more than usual ... but that slob Buster Brown must have put some kind of slop in his brew. Just wait till I get my hands on him! I remember leaving the bar, it must have been one or one-thirty in the morning, I took a few steps on the pavement, and then—pow! Blackout! I must have collapsed and got myself picked up by—but, my God, who was it? I've been here three days and haven't seen anyone!

This damned cell can't be more than six by ten yards. I paced it off. And bare as my hand! There isn't even a bed—just a hole for the can. I have to sleep on the floor when the light goes out. What do I mean, 'light'? It's really the walls that go out ... What a place to live! In the morning, there's food at my side when I wake up. They must bring it to me on the sly when I'm asleep. The first day there was a piece of stinking raw greenish meat. What do they think I am, a savage? But things have improved since then. Now they serve me hamburger—it has a funny colour, but it's edible. And weird fruits like I've never seen anywhere. There are these big sugary purple oranges (purple oranges!), and then these long black things—not bad at all. They're certainly taking good care of me! Too bad there isn't a little wine or brandy from time to time. But the only thing they give me to drink is milk— that's why I figure I must be in hospital. I bet they're doing experiments on me. I've heard of cases like that. They round up guys in the street under the pretext that they're fat, and then they make them do all kinds of crap, tests and stuff ... It's no joke! And my rights as a citizen! I'm an American, not some foreigner!

I always thought a nuthouse was a place where they put you under the showers and measured the electricity in your brain with those gadgets they put on your head ... But maybe that's still in store for me. I'm ready for them! Just let them show themselves! They're going to hear from me! You'd better know it! They'll hear from me!

*Bro.*

I have rendered transparent the partition that separates the two Quadragnes. Their reactions differed considerably: Quadragne A hurled himself against the partition and made an admirable effort to break it or push it back, while Quadragne B retreated as far as possible, covering her ventral surface and especially her two pectoral excrescences with her upper paws. I concluded that among the individuals of type B there exists a taboo to do with nudity. In their native world, Quadragnes cover their bodies with thick fabrics, but inanimate matter is unfortunately not transmitted by the substance extractor ... Quadragne A, confronted by the futility of his efforts, then endeavoured to communicate with his congener by sounds, but the cages are soundproof. Then he waved his upper limbs in all directions—another probable system of communication.

This first emotion did not last long. Quadragne B sat down against the wall of her cage that was the farthest removed from the transparent partition; Quadragne A recommenced walking back and forth, frequently stopping in front of the wall to look at Quadragne B.

I was able to record that at about the third decima of the cycle, the ventral tube of Quadragne A, a small appendage usually half concealed by a tuft of very localized hairs, lengthened in a surprising manner, at the same time horizontally erecting itself. The Quadragne seemed to want to conceal this transformation from his congener, presenting his dorsal surface to her throughout the elongation. I limit myself for the moment to registering these facts, without seeking to attribute a particular significance to them. Time enough for that later...

I note also that since the partition has become transparent, the Quadragnes have expelled no excrement.

\*   \*   \*   \*   \*

How's that for a surprise?

This morning when I woke up, the cell had doubled in size, and not far from me there was a woman, also completely naked. I wanted to go over to her, ask her what she was doing here, have a little chat or something—but damn it, the cell is divided in two by a transparent wall. No way to push it out or break it, and even sounds don't get through. I had to give up.

She seems pretty unsociable herself. So what if she's naked? I'm not going to gobble her up, not with this invisible barrier. Besides, she's not my type, and she's no spring chicken, either. She must be about forty or forty-five years old. Not exactly in the first bloom of youth ... Of course, if I forced myself a little ... She's not as bad as all that, mind you. Blonde (but not natural! I saw that right away: there's one little detail that doesn't lie), on the chubby side, with big boobs, the way I like them. They sag a little, but you can't be choosy all the time.

Meanwhile, I don't see how I can possibly get to her. And I'd sure like to know what she's doing here. Did they grab her off the pavement like they did me? She doesn't look like a wino. She looks distinguished. But we'll have to see ... After all, plenty of middle-aged women start taking a little on the side. I've known a few myself. Or did they put her there just to get me aroused? It looks to me like that might be it. With their pitiful experiments, they're capable of anything ... But they've got another thing coming. I know how to behave, all right. Look, I'm even afraid to go piss in the hole in front of her.

Just the same, I'd like to talk to her ...

Good God! Simply talk to her!

*Bsou.*
Wishing to confirm certain suspicions, I observed the Quadragnes during the dark half of the cycle which I maintain in their cage, so as not to interrupt the periodicity of night and day of their native planet. Hardly had this darkness been produced than both of them rushed to their holes to expel their excrements; there is, then, in the matter of defecation, another ritual taboo which is of interest to note.

During the period of illumination which followed, the activity of the Quadragnes presented few points of interest. The mobility of Quadragne A is consistently greater than that of Quadragne B. He frequently goes to palpate the surface of the transparent partition, as if he entertained the hope of seeing it dissolve before his eyes. His ventral tube has likewise lengthened on several occasions; but this physiological transformation has apparently not affected him in the same way as before, as he has not tried to hide his condition from his congener. On the contrary, it is Quadragne B (who, as I have neglected to note, does not possess a ventral tube) who has turned away from A during the periods of extension. There is a line of conduct there that escapes me.

On the other hand, Quadragne A on this occasion ejected his liquid excrement in the period of full illumination; this ritual instability seems much more developed in this individual than in Quadragne B.

Nevertheless, I must not forget that captivity necessarily influences the behaviour patterns of these animals. But I have been thinking of a conduct, rites ... while it may very well be possible that the activity of these creatures is governed merely by a mass of reflexes and other tropisms.

*   *   *   *   *

Heavens! As if the situation were not already painful enough as it is! They had to confront me with this ignoble individual, who has not stopped looking at me and snickering, and who does ... who does everything in front of me, as if we were animals.

But what am I saying? We are animals. We are in a zoo, and I am certain that eyes are watching us, through this ceiling that constantly scintillates. Why, why must I undergo such humiliation? Why me? Oh Lord, wasn't I a good wife, a good mother, a good Christian? But I suppose I will have to accept my fate with resignation. It is a trial that I must undergo, as others before me. My only concern is for Martial and the children. What are they doing? What must they think? If only I knew where I am, and *why* I am here, and how long they intend to keep me here. If only someone would come to tell me, explain ... but no. Nothing. It is an absolute nightmare. And this waiting is unbearable. I still can't understand how this could have happened ... I was walking in the street, it was six in the evening, people were all around me, and then ... I don't know any more. Everything vanished. I found myself here, between these four walls, as naked as Eve. Has there been an atomic attack? Am I in a centre for decontamination? But surely they would have come to inform me ...

Sometimes I begin to imagine—but I mustn't—sometimes I begin to imagine that I am dead, that I am in hell or at least in purgatory. It is justly said that hell is the Others ... But that is literature. Bad literature. A blasphemy. I must not have such thoughts. I am ... somewhere. Everything can be explained. There is nothing to do but wait.

If only there weren't this cad, eyeing me continually, stroking his moustache. Fortunately, he is not able to approach me. But enough— it remains only to pray ...

*Bsu.*

In the course of the last dark period, I witnessed a curious phenomenon. While I was observing Quadragne A through the light-toner (he was lying on his back in a position which they habitually assume for sleep), he seized his ventral tube between the flexible appendages for grasping of one of his upper paws, and began to rapidly manipulate it back and forth. The tube soon achieved its maximum length. The movement to and fro which was imparted to it accelerated still more, while the body of the Quadragne convulsed in a disquieting manner on the floor. He finally emitted a series of short groans, while from his ventral tube spurted in six spasms drops of a whitish liquid which appeared to be different from the habitual yellow liquid. This ejection—apparently accompanied by violent suffering—terminated, and the ventral tube was rapidly resorbed. Then the Quadragne turned over on his side and soon fell asleep. I do not know how to interpret this latest event.

I am now going to transfer myself to the Sphere of Gondonax to replenish my pharmacopoeia with vernamoual Double-Z. I will resume my observations when I return: it will be necessary to conduct tests on the practical intelligence of the Quadragnes, in suggesting to them by visual or material indices that it is possible for them to do away with the partition themselves.

*Cso.*

I manipulated the atomic structure of the transparent partition so that it will become permeable both ways however little one influences its molecular alignment by means of a simple Psy-O wave. I then materialized in the cell, by the side of individual A, a green gandarche which I caused to pass through the wall several times, so as to make it clear to the Quadragnes that it was possible to annihilate this apparently solid barrier by mind alone.

The results were nil. At the apparition of the green gandarche, Quadragne B emitted a piercing shriek and took refuge fearfully in a distant corner of its cell. This creature is definitely affected with hyper-emotivity. Quadragne A, without displaying the same kind of repulsion (after all, the gandarche is a charming animal) prudently kept his distance from it; then, as soon as he had registered the fact that the wall could be traversed, he threw himself against it—and naturally banged his head! He then tried to push it, but unfortunately it does not seem to have occurred to him that he was able to make it disappear by a simple effort of thought.

I then caused the green gandarche to disappear, and I materialized by the side of Quadragne A, who seemed to me nonetheless to possess faculties superior to those of his congener, the six elements of a multa-X series, which permit, however sloppily they are arranged, a passage to be opened in any inert matter even if it is atomically non-decynethisized. The Quadragne contemplated the elements for a long time, hefted them one by one, attempted to pile them up in the evident intention of clambering up to reach the suppose summit of the cage, and finally, after the scanty success of these initiatives, he hurled one against the wall, in the senseless hope of breaking it by simple impact.

I caused the elements to disappear in their turn, and as a last shift I activated the wall so that it would emit, in a gamut of colours perceptible to the imperfect eyes of the Quadragnes, and in an accelerated yet irregular rhythm, the three universal signals of the Recognition of Matter: Danger—Neutral—Welcome. No sooner had the projections begun than the two Quadragnes put their heads between their upper paws and turned their eyes away from the flashing wall, as if the syncopated signal dangerously injured their visual centres.

I soon stopped this, careful not to injure them. But I am very annoyed: I have abandoned any idea of testing the intellectual coefficient of these creatures, who must be placed quite low in the universal scale of intelligence. And to think that the Quadragnes are indexed as 'creatures with a fair measure of civilization!' There is nothing left for me to do but observe them in the position of physical contact: on Csou, I will eliminate the wall.

\*    \*    \*    \*    \*

They're crazy! Completely crazy! But what do they want? What are they looking for?

First there was this little animal that suddenly appeared in the cell, like an octopus, but green all over, with clusters of tentacles and hair everywhere ... And its eyes, waving around on stalks! Where the hell did they pick that up? What's worse, it got through that invisible wall and I couldn't. It's as if they're trying to drive us crazy!

The woman over there was scared out of her mind! Not me. I've seen a lot, after all. But I can't figure out how the octopus could get through the wall. It disappeared just as it came. Ffft! Gone! In its place, six big tubes arrived with bunches of—bunches of little tubes that branched out in all directions. I'm not a complete idiot. It was perfectly clear to me that it was a test, and that they wanted me to do something with these tubes. But what? ... In the end I just gave up.

And finally the invisible wall began to vibrate, vibrate ... with blinding colours, green, orange, red, spinning around, dazzling me ... I couldn't stand it. Fortunately, it's over now. They've given up. But it doesn't seem natural to me, all this stuff ... I've got my own theory: what if our kidnappers are Martians? That's right, Martians ...Martians or people from God knows what planet. Because with all these stories about flying saucers, you've got to be ready for anything!

   Yes sir! Martians!

*Csou.*
I have eliminated the wall. As I have been able to observe, it was totally invisible to these creatures, who register only a pitifully limited range of vibrations; nevertheless, Quadragne A, who was in the habit of going up to feel it continually, soon perceived its disappearance. He reacted to this with excitement, and crossed the former line of demarcation to approach Quadragne B. The latter seemed to display signs of fear, and retreated. The two Quadragnes then exchanged a series of modulated sounds from their head-mandibles: as I have noted elsewhere, it is their primitive mode of communication.

   What followed is more curious, and exhibits that character of fundamental strangeness which characterizes the vital norms of the Quadragnes. I did not really observe how the situation first became tense between them, but it is certain that hostilities were declared when Quadragne A started to run his upper paws over the body of Quadragne B. The latter tried to fend off these attacks by backing away and by disordered movements of her paws. Then the two Quadragnes, one pursuing the other, made several rounds of the cage in rapid propulsion. Quadragne A finally succeeded in pinning Quadragne B against a wall, holding her firmly to him with his two upper members, and pressing the sucker of his mandibles to his adversary's head (as well as the intermediary articulation). It was my initial fear that I was about to witness a scene of cannibalism—I prepared to turn on the ongdal gas—but it soon appeared to me that this mandible-play was quite superficial and presented no real danger for the assaulted Quadragne.

   Finally, Quadragne A introduced his ventral tube (which had in the meantime achieved its maximum length) into the small vertical cleft which Quadragne B possesses completely beneath her posterior parts, concealed under a hairy surface and through which she ordinarily discharges her liquid excrements. Quadragne A, holding his victim firmly upright, then began to jerk up and down in place, with the effect (of course I was observing the process with a powerful magnifying lens) of slipping his ventral tube into the interior of the cavity of Quadragne B. The back-and-forth movement achieved an accelerated rhythm, and the two Quadragnes began to moan softly. Quadragne B no longer seemed to be struggling, but passed her upper paws over the posterior parts of Quadragne A with a kind of gentleness. Then the two animals separated rather abruptly, without my clearly understanding the reason. I saw them squat against the wall of the cage, rather distant from each other. The ventral tube of Quadragne A had returned to its size that I will henceforth call 'in repose'. In the eyes of Quadragne B a colourless liquid formed and abundantly exuded.

\*     \*     \*     \*     \*

O Lord! ... What have I done? ... What has been done to me?

You are my witness that I resisted, that I did what I could to avoid ... what happened. But his young good-for-nothing threw himself on me like a wild animal ... And like an animal, he sated his basest instincts.

What a shame ... what terrible shame! And this, under those invisible eyes which, I well know, never cease from watching us. And under Your eyes, Lord! But I must not spend my time lamenting. One day this martyrdom will end, I know; I have faith. I have only to wait, to be calm, to think of my dear Martial, of my little Pierrot and little Annette ... and to pray.

\*     \*     \*     \*     \*

I couldn't resist ...

Put yourself in my place! For eight days I was stuck there, going around in circles. And then this naked woman in front of me all the time!

When I realized that the goddamn wall had disappeared, I ... and besides if she hadn't screamed, if she hadn't started running ... That's what excites me, broads who are scared.

Never mind ... it's okay now.

She's putting on her crying act, but in a few days she'll calm down and ask for it again. Yes sir! I've known them, ones like her. Middle-aged broads who haven't kissed anyone for a long time. It's hard to loosen them up, but after that ... real furies!

The stupid thing is that we can't understand each other. I would never have figured her for a foreigner. She must be French ... or Italian. Apparently Italian women don't care about getting old. And they're really hot for it.

Yes, I'd really like her to be Italian ... I never had an Italian before!

*Csu.*
The two Quadragnes appear to have reached a mode of peaceful co-existence. Towards the end of Csou, they resumed their oral communication—although the exchanges seemed rather brief to me—and when I made it dark in their cage, they lay down with each other, and mutually passed their upper paws over all the surfaces of the other's body, particularly over (and in) their excretory organs; the tube of Quadragne A again grew to the size which I will call 'in labour'. Again there was introduction, Quadragne A being extended horizontally on individual B, and the two animals were 'facing'. The same grotesque dance recommenced, the transition from a vertical position to a horizontal position having in no way modified the ritual. Then they rapidly fell asleep, very entangled. I ended the observation, quite puzzled and, I must admit, sufficiently disgusted.

\* \* \* \* \*

I'm ashamed to say it, but I feel myself taken with a sort of tenderness for this young rascal. Despite his violence and his lack of education, I am sure that he is basically good. The young people of today are like that, it seems: impulsive, unaccustomed to restraining their instincts. Headstrong, in a way ...

And what could I do, in the situation in which we find ourselves? Struggle, resist to my last breath? That would have been quite stupid and would have done no good. When one finds oneself in an exceptional situation, one must adapt oneself to exceptional contingencies. Rather than be enemies, it's better to be comrades, no longer having to ignore certain inconvenient needs.

Besides, if Martial were able to see me, I am sure that he would understand me, that he would pardon me and even approve. Poor Martial ... With him I have never ... But after all I am a good Christian, and there are some things it's better not to talk about.

Nevertheless, it would be foolish to be ashamed of our bodies. God has made us thus, capable of experiencing sorrow as well as pleasure. My modesty forbids me to insist on this point, but when enforced contact makes the simplest decency impossible, why desperately wish to go against the natural order of things? And then I should also put myself in the place of this young man, whom the sight of my naked body incites to lust. It is true that I am still young: I am just barely thirty-six years old. And I do believe that I am not unattractive ... To refuse my body in such a situation would be mere hypocrisy; I even believe that it would be contrary to the simplest Christian charity. One can only give what one has!

I only regret that we do not speak the same language. It would have been truly comforting to exchange ideas on this impossible situation. And then we would have been able to know and understand each other better ... He might have said nice things to me, told me that he finds me beautiful. But he's English, alas, English or American—and I have completely forgotten the few words of English that I learned at school ...

No matter! Words don't count for much in comparison with a simple presence. And his is, all things considered, as comforting as that of anyone. And thanks to you, my pet, I am no longer alone. Despite his long hair and his moustache, I almost find him handsome!

*Dro/Drou/Dru/Dso.*
I have kept the activity of the Quadragnes under constant supervision for four cycles, noting the periodicity and the frequency of their meals, their evacuations and their 'copulations'.

Copulation: this term was suggested to me by 11.427 Green In Sky Of Topaz Nadir, who has a certain amount of experience with 'bisexual' subjects (another new term!). It seems that the introduction of the tube and the subsequent dance are the preliminaries to semination, strictly speaking; Quadragne A releases his seed into Quadragne B, who is then 'fecundated'. All these rites, then, have simply to do with reproduction. I am quite willing to accept the explanation of Green In Sky Of Topaz Nadir, but I nonetheless note two things: why these repeated relations, when in principle a single releasing of seed is enough for the germination of a new being? On the other hand, if we grant that these so-called organs of reproduction are bound in with orifices of liquid evacuation, then copulation must not be a very enjoyable act for the Quadragnes ... In brief, there is more mystery in these animals than in all our philosophy!

To come back to more practical notations, I was able to observe, during the four illuminated periods and the four nocturnal periods which have just elapsed, that the Quadragnes copulated eleven times, always horizontally, the sole variants being found in their respective posture of domination, Quadragne A sometimes being on top, sometimes on the bottom. On several occasions, prior to the introduction of the tube, the Quadragnes reversed their position (I am tempted to represent this new caprice by the sign of a horizontal 69—which is not far removed from the symbol of infinity!) to devote themselves to buccal-reproductive contacts: at one end, Quadragne B absorbs in her buccal air-hole the tube of Quadragne A, while he introduces his retractile lapper in the cleft of Quadragne B. I think that these singular manoeuvres must be considered as a sort of symbolic toilet, or washing performed on the reproductory organs before the act properly so called: it is easily understandable, when one knows for what uses the said organs are otherwise employed.

Aside from these details, I have nothing in particular to note. The observation of the Quadragnes has become for me a sort of routine, and I no longer take very much interest in it. Moreover, I am going to break off for a while this tedious study, since we are nearing the megacycle of Fouge-Framme and I will have to put myself in stasis for recharging.

*    *    *    *    *

Bed and board, with a pretty woman whenever I want her—who could ask for anything more? A little something to drink from time to time, of course ... But I've crossed that one out.

The Martians are A-okay with me!

*Eru.*
Here I am again (with an index of 148!) at the cage of the Quadragnes. I have hardly observed them today, since the success of my charging stasis has impelled me to enter into contact with numerous other individualities of class F. Besides, I have resolved to materialize a dorzz with the help of 11.427 Green In Sky Of Topaz Nadir, to the limit of instability of our two influxes. This is infinitely more creative than the study of these two primitive organisms. Moreover, their activities seem to have become rarefied: the two Quadragnes remain squatting, each on his own side, against the wall of the cage and no longer seem to be prey to this reproductive madness which agitated them prior to Fouge-Framme. But perhaps now that Quadragne B has finally been fecundated (all this is perfectly clear to me since stasis, when I integrated in my circuits a spool on the customs of sexual beings), these two animals no longer feel the need to copulate.

*   *   *   *   *

How well I understand them!

They've started up again! Their filthy tricks, tests, whatever it is ... it's started up again.

My God, I really thought I was going to pop out of my skin, I was so scared!

There I was, peaceful, almost asleep—I have to say that I've started to have enough of the old girl—when the cage vanished. Yes sir! The walls, the ceiling, the floor ... pffft! All gone! Just me and the dame, standing there in mid-air! But the most incredible thing was, we didn't fall. At first I said to myself, This is it, they've seen enough of our faces, they've dropped us without parachutes from their cotton-picking flying saucer ... But no. We floated in a sky, a sky that was a funny violet colour. And then, all of a sudden, objects came flying toward us. Like balls of fire ... well, not exactly balls of fire ... I don't really know how to describe them. Comets, maybe, with wriggling tails of fire. They were coming right down on us! I thought it was curtains, that we'd go up in flames like a couple of Buddhist monks. The broad was screaming her head off—you should've heard her.

And then suddenly there were no more flaming balls. We began to descend very gently, like feathers. Far below us, in the purple void, I saw a luminous white circle that got bigger and bigger ... Actually, it wasn't getting any bigger; we were falling onto it, but very slowly. Finally we landed on it, and she throws herself into my arms, jabbering something or other in her French or Italian. I told her not to get excited, but of course she didn't understand me.

The white thing on which we landed was so big that I couldn't see where it ended. I told myself it might be a planet—not Mars, of course, because Mars is all red. I tried the ground with my foot. It was hard ... harder than the hardest rock. And so shiny that it made me cry just to look at it. We stood there a while without knowing what to do, and then all of a sudden something new appeared on the horizon. It was like a gigantic pink board that grew, and grew so fast that it soon became as big as a mountain. I had the impression that it was like a giant saw, cutting up the white plain and coming right toward us. We started to run, and suddenly we found ourselves in a kind of pink molasses. It wasn't liquid—we would've suffocated—but some-thing like a thick dust, and it made us cough. The pink board had overtaken us, but it wasn't as solid as I'd thought.

I didn't realize until later that the white plain had disappeared out from under our feet, and that we were floating in the molasses just like we'd floated in the sky. There were also piles of stuff moving around in this jelly. Stars, it looked like, that expanded and divided, stuff riddled with holes like sponges, things with lots of threads coming out of them, like big worms ... I asked myself if they were plants or animals ... or something else. I really thought for a minute I recognized a weird green octopus, like the one who appeared in the cage, but I'm not sure. Luckily, none of that crap got too close to us.

And then the molasses started to get thicker, and it was getting hard to breathe. My mouth and nostrils were full of it, and I really thought I was finished. Then we found ourselves floating along its surface, as if we were being carried along by a warm and very salty sea (because I don't know how to swim, is that it?). Above us, there was this purple sky again, very luminous, almost phosphorescent, which was really weird, since there wasn't any sun. We floated on our backs for a long time, and then bit by bit the molasses disappeared, but it wasn't like a swimming pool emptying out—it was as if it was slowly evaporating, breaking up into pools that moved over the ground like patches of fog. And we never got wet at all ...

Then we found ourselves standing on our own two feet again, but not on the white plain. On the contrary, the ground was as black as coal, and it didn't seem to be very solid, since our feet sank right through the surface up to the ankles. Like walking through a layer of very fine dust. After a minute, enormous balls began to roll all around us on the black plain. They came from the horizon, and disappeared as quickly as they had come. It was terrifying. At first I thought we were going to be crushed, but actually they were shooting by at some distance from us. They must have been a good couple of hundred yards in diameter, and they kept changing colour. Sometimes they were white, sometimes blue, red, yellow, orange, sometimes they took on a weird colour I wouldn't begin to know what to name. But the worst thing was the noise they made. A drumroll of thunder. Up until then we hadn't heard any sounds at all on this planet, even if everything did keep changing from one minute to the next. But this made a noise in my head loud enough to drive me crazy. Like bowling balls, except that we were right in the alley and the balls were as big as houses. And then like everything else it quietened down, and the last balls disappeared at the edge of the black plain. It was at this moment that I realized that the plain was tilting in the distance, all around the horizon. After a couple of minutes it looked like big walls of coal were rising toward the sky. Soon I felt like I was standing in the crater of a volcano, and then there was nothing more over us but a small bright circle, like a purple sun in the middle of all this blackness—and then it was absolutely dark. Much worse that the darkest night. Like being in a completely sealed-off room. I didn't know what to do, I felt her hands all over my shoulders, scratching me. I wanted to talk to her, but I couldn't even hear the sound of my own voice, as if I'd turned into a deaf-mute. I couldn't even hear her screeching. I think there must have been something there in the dark, because it began to stink, a real putrid odour, it choked me. I had to vomit ... but then the smell went away after a while and all of a sudden, in the dark, a cube appeared, just like that, a brilliant silvery cube that was absolutely visible even though it was pitch black. Naturally I couldn't tell how big or how far away it was. Then there was another, and another, a whole pile of them appeared in the dark and began to pile themselves up one on top of the other, like when a kid piles up building blocks. Lucky for us we didn't see the hand that was piling them up! Little by little the cubes were getting closer to us, and soon we were surrounded on all sides by these blocks, it wasn't dark at all any more, and I thought we were about to be crushed to death by the last block, which would fit right in the spot where we were. But luckily it remained empty, and it was a good minute before I realized that the part that had remained empty was in fact our cell, and that its walls, floor and ceiling were the sides of the blocks piled together.

Then the worst thing of all happened. But that—I can't talk about it. I can hardly think about it ... There aren't any words to explain the horror that appeared in the cell. My God! ... I'd seen my share of unbelievable things since I'd been on Mars ... But this! When I think of it, I get the shakes and my heart starts thumping again. The woman had a real nervous breakdown and almost took out one of my eyes with her nails while I was trying to calm her down. Luckily it didn't stay too long, but, my God! ... Where do they find these things? They seem to be real jokers, these Martians ... And why are they showing us all these monsters? Do they want us to die of fear?

I've had it up to here!

If I could just get out of this place ...

And now everything is quiet, but the broad's on my back again, blubbering, and she wants me to be her little lover boy. What a life ...

*Esu.*

Taking advantage of a position necessary for the growth of certain tardy radicles on the upper surface of the dorzz, I gave my attention to a new experiment on the Quadragnes. Not daring to let them out of their cage, I projected simulacra of environment of the A-1 Superior zone, so as to be able to observe their reactions to a model series of situations and settings forming the usual backdrop of our existence. I hoped in this way to obtain a positive result, which would perhaps have permitted me to integrate the Quadragnes in one of the three-dimensional inserts of the Sphere, in company with other familiar animals captured in the lower spheres.

Unfortunately, this experiment was a total failure: from all indications the Quadragnes are incapable of adapting themselves to a milieu that differs in the slightest from the surroundings of their primitive existence. In short, these stupid animals do not seem to be happy except in their cage ... Whether it was on the defalcating geyser of the transverse Arce-de-Creuse, whether it was in the nourmance of the Miol Vector or between the demionyctisized Olphases of the Pyrre-Bouge, the Quadragnes did not display the least glimmer of intelligence in attempting to understand their new environment. The cervical captours even registered the waves characteristic of the most total panic.

As a last resort—although the thought of physical contact with these repulsive animals hardly enchanted me—I materialized myself personally in their cage. The result was disastrous: the Quadragnes emitted piercing sounds and gave themselves up to frantic gesticulations, as if my presence inspired in them an active terror. I did not linger in this trying proximity. The Quadragnes are manifestly incapable of perceiving the radiance of a superior being ...

I am going to return to my dorzz, which gives me infinitely more satisfaction.

*Eso.*
(along with many others!) add to the file of incomprehensible enigmas which the behaviour of the Quadragnes gives rise to. Quadragne B, who seemed to me to manifest an abnormal agitation, performed a series of mimic actions on Quadragne A which ordinarily precede copulation (caresses of the upper paws, play of the jaws). Quadragne A disengaged himself, followed by his congener. After a new tentative on the part of B, A struck her violently and she went to squat in a distant part of the cage. B subsequently made a series of piercing sounds, while a clear liquid flowed from her eyes. She then stretched herself on the floor and began to rub her pectoral excrescences and inside her cleft with her upper paws, until she uttered

several of these plaintive sounds of copulation. At no point, however, did A intervene.

I do not seek to logically analyse these latest facts any more than the general activity of the Quadragnes, which seems to me to be governed by the most impenetrable incoherence and stupidity. I will have to consider some radical solution of their problem.

*    *    *    *    *

The broad is really starting to get on my nerves. I never have been able to stand the same woman for more than eight days.

My God, if they'd just let us go!

*    *    *    *    *

As if the waking nightmares which our torturers inflict on us weren't enough!... But now, my companion in misfortune has turned away from me. Lord! Why multiply my torments? Why have I been permitted to taste the joys of the flesh, to leave me prey now to the torments of frustration?

But perhaps it was a trial to which You subjected me? A trial in which I stumbled ... Like Eve tasting the forbidden fruits of the Tree of Knowledge, I innocently tasted the fruits of lust. I was ignorant of the most sacred law of the married woman. I have committed the sin of adultery.

Oh! Martial ... Forgive me!

*Esou.*
I have decided to end my observations here, for I am convinced that I will learn nothing more of interest from these two Quadragnes. The renewal of their atmosphere and the preparation of their nutrients takes considerable time, and there is no question of my continuing thus for such meagre results. During their next nocturnal unconscious period, I will expose them to a C+ ray, which will end their existence immediately and without pain.

I have nonetheless had the foresight to register the cervical influxes of these creatures. Perhaps one day it will be possible to decode them and retranscribe them into a clear language, which would permit a great step forward in the study and comprehension of the Quadragnes.

And who knows—perhaps later on, in the course of the next

transference to Lower Sphere C X 66, I might decide to amuse myself by capturing two other Quadragnes with the substance extractor. But for a change, I would take care to obtain two individuals of the same 'sex'—two A Quadragnes, for example. Observation of their cohabitation would doubtlessly hold other surprises in store for me.

Signed: Blue of Blue-Earth Peer

translated by FRANK ZERO

# The Good Ring
## SVEND ÅGE MADSEN

A man named Stig is ploughing. He stoops over even though his back resists the effort. When he straightens up again the ring that he has bent over to pick up lies in his hand, a ring made to fit a finger.

As soon as he has the ring Stig knows that it is no ordinary ring. He considers throwing it away so as not to tempt fate, but he simply cannot help examining it more closely. Although almost no air is stirring, it seems as if a gale is blowing through the circumference of the ring. He tries to put it on his finger but the blast is too strong and prevents him from doing so. Only when he turns the ring around and puts it on with the wind rather than against it does he succeed.

Stig goes on with his ploughing. He is tired, the soil is hard, and he is sweating. He would like to stop, but he still has a long way to go. Stig curses the bad luck that brought him to this place.

When finally he is on the way home after his heavy labour and is preoccupied with thoughts about the miserable way things are arranged in this world, he suddenly hears voices around him. Nothing of this kind has ever happened to him when he has been alone. He is alone now.

The voices come from his left hand. When he tries to distinguish between them he perceives one that reminds him of his own, a voice that in a cheerful tone utters some incomprehensible words, something like 'I believe the Brain is with me'. A second voice laughs uproariously while a woman squeals. A third mutters the same words over and over again.

'That's all I need', Stig says to himself. 'Now I'm going out of my mind.'

When Stig reaches home there is a woman in his house. She is complaining. The woman is Karen, and she is his wife. Dog-tired, he lashes out at her, but Karen ducks in a practised manner without once interrupting her flow of reproaches.

Stig wearily closes his eyes. When he opens them again he sees a letter lying in front of him. He opens it and finds, not to his surprise, that it contains a bill for a sizeable amount.

'Who arranged the world this way, anyhow?', he says to himself while casting a look of recrimination upward. 'And what have I done that I should deserve to drag out such a miserable existence here?'

In a sudden fit of anger he seizes a half-filled mug and flings it towards the wall. Karen dodges, although the mug is not thrown in her direction. She calms down, with just as much ill grace as she can muster up.

Stig picks up a fragment from the mug with which to scrape the scabs of the sores on his arm. The sores begin to bleed, but he pays no attention to them.

'Go out and get something fit to eat', he snarls at Karen. 'And don't come back until you've found something.'

Karen sputters and grumbles, but goes.

As soon as she is outside Stig locks the door. He rummages through the house and finds a rope that looks usable. He gets up on a rickety stool, manages to get the rope tossed around a crossbeam, then fastens it securely around his neck.

He shakes his fist at the world around him.

'Now I'm through slaving for you!', he mutters.

He leaps, the stool overturns, the rope goes taut. Whereupon the crossbeam breaks and Stig tumbles to the floor with a loud crash.

But he does not have time to complain, for when he falls something happens to the ring on his finger. It has grazed the floor, and now it begins to grow larger with incredible speed. It becomes so large that it slips down around Stig's arm. It continues to increase in size, and soon it is so big that he is drawn through it as if by a violent gust of wind.

\*    \*    \*    \*    \*

Everything is white, and there is nothing. Stig finds himself in nothing and on nothing. There is no earth beneath his feet, no sky above his head.

Until he discovers a spherical object in front of him. It is two or three times the size of his head.

'Just a moment', says the sphere, beginning to change form, 'Let me see now—these damned gadgets!'

Slowly two eyes, a nose, and a mouth appear on the surface of the sphere.

'Now you'll undoubtedly find me more to your liking', the mouth says with a smile.

The sphere resembles a child's drawing of a face. One eye is a little smaller than the other. Stig discovers that he has no aches or pains, that he is neither tired nor hungry. He puts his hand up to his throat.

'Where are we?'

'We are a short distance from a planet. I thought you'd find it agreeable here. If you're cold we can get a little closer to it.'

'No thanks, I feel fine. Was it you who brought me here?'

'Yes. It was my ring. You can call me Krr. There is such a sound in your language, isn't there?'

Stig nods. 'What are you?'

'I am a Brain', says the sphere. It wrinkles its forehead and smiles. 'You're familiar with the theory of evolution—first the amoeba, then fish and mammals, and then man. And little by little, less and less work for man to do, and more and more things to speculate about. In other words, less and less body and more and more brain. Eventually one becomes able to imagine anything. This, for example ...'

Suddenly Stig whirls around four times in space.

'Stop it!', he yells in exasperation.

'It's a little difficult to explain how it's done', says Krr. 'But this is approximately the place.'

A speck of light appears on the sphere to indicate the place.

'We Brains, of course, can read one another's thoughts. We switch on lights for those we want to reveal to others. Consequently we have no need for eyes or a mouth. These eyes that you see I have assumed merely for your sake—I don't actually see with them. Do they look natural?'

He blinks one eye.

'Couldn't you somehow have managed to keep arms and legs?', asks Stig, a bit unnerved by what he has seen.

'Yes, and there were some who did in the beginning. But in the long run it got them nowhere in their sports and what have you. And by the way, it's more convenient to imagine your way around than to walk here, there and everywhere.'

'Have you shifted me around in time?', asks Stig, feeling very uneasy.

'What? Oh, that nonsense of yours about time machines. You folks ought to understand that it isn't possible to make time machines. A person can't shift around in time that way, either into the future or the past.'

'But according to the theory of evolution, you would exist quite a while after I had been on the scene. And yet both of us are here now at the same time, aren't we?'

'Yes, but now you must try to keep your wits about you. We Brains are carrying out various kinds of experiments. We do a good deal of research, because after all we must try to become a little wiser.'

Krr smiles apologetically.

'We have human beings more or less like you, as well as the ingredients of human beings, preserved in—well, let's call them test tubes. And round about us we have a sea of planets at our disposal. You see, there are quite a number of points about our past that have not been explained. And so our historians are setting up worlds—staging them, you might say. They simply take a planet of suitable size, proper climate and so on. And then they populate it with an adequate number of our test-tube people completely endowed, both physically and psychically, as mankind was at a specific period in the course of history. They are brought together, assigned the proper roles in relation to each other, and then turned loose. And they immediately begin to put on a play for us that is altogether authentic from a historical standpoint. These people, of course, simply believe they are living a real life.'

'Are you trying to tell me that I come from a test tube?', Stig shouts. In his rage he wants to strike out at the sphere but finds himself unable to do so.

'We let our research worlds go on for a long time. Your planet may very well have been started at some particular time during the iron age and then allowed to develop until your own era. Or it may have been started a short while ago. It is only a question of furnishing you and the others in your world with a suitable number of remnants from earlier times. Then you can attribute a long past to yourselves.'

'That can't be so', Stig says quietly. 'You're the ones who come from another place. My world can't be unreal.'

'No, it's really not unreal. Reproductions also are real, you know.'

'Put me down on earth again this instant. I don't like the feeling of uncertainty that you're trying to arouse in me. And by the way, how does it happen that you're able to carry on a conversation with me? If the rubbish you've been giving me were true, you wouldn't be able to understand my language at all.'

'I'm a paleopsychologist, and my speciality is your era. Wouldn't you like to meet a few of my colleagues?'

'Are there many of you Brains?'

'Yes, all in all a fairly large number of us are scattered about here and there. But there may be a considerable distance between us.'

'Do you have many planets going?'

'Yes, you might consider it an appalling number. We think there are too few. But starting a new world is quite a long and complicated business, and sometimes it is hard to get the necessary appropriations. At present we have in operation three worlds that are alternatives to yours. Three, that is, which are in the same stage of development and which were started at the same historical base period as yours. But naturally all four—yours and the other three—each developed its own distinctive characteristics, even though they bear a strong resemblance to each other. You wouldn't have any difficulty feeling just as much at home on any of the other three as you do on the one I brought you from.'

Stig sees two spheres come bouncing toward them like two balls on an invisible tabletop. When they come to a halt in front of him they both begin to assume facial features, as Krr already has done.

One is a little taller and chubbier than Krr. It gives Stig a broad smile.

'How do you do?', it says. 'My name is Fffh. I've overheard most of your conversation. I'm a paleopsychologist, and for the time being I'm investigating a planet in the same stage of development as yours, just as the other two are doing. I'm glad to meet you.'

By this time the third sphere has managed to straighten out its face. It has obviously gone to more trouble than the others, for it has provided itself with a slight wrinkle across the forehead and little crow's-feet at the corners of the eyes and mouth.

'My name is Sst-Sst. Excuse me for not shaking hands. What an attractive body you have.'

Stig looks down at himself to determine whether the sphere is making fun of him, and to his surprise finds that he is very well satisfied with what he sees.

'Thank you—how do you do?', he replies. 'Tell me, how does one pass the time when he hasn't got a body?'

'We go in for sports—mental gymnastics', Fffh explains.

'Fffh has taken part in a rather famous guessing match', Sst-Sst adds.

'But without too much luck', says Krr.

'Why am I here?', Stig asks suddenly.

'Because you put on my ring', Krr explains.

'What's going to happen to me? Will I be put into a test tube?'

'Not at all. Nothing bad is going to happen to you. Just take it easy. And speak up if something doesn't suit you.'

Stig notices that various parts of the balls are lighting up now and then.

'We're only communicating with each other', Sst-Sst explains.

'You're limited to thinking in one direction—ahead, and one thought at a time. We think spatially. It would take too long if we were to explain all our thoughts to you. It would be as if you had to explore a big, pitch-dark house with nothing but the light from a match—some place where you knew you'd quickly get a view of everything in daylight.'

'Before I believe you I'd like to see some of your other worlds. If you won't show me other planets I'll know that mine is the only real world', Stig exclaims with firmness.

'We'll let you see three other planets that are in the same stage of development as the one you come from', says Fffh. 'Things there are so closely in accord with your thought processes that you'll be able to understand them. What you would see on the others would be beyond your comprehension anyhow.'

Stig begins to get uneasy when the three Brains apparently take his wish seriously. In front of him appears something that suggests a mirror. In it he sees unclearly a flickering image of three orbs swarming with life. He strains his eyes, trying to distinguish one from the other, but has to give it up.

'No, not all at the same time', he says. 'I can't see them all at once.'

'Well, just a moment', says Krr.

The planets disappear. Instead he sees in the mirror—or perhaps it is a door that the thing reminds him of—three persons, all of whom are hardly distinguishable from himself, although one seems a little more cheerful, the second a bit stouter, while the third has a few more wrinkles in his forehead. Stig nods his head in astonishment, and at the same time the other three nod to him.

'Have a good trip', says one of the Brains.

*　*　*　*　*

Stig is ploughing. The birds sing. He glances toward the sun and decides that he may as well go on working a little longer. He gazes happily at the handsome ring.

A little later he chooses to stop while the weather is still good. He sets out for home filled with contentment. He steps lightly and with every step feels the good earth beneath his feet.

'Is this me, or isn't it me?', he mutters to himself as he looks down at his strong, brown arms.

He decides to sing, and finds a stick with which he rhythmically taps the ground as he walks.

'Yes, it's me, because I want to be me', he sings, using a home-made melody that goes nicely with the sound of the birds. 'I'm happy because I want to be happy.'

Within shouting distance of the house he comes to a halt.

'Karen', he calls out. 'I've decided to stop now.'

In the doorway appears a pretty, cheerful woman. They run to meet each other. He reaches her first and seizes her in an embrace.

At the edge of a ditch they tumble to the ground. He holds her hand in his.

'I've chosen the prettiest woman as my own.'

She presses something soft against his lips and whispers: 'You're talking nonsense. It was I who chose you.'

Everything is completely serene as he feels the soft fullness of her body against his own.

'Just imagine!', says Karen. 'We've been permitted to live in the world that we ourselves prefer to live in. And allowed to arrange things exactly as we would like to have them.'

She gazes gratefully into space.

Hand in hand they walk toward the house.

'Should we have something to eat?', says Stig.

'Yes', she says. 'That's a good idea. Shall we eat outdoors?'

He nods and feels a deep satisfaction at having chosen to do what he wanted to do.

'I feel that the Brain is looking down at me', says Karen, who has gone into the house. 'It is nodding its head because I made the right choice.'

She depicts a circle in front of her face.

Suddenly a thought whirls through Stig's mind.

'Since we're only living in a world that we ourselves have chosen, how can we be sure that we made the right choice?', he says gravely. 'How do we know that we couldn't have done better? We could have arranged everything differently, you know, and in one way or another it might have been better. At any rate, we can't be sure.'

Karen looks at him in alarm. 'What are you talking about? If we had wanted the world to be different than it is, we would, of course, have chosen to have it different. Why do you say things like that? You never used to behave this way.'

'I'm not quite myself', Stig admits.

Together they carry the table out.

Stig fetches the chairs himself. He picks up a stool, but as he is going out he stumbles. As he falls the ring scrapes the ground. It begins to grow larger.

*   *   *   *   *

Stig rides his easy chair over to the service panel. He satisfies himself that the automatic plough is stopped.

'That's that', he says to Karen, who is lying on the autoerotic carpet.

He looks at the ring on his finger which the soil-purifying apparatus has just separated out and brought in to him.

'Please tune in for perivision, now that you're over there', says Karen. 'And set for three.'

Stig grunts and presses several buttons on the panel. The table is set for three. The announcer steps forth from the television screen and seats himself beside them in the chair that stands ready for him. Karen joins them.

The announcer greets them and takes a sip from his cup. Then he says: 'As you know, an event of major importance took place when it was discovered that preservatives could be incorporated into explosives. When the bomb is dropped on an area everything in it rigidifies and sets like cement, and the extent of the area depends, of course, on the force of the bomb. Afterward, as you know—and as you no doubt already have turned to your advantage—afterward it is possible to buy such an immobilized, bomb-stricken area, complete with people in the most lifelike postures, urinating and doing other piquant things. Furthermore, in taking over such an area you naturally extend help to the belligerent nation, so that its soldiers can get things cleaned up without wading around in corpses and doing other messy jobs of that sort. That's why we all have one or more bomb sites situated here and there to serve as ornaments. I like to draw a comparison with the ancient Egyptians, who kept their mummies—'

Stig switches off the sound.

'This wine—well, the label and the year are all right, but don't we have one made from grapes that were picked a little later in the day? I prefer those picked in the evening, you know.'

'Find out about that yourself, if you don't mind. And turn it on again. I'd like to hear it, but see if you can't get him to speak a little more dramatically.'

Stig again presses several buttons.

'... and what is far more interesting, far superior to the old static battlefields, a bomb that does not fossilize the area but allows it to carry on as usual. This bomb bears the same relationship to the old ones as motion pictures do to still photographs. You can buy such a living, animated war-stricken area. Did I say animated? Yes, not only do the people move but, I might add, you yourself will be moved. You can, of course, determine for yourself the size of the area you want. And I promise you will come to feel a strong attachment to your area. I am not exaggerating when I say that you will feel the closest ties to them. It will be like seeing your own relatives, your dearest friends, struck down by misfortune. Just think—an animated war-stricken area, not only life-like, not only automatic, but authentic. How thrilling, how different, how instructive! You can witness at closest range everything that goes on—see, for example, how a primitive native-born woman behaves—and all with a lifelike faithfulness on a par with the most subtle neoplastic-realistic novels. Your own war documentary. You have not lived until you have tried seeing death in this way. On the other hand, the price is just as high as we have been able to set it—17 debits.'

The announcer than alters his tone of voice completely and proceeds to comment on a toothpaste that confers new growing power on the teeth. Stig turns off the set, and the announcer vanishes.

Karen gets up and stretches. 'When are we going to get one of those?'

Stig sits toying with the duplicator. 'In any case, you'll have to do something first', he says, teasing her.

He adjusts the apparatus. In front of him stand two identical women. One Karen begins to undress. The other follows her example.

Stig starts the duplicator again and lets it run until three other women materialize, all exactly like the first two.

Together the five figures begin to pull off Stig's clothing. After he has been stripped naked he again presses a button on the device.

'No more', the six women beg. 'That's enough now.'

With a teasing smile he makes the apparatus produce two more women.

The eight bodies mill around him. Sixteen identical hands caress him here, there, and everywhere, sixteen cool, slender hands gently stroking his body.

For some time he lets the eight women minister to him while one tries to outdo the other in inventiveness.

When he tires of the sport he sets the device going in reverse, an soon there is but one Karen beside him.

With no need for discussion, she goes over to the multiplier and has herself transformed to twice her normal size. Stig moves closer to the giantess and with some effort pushes his way up into her. His head is in the familiar, dark, hot, pulsating surroundings. With a series of slithering manoeuvres he moves his head in and out several times. For a little while he wallows in her juices.

He lets himself slip out of her and moves on to her head, which is twice as large as a normal head.

'No, it won't do', he says.

Karen resumes her normal size.

'We aren't really living at all', he says. 'You're just as unreal as all your doubles.'

'What kind of nonsense is that? Anyhow, we have a good time. Any one of my doubles is just as good at satisfying you as I am.'

She leaves him in a huff. He is about to run after her but, unaccustomed as he is to walking, he stumbles over some of her clothes. As he falls the ring scrapes against the floor. It begins to grow larger.

*   *   *   *   *

Stig is sitting on the ground. They have seated themselves in a circle—many, many of them. All have their eyes closed and all are completely relaxed. They feel each other, they are each other. Stig feels a single large body which is the entire group and which inhales and exhales in unison like one large organism.

Until one of them says, 'Now we are waking up'.

They open their eyes and look happily around at each other.

'And now we are completely awake.'

They get up and move about. Their legs come in contact with the ground and carry them forward with light, buoyant steps. Their arm movements add to the effect.

'Am I dreaming or am I awake?', Stig's voice whispers within him as he moves to and fro. 'At last I'm fully awake again.'

Intense colours flicker before his eyes, the field stretches out into infinity. Everything is completely new and everything is familiar. New, fantastic shapes hover before him. Beautiful, familiar objects are within his reach.

A radiant young woman stumbles over a stone. The pain she feels is transmitted to him. He reaches out and helps her up. He feels her pain in his knee and banishes it with a cooling hand. He smiles at her gratefully.

Together they walk over to the tree. She reaches up and plucks a piece of fruit. She hands it to him, he takes it, holds it in his hand, turns it slowly around. It is a world with everything in it, it is everything they are familiar with, it is everything new.

'It is a world with everything in it, is everything we are familiar with, it is everything new', she says in a voice that simply floats off into space.

'It is the beginning, it is the end. Do you see it?', he adds.

'It is sleep, and it is the sleep that we call life, and it is the waking state that is ours', she says, and her smile dissolves into his.

They share the fruit, they touch each other's fingers and let their happiness flow from one to the other. They feel the group around them. They are themselves, they are the same person, and they are the group.

He shows her the ring he has just found. She touches it and carefully turns it round.

'Are we really awake?', says Stig.

'We are happy', says the cautious voice that clings around him.

'Is what we call our waking state nothing but a dream to other people?', says Stig.

'We are happy', says the cautious voice that clings around him.

Stig shuts his eyes and comes to life in the ordinary sense. He wants to grab hold of her, but in his mundane clumsiness he stumbles. As he falls the ring scrapes the ground. It begins to grow larger.

\*   \*   \*   \*   \*

Everything is white, and there is nothing, Stig is in nothing and on nothing. There is no earth beneath his feet, there is no sky above him.

'You have paid a visit to the three worlds that are in the same stage of development as yours and that were established under the same conditions as yours', Krr explains.

'I can tell that you are now a little more convinced that our account of things is correct', says Sst-Sst. 'But it's only reasonable that you should have time to get used to the thought.'

'You were in the three worlds at the same time, but we had to let you experience them one at a time', Fffh explains.

'There is something I don't understand', says Stig. 'Which of the four worlds is the authentic model, which of them brings us up to you? Which is historically correct?'

'We can't answer that question because it is not correctly put. There is not simply one truth. You people must have found that out, haven't you?'

'No', says Fffh, shaking all of his large head. 'That will only happen somewhat after his time, to its full extent, that is.'

'Incredible!', says Krr.

'We have to assure you that all four worlds are real, and therefore historically correct.'

'But then do you come from several different planets? Did you three originate in different places?'

'No, we all come from one world—the one you call Earth. But all four models of the Earth that you visited are authentic and exist simultaneously.'

'What is going to happen to me?', Stig asks, on his guard.

'We merely wanted to show you the various possibilities. Now you yourself must decide which world of those you visited you want to be put down on—that is, where you'll spend the rest of your life.'

Feeling cheered up, Stig looks at the three Brains.

'You—you mean I can make my own choice—any of the three places?', Stig stammers. 'Why, there can be no doubt about it ... And yet I don't want to do anything rash. It means too much to me, you know.'

Stig begins to consider the three possibilities. Throughout the conversation the three Brains have been flashing lights and transmitting thoughts to each other. They have a bet on, and they have brought Stig up to let him make his choice. Each has placed its money on the particular world that is its personal object to study, since each is convinced that it cannot help being considered the best.

'Why weren't you satisfied with showing me only one of them?', Stig says. 'Then I would have felt much more certain of my choice. You should have sent me to the first one—the one that resembled my own, where I was happy and could have things the way I wanted them.'

'Does that mean you prefer that one?', says Krr.

'No—just wait a moment. Those machines were really marvellous. I don't suppose I'd be allowed to mix things up a bit, would I? I mean a little of that happiness, a bit of the machines and a little of the colours. Such a combination would be utterly and fantastically good.'

Stig is made uncomfortable by the way the three Brains stare at him.

'Regardless of how I choose, I'll always be wondering whether I made the right choice.'

Although the Brains seem very patient, he feels hard pressed because of their overwhelming mental faculties.

'After all, you're not offering me worlds at all, but only images of them. How do you expect people to live in them? It's simple enough for you—you know that your world is the right one, whereas I ...'

'We're not actually so sure', says Fffh, suddenly looking serious. 'Our most recent investigations have turned up some disquieting material.'

Alarmed, Stig looks from one to the other of the superior beings to make sure they are not merely pulling his leg.

'But that doesn't concern you', says Sst-Sst. 'You won't remember this experience very long. It's all so improbable that you'll soon begin to think it's nothing but a story you heard. And fortunately you don't put much stock in stories.'

\*   \*   \*   \*   \*

Stig is standing on solid ground. He looks around.

'There is something that has to be done over', he mutters.

He grasps the ring on his finger. With some difficulty he pulls it off. For a moment he looks through it as if through a telescope, but nothing catches his eye. Then he violently casts it away. He hears a faint sound as it lands.

He blinks his eyes. 'That was a strange story', he says to himself. 'It's a good thing it's only a story—one that I wouldn't care for if it were true.'

He is annoyed because of the innate irascibility that has led him to throw the ring away. 'But that's the way things are in the world—a person no sooner gets hold of something valuable than he throws it away. Well, that's how it is, and there's nothing one can do about it.'

Although it strains his back to do so, he stoops over and picks up a sharp stone. With it he begins to scrape away the sores on his arm.

translated by CARL MALMBERG

# Slum
## HERBERT W. FRANKE

'We're not here to pass judgement on anybody', said Vertain, the chairman of the Commission. 'We're here to find out what happened. Just the facts: straight, accurate, and objective. Without any emotionalism. That's all.'

They sat in the Institute's little conference room, the specialists from the Office of Investigation and the members of the expedition team—the ones who had returned, that is. The only movement in the room came from a five-year-old girl whose image was projected onto the giant videoscreen. Although she was surrounded by toys, the child showed no interest in anything except the candy that had been set out for her. She played with the colourful foil-wrapped bonbons, alternately tucking them behind the pillows and stuffed animals and then retrieving them, only to find another hiding place after a cautious look around.

Vertain turned to the heavy-set man at the far right of the row of team members. 'Why don't you start off, Govin?'

'All right.'

Govin tore his eyes away from the child playing on the screen. In a slightly hesitant voice, he began to speak. 'You all know the background. The Institute for Ecological Research needed some data. A change in the composition of the outer air had been registered—there'd been an increase in carbon dioxide and nitrogen, and the bacteria count was up as well. Our job was to find out why. The government issued a special permit for us to go on to the mainland.'

The chairman filled in the silence with a question. 'Were you given adequate equipment?'

'Of course. We had everything we needed—food, water, respiratory filters, medication—'

'But no weapons', put in Petrovski, the chief technician at the Institute.

'No, no weapons; whatever for? At that point, we had no idea—I mean, who would have imagined that—out there—' Govin's glance involuntarily strayed to the window. A shaft of milky green light fell across the floor of the room. 'We thought the outside world was dead. After all, it'd been years since anyone had left the suboceanic cities.'

'That's just it', said Petrovski.

Vertain waved his hand, a gesture of impatience. 'Go on', he told Govin.

'We took three special vehicles, each one with its own supply system: living quarters below, a control cabin on the upper level, and a quartz dome. They were hermetically sealed against bacteria, and had some lead content—to act as a radiation shield. One tank for every two men. The sluice ferry dropped us off.'

'What did it look like—out there?', asked Ruarka, the biologist.

'At first everything looked just like the descriptions—ruins of suburbs, mountains of garbage, dust, fog ... And the sun—the sun was nothing more than a flat disc of haze.'

'Any animals? Plants?'

'No animals at first', Govin replied. 'Later on we came across some rats. Big fat ones, much bigger than the ones you read about in the Chronicles. There must have been a thousand of them gathered on an empty spot between the ruins of a wall. Murray and I climbed out to catch a few specimens. We had our protective suits on, of course, and were prepared for a real hunt, nets and all. But they didn't try to run away. In fact, they came right up to us. Didn't attack us, either. They sniffed at our boots, climbed up our legs—they even let us pick them up with our hands.'

'They've been examined in the meantime', Ruarka added. 'They're white rats, albinos. And they're well fed, almost as if they'd been fattened up.'

'That should have made us stop and think right there', said Govin. 'But we had to keep going if we wanted to penetrate several miles into the interior, as we'd planned. It was rough going, too. We kept hitting up against masses of viscous material, decaying garbage that would give way every once in a while. At one point Anthony's tank sank halfway into the muck, and that was some job, fishing it out with steel ropes.

'Later on we ran across our first hint about that change in air composition. We came on a river bed where the water had dammed up: a bridge had collapsed, there were garbage deposits, and the water seepage had created pools, like miniature lakes, their shores covered with a grey-green film of algae or fungi.'

'Some sort of symbiosis', Ruarka explained. 'Algae and bacteria with an unusual metabolic system. They release nitrogen and consume—'

Vertain broke in. 'Maybe all they need to see is the report. It's all stored in the data bank under UP 7/CURRENT.'

'I might just add that the presence of these organisms doesn't explain the increase in nitrogen', said Ruarka. 'Not by a long shot.'

There was a moment of silence. Vertain thumbed through the stack of photocopies in his mind.

'There might have been other clues farther on in the interior.'

'We never got that far', Govin reported. 'After that point, our problems began to mount up. First a building collapsed right in front of our eyes; we barely escaped being buried by the debris. Then Larry drove his tank into a kind of trough. There was some sort of murky liquid, pools of it, at the bottom. We thought it was water, but it turned out to be sulphuric acid. The chain drive gears were eaten away, and the tank stalled—we had to leave it behind. That meant we were working with two tanks and had to divide the living space among three men. It was a little tight, but that was no reason to turn back.

'The next night we had that business with the cobalt tank. We'd been keeping the Geiger counters running, and rarely ran into a hot zone. We'd been particularly careful about checking the areas where we planned to spend the night, of course, and we'd done the same thing this time. Everything was fine. But when we woke up the next morning, the needles were jumping like crazy. We got out of the radiation zone as fast as we could; then we took a look. Under Ed's car there was a lead tank containing cobalt.

'Uncovered. And the gama radiation field had reached our camp site.'

'You didn't suspect anything then?', Petrovski asked. A shadow fell across the faces of the team members: dark clouds of smoke were drifting past the window. Vertain switched on the lighting discs.

'Not exactly', Govin answered. 'We were in a basin, after all. The tank might have slid down by itself. Besides, we knew how careless the cities had been with radioactive residue.'

Ruarka put a hand up. 'Hadn't you been taking the safety precautions a little lightly yourselves?'

'We took every precaution imaginable', Govin assured him. 'We didn't *feel* as safe as we had in the beginning. But that's what made us wonder whether we weren't imagining things. There were certain— signs ...'

'What kind of signs?'

'Falling rubbish—the bridge that had just collapsed—tracks ... But they could just as easily have been caused by natural events.'

'What effect did the radiation exposure have on the men?', Doctor Griscoll asked.

'Slight nausea. That passed, though; only Larry never recovered. He'd been nearest to the tank.'

'And got the highest dose', Griscoll added.

'Then the accident happened. We passed several mountains of piled-up rubbish. They were burning—even from a distance we could smell it through our filters, and black clouds rose in the air. There weren't any open fires, though; they just smouldered. The wind kept blowing ash in our faces, and the air was hot. Nearby we found strange fleshy plants growing in the pools of water, broad green leaves tinged with pink. Ed climbed out to gather a couple. Suddenly there was a splash—this big greyish animal had his leg between its jaws, and he tripped ... more animals moved in, from all directions ... We were completely helpless.'

The biologist cleared his throat. 'Govin submitted photos. It's related to the crocodile, but larger.'

'Go on', Vertain commanded. 'What happened next?'

'There were five of us left. I don't think I have to tell you we turned around on the spot. As we were trying to move a pile of beams that blocked our path, Anthony heard this sound from a cellar, like somebody crying. He and I crept down a short flight of stairs and saw a man in rags, filthy, with matted hair. He was beating the child.'

As if on command, they all looked at the little girl on the screen. She had fallen asleep in an armchair, but tossed her body from side to side restlessly.

'The moment he saw us, he slipped away down some dark hole, and we let him go. The child was crying. Anthony tried to pick her up, but she scratched him, and I had to give him a hand. She fought us off like a wildcat—she even tore my respiratory mask off my face. Then I noticed that she—well, she stank. With all that filth around - what else could you expect? But Anthony lost his head. He took her along, gave her a shower and something to eat. After about an hour, she let Anthony hold her. Nobody else, just Anthony. We had to take her along; he wouldn't let up until we did. Then they started to attack us openly, and we got a look at them: men in rags, freaks and cripples with ugly faces. The gleam in their eyes was pure hate.'

'Maybe their reaction was normal enough. Maybe they were just trying to defend their property.'

'Maybe', said Govin edgily. He went on. 'We tried to find a way out of the rubble, but they must have realized we were about to escape forever. There was only one narrow pass left to get through, but they tried once more to stop us. They built up a barricade and started throwing stones. Then they started to shoot. There couldn't have been more than three or four shots, but one of them broke through the dome and got Anthony.'

Again there was a brief pause. Govin stared dully at the sleeping child. No one spoke. He ended his report: 'Up until that moment we hadn't made any real attempt to defend ourselves, but now—we might not have been equipped with weapons, but we did have the flamethrower that we used once in a while to level the path. So we used it this time to break through the barricades. Four hours later, we were picked up. That's about it.'

Vertain tore the dictation reel out of the output slot, smoothed out the paper and folded it. The official part of the agenda was over, but the men remained seated where they were.

'What now?', Petrovski asked. 'Those are human beings out there, and we were never even aware of their existence. They must be the descendants of the ones who didn't emigrate - the ones who chose smog, filth and pollution over the purity of suboceanic life. They clung to their world, to their lives in the cities; but they couldn't keep that world from decaying. No one ever dreamed that any of them would survive.'

Vertain expressed the question that burned in every mind. 'Is it our duty to help them? There can't be many of them. Should we take them in, open our safe, hygienic world to them—to others like that little girl?' He nodded toward the screen. The child shielded her eyes with her hand, as if to make herself invisible.

Govin was as perplexed as the rest. The child—would she be happy down here? His eyes wandered back to the window. The water outside was murky; clumps of bacteria and plankton drifted by, sludge from the sewage system.

Where did their responsibility lie? Out there? Or with those inside?

Vaguely, Govin recalled an old legend about the sea—something about turquoise waters, turquoise and crystal clear.

translated by CHRIS HERRIMAN

# The Land of Osiris
## WOLFGANG JESCHKE

### 1
### Master Jack

He came down the Shari River from the south out of the country of the Lagones and Bagirmi. He had three horses with him, two of which he used as pack animals. He rode the third himself, a small brown mare with a white blaze and dark brown eyes, a beautiful horse.

It was on the day of the feast of Id El Kebir, the Bairam. I remember it as if it were yesterday—a hot morning—there was the smell of warm blood and entrails, of freshly baked bread. That morning rams had been slaughtered in front of all the houses—even before the huts of the poor. The king, Allah be praised, had animals distributed to them for slaughter, so that no one in the town would be without his roast for the Easter celebration. The men had already begun to drink Laqbi early in the morning. They were lighthearted and merry and some of them were even slightly inebriated. Then news came that a stranger had ridden through the southern gate of the town.

Annur, the barber, brought the news. In spite of the heat, he had his melefa slung tightly around his shoulders. His toothless smile froze into a grimace. He rubbed his long nose and his small eyes—lively from curiosity and Laqbi—sparkled in his brown wrinkled face under his bleached barbusch that had once been red. 'So, so, one of light skin', my father said slowly, laying his knife and the bloody liver beside the head of the ram on the bench in front of our hut. He cleaned his hands on the blood spattered apron, which he had put on over his burnouse, wiping the sweat off his brow with his arm. 'A travelling doctor?'

'Not a Tabib', Annur said and looked with the eye of an expert at out ram. 'He says that he is a man of learning, a sort of stargazer.'

'Stargazer?'

The barber shrugged and snorted. 'At any rate, he comes from somewhere way down south, somewhere where there are not only blacks. In former times, whites are said to have lived there.' Annur sniffed in disgust and spat on the freshly swept clay floor in front of our hut. My father looked at him sternly. 'One thing is certain, he's an unbeliever', he continued scornfully, without even noticing our disapproval. 'Were Hassan in power—pah—such so-called scholars would have been forbidden entry into our town or would have had their heads chopped off and nailed to the city gate as a warning to all.'

'That is not the way to talk during our Easter celebration', my father reprimanded. 'The times of Hassan in which every light-skinned man was stoned or hanged, whether he was a mutant or not, are past—Allah be thanked. King Ahmed ben Brahim is a good ruler. He gave me this fat ram as a present.'

'Truly a fine animal', the barber had to admit with a touch of envy, as he belonged to those who had enough money to buy their own ram.

'Where is the stranger, Annur?', I asked curiously as I had never seen a white adult before.

'He's staying in the caravansary and has been brought to the king's palace by the guards of the city.' Then he turned to my father and said, 'According to a discreet, preliminary examination, he doesn't seem to be a mutant. When he comes out of the palace we will know more.' Then with a touch of doubt in his voice, he said, 'Maybe, he is really telling the truth—perhaps he does come from the south and not from the countries of the dead in the north. We'll know in time. One thing is certain, he's an unbeliever.' This time my father caught him with a reproachful look before he could spit on the floor. The barber pressed his lips to a thin line and made do with repeating sharply, 'One thing is certain!'

I ran in the direction of the caravansary in order to see the mysterious stranger. The sun was bright in the yard. The first things I saw were the saddles and packs near the stalls. Hazaz sat on a mat made of palm leaves in the shade and was mending a camel saddle. One would never have thought that such powerful hands could make such adept and quick movements. He stuck holes in the worn leather with an awl. He waved to me and rubbed his crocheted cotton Taqija which he always kept on his shaven head.

Abarshi and Sliman, the most famous vagabonds in town, crouched behind the packs of the stranger, pulled as if unintentionally on the straps and buckles and blinked to emphasize their boredom into the sun.

'Hands off!', Hazaz snarled without taking the tarred string from between his teeth.

'He's a white devil', Abarshi said as an excuse. 'Who knows what kind of diseases he's brought with him!' One eye clouded with a cataract stared accusingly at the dusty leather cases of the stranger as if it hoped to divine their contents with some hidden power, while the other eye glanced covetously around.

'All the more reason to keep your hands off!', Hazaz replied, pulling the string through the holes and hammering it into place with the wooden handle of the awl.

'Beware of the beast that arrives from the north, says the prophet. He is ill and carries with him slow invisible death', Sliman proclaimed with a dark frown, stroking his white beard which hung like plucked cotton around his chin. He looked so wise that he seemed about to turn into a marabout.

'The prophet never said anything of the sort, you cunning bastard', Hazaz replied. 'It was one of those drivelling preachers, who visit us year after year, poisoning the souls of our people while draining the last penny out of their pockets. Besides, the stranger doesn't come from the north, but from the south.'

'The devil has many dwellings, says the prophet', Sliman replied, uneasily balancing the weight of his bleached blue turban on his head. 'Allah's wrath will crush those who disobey his laws just as the crocodile whip crushes the scorpion who raises its sting.'

'Then take care, Sliman; if you don't keep your poisonous tongue still, you'll be mistaken for a scorpion.' Sliman fumed with rage and crouched down beside Abarshi in the shade. The noise of the crickets in the palm trees of the caravansary was like a persistent metallic shriek. Somewhere, under the roof of the stalls, pigeons cooed and we could hear the breathing of the stranger's horses.

'Beschir', Hazaz asked, 'have you done your good deed for the day on this holiest of all days?'

I looked at him sceptically as I had no idea just what he was trying to get at. 'No', I said hesitantly.

'Then feed the horses. I have given them water.'

'What's his name?', I asked.

'Jack Freyman. He's called Master Jack.'

I went into the kitchen and put on the tea. Then I gave the horses millet and hay and brushed them down. Ticks had nested in their hide and their legs were covered with leech wounds, like all the animals coming from the humid hot south.

A clatter of hooves was heard and we rushed out to the yard. A royal escort, the vizier himself, was accompanying the stranger. The vizier rode at the stranger's side under a canopy held by four slaves flanked by six cavalrymen of the king's guard in full armour riding horses with blue quilted armour, the slit toes of their curly pointed-toed shoes hooked into the stirrups. The visors of their helmets glittered in rivalry with the silver harnesses and the polished brass plates at the heads and necks of the horses. They made a magnificent sight.

I was disappointed by the stranger's appearance. I had seen light-skinned ones before, young eunuch slaves such as the barbarians make of the healthy children of the refugees. But this man's skin was almost as dark as that of a Tuareg. He was of medium height and strongly built. He looked more like a merchant from the west, with his black turban which hid his hair and his black beard. However, when he rode nearer and got down from his saddle I noticed that his eyes were as blue as the waters of an oasis reflecting the midday sun.

The cavalrymen loosened their shoes from the stirrups, sprang down from their horses and thrust their spears into the dust of the caravansary. I recognized one of them called Chalilu. He lived not far from us, but didn't seem to recognize me and stared straight ahead. Perspiration ran down his face from under his helmet, down on to the thick cotton armour. His round face, instead of registering the worthiness of his station, bore the expression of an imbecile.

Hazaz bowed before the Vizier, who took out an official document and began to read it aloud.

'By order of his majesty, the King, our Master, Jack Freyman Effendi, travelling scholar from the far off country of Zimbabwe and guest of our King is to receive a Bishari riding camel from his Majesty's herd as well as three pack animals of our best breed. Further, to accompany him to Darfur to protect and to serve him, he is to receive a guide familiar with the route and a camel herder. These men will also receive the appropriate riding animals from the King's herd. Further, he shall receive the following provisions for forty days from the stock of the caravansary: dates 40 pounds, millet 30 pounds, sugar 6 pounds, tea 5 pounds and salt 2 pounds...'

I looked the stranger over. He was wearing a white tunic such as is worn in the south and unusually cut trousers of light grey cloth, held up by a belt in which two knives were fastened, and falling over low boots of shiny leather. On a shoulder strap, he carried a quiver of short metal arrows. As he dismounted, he took a weapon from his saddle horn. It looked like a cross between a short-barrelled gun and a bow. I found out later that it was called a crossbow and that one could shoot more accurately with it than with many a gun.

As he turned his face towards me, I saw that his black beard was greying on the cheeks and at the corners of his mouth. His face seemed young. How old could he be? Forty or even older?

'Master Jack Effendi?', I said.

He hesitated and looked at me with a critical glance. 'Yes?', he asked.

'Give me your horse. I'll look after it.'

He handed me the reins.

And so it happened that Hazaz was chosen by the King himself to show Master Jack the way to the east and I, as I had often accompanied Hazaz as his camel herder, was allowed to follow him this time too. What a journey this would be! It would lead us through the land of the dead to the very edge of the world—and Master Jack beyond it.

## Extracts from the Journal of Master Jack

March 29th, 2036

*We have just reached Kotoko on Lake Chad. The brothers of Fort Sibut were right. It is mortal danger for a white man to let himself be seen north of the Niger River. However, it's no different south of the Zambezi. But how one could hold it against the people? The white race has destroyed its own world— brought itself to a spectacular end. The fact that they took countless other races to their deaths in the process and brought them unspeakable misery doesn't interest these people in the least. Should I expect gratitude?*

*In spite of this, I meet people everywhere with whom one can talk quite reasonably—chiefs, tribal princes, rulers—more sensible and wiser perhaps than the politicians and rulers of our race who were only capable of presenting one another with an expensive cremation.*

*King Ahmed ben Brahim is about my age. He has a natural dignity—a sense of humour—and is quick to understand. He asked me about my itinerary and I showed him the way on my map from Mt Darwin to the north into the former Zambia, down the Lualaba and the Congo, up the Ubangi and the Tomi past the ruins of Dekoa and Fort Lamy and down the Shari—the great western detour round the countries of the dead. He laid his hand on my map, on the point between Juba and Djibouti, between Asmara and Lake Victoria, where the bombs had fallen in the struggle for the horn of Africa.*

*He noticed at once that on the old map Lake Chad was shown larger than it is today. The latest satellite pictures show that the desert has extended even further to the south. I can confirm this. The king has just told me that the old caravan route to the Nile can only be covered with camels today. There is not enough water for horses. Only three centuries ago ox teams travelled through this old caravan route. I made him a present of a burning glass—these lenses are called Zimbabwe glasses here and are highly valued. I offered him my horses. He promised me his support, indicated he would allow me to use his camels and provisions and even offered me the prospect of a guide and a herder. He has already found a guide. His name is Hazaz, a big strong Nubian. He seems prudent and experienced and seems very reliable. His herder is a young boy called Beschir. He's quick-witted and intelligent and has a good hand with animals, but he is delicate, a bit small for his fourteen years, with sad dark eyes that reveal a sensitive character.*

*Here nothing is known about conditions on the Nile, except, at best, pilgrims' fables at second and third hand. Tales of horrible mutants, men with bodies of insects, heads of birds and white cannibals.*

The day before our journey started, I rode to the northwest to the lake where the king's herd grazed. The king's blacksmith was also there. The camels were being shod. Two slaves held a grumbling, snarling animal while the smith pressed its hooves against his loin cloth. He nailed Bu Raqabu, the strong hide of the sabre-horned antelope, to the animal's hooves. It was known to resist the rocks and sand of the desert better than steel. He laughed in relief when he had finished and poured the leather pail full of water over himself.

That night I led the animals, rebellious with restlessness, into the town, where they were to be saddled and loaded before sunrise.

Thus, it came to pass that we rode away from Kotoko towards the east through the land of the light-skinned Dagama on our way to the great contaminated river and to the ocean beyond the desert, to the holy city that had risen from the dead, over which Allah holds his protective hand.

## Extracts from the Journal of Master Jack

April 8th, 2036

*At last we are on our way. The king has kept his promise. Well-equipped with animals and provisions, we are setting off for the east, following the old pilgrim route which once crossed Darfur through Kordofan to Khartoum and from there on to Port Sudan. The names of these places are unknown to all here today. Has the route changed perhaps?*

*It is said that there are pilgrims who maintain that they were in Arabia after the oil war. Mecca had been rebuilt, at least the holy places. I mistrust their reports. I don't dare bring up the subject otherwise for it arouses a religious fanaticism that frightens me.*

*In spite of all this, I am confident.*

We rode through many abandoned villages and rested at dried-up springs. We crossed the sandy remains of the Lake of Fittri, in the land of the Bathra tribe. The lake looks like a mirror that has broken into smithereens, but this is only the layer of salt covering the clay earth that has cracked from the heat and glistens in the sun. Our camels left deep tracks. The air was damp and stifling and the camels snorted with fear. Islands seemed to float over the horizon to accompany us soundlessly along our route.

We detoured round the ruins of Abéché where there are supposed to be strange beasts and horrible pale mutants who know how to make themselves invisible. They are said to strangle travellers at night.

On the twenty-eighth day of our journey we reached the foot of the mountain and rushed to the spring called Bir Meschru, the Spring of the Skeletons. Many are said to have mysteriously died there. But that too is a lie. Just half an hour's ride from the spring, there is a place to the north, between isolated tamarisks and shittah trees, where there are hundreds of dead bodies. It is quite evident that they had not met with a mysterious death, but had been cruelly massacred. Few of them had become skeletons; most had mummified in the dry air and had become feather-light, rolling over in the wind. Although the sun had darkened their skin, it was obvious that they were white refugees that had been slaughtered. All their clothes had been stolen.

We rode back to the oasis and were all very depressed. The otherwise happy face of Master Jack had never been so earnest.

In the meantime, back at the spring, a second caravan had arrived and had set up its camp under the palm trees. There were two travellers with four camels, pilgrims from the west far beyond Timbuktu, on their way to the holy places. They begged us for tea and sugar. I was sure that they were from the Logon tribe from the cut of their faces and their clothes. I didn't believe a word they said, for the Logons are deceitful and covetous and are said to be magicians with the Evil Eye, who can change into hyenas in the night. They camped a stone's throw away from us.

The water of the spring was somewhat salty and tasted of sulphur. However, this was the richest source of water for many miles and our camels needed a rest. Thus, it was decided to rest for two nights and one day.

### Extracts from the Journal of Master Jack

May 5th, 2036

*We must have passed the former boundary between Chad and the Sudan long ago. As far as I can make out El Geneina doesn't exist any more. The mountain range to the east must be the Jebel Musa. Now, the caravan route leads up into the mountains. The way before us is difficult. Hazaz assures me that it can only be a three-day journey to El Fasher, the former caravan junction in Darfur. From there it will take us 30 days to En Nahud in Darhamar, another 7 or 8 days to El Obeid in Kordofan and then Khartoum will be within reasonable distance. Only two months if our journey continues so successfully. But who knows what perils await us? I have seen thousands today who once believed themselves fortunate. They had fled contaminated Europe and had succeeded in their flight across the Mediterranean. They had encountered unspeakable hardships in crossing the desert—were led by deceitful caravan guides into a supposedly safe place that turned out to be a trap and there they were slain. These horrors actually happened. I have seen these 'mutants' graveyards', as they call them, with my own eyes. The robbers and murderers even went about their horrible business with the approval of their governments, in order to prevent the plague resulting from biological warfare advancing further to the south, as it had completely depopulated the whole of the northern strip of Africa. The military was often put into action to shoot down the streams of refugees. What they didn't realize was that migratory birds had already carried the plague into the areas of the south— which abound in water—yes, even in the heart of Africa and that they returned with it every autumn.*

## 2
## The Labyrinth

It clouded over that night, but there was hardly a drop in temperature. I dreamt of the dead in the desert that the wind had set into motion. There had been children among them.

Some time or other in the night I awoke. Hazaz had put wood on the fire again and cowered in the darkness of the night. Today I know that he was then as conscious as I that something was wrong. The Logon tribe had taken on another form and were sniffing us out.

In the morning, fog covered the oasis and the sun was lost to view. I had a hard time finding the animals and herding them together. They had diarrhoea from the sulphurous water and their hides were damp from the fog. We crouched in silence around the fire and drank tea.

Master Jack went over to the pilgrims and spoke with them for a long time while Hazaz and I rearranged the packs on the animals and checked the saddles and their straps and put them in order.

Although it was the beginning of May, the wind came from the south and the suffocating heat became unbearable. It strained our hearts and hindered our breathing, making us at the same time exhausted and restless. The atmosphere was crackling and deceptive. Distance had no meaning. The mountains appeared nearer. The hours dragged on. Threatening clouds were gathering in the southeast.

'Herd the animals together, Beschir', Hazaz said. 'A storm is coming.'

Master Jack came back just as we were putting up our tent and securing it. 'There's going to be a thunderstorm', he called and, as if the heavens wanted to prove their point, a sharp crack of thunder echoed from the mountains nearby. The animals sought shelter under the sparsely growing siwak bushes. The sky darkened visibly. The wind throbbed in the acacia trees and the dry palm branches hissed like disturbed snakes. However, the storm made its way past us to the north. There, in the mountains, deep red lightning flashed and ripples of thunder were heard for a long time, while in the south, the stars began appearing one by one. Nearby hyenas were laughing. Shortly after, I must have fallen asleep.

I awoke to a scream. Before I could get to my feet, Master Jack was up, had grabbed his crossbow and quiver, and run out. I ran after him. My riding camel was only a few feet away and was no longer tethered. It seemed out of breath as if it had been chased around. It stretched its neck and sniffed. In the leaden-coloured light of the dawn, I discovered a second camel just a few yards away plucking at the branches with its hard lips and snorting excitedly. It was Master Jack's camel. It had its hobble on, binding its forefoot to the leg. The other animals were nowhere to be seen.

'This way, Beschir!', I heard Master Jack call. He crouched beside Hazaz on the ground. I couldn't see what had happened. I grabbed my camel by its reins and dragged it behind me. As I drew nearer I saw that the left side and sleeve of Hazaz's garment was dark with blood. It was the most horrible wound I had ever seen in my life! It gaped open three or four fingers wide, not bleeding. One could see the white of the bone.

I heard a deep sobbing that sounded like a foolish bleat. I was very much ashamed when I realized that the sound was coming from my own throat. But I couldn't help it. I sat down in the sand, as I could no longer stand up.

'I surprised them', Hazaz whispered, clenching his teeth. 'Those jackals! Those sons of bitches. . .'

'Keep still!', Master Jack ordered. He pressed the wound together. 'You should have woken us. You should never have acted on you own!'

With a throbbing cry, Hazaz buried his face in his right arm and lay on his stomach in the sand.

'Come here and help me, boy!', Master Jack's voice aroused me from my stupor. I felt the sweat break out on my neck and freeze in the cool of the morning. My whole body trembled as I helped to dress the wound with cloth from Master Jack's saddle bag and to splint the arm with a piece of wood.

'Don't bother about me!', Hazaz moaned. 'Catch up with them. They won't get far. Not with my camel. It will put up a fight. But the pack animals. . .'

'Was this done with the stroke of a sword?', Master Jack asked.

'It was a shangormango', Hazaz snarled. 'Thrown from not even ten feet away—the jackal wanted to throw it in my face. At the last minute, I shielded my face with my arm.'

We carried him carefully to our pack saddles. We made him a comfortable bed under a tamarisk tree. The sun was rising as we saddled our camels.

'What is a shangormango?', Master Jack asked as we looked for tracks. I wished I had been given the eyesight of Hazaz.

'A throwing iron', I said. 'Some are very adept with them. They can decapitate a man at a distance of thirty feet or slit the legs off a gazelle at fifty feet.'

Hazaz was right. His camel had resisted stubbornly. Its tracks were easy to recognize. When the two scoundrels saw us coming, they tried to get away on foot in different directions, knowing full well that even in the saddle they wouldn't have a chance against our swift riding camels. Their plan had failed the moment Hazaz prevented them from taking all the animals. Had they fled at that moment with their own animals, they would have perhaps been able to get away. But their greed got the better of them. These men were not robbers, but petty scoundrels, and stupid ones at that.

We set off after one of them and Master Jack soon rode him down. He let out a pitiful whimper and crawled towards me on all fours, perhaps hoping I would be more merciful. Master Jack handed me his crossbow and I took aim and crooked my finger round the trigger, when suddenly all anger and bitterness left me. I was filled with a great sadness and loathing for the pitiable creature lying face down before me. He crawled towards me like a misshapen lizard, stretched out like my own shadow. I just couldn't do it. I remembered the horrible wound. I just couldn't do it: Master Jack took the crossbow from me, unstrung it and hung it on his saddle.

'Listen!', he said to the man. 'We are going to take your animals as we have a wounded man to transport. As long as we are at the watering place, keep away! Should you dare to come anyway, I'll shoot you both!' Then he turned his camel around and we rode away.

The whimpering behind us turned into a great lamentation. The further away we rode, the angrier and nastier it became—directed, of course, at Master Jack's light skin and his race. I looked at Master Jack, but he didn't look back, took no notice at all. Perhaps he didn't understand. We herded the animals together, our own and theirs, and rode back to the oasis.

I was at odds with myself. Master Jack had been allowed by circumstance to see into my very heart. Was it the heart of a coward incapable of revenging his friend? As if he had heard my innermost thoughts, he said, 'You did the right thing, Beschir. His life is useless. His death would have been no less useless.'

I looked at him helplessly, but he smiled and nodded encouragingly. I pulled myself together and knew at that moment that I would follow this man to the very edge of the world. And I swore to myself to do so, come what may.

It was midday when we returned to the oasis. We noticed from afar that another caravan had arrived. We were frightened and expected to find Hazaz dead and our packs and provisions plundered. It would have been easy booty, but we were lucky. They were merchants from Darfur on their way to the west. They had looked after Hazaz and had given him something to drink. They told us that they couldn't understand what he was talking about and that he had often lost consciousness. They were astonished when they heard of our misfortune and kept shaking their heads in disbelief and repeating, 'Tsk, tsk'. However, they seemed much more preoccupied with their own troubles. During the night in the mountains, they had been caught in a storm and were drenched through and through. They had spread their coats, blankets and packs out to dry and sat jealously guarding their possessions. Later, however, they helped us gather boughs, branches, and rushes in order to weave them together into a sort of litter similar to those used by well-born women or for transporting valuable female slaves. We shall transport Hazaz in this. His condition is becoming more and more serious. He has not regained consciousness since our return..

## Extracts from the Journal of Master Jack

May 6th, 2036

*Yesterday, I wrote of our good fortune. Today, it has left us. Two camel thieves surprised us before dawn. However, they acted so stupidly that it didn't take long to regain possession of our animals. Unfortunately, our caravan guide was so badly wounded in the attack that I fear for his life. My antibiotics were lost in the Congo River along with my pistols and ammunition. All of which I could have used today.*

*Merchants who have just arrived from El Fasher said they left there three days ago. It would be wonderful if we could reach El Fasher in three days. Perhaps poor Hazaz would have a chance of getting medical help in time—if any is to be had there.*

*We shall remain here one more night. The spring just doesn't have enough water for the number of people and animals now camping here, but thanks to the rain in the mountains, the water level is rising rapidly. However, the water is too muddy. I hope the sediment will have settled by morning.*

*The two scoundrels have not shown their faces all day, although they were not at all intimidated by my threat. It's a good thing that there are now eleven more men here.*

\*   \*   \*   \*   \*

*I was proud of Beschir today. After the first shock, he proved alert and prudent, with great character. It would have been easy for him to let his revenge gain the upper hand. He's a good boy and I shall try to spend more time with him in future. Hazaz will no longer be in a position to look after him. But I shall take on this extra responsibility gladly.*

*I am not looking forward to meeting the notorious sovereign of El Fasher, the ruler of the Sudan. He is supposed to be partly of European descent. Those are often the worst despots in the countries which were once called the third world and which are the only countries in which human beings still live today.*

Hazaz has been lying in fever for the past two days and he keeps asking, 'Did you hear the fat one laughing? He laughed the whole night. The whole night.' I wipe the sweat from his forehead. His wound stinks. It has begun to fester.

'What does he mean by the fat one?', asked Master Jack.

'Oh, that is the hyena. Most of our fairy tales are about the stupid fat one who is taken in by everything, even squirrels and lizards, and always falls flat on his face.'

'Then he has every right to laugh! For we are the stupid ones this time', Master Jack said. He was right.

He is very worried about Hazaz's condition but tries not to let it show. I pray to Allah and implore him to let his cape of kindness be large enough to cover Hazaz with just one tiny corner.

We climbed for three days through ravines and rugged canyons and rocks as large as palaces. The road was difficult and the animals tired quickly.

Master Jack had built a frame on which we could set down the litter with Hazaz it in to load it on to another camel. We had to lean it against the rocks so that it wouldn't collapse as the animals were so tired and impatient to be rid of their loads that they fell to their knees before I could even loosen the straps and give the command to kneel. They are taking advantage of me and I have to use the whip to curb their growing stubbornness.

They notice the absence of Hazaz's strong hand.

Late in the afternoon of the third day of our journey, we reached the summit of the pass. Bare mountains as far as the eye could see, a labyrinth of stone. No plant, no animals, no sign of man's work. We rode on into the land that was not made for humans, a land that had frozen in the middle of creation as if Allah had lost interest in his work before separating the mountains and valleys. In spite of the merciless sun, this land is strangely dark and gloomy as if it were the bottom of an ocean. Sometimes the vultures sail over this land in elegant flight, creatures of a higher world descending to investigate the ocean floor, their sharp eyes looking for prey.

I have never been so far east. The loneliness of this expanse of land is so overwhelming. There is hardly a trace of the caravan route. The rocks are hard. The signs indicating the way to A'alam are often only two to three stones one on top of the other and one needs good eyes to make them out. Master Jack always stops and stares through his glass. In this desolate land there are no people. El Fasher cannot be far now.

The next morning we are surrounded by a patrol. Threatening figures on long-legged Mahari, racing camels of the famous Tuareg breed, with saddles and bridles of silver, covers and turbans with white and green tassles, the colours of the king. The cavalrymen are armed with lances and crossbows, some of them even with rifles. An officer with a laced jacket, with green and white epaulettes, orders his steed to kneel. After cross-examining us quickly, he lets his men dismount, shares salt and tea with us. He inspects the litter with a critical eye. Yes, there are doctors, Egyptians, Arabs and even light-skinned doctors. They will be able to give Hazaz the medical attention he needs. Under cover of the cavalrymen, we ride into El Fasher only four hours away. We are not given quarters in one of the caravan-saries, but are taken directly to the palace of the king, which he had built on a plateau in the north of the city. There are many soldiers and many light-skinned people. The market place is full of activity. Affluence is apparent, flourishing under power and common sense. Laughing faces—an oasis of colour in this dark wasteland—El Fasher.

The palace of the king: the sumptuous nest of a bird of prey, grandiose, a fortress against attack: beautiful, built of stone and clay, ornamented with coloured tiles. The sun has reached its highest point and casts straight, sharp-angled shadows, created by the many ledges, eaves and balconies over the facade of the building. Two burnt out tanks flank the entrance of the palace like frozen mastodons, their guns raised like threatening trunks.

In the courtyard before the palace we are told to unsaddle the camels. A doctor is called. He is a young Egyptian. Hazaz is then carried away. What will it cost? He has a wide nose and the corners of his mouth drop under his black moustache, an honest, trustworthy face. He lifts his hand as if testing the weight of the air while his eyes take note of our belongings—two camels, three, we'll see. We are given a room near the stables. Our animals will be looked after. Master Jack opens his packs, looks for fresh clothes and a present for the host.

**Extracts from the Journal of Master Jack**

May 10th, 2036

*El Fasher at last! It has not lost any of its significance as the former capital of Darfur. Even the size of the population has remained the same as before the war, unlike most of the cities of the Sahel Zone. However, it is no longer the hub of trade that it once was. Once, in former times, the caravans went through Bahr El Ghazal to the Upper Nile and through Equatoria to Ethiopia, to Uganda into Northern Kenya and then on to Somalia and came back with salt for the herds. Today, it is one of the most important stops between east and west, part of the old pilgrim route from Chad to Darfur and Kordofan to Nubia.*

*Achmed Ueled ben Muchtar, King of Sudan and as he calls himself, Emperor of the edge of the still inhabitable world and A'alam of Allah to the holy places, is apparently not the despot he is made out to be. He can thank his diplomatic skill and the tactical ability of his officers for his reputation as a cruel and severe despot. His reputation increases with distance. In the city itself, there is no trace of tyranny. The city is crowded with Europeans and refugees from Libya, Egypt and Arabia and many have the privileges of well-respected citizens. However, there are many light-skinned slaves, but they are well fed and certainly do not live in want. The troops as well seem to be predominantly Europeans.*

*The royal residence was designed by a French architect who had been received at court. It is an object of interest far and wide, sumptuously combining elements of European architecture with those of the orient. It is said that more than 3000 people live in this palace in which we also were received with such hospitality. Hazaz is being treated by a doctor. I hope that it is not too late and that the necessary antibiotics are available.*

*I am racking my brains thinking of a present for my host. I have a dozen magnifying glasses, two watches, a few yards of the finest asbestos cloth, four or five compasses and my telescope. I would not like to part with the latter. All this seems very meagre for a sovereign of whom it is said that he led plundering expeditions as far as the African Mediterranean Coast and is reputed to have returned home with fabulous treasures. Apparently, he even has an electric car and a helicopter. However, there is no fuel for the helicopter. But he is sure to send an expedition soon to the abandoned oil lines of Libya in order to get his toy moving.*

I have just visited Hazaz. He is lying in a white bed in a room with white walls. He is being looked after by a male nurse who was trying to put a glass tube into his mouth. His arm has been freshly bandaged and no longer stinks. But Hazaz, himself, looks as if he is going to die. His appearance frightens me. He didn't recognize me. The nurse pushed me out and as I tried to crouch just outside the door ordered me to go.

Yesterday, Master Jack was invited to the king's palace. Today, we have moved into the part of the palace reserved for guests. The rooms are high and spacious and the floors are laid out with the finest carpets. Many light-skinned men live in the palace, especially artists and technicians to the king. By no means all of them have been castrated as many have wives and children with them.

In the evening supper was served in the inner courtyard of the palace. Afterwards a light-skinned musician played a stringed instrument called a 'mandolino'. It is played by plucking at the strings and sounds very strange, sometimes like the cooing of turtle doves, at times sad and then again, merry. He sang this song to the music.

> 'If rain hovers over the land
> like a black muleta
> then, my friends, death is near...'

But the king called down to him, 'Not such songs! the rainy season is far off and death doesn't interest us at all.'

Everyone laughed and the musician sang some other songs. He has that red skin with white spots deepened by the light just like those who come out of the countries of the dead. On his bald head behind his left ear there is a wet wound which looks as though it will never heal and the whites of his eyes are a sickly yellow. But his voice is all the more beautiful filling the courtyard and making me forget the miserable appearance of the man.

He sang six or seven old songs from the past—I can almost remember the exact words of them. It was an amusing song about a little monkey who tried to reach the stars and in doing so set fire to the tree where he was sleeping and scorched his fur in the process. This was the refrain:

> The play is over,
> the monkey dead,
> the stars remain on high.
> The monkey's tree,
> and the man's own dream
> as dust now scattered fly.
> Thus perishes mankind too
> by his own hand,
> himself Eternity to deny.

A frail light-skinned deaf and dumb youth stood beside the singer. He had the shy fright-filled eyes of those who cannot hear. He watched the lively faces of those listening and turned again to stare at the lips of the singer. Each time the musician put his instrument down, he picked up his Jew's harp and put it to his mouth to accompany the song. This sounded very strange as he was always just one note behind because he followed the lip movement. It was this imperfection that made their playing together so charming.

A pilgrim, who had been to the holy places and was on his way home to the west, told Master Jack that between Omdurman and Port Said flying ships have often been seen travelling through the air hovering noiselessly over the desert. They have crews of giant beetles and are navigated by creatures with birds' heads. Such Egyptian beasts as one finds carved in stone in certain places arose from the mud of Lake Nasser when it dried up. Another reported that he had seen such a bird-headed creature with his own eyes. It had been killed near Atbara. A carnival showman had this thing that was neither man nor bird stuffed and exhibited at fairs up and down the countryside between Omdurman and El Obeid until the remains had stunk so fearfully that somebody burned them and chased the showman to the devil.

Although Master Jack is otherwise very smart, in such things he is terribly credulous. He listened patiently and asked what the flying ships looked like, asked about the colours of the plumage of the bird-headed creatures, asked about the beetles and the scarabs which according to the stories must have looked more like cockroaches. And he asked many other questions. The boastings of the pilgrims impressed me just as little as the other pack of liars—I didn't believe one word.

When I went to our guest chambers on the second floor, I met a man on the stairs who, judging from his clothes, had a high position at court. He refused to let me pass.

'Come here', he ordered.

I obeyed, stepped nearer and bowed. He slung his arm intimately around me and pressed me into a corner. His well-kept white beard smelled of sweet perfume, but his breath was pregnant with Laqbi.

'Listen, young man', he said in a drunken voice and grasped me tightly between the legs. I cursed in pain.

'Have you already got a teacher?', he tittered happily.

'I belong to Master Jack', I said in a tortured voice.

He let me go. I was horrified at the shamelessness of it all and ran away from him as fast as I could. As I ran up the steps I could hear him calling after me laughing, 'Who the hell is Master Jack?'

I awoke in the middle of the night. Someone was standing in the door. I recognized the weak profile, the bald head and the delicate figure. It was the youth who had played the Jew's harp. He looked cautiously to the right and left and then stared at me.

'What do you want?', I asked in a low voice so as not to wake Master Jack asleep in the next room. It then occurred to me that the youth couldn't hear me at all. His presence made me ill at ease. He raised both arms and made a few dancing steps setting his bare feet on the complex mosaic moonlight-flooded tiles, so that he seemed to be floating. I followed the movements of his feet with my eyes as though intoxicated. I felt reality slowly slipping away. Through the movement of the dance and the magic of the moonlight I was slipping into the realm of unreality. I pulled myself together and tried to shake off the growing numbness. At that same moment, the youth disappeared. I ran out into the corridor, but I couldn't find him anywhere. Where could he have disappeared to so quickly? Under a lantern at the end of the corridor, I saw a guard asleep at the table. His head rested on his crossed arms. I padded through the moonlight to the window and looked down on the courtyard in which the concert had taken place. It lay deserted, covered in a melancholy silver light. In the dark shadows pincered scarabs under the command of bird-headed pirate captains lurked to storm the sleeping palace.

'Beschir?', Master Jack called. I ran to the threshold of his room, but he didn't say any more. Had he called my name in his sleep?

Late that afternoon when Master Jack had been summoned to the king, I roamed through the upper floors of the palace. No one stopped me. I found a garden, a small paradise about a hundred feet long and forty wide surrounded by a building several floors high. Gravel paths led through the flower beds and hedges, the graceful pomegranate and peach trees, to a fountain in the centre. Its water sparkled in the midday sun falling wastefully on the large meat-like leaves of the water-lilies that had almost overgrown the little pond. The falling water gave the air a pleasant freshness. Several peacocks paraded with ornamental step over the grass and spread out their shimmering green and dark blue feathers into fans, stiff trains and rustling aureoles. I was fascinated. How could there be so much colour in this land of melancholy light and dark stone?

At the other end of the park, there was a draw-well; its cisterns were just being filled to feed the fountain. A great wooden treadwheel the height of at least three men turned creakingly while three slaves clad in loin cloths climbed up over the smooth worn treads to keep it moving. Their white bodies were wet with sweat and their heavy breathing was drowned by the splashing water. Then one of the black pails fastened one behind the other on an iron chain reached the top, tipped over and emptied its contents into a channel which led to the cisterns, then collapsed and dived below again.

I stopped and watched. In the narrow shade of the clay wall an overseer stood with a braided leather whip in his hand. Three other slaves crouched on the floor near him and were allowed to rest until it was their turn on the wheel. They looked me over with dull glances, but no one spoke. Only the creaking of the wooden wheel, the gasping of the climbing men and the splashing and falling of the water were to be heard. Suddenly the silence of the courtyard was interrupted by the brief cry of a woman which came from one of the upper windows of the palace. A second louder cry was followed by a third and a fourth, becoming a swelling rhythmic series of cries. Breathless cries and at the same time deep throaty groans. Then something strange occurred which was incomprehensible to me. One of the slaves who was brooding dully in the shadows had stood up, a muscular stooped man with dark hair and an unshaved face, had clenched both his hands into fists and held up his arms as though he were carrying a burden and jerked his hips back and forth in rhythm with the cries. With his eyes closed and biting his lower lip, he emitted a deep short grunt with each jerk while his loin cloth bulged. The whip came down with a slap on his naked shoulders, but it was a negligent, almost good-natured, blow and the man didn't seem to feel it at all. At that moment the cries broke off with a sharp high note and the slave stopped his movements as though he had been paralysed. His face had an expression I could not interpret, pained and yet happy.

The overseer bared gap teeth under his moustache and laughed and the two slaves crouching in the shadows joined unwillingly in his laughter. However, the others on the wheel kept climbing in dull preoccupied haste like a pack of confused apes in flight.

I smiled uncomfortably at the overseer for I could not guess the reason for his amusement. I quickly turned away and went further into the palace garden, past the pond and the splashing fountains emerging from the nostrils of the mighty stone hippopotamus which, half concealed by water lilies, raised its head above the water and stared at me with its blind little stone eyes.

I saw the deaf and dumb youth sitting on a stone bench under a pomegranate tree. For a moment I didn't know what to do. Was it a dream I had had in the night? Had the moonlight played a trick on me? Or did he really walk like a ghost through the corridors of the palace at night in order to give his mute inner world expression by dancing?

I sat down on the bench and laid the palm of my hand on the cool stone. The youth moved his mouth as if he wanted to say something to me, but he was only able to grunt. He raised his hands and grasped at his mouth as if to pluck the words he couldn't express forcibly from his lips. In his agony of wanting to say something, he rolled his eyes back so that only the whites could be seen. I was still sure he was trying to say something to me. However, it became clear that he was having a fit. He bent backwards and thrust his bald head backwards and forwards as if he wanted to break through some barrier. Then he lay thrashing about inclined over the bench, while in the corner of his crying wordless mouth foam gathered. I held him tight in fear of his falling off the bench. I fought with him finally covering his delicate body with mine. It had suddenly developed unbelievable power. I looked around desperately for help as I could no longer control him. I wanted to call the men at the well to get their help in my desperate struggle with the dark power that had taken over his body in broad daylight and was throwing it back and forth like a rag doll until I was completely out of breath.

Suddenly, I heard footsteps on the gravel path. I saw two small white hands cradling the head of the youth, stroking his temples and ears. It was as if they had worked a magic spell. The dark power left his body immediately, wiping away the stiffness of his limbs. Then to my complete bewilderment I realized that the body I was holding was that of a young girl. Directly before me, I saw the spotty bald head of the singer, the dreadful watery wound. I had to grit my teeth to keep from groaning but as I turned my head to release myself from the horror, I was looking into the still more fearful eye of a peacock—a great ringlike grey-rayed pool of protein behind which there was nothing. An attentive, absolutely expressionless peephole into a small stupid world governed by reflexes. Then, with a jerk of its head, the bird moved away and let me see the senseless magnificence of its plumage.

Slowly, ashamed, I removed my hands from the body of the girl and sat up. The singer—he seemed surprisingly tall as he stood before me—smiled at me apologetically.

'I thank you. She could have hurt herself', he said while helping her up. 'It overcomes her sometimes. I have told her time and again that she must not go into the sun.'

'But she was sitting in the shade!'

He shrugged his shoulders. 'That is our heritage', he said. 'The heritage of the great civilization. Thus perishes mankind too by his own hand, himself Eternity to deny.' He smiled.

The girl looked at me enigmatically with her bright eyes. I would have given anything to be able to make myself understood. If only I could have asked her something and if only she could have answered. But it was like talking to a star. It gives no answer but light.

'What is her name?'

'Simone.'

'A strange name.'

'So?' He took her in his arms. 'She cannot betray me. She can't even hear the cock crow.'

I didn't understand what he meant. When we left the palace garden, the overseer and his slaves had disappeared. The worn treads of the wooden wheel glittered in the sun. Water ran from the overflow of the filled cisterns and dripped onto the stone pavement. The black leather pails hung on the chain, full-bellied on the one side, loose and collapsed on the other.

A woman stood at one of the upper windows and looked down. I saw her mouth for a moment before she closed her veil. She smiled.

## Extracts from the Journal of Master Jack

May 25th, 2036

*We have been living in the palace of the king for two weeks now. He has asked to see me many times and I have had the opportunity of talking in detail with him. I would say he's in his mid-forties with a rare mixture of charisma, intelligence and foolhardiness. The condottieri are said to have been that way. He says he is descended from the caliphs and as far back as the prophets. However, it would not surprise me if the caliphs were called Stravros, Kostas, Spiros or something similar and if the prophet was called Pythagoras and owned bars in Beirut and Alexandria. He is the born adventurer and knows how to get along with the right people.*

*He also owns the most important scrap metal collection in the world. Both tanks before the gate of the palace are supposed to have been driven by Qadhafi himself when he took over Chad. He organized expeditions into the bombed and radioactively contaminated former oil wells in Libya. He says he brought back rich plunder from the dead cities of the Mediterranean, but they are mostly useless technical things that can never ever be put to use again: such as telephone installations and a complete air traffic control tower. However, he has the most important timepiece collection in the world. He is absolutely mad about time-measuring devices. He has all conceivable shapes and constructions—a collection spanning five centuries.*

*I told him about my expedition and our belief that somewhere in the Near East space activities were taking place which we could not identify. He thinks it is possible that creatures from outer space have landed on earth. 'It would be a wonder if we hadn't aroused any interest after the fireworks we set off here on earth!', he said. He insists on giving us a troop of soldiers to accompany us on our journey to the 'edge of the world' as he also calls it. In return for this favour, we should bring him one of the 'flying ships' home if we can find one.*

*He gave me the journal of his architect to read as a present. The one who built the palace. His name was Henri Fleurel. He died two years ago. It is written in French. I shall read it on our way through Kordofan.*

<br>

**3**

## The Edge of the World

In the morning, we visited Hazaz. His arm has been cut off. The emptiness under the sheet was horrible. I had so often admired that strong arm when he used the awl, saddled the camels, or, with the same strong hand, forced them to kneel—simply gone. I couldn't look and yet, as if paralysed, I stared at the empty space where his arm ought to have been. The doctor said that gangrene had set in too deep. The bone had been damaged and had splintered. There was a funny sound in my ears and I felt as if I were going to lose consciousness. I ran out of the door and stood at a window on the other side of the corridor breathing heavily. Hazaz is sleeping, he knows nothing of his misfortune. Why was I not able to slay those jackasses that morning?

I pray that Hazaz shall live. It is said that Allah's grace is boundless. All I ask of him is just a small corner, just enough to cover what is left of Hazaz.

Master Jack took me aside today and said that in a short time he must leave in order to reach the Nile at high water. It is for me to decide whether I shall continue with him. The journey will now be dangerous as we will be entering the last regions of the inhabitable world and now, more than ever, we shall meet up with contaminated animals and beasts with bodies of men.

'All pilgrims take on this danger', I replied. 'They do it for God!'

'But that is the difference', he said. 'They are religious fanatics. They are looking for danger in order to prove that God is with them. They are possessed.'

'And what do you want to prove, Master Jack?', I asked him.

He hesitated. Then he laughed and said, 'You're a smart boy, Beschir. Yes, I am possessed. I want to find out what is stationed in the northeast, who has set up a space centre there and why they are stubbornly ignoring the signals of our orbital tracking system, two stations of which are still working.'

'What is an orbal tracking system?'

'Orbital. The paths of the stars around the world can be controlled by it. We are a sort of caravan guide of the heavens.'

'All the stars?'

'What. . .? No, naturally only the artificial ones. The satellites of the earth. There are a lot of them up there and many are going to be giving out data for centuries, data that no one is capable of evaluating any more.'

'And what about Hazaz?', I asked after a while.

'I would have liked you to have stayed here with him to be at his side when he gets better. You could have joined a caravan on its way west and returned home. But Hazaz's condition is still very critical.' He stroked his hand over his sunburnt face and through his long dark hair. He didn't like the thought of leaving Hazaz behind. 'On the other hand. . .', he looked at me pleadingly with his bright-coloured eyes as if asking me to forgive him. My shyness made me avoid his glance. 'Should the worst happen, you would then be alone here. The loose morals being what they are in this palace, I would fear for your life. Lecherous bastards are always on the lookout for stray young boys to train as male concubines for themselves or to sell as eunuchs into slavery.'

I remembered with horror my encounter on the staircase, that encounter about which I had never uttered a word. 'I've decided. I'm riding with you, Master Jack!', I replied with resolution.

Everything had been packed. The Ghararas, light bags made of strong camel-hair yarn that the king had just given us as a present, were ready to be loaded. Just before leaving, we visited Hazaz. He was in good health and waved to us with the stump of his arm.

'Wait two or three days', he pleaded. 'And then I'll be able to ride with you.' But the doctor made it clear that Hazaz had a good chance of surviving only if his wound did not become gangrenous. There were hardly any medical supplies left and, if any were found, they had usually been spoiled by the heat.

We wished Hazaz luck and Allah's protection.

'I shall look for work and wait for you', he said. 'Until next spring if necessary!'

The doctor charged us three camels. I went to get them and brought them to him. I have not seen Simone, the young girl of the singer, again, although I have looked for her everywhere.

## Extracts from the Journal of Master Jack

June 5th, 2036

*It was with great regret that we left Hazaz behind at the palace. We are now on our way east at last. We could have joined a caravan, also on its way to El Obeid, with more than 200 camels, but it's moving too slowly for my liking. Even if we cut down our rests to a bare minimum, we have a stretch of 40 to 45 days journey before us. It's almost 1000 miles to Omdurman. Should it be necessary to penetrate even further north and make our way down the Nile, it will only be possible to get over the rapids during high water, especially over the first and second rapids near Wadi Halfa and Aswan as nothing is known about the state of things there since the dam disappeared.*

*We are making good progress on our way to the east. Our four escorts are adept hunters. We eat meat almost every day. They are unruly but apparently reliable boys. It would be nice if I could convince them to escort us further than Omdurman, but they have their orders.*

The king's four escorts have set a pace that puts a great strain on our animals, but Master Jack seems to be pleased. He is so restless.

Yesterday, Alkuttabu, the best hunter of our escorts, shot a gazelle at a distance of 250 feet with his rifle. Today, we found a dead desert fox. Its hide was rotten.

'Don't touch it!', Alkuttabu warned me. He heaped dry wood over the body of the dead fox and lit it. The smell was horrible. We rode on. 'Half a century ago', Alkuttabu said, 'there were more than a thousand lions here in Kordofan. I know, as this was my homeland.' He has the jet black skin of the Nuba and he is even taller than Hazaz. 'You'll hardly find one today. They prey on the weaklings of the herd and they are usually ill. That kills them, you know?' He likes to repeat, 'You know'. Each time he juts his massive black chin in my direction.

'Are you afraid of lions?', I want to know. He smiles. He has large white buck teeth with gaps between them.

'Yes, but only dead ones', he says laughing a high giggling laugh that one wouldn't expect from a man of his size and clicks his tongue delightedly.

He often looks to the southeast in the direction of the Nuba mountains, his homeland. If the wind comes from the south, the Samun as they call it, the one with the touch of poison, then he and his companions tighten their mouth scarves and a look of great discomfort comes over them.

To the south we occasionally saw the white haze of the swamp area of Bahr El Arab on the horizon. Now, a fire has been raging there for the past few days and the air is thick with flying ashes and the smell of burning wood.

'The shepherds have set fire to the bulrushes in order to smoke out the breeding places of the birds', Alkuttabu explains. 'But every winter migratory birds bring the plague into the country and thousands of cattle die.'

The farther we get to the east, the more particular our hunters become with their quarry. First the animal is checked for any outer deformations, then it is torn apart and the inner organs are carefully examined for any inflammation or tumours. Sometimes a look at the mouth and eyes is enough and the slain animal is then covered with stones or burned. The hunters won't let any vultures nearer than 50 feet, for now we meet with dying and bedraggled birds at every step. At the moment, there is enough healthy quarry, but the area is becoming more and more unreal and hotter than ever before. The haze over Sudd, the giant swamp area, the Bahr El Jebel, the white Nile and its numerous tributaries that flow into the plains of Bahr El Ghazal—all this blurs the horizon. The rainy season is drawing near.

En Nahud lies behind us, a desolate place with an abandoned garrison. We bought dates for the camels and sugar and salt. Master Jack measured the salt with his ticker, which he calls a geiger counter, and said that it was radioactively contaminated and that we would have to throw it away. Our escorts would have loved to beat the merchant who sold us the contaminated salt. However, Master Jack made sure they understood that the man could not have known himself and that he had probably been sold salt from Ethiopia or Somalia.

Master Jack reads a lot in a little book that the king gave him as a present. Yesterday evening, I know he was crying, I saw him. It really touched me.

'Why are you crying?', I asked him.

He closed the book and said, 'I am not crying. The light is already too weak to read by and I have been reading too long. My eyes are watering. There's a good boy, bring me another cup of tea, Beschir.'

I brought him a cup of tea. There was enough light to thread a needle by.

## Extracts from the Journal of Master Jack

June 24th, 2036

*We are progressing faster than ever expected. If we are lucky, the rainy season will only catch up with us in Omdurman. It ought to take us 20 days to get there if everything continues as well as it has so far.*

*The journal of Henri Fleurel, the architect of the king, is a shocking document which moved me to tears. Naturally, we know what happened, but the extent of the horror can only be really understood if all the ghastly details of the desperate exodus that the survivors from Europe went through are known.*

*Henri Fleurel was an architect in Perpignan, France. His wife and three of his children were lost in the war. Those who survived, his eldest daughter and her husband and a few neighbours, convinced that they were not radioactively contaminated or infected by the biological warfare, risked the crossing to Africa in a boat. They were not only shot at from land, but Algerian torpedo boats were constantly on guard to drive the numerous refugee boats away from the coast. It was only in Tunisia, where the authorities were more tolerant, that they were allowed to land. When they realized the extent of the danger in Tunisia too, the massacre began. Europeans, who wanted to exchange the valuables that they had salvaged for food, were brutally murdered. Or they isolated refugees into camps, but by then it was too late. They had brought the biological plague to Oran. The devilish plague developed in the war research laboratories, seeped in from the battlefields of Europe, depopulated the whole of North Africa within four months and spread like a bushfire through countries not even directly concerned with the war.*

*Countries like Sudan, Chad, Niger and Mali imagined themselves to be relatively protected by the desert belt in the north, but it soon became clear that the Sahara was the lesser of two evils for those who had fled the hell of nuclear war. Enterprising caravan guides, promising themselves rich plunder, told stories of missionary settlements in Uganda, in the Upper Congo, and in Rhodesia, supposedly organizing migrations to a safer place. The old tale of Prester John's Kingdom in the heart of Africa had survived for centuries and it was to this tale that the pilgrims turned, willing to believe anything, putting all their hopes into this paradise—a paradise that was as unreal as a paradise on the moon. Even if the pilgrims survived thousands of miles of desert after untold hazards, they then faced firing squads in Niger, Chad, or Sudan. The troops massacred them in the desert, after having been informed in time by the caravan guides who naturally kept a quarter of the loot collected for this service—in order—so the story went—to protect their own people from sickness and death. The refugees were given an ultimatum to pull back to the north at once—an absolutely deadly venture. Then the guns did the talking. If there was not enough ammunition, the Kabartu, honorary executioners, were put to work to smash the heads of those due to die with one full swing of their iron-clad clubs. They often worked for hours until exhaustion set in. Untold horrors must have taken place in such 'mantraps'. Most horrible of all, according to Henri Fleurel, was the screaming of the young boys who were rounded up and castrated to be sold as eunuchs.*

*'I know', he writes, 'that in these countries it has been a custom for centuries, especially at the large slave markets, to order barbers to carry out a total amputation with their razor and pour hot butter in the horrible wound in order to stop the bleeding. I shall never forget the smell of hot butter and burning flesh. I shall never forget the screams of castrated boys. If they lived through the ordeal they were then sold for a good price to the palaces of those in power as male concubines or eunuchs. Naturally, they had an explanation for this horror too. The genes of the young boys were radioactively contaminated—one couldn't take the risk. I understood—genocide is the worst kind of murder.'*

*Henri Fleurel and half a dozen scholars, 'selected' with the aid of a questionnaire before the journey to the supposed missionary settlements, survived the massacre and were sold to the court of El Fasher.*

*The mummies of Bir Meschru keep haunting me, robbing me of my sleep. The gold fillings in their teeth had been stolen.*

Master Jack has hardly spoken at all for the past few days. He seems very depressed. Even Alkuttabu's jokes don't have any effect on him at all. The Samun, the breath of poison, blows hot and stifling. Instinctively, we try not to breathe more than is necessary. How lovely a cleansing storm would be, bringing the Charief, the rainy season.

We ride into El Obeid. There are even more soldiers here. Many of the old caravansaries and the pilgrims' quarters are empty. The town lies in ruins, but the garrison is new and being enlarged. The flags of the king fly over it: green and white. We are given quarters in the barracks.

The stern reputation of the king can be felt here, though nothing of the freedom that rules in his palace. The laws in El Obeid are merciless. If anyone with any signs of the plague arrives, his left ear is cut off as a warning to others and he is run out of town. Should he dare show himself a second time, he is caught, clubbed to death and his body burned before the city.

The mutants are luckier. They are led before a Tabib, an official doctor chosen and paid by the town, who examines them carefully and then makes his decision. Should a man turn out to be a mutant, he is not allowed to spread his contaminated sperm, which means— off to the barber and castration.

Our escorts spent the day in a public bath. Master Jack went with them. They came back to the barracks very late in the night and were all very drunk.

Master Jack wasn't able to stand up alone. Alkuttabu helped me carry him to bed. The others started a fight with some soldiers who had complained about the noise. Since then, Keiki, our officer, has been going around with a bandage over his nose and a swollen eye.

## Extracts from the Journal of Master Jack

June 30th, 2036

*Today, just this quick note:*

1) *I believe that civilization will continue to exist. There are still public baths with hot water and other comforts.*
2) *I got myself stoned last night. I really needed it to wash down Fleurel's taste of hot butter.*
3) *The prostitutes of El Obeid are so unbelievably ugly that it takes several cups of Laqbi to overcome my disgust, which however (see 2) I finally succeeded in doing. I made them show me their left ears first.*

We only stayed in El Obeid for four days. Now we are on our way to Omdurman. The paths have been softened by two intense downpours. Red spiders with velvet-like bodies, Kul Ningilibe, which are called Fanna Kimme in this region, swarm by the hundreds of thousands over the ground all along the way as they usually do at the beginning of the rainy season.

But the mosquitoes bother us more than the spiders. We bought fantastic white fly swatters made of long baboon neck hairs from a merchant and we seem to do nothing else the whole day but swat around us to get rid of the pests. Their stings can be very dangerous. Who knows whose blood they sucked before?

The river is near. We can tell by the smell of the air.

# 4
# The River

Two days before we reached Omdurman, we overtook a caravan which had left El Fasher at the beginning of April. Two or three dozen pilgrims made up the caravan and they received Master Jack with hate-filled remarks and a display of anger. There was even one of those young Muhadshirin, who believe they hold the wisdom of the world in those small dried out gourds in which they keep their thin ink. I didn't like the travelling schoolboy the moment I saw him. He didn't have anything better to do than seek out Master Jack's company and fawn upon him, full of his own importance. Master Jack, in his guilelessness—Allah hold his hand wide over him— answered each question frankly and openly. The know-it-all scratched everything down on his Loah, his wooden writing block, and assiduously covered it with writing that looked like fly specks. The traditional goat skin that he wore stank and he himself even more, as if he had not washed since El Fasher.

Master Jack seemed not to notice the smell of this sanctimonious billygoat. The supposed learning and thirst for knowledge of the stupid babbler seemed to please him. He told him all about his orbital startrekking, about the heavenly caravansaries and the earthly satellites and other flying ships to be found under the stars at night.

Inevitably, as soon as we arrived in Omdurman and had unsaddled our camels in Messhid, the stinking billygoat rushed to the administrator of the mosque, who was at the same time justice of the town, and denounced Master Jack for blasphemy. Two guardsmen of the town arrived, put him in shackles and led him off. Keiki, Alkuttabu, Schuschan and Alifa were nowhere to be found. They had gone to the town and nearby garrison to look for better accommodation for us rather than the stinking pilgrim quarters. But it is not easy. The city is overrun with pilgrims waiting to join a caravan to the east.

I was powerless. I bellowed as loud as I could and kicked one of the guards in his fat arse. This only brought me a painful blow in my ribs with his spear and a reprimand from Master Jack who put up no resistance at all and let himself be led off.

Half the afternoon went by before our four escorts arrived. I was furious and told then what had happened. At first they were stunned by the news, then they set off in anticipation of adventure. I remained with our packs because everywhere I looked there were vultures.

## Extracts from the Journal of Master Jack

July 16th, 2036

*Today, something very unpleasant happened. A young man, who accompanied us on the last two days of our journey, whose apparent thirst for knowledge and interest in scientific and technical things flattered me, whose questions about our work on Mount Darwin I gladly answered, reported me to the local authorities for heresy. I was shackled and brought before a sort of religious court that had been set up on the spur of the moment. I was accused of having maintained that Allah does not guide the stars through the heavens at night. I had maintained that a group of white unbelievers were guiding them from some station that they had set up somewhere in the south on a mountain. The justice asked me whether I really believed all this and whether I knew that such blasphemous talk was punished with instant death. I must admit that I have met up with many dangers, but this time I really feared for my life.*

*   *   *   *   *

*Luckily, at that moment, our four escorts appeared in court, boxed the guards' ears for them and freed me from my shackles. I begged then to restrain themselves knowing their temperament and fearing trouble with the local authorities.*

*'In whose name are you forcing entry to this court?', the justice demanded.*

*I caught my breath as Alkuttabu aimed his rifle at the justice and pulled the trigger. The bullet hit the wall, barely two inches above the distinguished turban, and plaster rained down on his desk. Crying for help the justice took shelter under the desk.*

*'Next time I'll aim lower!', Alkuttabu bellowed in a thundering voice. Then he continued in his curious tongue clicking dialect, 'I am here by order of the king. This white scholar is travelling under the mandate of the king as the scholars of the king guide the stars around the earth at night.' And as if this weren't enough, he added, 'All the stars!'*

*The justice crawled out from under his desk and thundered back in a voice just as loud, 'Then it should have been your duty and obligation to take better care of this man. You should have made your presence legally known to me before rushing off to the brothels!'*

*Alkuttabu stared at him speechlessly and nodded his head in acknowledgement. In the meantime, Keiki and Alifa had already caught the young scoundrel, who had tried to disappear unobtrusively. They fastened him to a rack outside, cleverly designed to force the victim into a humiliating posture, and, with remarkable mathematical precision for desert boys, gave him one hundred strokes of the whip on each of his unwashed feet.*

*I fear that I put an end to his thirst for learning for a while. It will certainly be two weeks before he can continue his educational journey—unless Allah provides him with a sedan carrier.*

We were given quarters in the garrison, ugly flat buildings around a dusty inner courtyard. The courtyard becomes a filthy mire with every downpour. At night black worms crawl up along the raw whitewashed walls fleeing the damp. They wither up in the sun during the day and fall down, becoming plunder for the chickens, who take this gift from the heavens for granted.

It is not at all easy to leave Omdurman. The power of the authorities and the power of the king represented by our escort Keiki apparently ends on the banks of the river. The muddy river is rising.

This is the domain of Ngar Ba, the overseer of the river, as he is called by the captain of the harbour and the domain of the Tuweirat, the cavalry of the king which escorts the pilgrims' caravans to Port Sudan and back. The cavalrymen of the king are all, without exception, rascals and cut-throats who shamelessly enrich themselves on the pilgrims. Perhaps there is something in the name after all. Master Jack said it wouldn't surprise him if Kostas Ben Muchtar of El Fasher didn't have a hand in this lucrative business as it would be no problem for his garrison to do away with the riff-raff.

These so-called cavalrymen are thus allowed to ask a fortune for their service of 'Protection from highwaymen, monsters and mutants'; and to top it all off are not above demanding a present if they see something that takes their fancy. However, it is true that they are riding to the coast through a country in which all living things are contaminated, even the grasshoppers, and where all water is polluted and undrinkable. Whoever takes it upon himself to go beyond the edge of the inhabitable world, must take everything he needs until his return ... food, salt, sugar, water and more water.

We have to do the same.

We will make the journey to Atbara in a sailing vessel that will not be let down into the contaminated water until necessary. This time is to be decided by the overseer of the harbour, Ngar Ba, together with the Tuweirat, the cavalrymen of the king, who observe the river incessantly and estimate its danger. Funnily enough, the favourable time of minimum contamination always corresponds with the time when the maximum number of pilgrims have gathered, so that the vessel built for at the most one hundred people and two hundred animals, can then be loaded with two hundred pilgrims and three hundred and fifty animals.

Our request to make use of the services of the cavalrymen of the king only as far as Atbara was received with a benevolent shrug of the shoulders. This would be condescendingly permitted if the entire amount for the 'protection from highwaymen, monsters and mutants' was paid up to Port Sudan.

Our Keiki emphasized the word of the king with blows of his fist on the table of the harbour master and Alkuttabu menaced with an even faster clicking of his teeth—all to no avail. We had to pay. All our animals had been sold—for next to nothing, of course. Water costs ten times the normal price here, because it has to be brought from wells fifteen and twenty miles away. For who would want to drink the water of the White or Blue Nile?

When we calculated what we had left, both Master Jack and I had long faces. There was just enough to invite our four friends and escorts to a meal. It was an unforgettable evening. I swear I would have started clicking my tongue myself if I had been with Alkuttabu any longer.

The next morning they rode away. We boarded the sailing vessel. There was a pitiful boat made of mimosa wood attached to the stern with which we were going to attempt to ride the cataracts. We had had a new thatched roof put on it and our packs and provisions of water and food had been put on board. It cost the equivalent of eight goats to have it float harmlessly behind the sailing vessel—an amount that an experienced caravan leader in Kotoko would hardly make in a month.

The master of the harbour was called Abu Medf'a, Father of the Cannons, because he had had the two tanks that had once rusted in front of the president's palace in Khartoum brought over the river and set them up in front of his official residence on the harbour, where they continued to rust. He appeared in a gala uniform when our vessel set sail. A band played the national anthem of Sudan and the green and white flag of the king was hoisted. It can't be said that we didn't get our money's worth of show as we left the edge of the world and set out into the unknown, into the swollen waters of the White and Blue Nile, the first now grey-green and the second yellow.

## Extracts from the Journal of Master Jack

August 14th, 2036

*They are making a great fuss here about the contamination of the river. I have measured its radioactivity. Even now with the water-level at its highest and with the rainfalls washing most of the radioactive sand of Ethiopia, Kenya and Uganda into the rivers, the radioactivity is relatively harmless and can be tolerated without danger for weeks. On the contrary, the fuss is more of a lucrative business managed by the Father of the Cannons in cooperation with the Cavalrymen of the King and certainly with the King's permission and financial participation in the affair.*

*I told the master of the harbour that I had no intention of paying the enormous sum for the 'protection from highwaymen, monsters and mutants' and that I was capable of defending myself. I told him that we would take our little Kheasaht bark and set off on our own. This was a punishable offence and he threatened to seize our boat and our provisions if I dared try. These cutthroats know how to protect their monopoly and always talk about the dangers on the other side of the edge of the world, which, of course, only they are capable of controlling. They do go on here about the danger of the water. If it were not so filthy with mud and slime, I would drink from it just to prove them wrong.*

\*    \*    \*    \*    \*

*One of the Tuweirat, his name is Hassan, told me that there are people living further down the river. Of course, most of them are ill, but who is healthy on the edge of the inhabitable world? Most of them are said to be light-skinned. They must be approached with caution as they are extremely resourceful in their invention of deadly weapons.*

*He also told us about strange lights appearing in the north, shooting up into the sky and falling back to earth like giant meteors. This certainly proves that there are space activities nearby which we have also noticed. Am I getting closer to my destination? Are there really extraterrestrial beings? For which country in the Near East would have the know-how and technical possibilities after the war which it had not had at its disposal before the war? But in the form of Horus? In the form of scarabs? The forms of Egyptian mythology? An unlikely coincidence.*

*The Tuweirat said that he hadn't actually seen any scarabs or bird-headed creatures himself, but that he was sure they existed. They had risen from Osiris Land, the Kingdom of the Dead, filled with indignation that the realm of the Egyptians had been wiped out and that six thousand years of culture had been swept into the ocean.*

*There are no historians left to ponder over the whys and wherefores of the deadly blast. When it happened, the war was in full progress. During the Iranian Civil War, sparked off by Khomeini's death, the Soviet Union openly assisted the Mujahedin with weapons and supplies. Operating from a base in Yemen, the Soviet Union also caused the overthrow of the Saudi Arabian monarchy who were financing Bani-Sadr's mercenaries and ordered troop movements right up to the Iranian border.*

*The spark that set off the explosion did not go off in the Gulf, but in the Mediterranean. Just who it was who made a nuclear hell of the 'Nimitz' will probably never be clear. It could well, however, have been land-based atomic rockets fired by Qadhafi—for favourable oil delivery contracts, anything could be had in the 80s; after repeated humiliations in the Gulf of Sirta by the 6th US fleet, Qadhafi had threatened several times 'to give a slap in the mouth to the Jews in Wall Street and their third-class extra from Hollywood!' Whatever happened, there were units of the Soviet fleet nearby—and the direct confrontation then took place. While the flames of war overran the Mid-East and the Gulf Region within hours and Europe within days and finally, the whole world, Qadhafi put his mad idea into effect of 'drowning the capitalist jesters of the Nile', who kept threatening his border, and were only waiting for an excuse to take part in the invasion of the Libyan oil fields and make sure of a share for themselves. A few military planes actually succeeded in blasting the supposedly bomb-proof Aswan Dam—the rest, the dammed up waters took care of. 160 billion cubic metres—more than the Nile had carried in two years—thundered down the river valley. I have seen satellite pictures of this deadly wall of water, which fell as if in slow motion, wiped out Edfu, Luxor, Assiut, and finally Cairo before it poured over Alexandria and Port Said all the way to the ocean. The pressure of the waves, created by the masses of water, broke trees as if they were match sticks and whirled houses in its path as if they were leaves.*

*And then the silt came. Billions of tons of mud from the Nile, which had built up for two decades behind the 3600 metre long dam, was borne along with the outflowing water and covered the 40 million inhabitants of the valley like a brown shroud. It filled the Valley of the Kings, buried Cairo under a ten metre layer of brown loess deposit and covered the foundations of the pyramids.*

*Even the following year, the Eastern Mediterranean up to Crete and Rhodes was discoloured and the high water, at some points over the five metre mark, had changed the outline of the coast extensively. This delta stretched far to the north like the tongue of an animal who had died an anguished death.*

The Tuweirats and pilgrims have left us. They are taking the old route to Port Sudan. According to Master Jack, a thing on wheels had once rolled along it and, as unbelievable as it sounds, was able to travel the stretch of land to the ocean in one day.

The great sailing vessel had been made fast to a mooring. It is waiting for better wind. We, however, are moving ahead all the faster in the opposite direction because our wind is blowing from the south. Atbara is only a fort without inhabitants or garrison, because there is no water here except that of the Nile.

In the evening, we moor our boat at an island and sleep on the boat. Tomorrow, we shall attempt the fifth rapids. Apparently, we mastered the sixth with the great sailing vessel. I wasn't even aware of it. More than likely I slept through it.

'You are now leaving the country of the living', the captain had said ominously. 'It is of your own free will that you are withdrawing from Allah's hand and are now entering the ancient Land of Osiris, the Kingdom of the Dead, from where there is no return.'

That night, I closed the shutters of my life and could hardly sleep. I looked over the water moving and groaning along the shore as though it were really hurrying to the edge of the world to overflow into nothingness.

Suddenly, over the mountains to the north, I saw a flash of light rising into the moonlit sky, a small red gold tongue of fire which ripped a silver scar in the sky, a scar that soon disappeared, while the flash climbed higher, turning to the east and getting smaller and smaller on the eastern horizon.

I woke Master Jack and he followed the flash with his binoculars without saying a word. 'Definitely a rocket being shot into orbit. Beschir, we have almost reached our destination.'

All I could think of were the words of the captain and the edge of the world that the water of the river hurried to reach. I was frightened.

'Hey, Beschir!', Master Jack said the next day while he hoisted the sail on the mast and steered the boat into the middle of the river. 'Why are you looking so grim? Real adventure is just beginning! Let's move forward into the unknown!'

The unknown was rocky shores that became higher and higher and closer together and water that moved so fast tearing our Kheasaht with it and making us dizzy. Then, suddenly the shores drew away, opening to let the river flow lackadaisically ahead.

In the evening we moored at an island called Mograhd. From there we could see the ruins of Abu Hammed further downstream on the right. During the night we saw a fire on the left shore and heard human voices above the murmuring water.

I wondered how human beings could live beyond the edge of the world. Or are they dead out of the Land of Osiris? Questions one shouldn't ask at night. They weigh heavy on one like cold stones and sail away with the morning wind as if the sun had washed out their heaviness with its light.

However, the inhabitants of the river were very much alive, as we could see the next day. In a bend in the river, when we got too close to the shore, we were shot at with arrows that splashed harmlessly in the water.

Master Jack got out his crossbow and held his quiver at the ready. But from noon on, we couldn't spare a glance at the shore; we had our hands full trying to cope with the fourth cataract as we were pulled deeper and deeper into its witches' cauldron, the Battn el Hadjar, the belly of stone. The river was now completely surrounded by black rocks. The water foamed with such a thundering noise against them that we could only make ourselves understood by shouting loudly and at times the broad river divided itself into several branches so fast that Master Jack had no time to decide into which he should guide us. Our boat shot blindly forward chafing along the banks. It was pressed, cracking and moaning, against stones as large as houses, came to a stop and then was suddenly yanked further. I crouched, drenched through, in the middle of the boat and bailed out water like a madman while Master Jack stood at the helm keeping an eye on the fairway before the bow. I didn't know whether I was trembling more from cold or fear. However, Master Jack seemed to be enjoying the hellish ride. I had never seen him so happy.

And thus we sailed on into the evening. The sun had long set when we came to quieter waters and looked for a place to moor.

We threw caution to the winds and lit a fire from the driftwood, dried our clothes and cooked ourselves a hearty meal of white beans and fried meat. The sun sank like a bloated rotten gourd. The sky remained bright hours after the sun had gone down, as if the western horizon were in flames making the river molten copper.

'The weather is changing', Master Jack said. He was right.

The next morning a cold wet wind from the southwest blew in our faces and we couldn't set sail. We let ourselves drift along, past deserted villages and towns. Sometimes, we even saw people, a hand was raised, a spear, and once we saw a boat lying on the shore, but no boats were ever let into the river. No one disturbed us.

Three days later, we took the next cataract. Far less hellish and dark than the fourth. The river is permeated with huge boulders. The torrent foams over these pounding up and down just as it would at the stern of a large ship. On some of the rocks there are the ruins of fortresses and castles. Everything seems so dead. I wonder if Hazaz is alive?

## Extracts from the Journal of Master Jack

August 27th, 2036

*We have reached the basin that once was Lake Nasser, as one can see from the deposits on the shore. Palm trees and bushes line the shore. Sometimes human beings. I can detect many white men among them through my binoculars. Most are naked.*

*I am afraid to guide the boat to shore and meet them as, up until now, they have almost always reacted in a hostile manner, which is understandable. The struggle for survival must have been terrible, possibly including cannibalism. We shall keep to the middle of the river.*

*Sometimes, boats are to be seen, but we have not yet discovered any in the water. They are probably afraid of the contaminated river. However, the radioactivity is minimal. Perhaps biological or chemical substances. We haven't seen any fish yet. No crocodiles either.*

\*    \*    \*    \*    \*

*We are approaching Wadi Halfa*

The chute of the second cataract was the worst. The river tore along roaring and foaming between vertical walls left and right and we shot over it like an arrow. Hour after hour, I did nothing else but bail out water. Our boat, which groaned in all its ribs and joints, cracked and is leaking more and more. However, I am no longer afraid. Master Jack is a fantastic boatman. 'I have sailed down the Lualaba and the Congo', he said. 'There isn't a river that I can't master!'

We sailed for days between dried-out clay walls, the muddy deposits of the dam through which the river had dug a new bed. All the colours were in horizontal strips, red, ochre, brown and black. Master Jack explained that the different coloured strata indicate the years. The view is beautiful. It would be even more beautiful if there was not this terrible heat. There wasn't the faintest breath of air and we felt like chickens in an oven. I had to control myself not to jump overboard and take a refreshing bath. Master Jack warned me that it could have grave consequences. He was right. My hands and arms that had touched the river water while I was bailing out the boat had begun to itch.

Towards midday, we saw the rusty remains of a broad box-like iron ship hanging out of the clay bank into which it had been baked, the bows sticking up, the crushed superstructure turned downwards. Again and again, we came upon the bones of animals and human beings in the sand and in the shallow water near the shore. Once we found a crocodile on a high sandbank. It was dead as a doornail and dehydrated like a dried fish.

## Extracts from the Journal of Master Jack

September 1, 2036

*We are approaching Aswan. It is an unforgettable spectacle. The dam is one of the most impressive ruins of the world. It is as if one were gliding in the hold of a giant super-tanker towards the bombed out bow, ten kilometres long and three and a half wide, jutting up to the left and right about one hundred metres. The river, although it is swollen from the high waters and is held back by what is left of the dam, seems like a small channel between the mighty flanks. There, where the water has broken through and has cut itself a channel, rusty reinforcements jut out of the wound up to the crown of the dam, where trees, the remains of boats, and numerous dead bodies had been caught, mummified by the sun. We let ourselves drift cautiously through this gruesome canyon. The water flows in a low cataract over the remains of the dam wall and accumulated debris behind it into a shallow lake strewn with blocks of concrete and broken pieces of machinery, the edges and corners of which are worn smooth and round.*

*Aswan no longer exists.*

We spent the night just below the dam on a small island. In the morning, I brought Master Jack to shore. He climbed over the ruins of the dam the whole day, while I sailed the boat back to the island and roamed around it. It was sunset before he came back.

We stayed a second and a third day. Master Jack drew a lot of pictures in which every detail of the ruins of the dam could be seen.

The next day we hit upon a strange obstacle. It was a sort of curtain made of a white spun yarn hanging across the river from shore to shore. White root-like things held it to the shore. It spread over the surface and its web-like yarn seemed to hang deeply in the water. The most peculiar thing about it was that this structure moved as if it were alive. It pulsated, pulling itself together and then slackening again. We approached it slowly. It was a tenacious spongy web-like fabric over which the keel of the boat glided without any effort at all.

'Unbelievable', Master Jack said, feeling it and poking around with his ticker. 'I am sure that this web is alive and that it is capable of cleaning the water. Once over the obstacle, radioactivity is almost non-existent here. And the water seems to be substantially cleaner.'

We passed over four such web-like obstacles in the course of the day. The improved quality of the water changed the appearance of the shore. Dry clay desert became luscious grass, shrub and palm trees. Goats could be seen, and thatched huts, and people appearing suddenly between the huts. We proceeded with caution to one of the islands, moored our boat and looked for a place to camp. On the other side, on the left shore, we saw goats in the river drinking the water. A naked man was standing near them, leaning on his spear. Master Jack called out to him. He didn't answer and disappeared with his goats into the bushes.

For the first time we actually dared to take a bath in the river. It was heaven. Master Jack scooped up a pot full of water and boiled it for a long time. Then he drank a drop. I held my breath as I watched him and prayed to Allah not to let him drop dead before my eyes. My prayer was heard. However, I decided not to let Master Jack out of my sight for the next few hours.

Night had not yet fallen when we heard shouting from the watering place. We were afraid of being attacked and, in the encroaching dusk, stared across to where the screams had come from. Master Jack looked through his glass.

'It really is true', he whispered. 'It is true.'

'What, Master Jack?'

He gave me the glass and I looked through. With the artificial eyes the shore seemed much brighter.

I saw a confusion of bodies that encircled two creatures. They were hitting them with clubs, although the beings did not put up any resistance. The two figures looked like huge insects walking upright with dark brown shells and long feelers which grew over their faceted eyes like rams' horns and hung down over their shoulders and behind their backs, while their front limbs ended in scissor-like tools. It was amazing that these creatures, obviously so capable of defending themselves, hadn't made the least effort at resistance although they were being attacked with knives and spears. Finally, they were torn down and disappeared under a heap of naked human bodies. We could hear screams of triumph.

'What's that?', I asked breathlessly.

'Perhaps they are the ones I'm looking for', Master Jack answered. 'I undertook this long journey because of them.'

'Then, we have arrived too late, Master Jack', I said. 'They are dead!'

He lifted his glass to his eyes. 'My God', he whispered. 'Why are they doing that?'

At that very moment a flash of lightning bathed the river and shore in a white glaring light. Blinded, we clutched one another while thunder erupted around us. I had never experienced anything like it before. When it died down, we could hear the cries of pain from the drinking place, but neither Master Jack nor I considered it the right thing to do to hurry to the aid of these savages in the darkness. The crying and moaning could be heard all night long from the other shore. We kept waking up again and again and the light continued to reflect in our eyes.

# 5
# The Web

We ventured across at the first sight of daylight. Master Jack held his ticker carefully over the bow, but it didn't react. We couldn't find any signs of a fight. The first thing we noticed when we found the insect beings was that they in no way looked like scarabs or cockroaches. They were two-legged beings whose legs and bodies were covered with shiny dark brown exoskeletons. Their legs ended, like their upper limbs, in small, ribbed, three-membered pincers, which were obviously just as good for walking as for seizing or handling things. The strong armour of the backs and chests had been slashed through and hacked to pieces. There was very little left of the high domed heads and the large dark eyes except a grey and whitish mass of tissue. It was evident that the brains had filled most of the heads. They had been torn out and destroyed, probably so they could be eaten.

Nearby were eleven people, nine of whom were light-skinned. They were a pitiable sight. Most of them were still suffering from shock. They lay paralysed where the fire had thrown them down. A few had succeeded in pulling themselves up enough to crawl to the shore and scoop up water in the hollows of their hands to cool their blinded eyes.

We moored the boat and went to help the wounded. Master Jack bent over a slight fair-haired middle-aged woman who was cowering naked on the shore. Her once voluptuous breasts sagged like empty calabashes over the water.

'Can I help you?', Master Jack asked.

'Hey!', the woman cried and slanted her head to be able to hear while her blinded eyes sought Master Jack. 'Did I hear you right, young man? Did you ask me if you could help me?' She laughed a stifled laugh. 'Are you from the International Red Cross or from UNESCO or from one of those legendary relief organizations that we never heard of again?'

'Unfortunately not', Master Jack said. 'They no longer exist.'

'I thought so', the woman groaned with an ugly grin. 'I can't see any more because that thing spat its fire on us. Are you black or white?'

'What is that thing that spits fire on you?'

'That thing, it's that *thing*, you idiot. It's established its headquarters up there in the north and has covered everything with its web and lets its cockroaches swarm over the earth as though it had lost something.

'Listen!' She grabbed Master Jack's legs with vehemence. Master Jack put up no resistance at all, while I stared at the sagging breasts with a mixture of fascination and disgust. 'I don't know who you are, but if you have any power at all—please kill it! That thing is responsible for bringing the holocaust to our planet to conquer it. It has destroyed mankind as if they were vermin.'

'We destroyed ourselves, I understand.'

'Nonsense! Never! They ordered the whole thing to happen. We are vermin to them. It doesn't respect mankind any more than it respects vermin. No more than you respect a worm or a sparrow that picks crumbs from the dirt at your feet. It respects you even less. It respects you like the dirt under your feet.'

'You can't complain. The water is being decontaminated as far as I can see...'

'Not for us! For its brood of insects that swarm out of the earth. And it has just as little respect for them. It doesn't send them after us. It's only interested in the brains that it rummages around for in the earth.

It is only interested in seizing the soul of the earth and loading its ship with it.'

'Whose brains? Whose soul?'

'The brains of the people. The soul of the dead earth.'

'Who says so?'

'Those who have talked to it. But don't believe', she mocked, 'that you will get an answer from it so easily. Go up the shore! One of its ships is stranded there. Ask it! You'll get no answer. It will send its fire if you touch its biomass by mistake.'

'Biomass?'

I was inspecting one of the strange containers that the insect beings had carried with them. When I laid my hand on the spongy, water-filled tissue, it twitched convulsively. Suddenly, out of the corner of my eyes, I saw how one of the men crept up on Master Jack from behind with a knife in his hand, while the woman still held on to his legs tightly. It dawned on me that it was a deadly trap. I grabbed one of the spears lying on the ground and hit the idiot over the head with the shaft as hard as I could. He sank down without saying a word. The woman began to shriek, pulled Master Jack down and threw herself over him. I hit her over the head so that Master Jack could tear himself away and she screamed and kicked blindly around her while her breasts bobbed up and down. The pitiable figures, insofar as they could rouse themselves, crawled threateningly towards us. I jumped into the boat and began to row wildly, Master Jack waded up to his hips in the water before he could pull himself into the boat. He gasped for air.

'It's a man's duty to help his brother!', a tearful voice cried after us from the shore. It was a young man, but with his bald head and his mottled skin he looked like an old man. 'Whoever does not help his brother is on the side of that thing!'

'My goodwill to mankind is not that great. I am not willing to let myself be plundered and possibly eaten by you!', Master Jack shouted across to him.

'Be damned!', the young man called and the woman laughed her shrill laugh. I rowed as fast as I could.

Half a mile downstream Master Jack manoeuvred back to shore.

'I want to find out what this ship is doing here.'

We dragged our Kheasaht up on land and hid it in the bushes. After we had covered our traces as best we could we set off up on the slope overlooking the river. An hour later we reached the edge of the desert plateau and saw the strange ship no more than 500 feet in front of us.

It looked surprisingly fragile and was not half as impressive as I had imagined after all the tales we had heard about it. It measured perhaps 15 or 20 feet from bow to stern and was rather flat and raft-like without any high superstructure except for the small dome right around the stern.

'Almost like the cuttlebone of a cuttlefish', said Master Jack, who had stopped dead in his tracks beside me. A canopy had been set up over the stern and it fluttered in the wind. It was an unusually intense light colour of blue that had something unreal about it in the grey-brown surroundings.

Looking at the structure, I felt that I was confronted with a pitiable creature which had somehow foundered and was in difficulties. Twenty-five or 30 insect beings were crawling around the ship evidently trying to get the thing in the air again, as the keel of the ship was grounded. A bird-headed creature stood in front of the ship, absolutely motionless, its arms crossed over its chest, staring at us silently.

I looked at Master Jack. He stuck his chin out with a determined look, placed the crossbow he had automatically reached for back over his shoulder and marched ahead. I followed him. My steps weren't long enough to keep pace with his. With every step we took—and this we didn't know at the time—we left reality, as we knew it, behind us forever.

## Extracts from the Journal of Master Jack

September 5th, 2036

*It's really true after all—the proof—extraterrestrial beings right in front of us! Although, for the past two years, I had always thought it possible and for the past few weeks was absolutely convinced that an immediate confrontation would take place, it now seems unreal and absurd.*

*The situation is more than banal in a distorted sort of way. Shall I pose as representative of what remains of civilization and bid them welcome with a speech full of empty words like the mayor of a city receiving the local magistrate of a foreign town, to seal twin-city friendships? I see myself rather in the role of father of a family whose visitors have arrived unexpectedly and who suddenly remembers that a fire has been raging in the living room.*

*Excuse us, please, but an accident has just happened in our historical development. We were faster in finding a solution to our arms problems than in finding a solution to certain racial and ideological problems. Some maintain that a death wish also played a role, a certain pleasure in the destruction of the world. I think they exaggerate. The truth is that the half-hearted as well as under-financed peace research proved useless when the run on the last resources of the world began. Then some of the veneer of civilization chipped off. Just look around you—you can see for yourselves. Fifty years ago, we were three or four billion more inhabitants. But let's not get petty about it. The truth is we can't estimate just how many are left that easily. One thing is certain—enormous areas of this once so beautiful planet will be uninhabitable for generations to come, some areas forever. We now have several million mutants with whom we shall have the greatest difficulties coming to terms, because our already contaminated gene pool will be messed up even more. Seeds of future discontent have already been sown. But let's not look at the whole of history in a negative manner. Let's try to be constructive. Let's say it had a regulative, if not cathartic function. We have bombed ourselves back to a level of civilization when we are—I hope—or are you of another option—more able to cope at our present stage of evolution. Don't judge us too hard; do be fair. We are on the point of rolling up our sleeves and cleaning up the mess. Let me bid you welcome. Do make yourselves at home ... oh, pardon, I really didn't mean to offend you. It just slipped out. The Horus stood directly in front of me, a fascinating creature. Exactly as I had seen him in so many Egyptian drawings. The overly slender human figure with dark skin, the long delicate arms and legs, the beautiful sexless body, so perfect that it had something artificial about it, something artistic, the head with its superb blue green metallic plumage falling to its shoulders. However, most impressive of all were his eyes, hard, impenetrable black with an expressionlessness as unfathomable as polished obsidian. In spite of this, its eyes showed a certain intelligence, the uncompromising, cruel intelligence of a spy who was not impressed by appearances, eyes that in their robot-like, target-seeking field of vision absorbed every photon, but never gave any information about the receiver of all this data.*

*Between the curved, black, half-questioning open beak was the blue-black swollen curve of its tongue.*

*Horus, the falcon-headed one. Were the story tellers of Omdurman right? Have the gods of the ancient Egyptians risen from the Kingdom of the Dead, that realm to which they guided the souls and bodies of the pharaohs? Have they returned from the land of Osiris?*

THOSE WERE THE BIOPRINTS OF ANOTHER VOYAGER. *I looked around and saw no one. Beschir looked at me terrified.* BUT HE ALSO CARRIED WITH HIM THE ONE YOU CALL HORUS.

*'What's the matter, Master Jack?'*
*'Didn't you hear the voice?'*
*'No, I didn't hear anything at all.'*

I ALWAYS FORGET THAT FOR YOU HUMAN BEINGS WITH EYES THERE MUST ALWAYS BE SOMETHING VISIBLE IN FRONT OF YOU OR ELSE YOU ARE IRRITATED. SIT DOWN, I'LL ARRANGE SOMETHING VISIBLE. THAT DEFECT SHALL BE FIXED IMMEDIATELY FOR I WELCOME YOU ABOARD.

*With a penetratingly shrill clatter as if glass pearls were bouncing against one another at an amazing speed, the bow raised itself from the ground and sprang to and fro while the stern remained in the sand. Then the clatter died down and the bow fell back into the sand. In another attempt, this time with double the effort, the ship finally succeeded in getting into the air and hovered noiselessly about three metres over the earth.*

*The Horus raised its head as if listening to a voice that could not be heard by humans. Then he gestured to us that we should board the ship.*

*A sling was let down and I grabbed hold of it. It cramped itself together like a muscle and pulled me on board. Beschir and the Horus followed. The bottom of the ship seemed to be made of a spongy substance, the whole length of which was about twelve and the width four metres. Two to three dozen tentacles hung from it, some of them reaching the ground, while the upper part was tough and hard like a tortoise shell. However, it changed the moment we were let down and became elastic. Smoke began to rise between Beschir and myself, then a silky red feathery star blossomed forth from the smoke changing its form constantly until it took on the form of a sea creature. It swayed and waved in an invisible current.*

THAT IS THE TENTACLE CROWN OF ONE OF THE TUBE-DWELLING WORMS OF THE REGION, *the creature said.* IN FACT IT IS VERY LIKE THE SHAPE I HAD FOR ONE GENERATION OF MY LIFE—A SHAPE WHICH I TREASURE VERY MUCH. I AM KA TEN, A VOYAGER AND I HEARD YOUR SARCASTIC 'FATHER OF THE FAMILY GREETING.' I LIKED IT BECAUSE IT WAS VERY TRUE TO FACT. I HAVE NEVER MET NATIVES HERE WITH WHOM I COULD CONVERSE. COME WITH ME TO THE NORTH AND BE MY GUEST. I HAVE READ YOUR MIND AND PRESUME THAT THIS WAS YOUR DESTINATION ANYWAY.

*'Yes, you are right. We have been observing space activities in this region since the spring of 2034, but none of our signals were answered. Why...?'* I RECEIVED THEM. IS THERE ANY REASON WHY I SHOULD HAVE ANSWERED? *It was the mouth of the tentacle crown that asked.*

*I knew no answer.*

*The insect beings went to pick up our packs and bring them on board.*

\* \* \* \* \*

Since we have been on board the flying ship, a feeling of unreality grows in me and the fear that I shall lose myself to this unreality. There are the insect beings, who take no notice of us, crouching in the slipstream with their feelers lying flat on their backs. There is the bird-headed creature, its arms crossed over its smooth blue-black breast, standing at the bow and keeping watch. But above all there is the mouth of the wavering blossom of the sea speaking to us.

All this is frightening.

I looked up at Master Jack. His face was strange and was flooded with the blue light of the awning.

'You think you are dreaming', he said.

I nodded. We were surrounded by the desert, but nearby, not even a thousand feet, water began in which far off mountains hovered. The Lake of the Devil. Naturally, I knew what it was. I knew that it was a mirage and yet I was panic-stricken. The ghostly ship hovered, groaning in the wind, over the centre of a grey island of light that had broken away from the land rising in the bottomless sky, a sky that had frozen into an expectant stillness. Then the island of light became smaller until in the end it dissolved into the air.

'Master Jack', I gasped and covered my eyes. 'Please help me!'

The vision wouldn't move away. The succulent flower swayed and waved. The bird-headed creature turned towards me. I saw his toes for the first time. Instead of toenails, there were bent blades like polished blue steel.

I fell down on to the shuddering tortoise shell of the ship which changed its form instantly under my very back, felt the pulse of the ship and stared up into the bright, fluttering sky of the canopy while I lost consciousness and the shrinking island of myself was flooded over completely by an oppressive darkness.

**Extracts from the Journal of Master Jack**

September 12th, 2036

*Although the race of the voyagers comprises only a few thousand individuals, they have managed to infiltrate on a massive scale. They do not have any particular form, but go through different generation-changes, taking on physical forms in the water, on the land, and in the air. Forms that they can consciously manipulate after they reach a certain age, so that they can take on any form necessary at any particular moment. By means of a highly developed cloning technique and gene manipulation they are almost immortal, and because of their supernatural mental powers are in a position to live in more than one body. Shortly after their appearance in the evolution of their planet, they caught on very quickly to the fact that they could use every living thing in their world as a biomass and remodel it for their own purposes. Everything from daily commodities to cars consists of genetically modified beings, whose form and function has been adapted to each individual need … their bioprints.*

*This highly developed art of gene manipulation made them ideally suited for space technology. The only part of the brain that travels is the part that contains the ego, with its storage zones of all the experiences the individual has lived through, all the experiences that make up the ego. All the rest on board is biomass—gene material necessary for building individual bodies and billions of identical clones that are used as helpers.*

*Just like the heraldic animals on coats-of-arms, each voyager carries his special bioprints around with him and surrounds himself with them. They are often fantastic constructions, biological works of art, whole biosets that in their composition are exactly tuned to one another, complement one another and form minibiospheres with their own chain of nourishment.*

So this is the palace of the traveller of the stars, the voyager as he calls himself. I am looking along the white wall that stretches far into the night, into the maze of corridors of foam and webbed tissue which reaches far into the earth and in which hundreds of thousands of his insect servants are swarming in order to search for whatever is to be found in the buried city. They are called biotans, according to Master Jack—artificially bred animals and demibeings.

One of these mute beautiful beings in his brown armour is standing expressionless in front of my chamber and is looking at me with his soft, yet vulnerable eyes. He seems to be able to read my mind and hurries away to fulfil every wish immediately. Perhaps he really does read my mind, just as the traveller of the stars reads Master Jack's, and sends the answers to his questions to his brain.

It is pleasantly cool here in the web-like interior and, whether it is day or night, the walls of the corridors and chambers glow with light as if they were transparent and the bright sky were filtering through them.

## Extracts from the Journal of Master Jack
September 19th, 2036

*Six thousand years ago another voyager was stranded here. The reason is unknown. He had programmed the ship that waited in orbit to make its way home automatically if he did not return after a certain period of time. The ship went back without him. Ka Ten then set off to try and salvage his experiences, for he had roamed through unexplored regions of the galaxy for more than thirty thousand years. His brain must hold incalculable treasures of knowledge.*

*The most efficient natural knowledge carrier is the gene. Nature did not have enough time to develop methods of microminiaturization for memory and consciousness. For this purpose, all higher forms of life require the electrochemical storage capacity of what are still relatively large areas of the brain.*

*Our voyager is looking for this brain.*

WHEN EF RE REALIZED THAT HE HAD FOUNDERED, HE WAS CONFRONTED WITH THE PROBLEM OF SAVING HIS EGO. HE HAD TO MAKE SURE THAT HIS BRAIN WOULD SURVIVE UNTIL ANOTHER VOYAGER COULD FIND IT AND COULD REVIVE HIS EGO BY TRANSFERRING IT TO A CLONE. IT SURELY CAN ONLY BE FOUND UNDER ONE OF THOSE GIANT STONE TIME MACHINES THAT HE HAD HAD BUILT. ONLY THERE WOULD IT HAVE HAD A CHANCE OF SURVIVING THOUSANDS OF YEARS WITHOUT BEING DESTROYED BY ALL THE WARS AND NATURAL CATASTROPHES.

*'But why should he have had so many built?'*

FROM OUTER SPACE, ONE OF THEM CANNOT BE DETERMINED IMMEDIATELY AS AN ARTEFACT. TWO COULD BE A QUIRK OF NATURE. THREE—ALL IN A GEOMETRICAL ROW—NEVER. EACH VOYAGER WILL BE ABLE TO INTERPRET THE SIGN IN A MATTER OF MINUTES.

*'But dozens of pyramids were built in this country. Most of them truncated and not too beautiful to look at...'*

*That answers your question. There must have been imitators among the natives that he created. Perhaps he created a native clone and it produced human offspring. It is possible that he taught them how to preserve their gene material and their egos in order to salvage them at some time in the future in case they themselves foundered. He could have taught them how to preserve their gene material in the cells by mummification to prevent it from decaying. He also must have taught them that the brain, once taken out of the skull, must be preserved very carefully. But after his accident, the knowledge was perverted or couldn't be understood any more. The bird-headed creatures, who were originally given the tasks of preserving the brains, died out and only symbolically guarded the urns in which the brains and inner organs of the dead rotted and they chiselled the 'names of the stars' of the dead into the sarcophagus, the 'names of the eternal beings' who had long since become transient.*

I roamed through the labyrinth of the traveller of the stars. The light in the interior of the web was always mellow. The walls gave off light whether it was dark outside or whether the day burned with desert sun. A fresh breeze flowed through the rooms and corridors, halls and chambers. Everything seemed very much unfinished, set up provisionally to be finished if necessary later.

There was a continual coming and going in all the corridors. The insect beings swarmed up and down with silent industriousness. They received the commands of the bird-headed ones via their feelers and worked with an accuracy and quickness that frightened me. They transported things they had found under the buried city. They were measured and catalogued. Works of art, technical equipment, anything and everything which seemed worth knowing and keeping for posterity.

I was in the control centre of the palace where the bird-headed creatures sat with their special bioprints and all kinds of equipment, from where a continual data stream flowed to the space ship stationed just above us in the sky. There was a droning as in a beehive. It filled the rooms. Light zones flared up and went out again, clusters of storage crystals changed colour when their inner structure changed, when knowledge was poured into them or taken out of them in order to make room for more knowledge.

I also discovered a room full of timepieces that the insects had dug out of the city. It was a rare collection which by far surpassed that of the king's palace in El Fasher. If you want to judge just how far a technical civilization has advanced, the voyager said, then have a look at their timepieces.

Sometimes, roaming around, I was sure that I had seen human beings, but they proved always only bird-headed creatures, who for scientific purposes had covered themselves in webs that looked like splendid old garments. At times their eyes had been altered by complicated lenses that looked like Master Jack's binoculars which could be altered as needed.

Once, a young woman sat across from me. She didn't move at all and kept looking at me thoughtfully, supporting her chin with her hand. At first, I thought that I had frightened her and wanted to lay my hand reassuringly on her shoulder, but, to my utter astonishment, my hand sank through her. The girl was only a figure made of light which one could actually walk through. Her eyes looked like round transparent glasses. If you looked through them you could see a glare of fire as in a forge.

## Extracts from the Journal of Master Jack

September 28th, 2036

*'But how could he have foundered?', I asked the omnipresent one. 'With his ability for manipulating life, he must have been immortal here too.'*

HE WILL BE ABLE TO TELL US AS SOON AS WE HAVE HELPED HIM REGAIN CONSCIOUSNESS. EF RE WAS ALWAYS A GAMBLER. HE OFTEN TOOK UNNECESSARY RISKS AND ACTED THOUGHTLESSLY. IT IS POSSIBLE THAT HE CUT HIMSELF OFF FROM HIS SPACESHIP THROUGH CARELESSNESS. IT COULD HAVE JUST HAPPENED IN A MOMENT OF INATTENTION. HE WAS MORE CONCERNED ABOUT HIS OWN SPLENDOUR THAN HIS OWN SAFETY. HE HAD A SPECIAL PREFERENCE FOR BIZARRE GENE MATERIAL. HE CARRIED CREATURES AROUND WITH HIM IN HIS BIOMASS WHO HAD NO OTHER FUNCTION THAN TO IMPRESS THE NATIVES. IF HE ENTERED A WORLD, HE DID SO ONLY WITH THE MOST COLOURFUL POMP AND SPLENDOUR POSSIBLE. THAT'S WHAT HAPPENED HERE. ONE HEARS, WHEREVER ONE GOES, THE DESCRIPTIONS OF HIS GROTESQUE BIOTANS. HE SEEMS TO HAVE USED THEM TO MAKE A LASTING IMPRESSION ON THE NATIVES.

I MAKE DO WITH TWO HELPERS: THE WORKERS I HAVE BRED OUT OF A VERY OLD AND UNIVERSALLY ADAPTABLE INSECT RACE, WHICH HAD A HIGHLY TECHNICAL CIVILIZATION WITH SIMPLE FUNDAMENTALS AT THEIR DISPOSAL OVER 500 MILLION YEARS AGO, AND THE GUARDS—WHO ARE AN IDEALLY DESIGNED HYBRID FORM MADE UP ORIGINALLY OF DIFFERENT RACES. EVERY VOYAGER CARRIES THEM WITH HIM IN HIS BIOMASS. YOU CAN RECOGNIZE THEM BY THEIR QUICK ABILITY TO LEARN. THIS PERMITS THEM TO TAKE UP DIRECT THOUGHT CONTACT WITH EVERY BIOLOGICAL OR ELECTRONIC INTELLIGENCE IN A MATTER OF SECONDS—OR TO CONNECT THEMSELVES TO IT IN ORDER TO GAIN A MAXIMUM OF INFORMATION AND TO PROCESS IT. WHEN I MAKE CONTACT WITH YOU IT IS ALWAYS THROUGH THESE BIOTANS.

*I looked at the bird-headed creature who always accompanies me. Is it always the same one?*

I awoke in the middle of the night because a great commotion seemed to have taken over the whole palace. I went to Master Jack's chamber but he was not there. He arrived a few minutes later and reported excitedly that the brain of the voyager had been found. It was still intact.

## Extracts from the Journal of Master Jack

October 14th, 2036

*Now that the brain of Ef Re has been found, the omnipresent one is making ready for departure. The storage crystals on board the mother ship are insatiable. They store into the smallest possible space all the knowledge that the biotans have dug out of the rubble of buried museums.*

*Naturally, I have not been able to hide my wish to accompany him from the omnipresent one. But how will this be possible? He travels simply as a brain, leaving everything else behind him. He can create any form for himself from the gene material he carries with him and thus can travel with a minimum of biomass. What fantastic storage capacity! Such enormous amounts of genetic, chemical and electrophysical information in such a small space!*

IF YOU DECIDE TO TAKE THIS STEP, YOU MUST BE CONSEQUENT AND GIVE UP EVERYTHING YOU EVER HAD BEFORE AND THROW IT BEHIND YOU. THIS LAW GOVERNS THE COSMOS.

*'What could I give up?'*

ALMOST EVERYTHING. EXCEPT PART OF YOUR BRAIN, ESPECIALLY THE CERE-BRAL CORTEX. TECHNICALLY, THERE IS NO PROBLEM. ONLY THE YOU THAT STAYS HERE WILL HAVE PROBLEMS. YOU WILL HAVE THE FEELING OF LOOKING SIMULTANEOUSLY THROUGH TWO WINDOWS OF YOUR CONSCIOUSNESS WATCHING YOUR REAL EGO REMOVE ITSELF FROM YOU FOREVER. WOULD YOU WANT TO DARE THIS? DON'T SAY YES WITHOUT THINKING IT OVER CARE-FULLY. IT'S NOT JUST AN ADVENTURE. IT IS POSSIBLE THAT YOU WILL REGRET IT. IT IS A MADNESS OF A VERY SPECIAL KIND.

I sleep very uneasily since I learned of Master Jack's innermost plans. It is very seldom that I even see him. When I do he talks a lot of bewildering nonsense and seems to be overjoyed. 'Be prepared to give away all things of this earth.' I see a web before me in which millions of Master Jacks crawl around. They are all speechless.

'This is the fantastic maze of a strange technology', he raves enthusiastically. 'A technology of biology and parapsychology.'

When can I leave this mad maze? I yearn for real human beings. The palace of the traveller of the stars is really like a web. Each impulse is transmitted somewhere where it is registered, and sets off a reaction.

## Extracts from the Journal of Master Jack

October 17th, 2036

WE HAVE A LONG JOURNEY BEFORE US THROUGH UNEXPLORED SPHERES. WE
SHALL HAVE A LOT OF TIME TO ANALYSE THE DATA THAT WE HAVE TAKEN ON
BOARD. YOU COULD BE OF GREAT HELP TO ME IN THIS.

*I am prepared.*

*From the beginning of time man has always contemplated the intellectual
being, the bodiless ego, the winged soul. What nonsense! The encephalo-
graphic basis is necessary: the stimulated molecules, the brain, the electrochemical short and long term storage space, a biological organ capable of
analysing all matter, the sensorium. This instrument reacts to impulses that
signal threat to or conservation of life, it 'tickles the nerve', manifesting itself
in hormones.*

*Individual consciousness cannot be duplicated. The brain is the ego, unique,
indelibly marked by life, the pergament of the whole with all its conscious and
unconscious enigrams, with all its erasures and ink spots. Nevertheless, I am
prepared.*

Today, I was in the control centre of the palace. It has changed
completely. The walls have been torn down and high, arched
windows let through the light of skies full of stars. The sky glows
from time to time, lighting up the dark dusty haze and shrouding the
dark red suns. Strange constellations glow through another arched
window. Giant stars, clustered together, are linked sometimes with
multi-coloured bridges of dark matter and light. The control centre is
empty. The bioprints have disappeared. Darkness reigns and the
glowing lights intensify the impression of unreality.

Master Jack says that we have been connected to the bird-headed
creatures. My head is in fact about to split with the twittering of birds.
They are confusing tones that I don't understand and they frighten
me because they too are full of fear. The time for takeoff is getting
nearer and nearer. Nervousness is growing. The traveller of the stars is
moving on, leaving his biomass behind.

Bioscap.

Why did he create these mute beings? They live in a world that is
far worse than the noiseless world of Simone.

I swore I would follow Master Jack to the edge of the world.

Now I am standing at the edge of the abyss.

## Extracts from the Journal of Master Jack

November 19th, 2036

*What is this fist-sized cylinder that keeps reverberating in front of my brain? Subtly wired to the cerebrum and cerebellum, it pulsates life. A droning object, full of all my memories, like a recorder with the voice of a corpse, noisy impressions of a living tongue, spoken with the breath of someone who once was formerly alive.*

*Oh yes, I can certainly breathe. I have a pair of bellows sensitively guided by biomatical microprocessors. Yes, and a living heart that receives an impulse every 0.8 seconds, which gives it the signal to contract and—immanent to the system and obeying the necessary metabolic processes—gives it a powerful feeling of life. I have the best possible biomatically guided digestive system, which still gives a feeling of well-being although it is superfluous. It is really not my fault if this cylinder which pulsates inside my forehead still has difficulty identifying itself with me. A clever hormone guided drug deposit helps it with this task. For who am I then?*

*That is a difficult question.*

*In moments of lucidity, I know that I am not the one travelling to the stars.*

*I am the 'dispensable' part of me. The necessary system for preserving life in the wilderness. The shabby scrap material of myself that was. Even if this droning metal in my skull never becomes tired of assuring me of my ego and my hope.*

Master Jack asked me—it was his last wish—to accompany anything left of his former self back to the south.

We are sailing up the river together with a fair wind between the horrible walls of dark mud where the dead still go about their daily affairs. They hardly ever take any notice of us. For them, we are just travellers going back to another world, a world forbidden to them. They don't seem to mourn its loss.

I awoke and looked through the arched windows of the star traveller's control centre. The desert lay covered by a night full of bright stars. I could feel a hand on my shoulder. 'Wake up Beschir! It is almost morning. We must be on our way. The spaceship is going to take off soon and all this will be consumed by fire.'

Through the eastern windows, we could see the tender green of daybreak over the horizon. It was a sight that can be seen only on very clear days in the desert.

I got up.

'Is that you, Master Jack?'

'Yes, it's me. What's left of me', he said. He didn't have to convince me. His eyes, otherwise as clear as the sun, were filled with a darkness only to be found between the stars.

The traveller of the stars gave us a present of one of his ships with a crew of a dozen insect beings and one bird-headed creature cowering in the semi-darkness of the early morning.

With a great clatter, the powerful ship raised itself into the air and made its way off to the south.

Towards noon, a roaring sound erupted behind us accompanied by a stream of sparks which were consumed in their skyward flight.

In the evening, the first insect being dies and is blown overboard by the slipstream. We glide over the desert. Master Jack is crouching at the bow. In his eyes, there is the light of the stars.

The next morning, the deck of the ship is covered with empty insect shells and broken off feelers. The bird-headed creature is leaning against the helm, half-decayed. I sweep the chimeras overboard. I roll the stinking bird-headed remains to the stern and throw them off, taking over the helm myself.

### Extracts from the Journal of Master Jack
November 22nd, 2036

*Is this my handwriting? It really is. But aren't I trying to imitate the writing of someone else?*

*It is a madness of a very special kind.*

*Sometimes, it is as if I were not sitting at the bow of the ship which Beschir is guiding like an experienced sailor. It is as if I were sitting at an arched window with a view of the earth. The planet has hardly changed since the satellite pictures taken by the Apollo astronauts. A blue green oasis in the wilderness of the universe. The planet disappears far below us.*

I can feel the powerful heart of the ship. The powerful heart of a young animal rising, pounding against the force of gravity and groaning against the force of the wind.

### Extracts from the Journal of Master Jack
Sidereal Time

*At times, it is as if I were not here on board the spaceship, but on the ship Beschir is courageously sailing through the desert close over the surface of a sea of air. In the depth of my tank of impressions, my biosensors register that the sun is shrinking. Right next to the sun, I can make out the shape of Beschir, leaning at the helm. His dark face attentively looking forward. We are both leaving the solar system.*

I sail this ship, this bark of our illusions, under a sky of burning stars, fly through grasshopper swarms and over the swell of the sand ocean, over the bone yards and Golgothas of civilization, through clouds of faded hopes and passions, over the ash fields, through a burnt out day and into the night and on up into the cool morning twilight. While a moon, sick and wasted like a rotten orange, stumbles morning after morning into the day.

I shall lay this ship, this bark of our illusions, at your feet, my King, at the bottom of the ocean that you rule over. For how shall I follow the course of a navigator who sees stars other than those I should navigate by? He crouches in the bow and keeps looking for flashes of light somewhere far over our horizons.

I shall lay this ship, my King, at the bottom of your ocean. An ocean without light even at the height of day. I shall lay this young powerful animal that pounds against the force of gravity and groans against the force of wind at your feet, my King.

I, however, widely travelled sailor that I am, must first explore my home waters once again, so that I, unlike Odysseus, do not succumb to the delusion that I am on my own shores only to be shipwrecked on foreign ones. For that is the problem—to seek new paths.

I am afraid. Not the animal fear of life being threatened, but the fear of the experienced caravan guide, who knows that the A'alam he sees could lead him to an abandoned path whose wells have long since run dry.

### Epilogue

A place is assigned me in the realm of the dead.
Where I issue orders to the blessed spirits
(Whose residence remains hidden)
And to the servants of the double-headed lion god.
In the boat of the Khepra god, I speed through the firmament
Singing songs of praise. A breath of life nourishes me
And invests me with magic power.
As I travel through heaven in the Ra boat,
This god prepares my way and opens the gates of Geb...
And I embark in the boat of the sun god.

In your stead, I sail through the mansions of heaven
Midst the throng of spirits that surround it.
Truly, I live all the days of life, though dead,
I feel strength course through my veins
Like the double-headed lion god...

—Papyrus Nebseni


Mount Darwin Observatory
May 25th, 2039
Report

MASON (Radar Operator): 'I can now verify the sensor indications.'
STEPHENS (Chief of Security): 'Please verify.'
MASON: 'I've got seven points on the monitor. Camera?'
HARDY (Camera): 'Got 'em on the zoom. Four horses. Three people. Can't make them out exactly.'
MASON: 'Give alarm stage four.'
STEPHENS: 'Roger.'
HARDY: 'A man, dark-skinned, around his mid-fifties, one arm. A young man about seventeen or eighteen. Both leading horses. A white man about ... my God, I've got him right in focus! It is Jack ... Jack Freyman! Turn the fence off!'
STEPHENS: 'Alarm off. Radar operator, turn the fence off!'
MASON: 'Roger.'

I wrote this in the winter of 2048 at the Mount Darwin Observatory at the request of Mr Stephens and Dr Hall. I am standing at my writing desk while Hazaz is pouring me tea. Master Jack is sitting at the window, touching his scar and looking through the displaced gates of his perception into the bright heart of the galaxy.

I have recorded this above all for him because I love him and for the caravan guides of the stars who have taught me not only to read and write but much more for our common future.

Beschir ibn Hassan el Sadun
November 19th, 2036

translated by SALLY SCHILLER

# Captain Nemo's Last Adventure
## JOSEF NESVADBA

His real name was Feather. Lieutenant Feather. He was in charge of transport between the second lunar base and the airfields on Earth, both direct trips and transfers via Cosmic Station 36 or 38. It was a dull job, and the suggestion had been made that the pilots of these rockets be replaced altogether by automatic control, as the latter was capable of reporting dangerous meteorites or mechanical breakdowns sooner and with greater accuracy, and was not subject to fatigue.

But then there was the famous accident with Tanker Rocket 272 BF. Unable to land on Cosmic Station 6, it was in danger of exploding and destroying the whole station, which would have held up traffic between the Moon and the Earth for several weeks and brought the greatest factories on Earth to a standstill, dependent as they are on the supply of cheap top-quality Moon ore. How would the Moon crews carry on without supplies from Earth? Were their rations adequate? How long would they be cut off? Everyone asked the same questions; there wasn't a family on Earth who didn't have at least one close relative on one lunar station or another. The Supreme Office of Astronautics was criticized from all quarters, and it looked as though the chairman would have to resign.

Just then the news came through that an unknown officer, one Lieutenant Feather, had risked his life to land on the tanker rocket in a small Number Four Cosmic Bathtub (the nickname for the small squat rockets used for short journeys). After repairing the rocket controls, Feather had landed safely on one on the Moon bases. Afterwards he spent a few weeks in the hospital; apparently he had tackled the job in an astronautical training suit. On the day he was released, the chairman of the Supreme Office of Astronautics himself was waiting for him, to thank him personally for his heroic deed and to offer him a new job.

And so Lieutenant Feather became Captain Feather; and Captain Feather became Captain Nemo. The world press services couldn't get his Czech name right, and when news got out that Captain Feather was going to command the new *Nautilus* rocket to explore the secrets of Neptune, he was promptly rechristened Nemo (Jules Verne was en vogue just then). Reuters even put forth another suggestion: Captain Feather de Neptune (it was meant to look like a title of nobility). But no one picked up on the idea.

Readers all over the world soon got used to Captain Nemo, who discovered the secrets of Neptune, brought back live bacteria from Uranus, and saved the supplies of radon on Jupiter during the great earthquake there—or rather, the planetquake. Captain Nemo was always on the spot whenever there was an accident or catastrophe in our solar system—whenever the stakes were life or death. He gathered together a crew of kindred spirits, most of them from his native Skalice, and became the idol of all the little boys on our third planet (as the scientists sometimes called Earth).

But progress in automation and the gradual perfection of technical devices made human intervention less and less necessary. Feather/Nemo was the commander of the rescue squads on Earth, but for some years he had had no opportunity to display his heroism. He and his crew were the subjects of literary works, the models for sculptors and painters, and the most popular lecturers among the younger generation. The captain often changed his place of residence—and his paramours as well. Women fell for him. He was well-built and handsome, with a determined chin and hair that had begun to grey at the temples: the answer to a maiden's prayer. And unhappy at home; everybody knew that.

That was really why he had become a hero. At any rate, a psychologist somewhere had written a scholarly article about it: 'Suicide and Heroism. Notes on Cause and Effect'. That was the title of the study. The author cited the case of Captain Nemo: if only this great cosmic explorer had been more happily married, he said, if instead of a wife from Zatec, where the hops grow, he had married a wife from Skalice, where they are brought up with the vine, if only his wife were not such a narrow specialist in her own field (she was a geologist), but had the gift of fantasy, and if only the son had taken after his father—Mr Feather would be sitting quietly by the family hearth, and no one would ever have heard of Captain Nemo. As it was, his wife was of no particular use to him, and he was always trying to slip away from home. His son was nearsighted, had always had to wear thick spectacles, and was devoted to music. He was also composing symphonies that nobody ever played; his desk was full of them by now, and the only thing he was good for was to occasionally play the harp and to teach youngsters to play this neglected old instrument at music society meetings. The son of a hero, a harpist—

that was another good reason for Captain Nemo to be fed up with life. And so he looked for distraction elsewhere. His most recent affair was said to have been with a black girl mathematician from the University of Timbuctoo, but everyone knew that even this twenty-year-old raven beauty could not hold him for long. He was famous for his infidelity—a relatively rare quality at this stage in history, since people usually married only after careful consideration and on the recommendation of the appropriate specialists, so that the chances of a successful marriage were optimal. Naturally the experts always tried to adjust the interests of those in love. Heroism was no longer considered much of a profession; it was a bit too specialized, and in fact no longer fulfilling. Today's heroes were those who designed new machines or found the solution to some current problem. There was no longer any need to risk one's life. Thus Captain Nemo had become somewhat obsolete in the civilization he had so often saved from destruction; he was a museum piece women admired because they longed for excitement, because they still remembered that love-making and the begetting of children were the only things that had not changed much since men emerged from the jungle. Feather and his men were the constant recipients of love letters from all over the Earth—in fact, from all over the solar system. Needless to say, this did nothing to make their own marriages any more stable, quite the reverse: because they were so popular, they longed to be able to return over and over again as conquering heroes. Finally even the raven-skinned girl in Timbuctoo began to think of setting up house as the necessity for heroic journeys began to dwindle: even this adventurous young lady wanted to bind Nemo with love, just as the geologist from Zatec had managed to do once upon a time. But that was not what the captain wanted at all. That would mean the end of adventure, and the beginning of old age and illness. He could not imagine what he would do with a happy marriage; he would have to upset it so as to have a reason for flying off again and risking his life, just as a drunkard invents a reason for getting drunk. Nemo knew the stories of all the great adventures of the past, he knew how to build up a convincing argument, and he used to say that in the end humanity would realize that this vast technical progress that kept them living in ease required, demanded an equally vast contrast; that man must give rein to his aggressive instincts; that men need adventure in order to remain fertile—in other words, that risking one's life in the universe (or anywhere else) was directly bound up with the fate of future generations. It was an odd sort of philosophy; very few people took it up, and as time went on there were fewer and fewer arguments in its favour. In fact, for the last five years Nemo and his men had simply been idle. The men were discontented. And so they were all delighted when one night quite suddenly their captain was called to the chief ministry, just like in the old days of alarms.

## Pirates

'This time, Captain Nemo', the minister addressed him ceremoniously, 'we are faced with an unusual and dangerous mystery. For this time it is apparently not only Earth that is threatened, but the sun itself, the source of all life in our solar system, the source of all we see around us.' The minister solemnly signalled to the assistant secretary of science to continue. Nemo and his adjutant were sitting facing them on the other side of the conference table. The four men were alone in the room. The assistant secretary walked over to a map of the Universe.

'Of course we didn't believe it at first, but we were wrong, gentlemen. The facts you are about to be given are well founded. About a year ago, one of the universities sent us a paper written by a young scientist about the incidence of novas. The papers quoted old Egyptian astronomical maps as well as recent observations in the constellation of Omega Centauri and the galaxy of Andromeda. The writer concluded that novas do not simply explode of their own accord, but that they are touched off according to a plan. Like someone going along the hilltops who lights a beacon to signal back to the valleys below. Some sort of rocket seems to have been entrusted with the task—or a satellite with an irregular course, something moving independently through space and destroying the stars one by one. It is interesting to note that a similar idea occurred to the writers of antiquity. Since according to this paper the next victim of these cosmic pirates would be the immediate neighbourhood of our own solar system, we quickly set up a secret telescope near Jupiter, without the knowledge of the public, in order to observe the regions in which this body appears to be moving. Today we reviewed the information provided by that telescope.' The assistant secretary picked up a long pointer and turned back to the astronomical map. The minister could control his excitement no longer. He leapt to his feet.

'They're coming!', he shouted. 'They're coming closer! We've got to catch them!' He was so excited that his chest was heaving, and he had to wipe his brow with his handkerchief. 'Damn them', he said and sat down again.

'If the reports from ancient Egypt are reliable, this body has been wandering around the universe for about nine hundred thousand years', the assistant secretary of science went on. 'We've managed to calculate the precise course it has followed to date. It cannot possibly be the satellite of some distant sun—it's a body that moves under its own power.'

'Its own power? Then it *is* a rocket', Nemo's young adjutant breathed.

'But seven thousand times the size of any rocket we are presently capable of constructing', said the assistant secretary. 'And it detonates the stars from an immense distance. In one year our sun will come within its orbit. In one year, it can cause an explosion of our solar system.'

'What are our orders, sir?', said Nemo briefly, taking out his notebook as though it were all in a day's work to tackle cosmic pirates seven thousand times his own size.

'Orders? Don't talk nonsense', the minister burst out. 'How could we send anyone to attack it? You might just as well send an ant to deal with an elephant.'

'Why not, if the ant is clever enough and you give it enough oxygen?', Nemo laughed.

'There's no question of building a miracle missile for you', the minister went on.

'We can give you the latest war rockets equipped with radioactivite missiles, but of course they're over a hundred years old', the assistant secretary said. The young officer at Nemo's side frowned.

'Haven't you got any bows and arrows?' Nemo savoured his joke. He was notorious for telling funny stories when things were really dangerous.

'This is a serious matter, Captain Nemo', said the minister.

'I can see that. Your automatic pilots are no good to you now, are they? You can't send them out that far because they'd never be able to keep in touch with you, I suppose. Only a human crew can fly that kind of distance.'

'Naturally.' The assistant secretary looked grim. 'That's why it's a volunteer's job. Nobody must be allowed to know anything about it. We don't want to frighten the public now, when people have only been living without fear of war for a few generations. We'll issue a communiqué only if your mission fails.'

'You mean if we don't manage to render them harmless?'

They explained that it was not a matter of rendering the aliens harmless. It would be far better if they could come to terms and avoid making enemies in the universe unnecessarily. But they did not want to tell Nemo what to do: they appreciated to the utmost not only his heroism, but his common sense as well. The moment the pirates turned away from our solar system, they assured him, everything would be all right.

'We shall send in a report, I suppose?', the adjutant asked.

'I hardly think so', said Nemo.

'Why not?' The adjutant was just over twenty. The other three looked at him—the minister, his assistant secretary, and Captain Nemo.

'My dear boy, there's such a thing as relativity, you know. By the time you get anywhere near that thing, you'll have been moving practically at the speed of light, and more than a thousand years will have passed on Earth.'

'A thousand years?', the adjutant gasped, remembering that a thousand years earlier Premysl Otakar had been on the throne of Bohemia.

'It's a job for volunteers only, Captain Nemo.'

'It's a magnificent adventure—'

'And I'm afraid it will be our last', Captain Nemo replied, getting to his feet and standing at attention. He wanted to get down to the details of the expedition.

'What do we tell the folks at home?' His adjutant was still puzzled.

'Surely you don't want to upset them by suggesting that in a year or two somebody's going to blow our Sun to bits? You'll set out on a normal expedition, and in a month we'll publish the news of your death. Or do you think it would be better for your loved ones to go on hoping for your return, until they themselves die? Your grandchildren won't know you, and in a thousand years everyone will have forgotten you anyway.'

'If we get the better of the pirates', Nemo laughed. 'If not, we'll all be meeting again soon.'

'Do you still believe in life after death?', the minister smiled.

'An adventurer is permitted his little indulgences', Captain Nemo answered. 'But if you really want to know—no, I don't believe in it. That's precisely why I love adventure: you risk everything.'

'But this isn't an adventure', his adjutant interrupted in an agitated voice. 'This is certain death. We can't destroy an entity that has detonated several suns in the course of the ages from an enormous distance—and even if we managed to do it, we'd be coming back to a strange land, to people who won't know us from Adam ...'

'You will be the only human beings to experience the future so far ahead', said the minister.

'And it is a volunteer expedition', added the assistant secretary pointedly.

'If you can suggest any other way out, let us hear it. The World Council has been racking its brains for hours.'

'And then they remembered us. That's nice.' Captain Nemo felt flattered. 'But now I'd like to know the details ...' He turned to the assistant secretary like the commander of a sector ready to take orders from the commander in chief of an offensive.

### Farewell

'Can't they leave you alone?', Mrs Feather grumbled crossly as she packed her husband's bag. 'Couldn't they find anybody younger to send? You'd think they could find somebody better for the job when you're getting to fifty ... I thought we were going to enjoy a little peace and quiet now, in our old age, at least. We could have moved to the mountains, the people next door are going to rent a cottage, and we could have had a rest at last ...'

'There'll be plenty of time to rest when we're in our graves', Captain Nemo yawned. Ever since he'd come home he'd been stretched out on the couch. He always slept for twenty-four hours before an expedition. He used to say it was his hibernation period, and that the only place he ever got a decent rest was in his own house. And his wife knew that whenever he came home he would drop off somewhere. In the last few years, though, he'd been stopping by on Sundays and at Christmas as well.

'For Heaven's sake, Willy, are you going to carry on like an adolescent for ever? When are you going to settle down?'

He got to his feet in anger. 'I wish I knew why you never let me get a bit of rest. If you had any idea how important this expedition is—'

'That's just what you said before you went to Jupiter and Neptune, and then there was the moonstorm business and the time those meteors were raining ... It's always the most important expedition anyone's ever thought of, and it's always a good reason for you to run away from home again ...'

'Do you call this home?' He looked around. 'I haven't set eyes on the boy since morning.'

It appeared his son had finally found a music group that was willing to perform one of his symphonies, and they'd been rehearsing ever since the previous day.

'You mean he isn't even coming to say goodbye to me? Didn't you tell him?'

'But he's getting ready for his first night at last, don't you understand?' His mother tried to excuse him.

'So am I', answered Nemo, who did not quite know how to describe his gala last performance. But in the end he tried to find his son. To listen to the rehearsal, if nothing else.

The concert hall was practically empty; one or two elderly figures were dozing in the aisle seats. The orchestra emitted peculiar sounds while young Feather conducted from memory, absorbed in the music and with his eyes closed, so that he did not see his father gesticulating at him from one of the boxes. He heard nothing but his own music; he looked as though he were quite alone in the hall. Nemo went out and banged the door in disgust. An elderly attendant came up.

'How do you like the symphony?', he asked the old man.

'It's modern, all right; you've got to admit that.'

'Yes, but I wanted to know whether you liked it.' At that moment, a wave of particularly vile noise came screeching out through the door, and Nemo took to his heels.

In front of the hall, the girl from Timbuctoo was waiting for him. She had flown over that morning by special rocket. He recalled how she had wept the last time he'd refused to marry her.

'We're off to repair some equipment between Mercury and Venus', Nemo laughed. 'We'll get pretty hot this time. When I get back, Timbuctoo won't even look warm by comparison.'

'I know you're not coming back, Captain.' She had always called him Captain. 'I was the one who passed the report on to the authorities.'

'What report?'

'About the cosmic pirates seven thousand times our size', she smiled. 'I thought it would be an adventure after your own heart at last. I could have sent the whole thing back, you know—a very young student submitted it. I could have won a little more time for us to spend together. But we have our responsibilities, as you've always told me.'

'You're perfectly right.'

'But we must say goodbye properly. I'm not coming to see you off; I want to be alone with you when we part . . .'

So once again Nemo did not go home to Mrs Feather, nor did he see his son again before he left. His adjutant brought his bags to the rocket, since he hadn't found the captain at home. Nemo turned up looking rather pale and thin, and the crew commented on it, but he had always been like that whenever they were about to take off, and he was used to their good-natured jokes.

This time the ministry prepared an elaborate farewell. No expense was spared. The World Government Council turned up in a body, together with all the relatives of the men, and crowds of admirers: women, girls, and young boys. Enthusiastic faces could be seen between the indifferent countenances of relatives, who were used to such goings-on, and the serious, almost anxious faces of those who knew the secret behind this expedition. The minister's voice almost shook with emotion as he proposed the toast. He did not know how to thank the crew enough, and promised that their heroism would never be forgotten. His hand was trembling by the time he gripped Nemo's in farewell, and he actually began to weep.

Once the relatives and curious onlookers had vanished, the crew had a final meeting with the leaders of the world government.

'All our lives are in your hands—the lives of your families, your children and your children's children, for generations to come. Men have often died for the sake of future generations, and often the sacrifice has been in vain. You can rest assured that this is not the case today. That's the only comfort we can offer you. I wish I were going with you myself, but it would cause too much talk, and we can't risk a panic. Still, it's better to fight than to wait passively in the role of victim.'

Then they played famous military marches in honour of the crew—itself an international team—but the gesture fell a bit flat; not a tear was shed at the sound of Colonel Bogey or the Radetzky March. With sudden inspiration, the bandmaster struck up the choral movement from Beethoven's *Ninth Symphony*, and the band improvised from memory as best it could. In those few moments, everyone present realized that for more than a generation man had been living in the age of true brotherhood, and that fear had suddenly reared its head again.

## The Flight

In half an hour they had gained the required speed—the rocket had been adapted for its job after all. When sixty minutes had passed, the adjutant brought a telegraph message to the commander. On Earth, where several years had already passed since their departure, an official communiqué reporting the loss of the *Nautilus III* had been issued.

'So now we're dead and gone.'

'Am I to inform the crew?', the adjutant asked in embarrassment.

'Of course. We need have no secrets from each other here.'

The first reaction of the crew to the news of their own deaths was a roar of laughter. If you survive your own death, you live long, as the saying goes. And it was a fact that if they survived their meeting with the space pirates, they would return to Earth as thousand-year-old ancients, ancients at the height of their powers. But the topic soon palled, and the usual effects of space flight appeared. The men began to be tired and to feel sorry for themselves, to be touchy and depressed. There was only one way to deal with this state of affairs when humour failed. The captain always pointed out that if it didn't matter to anyone that the flight from Prague to Moscow made you age two hours in the old days, why should you mind ageing a couple of years? The main thing was not to feel any older. But when his jokes failed, he had to make the day's routine tougher. Hunger and fear left no room for useless brooding. For this reason, the captain had made it a practice to invent all kinds of problems in the spaceship (which was in perfect order, of course). One day the deck equipment threatened to break down, and had to be adjusted while it was running. All the parts were changed, one by one; general rejoicing followed. The next time he thought up an imminent collision with a meteorite: all supplies had to be moved from the threatened side to the other side, and after the supposed danger had passed, everything had to be put back in its place again. A third time he invented an infectious disease the men must have brought on board with them and which required reinoculation for everyone; or the food would be infested, which meant going on a diet of bread and water for two days. The captain had to continually think up minor forms of torment to liven their days and keep the men occupied so there was no time for brooding.

But there was no one there to think up a way to lift Feather's days. He had to bear everything alone: the feeling that their expedition and his own life were utterly senseless, that he was to remain alone forever; despair at the hopelessness of the task he had undertaken and at the hopelessness of the life he had left behind him on Earth. He and the ship's doctor had made a pact: whenever the doctor thought the captain's depression was reaching alarming proportions, he would discover an attack of gallstones that called for special radiation treatment in the sick bay. And then while the captain got very drunk in the sick bay—he refused all medication but whiskey—his adjutant took over command of the ship. In two days the captain had usually got rid of his hangover and came up on deck again to think up some new danger to throw the men into a sweat, to be overcome and to provide cause for celebration.

After his most recent hangover, however, Nemo did not have to bother to think up a new trick. The meeting with the pirate ship seemed imminent at last. They could see it now—a rocket that looked more like a blimp, shaped like a cigar and about the size of a small planetoid: half the size of our moon. It was moving very slowly in the direction of our solar system. There could be no doubt about it: it was aiming at the sun.

Nemo gave orders for a message to be sent down to Earth at once by means of their special equipment. It was an experiment, for the chance of communication at that distance was extremely dubious. Then he called all hands on deck. The crew had to take turns at the machines and sleep in their space suits with weapons ready. He turned the heaviest long-range catapults on the giant, and slackened speed.

## The Encounter

There were several courses open to them. They were all discussed by the staff officers, and the computers offered an endless list of possible combinations. They all really boiled down to two: either to attack the ship outright, or to come to terms.

In view of the damage the pirate ship had already done in space, most of the officers were in favour of direct attack. The test explosions were still very much alive in their minds, and they could not imagine anything in the whole of the universe that could stand up to their nuclear weapons. There was, of course, the question whether the attacking ship could survive the explosion. Would the *Nautilus* hold out? No one could offer an answer, because no one had any idea what material the pirate ship was made of. It was also quite possible that the crew of the super-rocket would be reasonable, intelligent and willing to reach an agreement. But suppose the pirates seized and killed the emissaries? That was the risk involved in the second alternative. The first, however, involved an even greater risk: they would all be blown to pieces.

Nemo finally decided to fly to the strange vessel in the company of a few of his most stalwart men, armed to the teeth and ready to open negotiations. They set off in an old-fashioned Cosmic Bathtub—the one in which he had first made his name.

They were all amazed to see that the rocket was very similar to certain types that were used for transport on Earth, only many times larger. They flew around it like a satellite and found no sign of life. Either there had been no lookouts, or the pirates were willing to come to terms. Or they were all dead, thought Nemo.

'We'll land there by the main entrance.' He pointed to an enormous gap yawning in the bow. The entrance was unguarded, and the five men easily found their way inside. Roped together and maintaining radio contact with the Bathtub, they went down into the bowels of the rocket one by one. The first to disappear was the adjutant. He came back in a few minutes. His eyes were staring wildly and he was spitting blood, as far as they could make out through the thick lenses of his space suit goggles. They had to send him back to the Bathtub at once. No one felt like going down after that. They stood there hesitating, their feet weighted down and little batteries in their hands to allow them to move about; their automatic-rifles were slung over their shoulders. No one stirred. Then Nemo himself stepped forward and slowly sank into the abyss.

He was barely ten feet down when a persistent thought began to circle in his mind, as though somebody were whispering to him:

'We are friends ... we are friends ... we are friends ...', he seemed to hear. But of course he didn't really hear anything. It was like having a tune stuck in the mind. The words went on and on in his head like a broken phonograph record.

He began to feel frightened by the words as they swirled around. At last he landed on a sort of platform. The moment he felt his feet touch ground, the opposite wall began to open; it was several yards thick. He shut his eyes and went quickly through the opening. At first he threw a thin stream of light ahead with his flashlight, but in about three minutes he was blinded by light.

He was at the side of an enormous hall—impossible to see how far it stretched. And up front was a group of monsters.

At least they looked like monsters to him. But he was equally sure that he looked like a monster to them. What surprised him most, though, was that the creatures were not all alike. One was almost the size of a whale and looked something like a swollen ciliaphore; another was covered with flagella, while another featured eight feet. They were all transparent, and he could see a strange liquid pulsating through their bodies. They did not move. If it had not been for the liquid, he would have thought they were dead.

'They're only asleep—frozen. You can wake them up if you warm them, they'll wake up right away ...' He heard the words in his mind. He had already realized that they came from micro-transmitters on the brain surface. He switched his battery off. He did not want to wake them up; he did not even want to warm the place they were in with his torchlight. He gave a couple of sharp tugs at the cable he had fastened to his body. The minute the men pulled him up, he heard the insulating wall close behind him.

'They really are monsters', he said to the others, taking a swig of whiskey. 'Enormous protozoa. When I was a boy, someone showed me a drop of water under the microscope. It's like a drop of water seven thousand times enlarged', he added, and almost believed his own words. They hurried off to the Bathtub, and returned to the rocket to call a staff officers' meeting.

'My suggestion', said the adjutant, who had come to himself in the meantime, 'is to fix all the explosives we've got to the surface of their rocket, fix the time fuses for a week from now, and get back to Earth as quickly as we can.'

'But suppose they're friendly', Nemo objected. 'We have no right to destroy them just like that. Suppose they're bringing us a message—or a warning?' Finally, he decided to fix the explosives to the giant ciliaphore spaceship, but to attempt to negotiate at the same time. 'Who wants to come along with me and talk to them?', he asked at last. He looked at his hardened band of adventurers, but not one of them could meet his eye. It was the first time in all those years that they had felt fear. The adjutant had been in a terrible state when they got him to sick bay. He had raved about monsters and terrible creatures, and they could see what horrors he had gone through.

'I'll go with you.' It was the adjutant himself who spoke. They were all astonished. 'I've got to make good ...'

## The Sphinx

The two men stood at the edge of the great hall, near the whale-ciliaphore and the elephant-flagellula, with the giant podia of the third creature lying in the background. They didn't even try to distinguish the rest of the monsters. Once again they heard the two messages echo in their minds. Slowly, they began to warm the air. They had brought an active accumulator with them, and in less than an hour the liquid in the ciliaphore's body had begun to course more rapidly, while the unknown creature's podia began to tremble and the flagellula stretched itself with lazy delight.

Up to this point the crew of the *Nautilus III* had been able to follow the encounter, because the adjutant had taken a television transmitter with him, but when the flagellula moved a second time the picture seemed to mist over, as though water were pouring over it, and communication was interrupted.

The second officer immediately called a meeting. Since the two emissaries had ceased to respond to signals on the cable, the men on the *Nautilus* wondered whether they should attack. Finally they decided to send another party. The men who went discovered that the wall was closed. It would not open, and even withstood the oxyacetyle lamps they had brought along with them from the spaceship, and which were capable of dissolving any material known to man. They decided to wait by the entrance to the giant rocket for an hour longer, and then to attack.

Precisely fifty-nine minutes later the two men inside were heard again. They came out and boarded the Bathtub. When they reached the *Nautilus*, Nemo called the whole crew on deck and gave the order to return home.

'What about the explosives?'

'We can leave them behind. They know all about it, anyway', and he shut himself up in his cabin with the doctor and the adjutant. They spent nearly ten hours in consultation.

Meanwhile, the men observed that the crew of the giant rocket was not idle. The enormous cigar-shaped vessel seemed to bend suddenly, straightened itself out, and moved off at top speed in the direction from which it had come, away from our Sun. The *Nautilus* had apparently succeeded in its task. But the mystery of the giant pirate ship had not yet been solved. They were all impatient to hear what the captain would have to say, and hurried on deck for evening roll call.

'I'm afraid you're going to be disappointed', Nemo addressed them. 'We only spoke a few words to the foreign ambassadors. They answered us by telepathy, and I must say they seem to have made much greater progress there than we have. We asked them whether they were flying toward our solar system, and why. They explained that a long time ago they had been sent into space from their planet to visit our system, which according to their reports seemed to be the only one in the universe inhabited by intelligent animals—that is to say, by living creatures who are aware of themselves, their surroundings and their own actions.

'We asked them what they wanted, and why they had undertaken such a long journey to see us—whether there was anything we could do to help them, whether they wanted to move to our planet—and of course we pointed out immediately that it would never work out. It seemed to us, you see, that nothing short of mortal danger could have sent these creatures on so long and difficult a journey.

'They replied that they wanted to know our answer to the fundamental question of life.' The captain blushed as he said that, like a schoolboy who has suddenly forgotten the answer when the teacher calls on him. 'I'm sorry. I know it sounds silly, but that's really what they said ...' He glanced at his adjutant, who nodded and repeated:

'They said they wanted to know our answer to the fundamental question of life.'

'Naturally we didn't know what they meant', the captain went on. 'We thought they were asking us about the purpose of life. Everyone knows that the purpose of life is to transform nature. But that didn't seem to be what they wanted. Maybe they wanted to find out how much we know about life. So we offered them the doctor's notes: we have mastered the problem of tissue regeneration; we can prolong human life and heal even the most seriously damaged animal. But that wasn't what they wanted either. *The fundamental question of life!* They seemed to be shouting the words at us, like a crowd at a football game, or a pack of mad dogs. They wanted to know the answer. And we didn't even know what they meant.'

'The fundamental question of life.' The adjutant interrupted him. 'Of course it occurred to us that it might all be strategy, a way of distracting us by philosophical arguments. They couldn't expect us to believe they'd been en route from some damn spiral nebula for at least two hundred thousand years, or that they were tagging the stars as they went so folks back home would know they were going on with their task; they couldn't expect us to believe they'd volunteered to be put into suspended animation just to ask the kind of question that no one on Earth bothers with except idlers, drunkards and philosophers. I thought it might be a trick—that they were really out to take us prisoner and destroy the rocket. I tried to give you orders—'

'And that's just what you shouldn't have done!', Nemo shouted at him angrily. 'The ciliaphore next to us immediately opened the insulating door and pushed us out.' "Tell them we have detached their explosives", he said. "It is clear to us that life in your solar system is not yet completely reasonable..."'

'We would have attacked if they'd kept you one minute longer.'

'You're all fools', answered the captain. 'Fools and idiots. Nothing would have happened. Can't you understand that these creatures are much more technologically advanced than we are? We were at their mercy, and they spared us, simply because they gave up killing and destruction long ago. They're interested in other things.' He was silent for a moment and then apologized quickly to the crew. 'It was an unnerving experience, and I'm getting old. You know I've never shouted at you before. But I've got the feeling those creatures could have told us much more. Perhaps life asks more questions, the more perfect it gets.'

'The main thing is, we saved our homes', said the second officer.

'Saved them? From what? Questions aren't dangerous to anyone.'

'They're starting up again!' The doctor ran in from the watch room without knocking or saluting. 'They're not going back to Andromeda—they're heading out into space again. And they're slowing down.'

'That means they still think they'll find the answer to their questions somewhere in the universe.'

'Fundamental questions, sir', his adjutant reminded him.

'Fundamental questions.' Captain Nemo was still angry with his adjutant. He turned to the crew and read the orders for the next day. Never before had they heard him speak so quietly.

'He's getting old', they said to each other. But they were wrong. The captain had just begun to think.


## Nautillus 300


On the journey home no one bothered to think up any problems for the crew, and no one bothered to keep the men from worrying. The captain sat in his cabin all day long, watching through the window the dark void that surrounded them, the mysterious depths of eternity—perhaps not so eternal after all—the utter infinite. The cooks began to hand out better food, the officers relaxed; roll call was held when the men turned up for it, and nobody bothered much about the flight itself. At first the men were contented; then they began to feel afraid, lost their appetites—the mess hall was next to empty at mealtimes—suffered from insomnia and were prey to disquieting thoughts. And in this state they landed. Needless to say, the rocket returned to the point where it had taken off. It was late evening; as far as they could see, there had been no changes at the base since the day they left. The moment they landed, old fashioned luggage trailers drove up from the hangars and men in overalls helped them down and into the trailers. They smiled and shook hands with the newcomers warmly, looking very friendly. But that was all. There was no crowd of welcoming officials, no reporters, no curious onlookers and not even a government delegation complete with military band. Nothing. Just a run-of-the-mill arrival, as though they had come back from a stroll around Mars. The captain felt injured.

'Didn't you know we were going to land?'

'Of course we knew. You interrupted traffic on the main line to Mercury. We had to take five rockets off, since we had no guarantee you'd be on time.'

'We're always on time!', the captain shouted angrily. 'Is there no higher officer coming to thank us?', he added in a haughty voice.

'Tomorrow, tomorrow morning. In your quarters', replied the man he had been talking to. He was tall, with an ashen face, and did not look well. He asked the crew to take their places in the trailers and take only essential luggage with them. They drove off with mixed feelings. This was not the way they had imagined their return to the Earth they had saved.

'We might just as well have sent the monsters instead. They'd probably have made a bigger impression.' They had just turned into the main road when they heard an explosion behind them. The captain swung around to look. At the base, someone had set fire to the *Nautilus*: the tanks had just gone up. Nemo and the men with him beat on the door of the truck in a rage, but the trailer only picked up speed.

'And we didn't even bring a gun with us', the second officer growled. The captain's adjutant leaned over and tried to jab a penknife into the rear tyre as they drove along at top speed. A voice came from the loudspeaker:

'Please behave reasonably, men. We must ask you to remember that you come from an era that sent several rockets a day into space. If we tried to save all of those that return to Earth, there would soon be no landing room left. You are the three-hundredth crew to have returned after hundreds of years in space. We cannot understand why you people were so anxious to fly around—in fact, we find it incomprehensible. But we do try to make allowances, and you must also try to understand our position.'

The adjutant gave up: the trailer had solid rubber tyres, and now they were drawing up in front of the camp. It was a huddle of low buildings similar to those of the era they had known. Porters came running toward them and picked up their bags. They all looked pale. The captain liked their quarters.

'I should like to thank your commanding officer', he said to the drivers.

'You must wait until tomorrow', they smiled shyly. 'Tomorrow morning, please.' And they saluted and drove off.

As Nemo approached the dormitory he heard loud laughter. He opened the door: his men were standing silently, hesitantly by their bunks, and in one corner lay an elderly bearded fellow in the tattered remains of an astronaut's suit, rocking with laughter.

'He says—'

'Do you know what he's been telling us?'

'—that they aren't men', the captain heard someone say.

'Robots or something like that ...''Black and white servants'' ... ''Grey doubles'' ...'

Nemo strode over to the old man, who was holding his sides in uncontrollable laughter, and dealt him several resounding slaps. The man jumped to his feet and clenched his fists. But a glance at the captain's broad shoulders calmed him down, and he could see that the rest were all against him.

'They don't even know what *this* means—brawling', he snapped. 'And they don't like it if we fight.'

'Who's ''we''?', asked the captain.

'Who we are? The small crew of a private rocket from California that set out to see whether there was anything to be exploited on Mercury. Only our joystick went out of action and we bounced back and forth between Mercury and Earth for years before someone happened to notice us and bring us down. I can tell you we felt pretty foolish when we found out that the people who had saved us, who played cards with us and drank grapefruit juice with us all the way here were really machines from a factory. Yes, gentlemen, you'll hear all about it from Dr Erasmus tomorrow. Just wait until morning.'

## The Fundamental Question of Life

'You've come back to Earth at a time when technical progress has been completed', Dr Erasmus told them the next morning. He was almost paler than his black-and-white servants. 'Man began to invent machines to save him drudgery. But work was really ideal for man. Man is best suited to do his own work; the only thing he cannot stand is the humiliation. As soon as machines had been invented that could in fact do all jobs, there was only one problem left: what the machines should look like. It didn't seem appropriate to create models of attractiveness; some people might fall in love with their own servant-machines, might hate them, punish them, take revenge on them—in short, transfer human emotions to their relationships with the machines. It was also suggested—this simply to give you the whole picture—that the form of a monkey or a dog be used. But the monkey was not considered efficient enough, and the dog, though he has been man's companion for ages, cannot clean up after man, or do his work for him, or look after him so well that man can devote himself to the two things only man can do: create and think. Finally, the servants were built, in black and white, and each man was given one so like himself as to be indistinguishable from himself, a grey double, as it were, who did all his work and looked after the man in whose image it was made. You can order doubles like that for yourselves, if you like our society and decide to try to adapt to it. You won't need to take care of anything; all the servants are directed from a common computer centre which follows a single chief command: *look after humanity*. Thus the technical problems have been solved for good, and man is free of work for all time.

'Of course, if you prefer to go on living in your old way—many elderly people do find it difficult to adapt themselves to something new—you can remain here. This camp has been set aside for you and anyone else who may return to Earth from space.'

It sounded so strange. 'What did people do with their time, then?' Nemo asked.

'I can show you', answered Dr Erasmus, and switched on the

telewall. They saw a garden, where Dr Erasmus's double was strolling along deep in discussion with several friends. Only then did they realize that the man they were watching on the telewall was the real Dr Erasmus and the one talking to them his grey double. Dr Erasmus on the telewall suddenly turned around and smiled at the crew, waving a friendly hand before going on with his talk as though there was nothing more important on Earth ...

The crew of the *Nautilus* decided to have a look at the new society. Dr Erasmus's double smiled: everyone started out this way; but, alas, not all retained their initial enthusiasm.

The captain's first errand was to the Historical Institute. There he asked to see the records of his last flight—the date of their take off and the date on which their death was announced. He could find nothing to fall back on. There was no mention of cosmic pirates anywhere; the minister had been so afraid of creating a panic that he had forgotten to leave any evidence which could help the men now.

'Look up Feather for me', he ordered. The double looked at him in perplexity. 'Leonard Feather, the famous hero, also known as Nemo', the captain went on, looking around to see if anyone he knew happened to be listening. But the double still looked blank.

'Don't you mean Igor Feather?' Igor was the name of the captain's half-blind son. 'Dvork, Janaek, Feather? The three greatest Czech musicians?', the robot asked politely.

'Musicians?'

'Composers, that is ... Feather is certainly the greatest of the three, as every child knows today. The house where he was born has been preserved for a thousand years in its original state; concerts and evening discussions on music are arranged there. You will find the place full of people', the robot stressed the word *people*. And so the captain came home after a thousand years.

Fortunately, there was no concert scheduled for that day. He was afraid that even after so many years he would not have been able to stand the caterwauling. Their old home now stood in a park, and all the adjacent houses had been torn down. While he was still a long way off, he could see two gold plates gleaming on the front of the house. One commemorated his son and the music he had written, celebrating the young man's service to the cause of music. The other—Nemo approached it with quickening pulse—commemorated his wife. No one had put up a plaque to the memory of Captain Nemo. He looked around thoroughly, but he could find no mention of himself.

'She died a year before the first performance of Igor's concerto in Rudolfinum Hall ...', somebody said behind him. He started and looked around to see his adjutant walking out of the shadow of the bushes. 'She had to take care of your son, who had gone completely blind. She looked after him for twenty years, and he died in her arms. She didn't even live to see his name established: he became famous a year after her death. That woman was a saint, sir.'

'Why are you telling me this?'

'Because I loved her.'

'You never said anything about it.'

'Of course you never saw anything strange in my coming to see you at home, but I was happy just to be near her. And you deceived her with that black girl who got married a week after you started out on your last flight.'

'That's a lie.'

'It's the truth. She had twelve children. You can trace her descendants if you like. There'll be hundreds of them by now. I was one of your officers on the *Nautilus* only because of your wife, sir. I wanted to show her it wasn't so hard to be a hero, and that I could stand as much as you could, even if my shoulders weren't so broad. But she only loved you. And you loved that other girl.'

'Another one of life's puzzles, isn't it? Another fundamental question.'

'There's no question about it. It's a fact. You helped to kill her ... It's a filthy business, and that's the truth. You behaved shamefully to her.' His adjutant had never spoken in that tone before. Nemo turned on his heel and walked away. He saw that once more he would have to do something for his crew, find them another difficult task, for this new age was too much like those empty days out there in space.

In the Astronautics Institute they would not even hear of taking him on. 'We have our own robot crews. Why risk your life? Why bother with things that can be done better by machines, while you neglect those things that only the human mind can do?'

'Here are my papers.' He showed them his records like a desperate man who had aged prematurely. 'I can pilot a rocket as well as any of your robots. And I've got a crew of men who'll follow me to Hell if need be.'

'No human organism could hold out in our current programme of space flight. We have no job you could do. We're investigating the curvature of space, the qualities of light, whether even higher speeds can be reached—all tasks beyond your powers. Devote yourself to philosophy, art, aesthetics. That's the coming field, after all ...'

'I'm too old', replied the captain, rising from his chair. The grey robot said he was sorry. The wall of his office yawned and his human image leaned into the room. He was about fifty, a Bohemian with a palette and brush in his hand, and an enormous canvas behind him. He had a ringing voice.

'If anyone says that the time for philosophy has not yet arrived, or that it has passed, it's as good as saying that the time for happiness has not yet come, or that there is no longer any such thing ... That's Epicurus, my friend, wisdom that's thirty-five hundred years old. Find yourself something creative to do. Everyone has some sort of talent—something that makes him aware he is alive, that proves his own existence to him, something he can express himself best in. Leave those technical toys to machines and children; there's nothing in them to interest a grown man. We have more serious problems. The most urgent are the fundamental questions of life ...' Nemo had heard that before.

'Has anybody found any answers yet?', he asked.

'My dear sir, humanity is still too young for that. It's not like smashing the atom or orbiting around Jupiter. These questions need time and patience, they require a man's whole being. The answer is not only given in words, but in the way you live ...'

'I'm too old to change. I'm prepared to turn up at the old take-off ramp tomorrow, with my whole crew', Captain Nemo decided with finality.

The painter shrugged his shoulders, as if to say he was sorry that he had wasted his time. He turned back to his canvas, and the wall closed behind him. His grey servant bowed the captain out.

'As you wish. But I've warned you: it is suicide.'


## The Final Answer

The captain could not sleep in the morning. He recalled how little enthusiasm his men had shown the evening before, how unconvinced some of them were that it would be better for them to move off. Still, in the end he managed to persuade them, and they had promised to come. He dashed out before it was light and stumbled up to the ramp on foot. Robots were already hard at work there. The rocket they were preparing for flight did not look anything like a rocket: it was more like a globe, or a huge drop of liquid. It made him feel a twinge of fear. The firing mechanism was altogether different as well; he could not understand how it worked. The grey robots let him go wherever he wished and look at anything he cared to look at. Their smiles were strangely apologetic, as though it were not quite right for such a serious-looking man to be wasting his time with such foolishness as rockets. Nemo went back to the rendezvous point. His men were coming up in the morning mist, one by one. They were wearing their old suits again. This time they would be leaving without the fanfare, without the flags, but it would be better for them all. They couldn't possibly stay on Earth, they would never be able to adjust to this strange life ...

That was more or less what he said to them on the little rocket base. The mist almost choked him and he had to clear his throat. Then he read off the roll: the men were to answer to their names and step forward to shake hands with him. They answered and stepped forward to shake his hand.

But they were robots. They were the grey doubles of his men, who had sent the robots rather than come themselves. Not one of those ungrateful sons of bitches had reported for duty. The captain rubbed his eyes. It must be the mist, he thought. And he sat down on the nearest stone because he found himself somehow unable to breathe properly.

'Captain Feather?' A broad-shouldered fellow bent over him. He was wearing a beautifully brushed uniform, covered with gold braid, such as Nemo had never seen before.

'Yes.' He looked at him closely.

'They sent me over from the central office. With your permission, I'll take over the command...' Yes, of course, it was himself. Just a bit greyer, that was all.

'If you wish. If they wish', answered the captain, who felt defeated. His double saluted respectfully and stood smartly to attention just as Feather always did. In a short time he heard his own voice coming from the rocket, giving brief, staccato commands, reports and orders, just as he had done in previous years. In a few minutes the rocket silently moved away from the ground—*what kind of fuel do they have in there?*—and slowly rose toward the clouds. He waved after it. And looked around, just in case anyone was watching. It was silly, after all, to wave at a machine that worked so precisely all by itself.

He turned away and went slowly back to his old home. This time there were crowds of people in the house. His son's last symphony was being performed. He recognized those strange sounds that had upset him so much before he had left on his last flight. But now they no longer seemed so odd: he found himself beginning to listen attentively. He remained where he was, standing by a tree, at a considerable distance from the audience; the breeze carried snatches of music to him. Far up in the sky he saw the rocket pass out of sight.

And it occurred to him suddenly that if his son had stood before those pilgrims from distant galaxies, he might have been able to answer their questions.

'I must tell them not to send rockets out to look for the answer to the fundamental question of life', he thought. 'We must find the answer down here, on Earth.'

The orchestra fell silent and the harp sang out alone. It reminded him of something very beautiful.

translated by IRIS URWIN

# The Altar of the Random Gods
## ADRIAN ROGOZ

Everything began in a fit of absentmindedness. Homer probably didn't even know that Lethe's quiet waters have their source in our world. And, since every effect has a cause (which in turn is an effect), it may be that forgetfulness made its appearance with the first stirrings of life, as did life's negation, death.

Homer Hidden was sitting in the cabin of an express car that was taking him from Mobile across Alabama to Huntsville on the Tennessee border.

His eyes were fixed on the tachometer needle which hovered around the 590 mph mark, but his thoughts were moving into the past, a time of cruel agitation for him, and into the even more difficult future that awaited him at Houndsville, as he had ironically dubbed the city of his destination. Yet, though his thoughts were grim, they gave him no hint of the terrible thrill in store for him in the next four minutes. How could his weak mind, which had so little insight into his own nature, have doubted the competence of the tiny electronic brain which was guiding him, cushioned on air, over the concrete-and-titanium super-highway? Why did he have to quarrel with Barbara, throw aside his past life and leave Mobile? Life itself moved at dizzying speed! Homer sat there, slack-jawed, hardly realizing that his car was now flying at 600 mph even though it seemed motionless. The deceptive thing (some would say 'the paradox') about speed was that whatever its degree, you soon got used to it and ceased to be conscious of it. Then they increased the speed. This was what made a mess of life for Homer: the continuous, mad acceleration.

Homer looked at his watch. There was still time enough before he reached his destination, he thought: time enough to be bored. He didn't suspect that he had only three minutes now. 'Progress', he muttered, as though it were a dirty word. Barbara, too, invoked progress, but she was really concerned only with status. Status was another illusion, as soon as it became an obsession and led you to ruin. Without thinking, he pushed the visibility button on the wall. Before him appeared the exciting panorama of a line of pylons with thousands of cars travelling atop them, but the picture left him cold now and even made him squeamish. Besides, the rules for travel on the expressways recommended that those with weak nerves should not look at the trajectory of the cars. To the left he could make out the dozens of colours that indicated different speeds: many-coloured blobs that stayed to the rear if they were slanting off to out-of-state destinations. To the right was a cliff that towered over the waters of the Tombigbee River. In front of and behind Homer, cars travelling at the same speed as his seemed to be vibrating and stationary. Sometimes the cars came within a hundred feet of each other, but they could not collide since the motors produced air cushions in front and back as well as beneath the cars. In addition, there seemed to be a kind of telepathic communication between the electronic brains operating over the same roadway; thanks to this interconnection the speeds were regulated relative to each other.

In case of accident the cars were usually parked in a vertical position. But Homer was suddenly terrified at the thought of a mad chaos which a single collision would cause. There was only a minute and a half now to the fatal moment, and under the influence which a dreaded future exercises on our minds, Homer began to feel uneasy. He suddenly sensed how irreparable his break with Barbara was, and immediately, stimulated as it were by his emancipation from the iron necessity he had felt weighing on him hitherto, he found himself filled with immense and unreserved love for her. Her green eyes and chestnut hair—43 seconds, 42—her scarlet mouth and the downy nape of her neck—38 seconds, 37—her breasts and shoulders and knees, that had all the innocence of things forever vanished—29 seconds, 28—again her cascading hair, no, done up in a coil and then cascading down; and the mouth that asked for unheard-of things—23 seconds, 22—again her eyes, ever larger, ever deeper; her whole figure with its different postures, as though she were always poised for play yet serious as though for a ritual—17 seconds, 16—he seemed now to see her across a dark, impassable stream—13 seconds, 12—'Impossible!', he groaned in despair; one of them must surely die for the other!—9 seconds, 8—'Barbara, come back!', he shouted, though it was he that had gone away—5 seconds, 4—but he was already annihilated, and only the great inertia of desire had made him move his arm like one entranced—3 seconds—and his hands—2 seconds—and his finger which reached out to touch the return button—1.5 seconds—but fell instead on the accelerator—1 second—and in a flash of realization he absurdly shouted 'Stop!' —zero!

These days the manual operation of a hovercraft flying at full speed was as rare as the pulling of an emergency cord on the trains of long ago. You could ask for a change of lane or for parking, both manoeuvres being effected by a shift of the craft to a vertical position; in any case, the commands could not be obscure or contradictory. On most routes no passenger intervention was possible since the entire trip was programmed; in the case of a major crisis the whole vehicular system simply ejected the damaged car. But many technocrats had palaces along the Gulf of Mexico, and so the route Homer was travelling was a privileged artery. This is why the mechanical pilot, receiving the wrong command, tried to satisfy the client. But then came the second, senseless command.

For a few fractions of a second the electronic brains along hundreds of miles of skyway emitted insane signals. They seemed to be trying desperately to understand the two contradictory manoeuvres, to put them into the system, lessen their effect, isolate the catastrophic accident. Over hundreds of miles the instrument boards sounded the alarm. The most surprised passengers were those at the head of the immense column, for they were suddenly subjected to frightful overloads. The lead cars received the first command and accelerated. One after another they leaped forward like jets of water. Guardpilots flying over the convoy were open-mouthed at the sight. But then, almost simultaneously, came Homer's 'Stop!' Overtaxed by these successive commands or finally grasping their illogicality, the mega-route system decided that Homer's car should leave the caravan.

What happened, in fact, was that Homer's cabin was catapulted vertically upward, while the rest of the car disintegrated. Then began the sequence of events that would make Homer famous.

Normally (in a 'normal' accident!) Homer's cabin, once catapulted aloft, should have become a small plane with enough power to travel a few miles. But it didn't happen that way. Because of the extraordinary pressure exerted on them, the cars behind Homer's were also catapulted upward. To travellers on other roadways the maximum speed lane seemed suddenly to explode and to toss up a cloud of beetles. The others landed safely outside the super-highway, but Homer's cabin struck the one immediately following it. The impact was appalling. Barbara's eyes leaped from their sockets, then grew dark. The brain that had summoned up her image had the terrifying sensation of coming apart. In the collision of the two machines Homer's capsule was damaged; it had the misfortune (a relative thing!) to break one wing. The capsule then plunged down on to the nose of another car on the maximum speed lane. The shock caused this car in turn to be suddenly transformed into a flying cabin. Like a puck, Homer's inert capsule was catapulted into the clouds a second time. It crossed the line of cliffs and arrowed toward the river, where a huge helicopter was buzzing pleasantly above the water. Less than a minute had passed since the mad scene had begun, but the helicopter pilot was already alerted. His television cameras were zooming in on the super-highway, for transmission to the world's sets, at the instant when Homer's capsule burst upon the screen.

As chance would have it (but chance, again, is a relative thing!) Homer was still unconscious when his capsule was split in two, like an apple, by one of the helicopter's giant rotors. Millions of viewers watched in astonishment as the man fell like a die tossed from the cup.

Just as the immense sword sliced through the foreign body, a huge metallic arm with a plastic net was shooting out, ready to catch Homer. But chance was cleverer than technology. One half of the split cabin pushed the net aside as it fell, and the man was pushed through the torn side of his half by the speed of the falling ruin. At the same moment the shock brought him back to consciousness. He almost lost it again straight off.

It was a nightmarish awakening to find himself plummeting towards a shapeless, seething something-or-other. Around him a crowd of machines were whizzing at great speeds, trying now to avoid the poor human body. During his frightful, fantastic somer-saults in the air, Homer saw—or thought he saw, for in the few seconds since he had recovered consciousness, his mind seemed suspended in a void—heaven and earth sickeningly intermingling above an abyss of foaming waters that were sucking him inexorably down.

Before he touched the surface, Homer, who couldn't swim, had enough presence of mind to pull the collar of his suit over his head, like a cowl, and sleeves over his hands, like gloves. He knew that these would keep him from drowning: as soon as he entered the water, his body would be covered with a membrane that would isolate him and also draw oxygen from the water.

But so violent was his fall that the poor fellow was knocked groggy again. Perhaps he struck something at the bottom of the river (if so, we'll never know exactly what it was), but in any event his protective envelope was torn open while he was still half-unconscious.

At this point, chance, which was to make Homer famous, again took a hand; on the river bottom there was a factory and Homer landed near it, with the current carrying him on to a mass of radioactive mud which the factory spilled out towards the river bank.

\* \* \* \* \*

When he came to, Homer found himself stretched out on a sandy slope; a cement projection had kept him from rolling into a basin of green-black mud left by the waves.

He crawled up the slope a bit. To either side of the Tombigbee the unbroken streams of cars glittered hypnotically. Overhead, the majestic sun was setting above these man-made inverted rainbows. Homer felt alone and shattered, though without pain. The beauties spread about him meant nothing to him. He moved on, stumbling and leaning on the translucent handrail. His brain seemed to contain a palpitating little sun, that faded and brightened in his arteries. He asked himself no questions but moved forward with a kind of dumb stubbornness, babbling sounds that had no meaning, except perhaps to him.

When he reached the temple of the random gods, he was exhausted. He entered the building as though it were a refuge, completely forgetting the sarcasm he had formerly heaped on the gods of these cybernetico-statistical altars. (Some young enthusiast, a few years earlier, had constructed robots with immensely complex circuits and astonishing memories, and installed them in every home on the continent.)

Homer leaned against the wall. A pleasant coolness bathed him; the pure (conditioned) air smelled of snow, ozone and spring flowers. A smiling Barbara came to meet him, her cheeks rosy from a just-ended game of tennis. Soft electronic music made her image waver. Then he heard the hum of a loudspeaker and a metallic voice spoke: 'Come closer'.

Beside the altar was a lighted zirconium lamp; Homer limped towards it. Behind the altar were three windows of water-green glass, covered with elegant equations like arabesques on a Persian carpet. Under the arch of each window was a large crystal parallelepiped containing sextillions of cells. Two eyes, two ears, two nostrils and a mouth gave each of the three random gods a disconcertingly human appearance. They looked like three likeable (if grotesque) monsters, but Homer stared at them with the superstitious terror of a trapped animal.

'Lean on that railing near you', came a kindly invitation from the middle parallelepiped; his pedestal bore a plaque: 'The God of Nothingness'.

Tell us what happened to you', said the parallelepiped on the right, 'The God of Concentration'.

Some hoarse sounds, like sobs or strangled cries, were all that Homer could produce.

'Enough!', said the god. 'From your memory traces and from information we gathered before you arrived, I have put together almost your entire history. Nod if you understand me.'

The man nodded, but his eyes were unfocused.

'It's an unusual case', the left-hand parallelepiped said with a joyous piping sound; he was 'The God of Speed'. 'I suggest that the remnants in his mind be amplified, translated and emitted by a human voice.'

A red microphone above Homer switched on and from it came words spoken with obvious effort: 'What's happening to me? What do you want?'

'Fine!', said the God of Concentration with a chuckle. 'All your questions will be answered, even the ones you don't know how to ask.'

'But we won't ask you any questions or, more exactly, any more questions', chimed the God of Nothingness in a sweet tone of voice. 'Your very coming has provided us with the most precious thing in the world: an absurd improbability come true! Here are the facts.'

'Amid all the thousands of cubic parsecs, Earth is a rare occurrence.' It was the right-hand brain that was speaking now. 'The need of very special solar characteristics means a probability of $10^{-5}$ that any galaxy will have an Earth. But a planet inhabited by rational beings imposes new conditions: the proper distance from the sun, a magnetic field to block harmful radiation, an extensive liquid broth to allow life to germinate, a favourable atmosphere. These and numerous other conditions reduce the probability of such an Earth to $10^{-10}$.'

'Maaad-ness, maaad-ness, maaad-ness', came Homer's amplified inner voice, like a bell wildly tolling to rouse a burning village.

'You're right, of course', said the middle God, serious and scratchy. 'This exceptional concurrence of circumstances is required if you Earth-worms are to make your appearance. First had to come the great reptiles, preparing the way for the small mammals. A few thousands of these at the dawn of time made it possible for you men to cover the earth with your millions of bodies and their upper ends like barely rational pinheads.'

'What am I doing here? What do you want with me?', Homer wailed. It sounded as though his spirit were floating free of his body.

'You came to us because an almost zero-degree probability was verified', hummed the middle God again, calmly and with a touch of admiration in his voice. 'You're quite an exceptional case!'

'A collision of two cars on the present traffic lanes can occur only once in ten years', the God of Speed explained in a friendly way. 'A collision of one car with two others can occur only once in a century. The probability that the same car should in the next moment strike another flying machine is once in a thousand years, and the additional splitting of your capsule by a helicopter rotor only once in ten thousand years. Your escaping alive at this point increases the index to one hundred thousand years. The chance of your half-cabin breaking through the rescue net—a million years. Your not being killed—ten million. Your being roused from a faint by your fall—one hundred million. The possibility of your managing to pull closed your protective membrane—a billion. The likelihood of falling in water and not on land—ten billion.'

'That makes you as old as a solar system', commented the God of Concentration.

'The good luck to be carried from the river bottom by the factory outflow—one hundred billion.'

'As old as a galaxy!'

'And the probability of reaching us alive—a thousand billion years.'

'As old as the universe!', murmured the God of Nothingness by way of conclusion.

At the beginning Homer had held on, as best he could, to the railing in front of the altar. But now he was hanging there like a rag doll, arms limp and legs awkwardly spread, held up under the arms by a metallic bar.

'Aren't you Barbara Hamilton?'

'Yes', said a surprised female voice, 'but how did you know that?'

The amplifier was reproducing the sound track of Homer's memory.

'Adrian Gord spoke of you once and I imagined you just as you are.'

'Incredible!'

'You're exactly like my image of you.'

'How nice!'

'Doesn't that prove we're made for each other?'

'Really?', said the woman's deep and now somewhat startled voice.

Before Homer's clouded and inflamed eyes the windows became the lights of the distant city and the altars a happy, moving merry-go-round.

'Analyse the delta waves!', requested the God of Concentration.

Two metallic arms, deft and impersonal, came down from some recess or other and grasped the human lump under the arms; Homer was gone in spirit into the green fields of his youth.

'Can't this fleeting moment stay forever? How angelic those violins are! What sweet sensations sweep through me!'

'You have only five minutes to live', said the God of Speed in the impersonal command tone of a space-flight dispatcher, as multi-coloured waves, along with other invisible ones, eagerly crisscrossed over Homer's body.

The 'voice' that was reproducing the inner words of the man crucified upon the metallic arms was no longer human at all. It sounded like a magnetic tape running at dizzying speed. But it was expressing a whole existence; run slowly it would probably have taken as long as Homer's life had.

'Homer Hidden', intoned the husky voice of the God of Nothingness, 'you're a being that comes but once in a universe. Be glad that you occurred!'

'Integral amplifiers on!', ordered the God of Speed.

Homer's field of vision suddenly had no boundaries and Barbara's smile filled the firmament.

Then the man trembled in the sensitive metallic arms and these, as though surprised, opened their grip. Homer collapsed at the foot of the altar, and a ribbon of blood leaped from his mouth.

'Strange, the fixations that even the rarest of mortals entertain!', exclaimed the God of Concentration. 'But what a splendid occurrence this was, just the same!'

The bundles of light that had continued to touch Homer's body withdrew hesitatingly.

'I told you once before that you've been infected with that useless feeling for beauty', said the God of Nothingness in his coldest voice.

translated by MATTHEW J. O'CONNELL

# Good Night, Sophie
## LINO ALDANI

Grey and blue overalls were running along the street. Grey and blue, no other colours. There were no stores, no agencies, there wasn't a single soda-fountain, or a window full of toys, or even a perfume store. Once in a while, on the fronts covered with soot, encrusted with rubbish and moss, the revolving door of a shop opened. Inside was dreamland: Oneirofilm, happiness within everybody's reach, to fit everybody's pocketbook; inside was Sophie Barlow, nude, for anyone who wanted to buy her.

\*     \*     \*     \*     \*

There were seven of them and they were closing in from all sides. He swung violently, hitting one of them in the jaw, which sent him tumbling down the green marble staircase. Another, tall and brawny, appeared below, brandishing a bludgeon. He dodged the blow by hunching quickly, then grabbed the slave by the waist, hurling him against a column of the temple. Then, while he was trying to corner a third one, a vice of iron seized his neck. He tried to free himself, but another slave tackled his legs, and still another immobilized his left arm.

He was dragged away bodily. From the depths of the enormous cavern came the rhythmical notes of the sitars and tablas, an enervating, obsessive music, full of long quavers.

They tied him naked in front of the altar. Then the slaves fled into the galleries that opened like eye-sockets of skulls in the walls of the cavern. The air was filled with the smell of resin, a strong odour of musk and nard, an aphrodisiac atmosphere emitted by the burning torches, tripods and braziers.

When the dancing virgins appeared, the music stopped for a moment, then took up again, more intensely, accompanied by a distant choir of feminine voices.

It was an orgiastic, inebriating dance. The virgins passed by him one by one, they grazed his stomach, face and chest with their light veils and the long, soft feathers of their headdresses. Diadems and neck-laces flashed in the half-light.

At the end the veils fell, slowly, one at a time. He saw the swelling of their breasts, almost felt the softness of all those limbs that were moving in front of him in a tangle of unsated desire.

Then, the long, freezing sound of a gong interrupted the dance. The music ceased. The dancers, like guilt-ridden phantoms, disappeared in the depths of the cave, and in the profound silence the priestess appeared, exceedingly beautiful, wrapped in a leopard cape. She had small bare pink feet, and between her hands clasped a long bluish knife. Her eyes, black, deep, constantly shifting, seemed to search his soul.

How long did the intolerable wait last? The knife cut his bonds with devastating slowness, her great black eyes, moist and desirous, continued to stare at him, while a jumble of words, whispering, murmuring, came to his ears in a persuasive, enticing rhythm.

She dragged him to the foot of the altar. The leopard cape slid to earth, she stretched out languidly and drew him to herself with a gesture at once sweet and imperious.

In the cavern, a conch shell of sounds and shadows, the world came and went in an ebb and flow of sighs.

\*    \*    \*    \*    \*

Bradley turned off the machine and removed the plastic helmet. He came out of the booth, his hands and forehead damp with sweat, his breathing heavy, his pulse accelerated.

Twenty technicians, the director and the principal actress rushed to the supervisor, impatiently surrounding him. Bradley's eyes moved around, looking for an armchair.

'I want a glass of water', he said.

He stretched out gingerly on an air cushion with a long, sloping back, drying the beads of perspiration, and breathing deeply. A technician made his way through the group and handed Bradley a glass, which he emptied in one gulp.

'Well? What do you think of it?', the director asked anxiously.

Bradley waved impatiently, then shook his head.

'We're not there yet, Gustafson.'

Sophie Barlow lowered her eyes. Bradley touched her hand.

'It has nothing to do with you, Sophie. You were terrific. I . . . only a great actress could have created that last embrace. But the Oneirofilm itself is artificial, unharmonious, unbalanced . . .'

'What's wrong with it?', the director asked.

'Gustafson! I said the film is *unharmonious*, don't you understand?'

'I heard you. You say it's "unharmonious", unbalanced. Okay, the music is Indian, four hundred years old, and the costumes are from central Africa. But the consumer isn't going to notice such subtleties, what interests him is—'

'Gustafson! The customer is always right, never forget that. Anyway, this has nothing to do with music or costumes. The problem is something else: this Oneirofilm would rattle even a bull's nerves!'

Gustafson frowned.

'Give me the script', said Bradley, 'and call the aesthetic technician.'

He rifled back and forth through the pages, muttering unintelligibly, as if to reconnect the ideas.

'All right', he said at last, closing the bundle of pages suddenly. 'The film starts with a long canoe trip, the protagonist is alone in a hostile, strange world, there's a struggle with the river's crocodiles, and the canoe capsizes. Then we have a trek through the jungle, rather tiring, a hand-to-hand fight with the natives. The protagonist is shut up in a hut, but during the night the chieftain's daughter Aloa comes in, and provides him with directions to the temple. Then there's the embrace with Aloa in the moonlight. Speaking of which, where's Moa Mohagry?'

The technician and the director moved apart, and Moa Mohagry, a very tall Somalian woman with sculpturesque curves, stepped forward.

'You were great, Moa, but we're going to have to do the scene over again.'

'Again?', Moa exclaimed. 'I could do the scene over a hundred times, but I doubt it would get any better. I really gave it all I had, Bradley . . .'

'That's exactly what Gustafson's mistake was. In this Oneirofilm the major scene is the last one, when the priestess seduces the protagonist. All the other scenes are going to have to be toned down—they should serve as atmosphere and preparation. You can't make an Oneirofilm composed of nothing but major scenes.'

He turned to the aesthetic technician.

'What's the sensitivity index in the median sampling?'

'In Aloa's scene?'

'Yes, in Aloa's scene.'

'84.5.'

'And in the scene of the last embrace?'

'Just under 97.'

Bradley shook his head.

'Theoretically it would be okay, but in practice it's all wrong. This morning I screened the scenes in the first part, one at a time. They're perfect. But the film doesn't end on the riverbank when Aloa gives herself to the protagonist. There are other, rather tiring episodes: the ones I just screened, then another trek through the jungle, and the fight with the slaves in the temple. By the time the consumer gets to this point in the film, he's exhausted, his sensory receptivity is down to a minimum. The virgins' erotic dance only partly solves the problem. I saw the film in two takes, and so I was able to appreciate the last embrace with Sophie in all its stylistic perfection. But, please, let's not mix up absolute index with relative index. The crucial thing is relative index. I'm positive that if we distributed the film the way it's put together now, the total receptivity index would fall by at least forty points, in spite of Sophie's performance.

'Bradley!', the director implored. 'Now you're exaggerating.'

'I'm not exaggerating', the supervisor insisted in a polemical tone. 'I repeat, the last scene is a masterpiece, but the consumer gets there tired and already satisfied, in such a condition that even the most luscious fruit would taste insipid to him. Gustafson, you can't expect Sophie to accomplish miracles. The human nervous system has limits and laws.'

'Then what should we do?'

'Listen to me, Gustafson. I was a director for twenty-five years, and for six years I've been a supervisor. I think I've had enough experience to give you some advice. If you leave this Oneirofilm the way it is, I won't pass it. I can't. Beyond not pleasing the public, I would risk undermining the career of an actress like Sophie Barlow. Pay attention to me, dilute all the scenes except the last, cut the embrace with Aloa, reduce it to a mere scuffle.'

Moa Mohagry started angrily. Bradley took her wrist and forced her to sit on the arm of his chair.

'Listen to me, Moa. Don't think that I want to take away the right moment for you to make a big hit. You have talent, I know it. The riverbank episode shows true zeal and temperament, there's an innocent primitive passion there that would not fail to fascinate the consumer. You were fantastic, Moa. But I can't ruin a film that's cost millions, you understand, don't you? I'm going to suggest to the production committee a couple of films that will star you, Moa. There are millions and millions of consumers who go mad for Oneirofilms in a primitive setting. You'll make a big hit, too, I promise you. But not right now, it's not the right moment ...'

Bradley got up. He felt faint, his legs weak and tired.

'Please, Gustafson. Also tone down the slaves' fight episode. Too much movement, too much violence. The waste of energy is enormous ...'

He went tottering off, surrounded by technicians.

'Where's Sophie?', he asked as he got to the back of the room.

Sophie Barlow smiled at him.

'Come in my office', he said. 'I have to talk to you.'

\*    \*    \*    \*    \*

'All right, I'm not saying anything new, they're old words, stale, you must have heard them a hundred times at school and during your training course. But it would benefit you to give them some thought.'

Bradley was walking back and forth in the room, slowly, his fingers laced together behind his back. Sophie Barlow was slouched in an armchair. From time to time she stretched out a leg and stared at the toe of her shoe.

Bradley stopped for a moment in front of her.

'What's the matter with you, Sophie? Are you having a crisis?'

The woman made a nervous, awkward gesture. 'Having a crisis? Me?'

'Yes. That's why I called you into the office. You know, I don't want to read you the riot act. I simply want to remind you of the fundamental precepts of our system. I'm not young any more, Sophie! You're running after a chimera!'

Sophie Barlow squinted and then opened her eyes as wide as a cat's.

'A chimera? What's a chimera, Bradley?'

'I told you, I can spot some things right off. You're having a crisis, Sophie. I wouldn't be surprised if it had something to do with the propaganda that those pigs at the Anti-Dream League put out by the truckload to undermine our social order.'

Sophie seemed not to pick up the insinuation. She said:

'Was Moa's performance really that good?'

Bradley passed a hand behind his neck. 'Absolutely. Mohagry will make it big, I'm convinced of it ...'

'Better than mine?'

Bradley snorted. 'That's a meaningless question.'

'I made myself clear. I want to know which of us you liked better, me or Moa.'

'And I repeat, your question is idiotic, lacks common sense, and just goes to confirm my suspicion—in fact, my conviction—that you're going through a crisis. You'll get over it, Sophie. All actresses go through this phase sooner or later. It seems to be a necessary stage ...'

'I would like to know just one thing, Bradley. Something that's never said in the schools, something nobody ever talks about. *Before*. What was there before? Was everybody really unhappy?'

Bradley took up pacing around the armchair.

'Before, there was chaos.'

'Bradley! I want to know if they were really unhappy.'

The man stretched out his arms disconsolately.

'I don't know Sophie. I didn't exist at the time, I wasn't born yet. One thing is sure: if the system has asserted itself, it means that objective conditions have allowed it to do so. I would like you to be aware of one very simple fact: technology has permitted the realiza- tion of all our desires, even the most secret ones. Technology, progress, the perfection of instruments and the exact knowledge of our own minds, of our own egos ... all of that is real, tangible. Hence even our dreams are real. Sophie, don't forget that only in very rare cases is the Oneirofilm an instrument of comfort or compensation. Almost always it is an end in itself, and when just now I had you, I enjoyed your body, your words, and your odours amid a play of exotic emotions.'

'Yes, but it's always artificial ...'

'Okay, but I wasn't aware of it. And then, even the meaning of words evolves. You use the word *artificial* in the pejorative sense it had two centuries ago. But not today, today an artificial product is no longer a surrogate, Sophie. A fluorescent lamp, correctly adjusted, gives better light than the sun. This is true of the Oneirofilm as well.'

Sophie Barlow looked at her fingernails.

'When did it begin, Bradley?'

'What?'

'The system.'

'Eighty-five years it's been now, as you should know.'

'I do, but I mean the *dreams*. When did men begin to prefer them to reality?'

Bradley squeezed his nose, as if to collect his thoughts.

'Cinematography began to develop at the beginning of the twentieth century. At first it was a question of two-dimensional images moving on a white screen. Then, sound, the panoramic screen, colour photography were introduced. The consumers gathered by the hundreds in special projection halls to watch and listen, but they never *felt* the film, at most they experienced a latent participation through an effort of fantasy. Obviously the film was a surrogate, a real and proper artifice for titillating the erotic and adventurous taste of the public. However, movie-making then represented a very powerful instrument of psycho-social transformation. Women of that period felt the need of imitating actresses in their gestures, vocal inflections, dress. This was no less true of men. Life was lived according to the movies. First the economy was conditioned by it: the enormous demand for consumer goods—clothes, cars, comfortable housing—was of course due to real exigencies of nature, but also and above all to the ruthless, indefatigable advertising that harassed and seduced the consumer every minute of the day. Even then, men longed for the dream, were obsessed by it, day and night, but they were far from achieving it.'

'They were unhappy, right?'

'I repeat, I don't know. I'm only trying to illustrate for you the stages of the process. Toward the middle of the twentieth century the standard woman, the standard situation was already in existence. It's true that there were directors and producers in those days that tried to produce cultural films, ideological movies, to communicate ideas and elevate the masses. But the phenomenon lasted only a short time. In 1956 scientists discovered the pleasure centres of the brain, and through experimentation revealed that electric stimulation of a certain part of the cortex produces an intense, voluptuous reaction in the subject. It was twenty years before the benefits of this discovery were made available to the public. The projection of the first three-dimensional movie with partial spectator participation signalled the death of the intellectual film. Now the public could experience odours and emotions; they could already partly identify with what was happening on the screen. The entire economy underwent an unprecedented transformation. The human race was starved of pleasure, luxury and power, and only asked to be satisfied at the cost of a few pennies.'

'And the Oneirofilm?'

'The Oneirofilm came out, fully perfected, only a few years later. There's no reality that surpasses dreams, and the public became convinced of this very quickly. When participation is total, any competition from nature is ridiculous, any rebellion useless. If the product is perfect, the consumer is happy and the society is stable. That's the system, Sophie. And certainly your temporary crises are not likely to change it, not even the melodramatic chatter of the Naturists, unscrupulous people who go around collecting funds for the triumph of an idea that is unbalanced to start with, but for their own personal profit. If you want a good laugh—last week Herman Wolfried, one of the leaders of the Anti-Dream League, appeared in the offices of the Norfolk Company. And do you want to know why? He wanted a private Oneirofilm, five famous actresses in a mind-blowing orgy. Norfolk has accepted the commission and Wolfried is paying for it through the nose, so much the worse for him.'

Sophie Barlow jumped up.

'You're lying, Bradley! You're lying on purpose, shamelessly.'

'I have proof, Sophie. The Anti-Dream League is an organization out to dupe simpletons, incurable hypochondriacs and passéists. Perhaps there is some remnant of religious sentiment behind it, but at the centre of it is only greed.'

Sophie was on the verge of tears. Bradley moved toward her solicitously and put his hands on her shoulders in a tender, protective gesture.

'Don't think about it any more, Sophie.'

He guided her over to the desk, opened the safe, and got out a small, flat, rectangular box.

'Here', said Bradley.

'What is it?'

'A present.'

'For me?'

'Yes, actually it was to give you this that I called you into the office. You've made twenty Oneirofilms for our production company, an inspiring goal, as it were. The firm is honouring you with a small recognition of your worth ...'

Sophie started to unwrap the present.

'Leave it', Bradley said. 'You can open it at home. Run along now, I have a lot to do.'

There was a line of helitaxis just outside the building. Sophie got into the first one, took a magazine from the side pocket of the vehicle, lit a cigarette and, flattered, contemplated her own face on the front cover. The helitaxi rose softly, steering for the centre of the city.

Her lips were half-open in an attitude of offering, the colour, the

contrast between light and shadow, the expression ambiguous ...
Each detail seemed knowingly graded.

Sophie looked at herself as if in a mirror. At one time the job of
acting had presented various negative aspects. When she made a love
scene, there was a flesh and blood 'partner', and she had to embrace
him, tolerate the physical contact, kisses, words breathed straight into
her face. The camera photographed the scene which the spectators
then later saw on the screen. Now it was different. There was 'Adam',
the mannequin packed with electronic devices having two minute
cameras conveniently placed in his eyes. 'Adam' was a wonder of
receptivity: if the actress caressed him, the receptivity valve registered
the sensation of the caress and fixed it, together with the visual image,
on the reel of Oneirofilm. Thus the consumer who would later use
that reel would perceive the caress in all its sensory fidelity. The
spectator was no longer passive but the protagonist.

Naturally, there were Oneirofilms for men and Oneirofilms for
women. And they were not interchangeable: if a male consumer,
plagued by morbid curiosity, inserted in his reception helmet a reel
meant for female consumption, he would get an atrocious headache,
and also risk short-circuiting the delicate wiring of the apparatus.

Sophie told the pilot to stop. The helitaxi had gone barely a dozen
blocks, but Sophie decided to proceed on foot.

Grey and blue overalls were running along the street. Grey and
blue, no other colours. There were no stores, no agencies, there
wasn't a single soda-fountain, or a window full of toys, or even a
perfume store. Once in a while, on the fronts covered with soot,
encrusted with rubbish and moss, the revolving door of a shop
opened. Inside, on the smooth glass counters, there was the *dream*,
happiness for everybody, for all pocketbooks, and it was Sophie
herself, nude, for anybody who wanted to have her.

They marched on. And Sophie Barlow marched along with them,
an army of hallucinated people, people who worked three hours a
day, prey to the spasms that the silence of their own shells yearned
for: a room, an Amplex and a helmet. And reel after reel of
Oneirofilms, millions of dreams of love, power and fame.

In the middle of the square, on a large platform draped in green, the
fat man was gesticulating emphatically.

'Citizens!'

His voice raised itself as loud and clear as a dream speech, when the
dreamer has the whole world singing hosannas at his feet.

'Citizens! An ancient philosopher once said that virtue is a habit. I am not here to ask the impossible of you. I would be a fool if I expected to renounce it immediately and completely. For years we have been slaves and succubuses, prisoners in the labyrinth of dreams, for years we have been groping in the dense darkness of uncommunicativeness and isolation. Citizens, I invite you to be free. Freedom is virtue, and virtue is a habit. We have cheated nature too long, we must rush to make amends, before we arrive at a total and definite death of the soul ...'

How many times had she listened to speeches like that? The propaganda of the Anti-Dream League was sickening, it had always produced in her a profound sense of irritation. Lately, however, she had surprised and bewildered herself. Perhaps because she was an actress, when the orators in the squares spoke of sin, perdition, when they incited the crowds of consumers to abandon the 'dream', she took the accusation as if it had been personally aimed at her; she felt a responsibility for the whole system. Perhaps behind the orators' emphatic tone there actually was some truth. Perhaps they hadn't told her everything at school. Maybe Bradley was wrong.

On the platform the fat man ranted and raved, pounding his fist on the wood of the lectern, red in the face, congested. Not a soul was listening to him.

When the veiled girl came out of a small side door, there were some in the crowd who stopped for a second. From the loudspeakers issued the sound of ancient oriental music. The girl began to take off her veils, dancing. She was pretty, very young, and made syncopated, light, eurhythmic gestures.

'An amateur', Sophie said to herself. 'A would-be actress ...'

When she was standing naked in the centre of the platform, even the few men who had stopped to wait moved on. One or two of them laughed, and shook their heads, disappointed.

The Anti-Dream League girls stopped the passers-by, they approached the men, thrusting out their breasts in an absurd, pathetic offer.

Sophie lengthened her stride. But someone stopped her, grabbing her arm. It was a tall, dark young man, who stared at her with steady black eyes.

'What do you want?'

'To make you a proposition.'

'Speak up.'

'Come with me, tonight.'

Sophie burst out laughing.

'With you! What for? What would I get out of it?'

The young man smiled faintly, patiently, a smile tinged with security and superiority. Clearly he was accustomed to this sort of refusal.

'Nothing', he admitted unperturbed. 'But our duty is to—'

'Cut it out. We'd spend the night insulting each other, in a pitiful attempt to achieve "natural harmony" ... Dear boy, your friend up there on the platform is spewing forth a pile of nonsense.'

'It's not nonsense', the young man retorted. 'Virtue is a habit. I could—'

'No, you couldn't. You couldn't because you don't want me, and you don't want me because I'm real, true, living, human, because I would be a surrogate, a substitute for a reel of Oneirofilm which you could buy for a few pennies. And you? What could you offer me? Silly presumptuous young ass!'

'Wait! Listen to me, I beg of you—'

'Goodbye', Sophie cut him short. And continued her walk.

The words she aimed at the young man had been too harsh. It had been a uselessly hostile reaction; she might have rejected his proposition neither more nor less vehemently than the other passers-by did, with some grace, or better, with a self-sufficient smile. In the last analysis, what right did she have to insult him, perhaps to hurt his feelings? He was acting in good faith. But what about the leaders? Bradley has assured her a number of times that the directors of the Anti-Dream League were a band of swine. What if Bradley had been lying to her all along?

The suspicion had now been plaguing her for several weeks. All those speeches in the squares, the manifestos on the walks, the propagandistic pamphlets, the public proposition to experiment in natural relations with the League's activists ... Was it possible that the whole thing was a lie? Perhaps there was some truth in what the orators and lecturers maintained, maybe the world was rotten to the core, and only a few enlightened men had eyes to see the horror and assess such decadence.

Man as an island: they had all been reduced to this. On one side the producing class, a class that kept power and to which she herself belonged in her capacity of actress; on the other, the prostrate, blind army of consumers, men and women avid for solitude and darkness, silkworms coiled up in the silken filaments of their own dreams, pale bloodless larvae poisoned by inaction.

Sophie had been born in the glass. So had everybody else, for that matter. She did not know her mother. Millions of women, once a month, went to the Bank of Life; millions of men achieved orgasm by means of the Dream and donated semen to the Bank, which sorted it carefully and used it according to rigorous criteria. Marriage was an archaic institution. Sophie had been the child of a dream, of an unknown, anonymous man who in a dream had possessed an actress. Every man over forty could be her father, every woman between the age of forty and eighty her mother.

When she was younger, this thought had disturbed her greatly, then bit by bit she had got used to it. But lately all the doubts and anxieties of her adolescence had reared up again, vultures that patiently circled above, waiting for one of her moments of weakness. Who was that young man who had stopped her on the street? A champion of superior humanity, or a fool?

Certainly, if he had said to her, 'I recognize you, Sophie Barlow. I recognize you in spite of your standard suit and your dark glasses.' Or if he had said, 'You're my favourite star, you're the obsession of all my days ...' Or even if he'd said, 'I want to get to know you, whoever you are, just as you really are ...'

Instead, that lout had talked about duty. He had asked her to spend the night with him, but only to pay obeisance to the presumptuous new morality: Virtue is a habit. A habit, a routine of natural relations. Love one another, ladies and gentlemen, come together in self-denial! Each of your acts of love will contribute to the defeat and destruction of an unjust system. Unite yourselves, come together in reality, the sublime joy of the senses will not delay in manifesting itself! An exultation of sounds and lights will fill your souls, will glorify your bodies! And our children will once again be formed in the warmth of the womb, not in the cold glass of a test tube.—Wasn't this what the fat man on the platform had been preaching?

She went into a crowded store and made her way over to the sales counter, where hundreds and hundreds of Oneirofilms were neatly displayed, packed in elegant plastic boxes. She loved to read the descriptions printed on the covers, to listen to the conversations that the shoppers sometimes had with each other, or the zealous advice that the salesman whispered in the ears of undecided customers. She read a few titles.

> *Singapore*: Eurasian singer (Milena Chung Lin) flees with the Spectator. Adventure in the underworld of this eastern port. Period, mid-twentieth century. Night of love on a sampan.

> *The Battle*: In the role of a heroic officer, the Spectator
> infiltrates an enemy encampment and sabotages its munitions
> dump. A last battle, bloody, victorious.
> *Ecstasy*: The private jet of a Persian princess (masterful perfor-
> mance by Sophie Barlow) crashes in the Grand Canyon.
> Princess and Pilot (the Spectator) spend the night in a cave.

Descriptions in greater detail were to be found inside the boxes.
There was no danger that an exact knowledge of the contents on the
part of the consumer would lower its desirability index. Mental
projection inside the Amplex was accompanied by catatonic stupor
in which the memory of each independent episode never connected
with the next to form a whole. One could not know, experiencing the
first episodes, what would happen in the second and following
episodes. Even if plot descriptions were learned by heart, even if
one saw the same film twenty times, the conscious ego, the everyday
ego was sacrificed to the urges provoked by the reel: one ceased to be
oneself in order to assume the personality, the mannerisms, the voice,
the impulses suggested by the film.

A salesman sidled up to her solicitously.

'May I help you to choose a gift?'

Sophie suddenly noticed that among the mob of buyers there were
no other women. This was the men's department. She moved off
toward the opposite counter, mingling with women of all ages,
lingering before the enormous photographs of the most popular
actors.

> *Outer Space Belongs to Us*: Commander of a spaceship (Alex
> Morrison) falls in love with the lady doctor on board (the
> Spectator), the rocket changes course to discharge the crew on
> one of Jupiter's moons, and the Commander heads off with
> his lover. Trans-galactic crossing.
> *Tortuga*: Period, mid-seventeenth century. Gallant pirate
> (Manuel Alvarez) abducts noblewoman (the Spectator). Jea-
> lousy and duels. Love and sea voyages under a fiery sky.

'What's it like?', asked a tall girl, her buxom body suffocating in a
pair of overalls too small for her.

'Fascinating', her companion asserted. 'I bought four more copies of
it right away.'

The other girl looked sceptical. She stretched her neck over the
counter, stood on the tips of her toes to read the descriptions on the

furthermost boxes. She said something in a low voice, and her companion answered in a whisper. Sophie moved off. She spent a few minutes in the 'classics' section, giving a fleeting glance to the back of the shop where men and women crowded together to buy the so-called 'convenience' Oneirofilms.

When she had been younger, at school, they had told her that in former times men considered taboo anything that had to do with sex. It was highly improper to write or talk about the many aspects of love life. No woman would ever have described her desires and her sexual fantasies to a stranger. There were pornographic publications and photographs, many of which were illegal. People who bought them did it on the sly and always with a feeling of guilt or embarrassment, even when they had been passed by the Censor. But with the advent of the 'system' the primitive custom of sexual modesty had become obsolete. Modesty existed, if at all, in some kinds of dreams, in 'convenience' films made for the over-fifty set, where the consumer seduced or raped a teary, red-faced, trembling young girl. But in real life it had disappeared, or at least verbal modesty had. Without a shadow of embarrassment or discomfort, anybody could ask for an erotic film, the same as any other film about war or adventure.

But what about real and proper modesty? Among the many who crowded round the counters to buy the luxury in a box, who would have had the courage to disrobe in the middle of the mob? Only those activists of the Anti-Dream League, who were completely unselfconscious when they propositioned people, but perhaps not quite so unselfconscious when faced with performing what they themselves considered a weighty duty. The truth was, for nearly a century men and women had lived in a state of almost complete chastity. Solitude, the measured penumbra inside the narrow walls of their habitations, the armchairs with built-in Amplex: humanity had no desire for anything else. Faced with the greater attractions of dreams, the ambition to own a comfortable house, elegant clothes, a helicar, and other amenities had simply gone by the board. Why beat one's brains out collecting real objects when, with an Oneirofilm that cost but a few pennies, one could live like a nabob for an hour, near stupendous women, admired, respected, served hand and foot?

Eight billion human beings vegetated inside squalid beehives, isolated in mean little holes, nourished by vitamin concentrates and soybean meal. And they felt no desire to consume anything real. After the bottom fell out of the market, the industries producing consumer goods had been abandoned all at once by financiers, who transferred their funds to companies producing Oneirofilms, the only merchandise for which there was any real demand.

She looked up toward the shining chart, and was disgusted at herself. The numbers spoke clearly. The sales chart was most eloquent. Her own Oneirofilms were the ones must in demand, more than everybody else's put together.

Sophie left the store. She walked homeward, her head bent, her step slow and listless. She didn't know how to judge that crowd of men who moved all around her, without recognizing her. Were they her slaves, or was she theirs?

\*   \*   \*   \*   \*

The videophone rang: a streak of light in an abyss of black velvet, a peal from lofty cathedral spires in a sleepy, grey dawn.

Sophie stretched out a hand toward the pulsator-button.

A red snake zig-zagged onto the screen, lingered, seemed to explode; finally it resolved itself into Bradley's image.

'What do you want?', Sophie whined, her voice slurred with sleep. 'For God's sake, what time is it?'

'It's noon. Wake up, my girl. You have to go to San Francisco.'

'To San Francisco? What for? Are you out of your mind?'

'We have a co-production contract with Norfolk, Sophie. It was set for next Monday, but time presses. They need you now.'

'But I'm still in bed, I'm deathly tired. I'll leave tomorrow, Bradley.'

'Get dressed', the supervisor barked. 'A Norfolk jet will be waiting for you at the West airport. Don't waste time.'

Sophie was fuming. This extra work wasn't scheduled. What she wanted to do was spend the rest of the day in bed, resting. She struggled out from under the covers, her eyes still shut, and sluggishly, halfheartedly undressed in the bathroom. The metallic jet of the cold shower made her shiver. She dried herself, dressed hurriedly, and left the house on the run.

She knew the methods of those types at Norfolk. They were worse than Bradley, real nitpickers. Always ready to find fault even with the scenes that had come off well.

In eight minutes, the helitaxi deposited her at the entrance to the airport. She entered by the door that led to the runway for private aircraft, and looked round for the Norfolk jet.

The pilot emerged from an outbuilding and walked over to meet her with a bouncy step.

'Sophie Barlow?'

He was tall, with light blond hair and a bronze complexion, a face that looked as if it had been baked in an oven.

'I'm Mirko Glikorich, from the Norfolk Company.'

Sophie said nothing. The pilot did not think her worth a glance, and spoke staring at an indefinite point somewhere out in the airfield, two cold, aggressive eyes of a fine grey colour like anthracite. He took Sophie's suitcase and marched off toward the main runway, where the Norfolk jet was being prepared for take-off. Sophie had a hard time keeping up with him.

'Hey!', she exclaimed, balking like a thoroughbred. 'I'm not a runner. Couldn't you walk a little slower?'

The pilot kept moving, without so much as turning around.

'We're late', he said curtly. 'We have to be in San Francisco in three hours.'

She was breathless by the time they reached the aircraft.

'Do you mind if I sit in front with you?', asked Sophie.

The pilot shrugged his shoulders. He helped her up, settled himself into the cockpit, and waited for the signal from the control tower.

Sophie looked around, full of curiosity, a bit intimidated by all the dials and switches on the instrument panel. The pilot whistled softly, impatient. Sophie groped around in the pocked of her seat and pulled out a dozen magazines. They were all at least several weeks old, some from the year before, dog-eared. Her face was on the cover of each of them. There was also an Oneirofilm catalogue folded open to the page that listed the films starring Sophie.

'Are these your things?'

The pilot didn't answer, but looked stiffly ahead. The take-off had been gentle as a feather, and Sophie hadn't felt it at all. She glanced out the window and barely stifled an 'Oh!' of surprise. A sea of houses extended itself beneath them; like a downy eyelid, the grey shell of the countryside opened up before them.

'Are these yours?', Sophie insisted.

The pilot turned his head slightly, an imperceptible movement, a lightning glance. Then he stiffened again.

'Yes', he said through his teeth.

She tried to hide the intimate gratification that always pervaded her when she met one of her ardent fans.

'What did you say your name was?'

'Glikorich', the pilot growled. 'Mirko Glikorich.'

'That's a Russian name, isn't it?'

'Yugoslav.'

She watched him for a while. His lips were narrow and taut, his profile straight and sharp ... Mirko looked as if he had been chiselled in rock, mute, motionless. Sophie grew impatient.

'Can I ask you a question?'

'Speak.'

'Before—at the airport. You came to meet me and asked me if I was Sophie Barlow. Why? You know me, don't you? These magazines and the catalogue. I'll bet you're a fan of mine. Why did you pretend not to recognize me?'

'I didn't pretend. It's different, seeing you in person. In the end I recognized you because I knew you were supposed to turn up at that entrance at the airport. But in the middle of the crowd, no; you could have passed me without my noticing.'

Sophie lit a cigarette. Maybe the pilot was right: in the crowd nobody would notice her, even without her dark glasses. She felt a kind of dull anger toward the man beside her. But she kept making an effort to talk to him. Mirko proved to be dense as a jungle, impenetrable, diffident.

'Why don't you turn on the automatic pilot?', Sophie asked. 'I'm bored, Mirko. Say something to me.'

The pilot remained impassive. He blinked once or twice, and stuck out his chin.

Sophie caught his arm. 'Mirko! Pay attention to me! Turn on the automatic pilot and have a cigarette with me.'

'I prefer to leave it on manual.'

Sophie lit another cigarette, then another, using the butt of the second. She leafed through a magazine, worrying the pages in a fit of uncontrollable nervousness. She started to sing to herself, tapping her foot against the rubber lining of the cockpit. She snorted, fidgeting, and finally pretended to feel nauseated.

Mirko felt around inside the pocket of his flying suit and handed her a tablet.

Sophie was furious.

'Idiot!', she cried. 'I won't stay here a moment longer. I'm going back in the cabin.'

The little living room behind the cockpit was attractive. There was a couch, a stowable berth, a little table and a bar.

She poured herself a drink, a tall glass of brandy, which she gulped down at once. She poured herself another immediately, and the edges of objects began to vibrate in a bluish, inviting fog. She lowered herself to the couch, thinking of Mirko, a consumer like all the rest, an imbecile. She couldn't wait to get to San Francisco, make the film, and fly back to New York.

Now she sipped the brandy with less gusto. As she set the glass on the table, she began to feel groggy.

Suddenly, the arm of the couch was shoved against her, and an abyss seemed to open beneath, as when an elevator begins to move. She watched the glass start to slide along the tabletop, spill on the rug ... Then; a pain in her shoulder, her forehead knocked against something ... Fog. Red and blue globes. Roaring of motors gone wild.

'Mirko!', she cried, raising herself. The door to the cockpit seemed bolted shut. She squeezed the hostile handle and, lurching, tried to pull the door open. An emptiness inside her chest, a moment of balance, then the absurd feeling of weightlessness. She saw Mirko's back, his hands tense on the throttle, the clouds racing towards them like dream vapours.

Now Mirko was talking. In fact, he was shouting, but she wasn't aware of it. She pressed herself against the back of her seat, clenched her teeth and braced herself for the crash.

The aircraft plummeted like a corkscrew.

When she opened her eyes next, she saw a white cloud in the middle of the sky. A vulture circled far up. She was lying stretched out on her back, and something moist and fresh was pressed against her brow. She raised an arm, touched her face, temples, and removed the handkerchief soaked with water. Then she rolled over on her side.

Mirko was on his feet, over by the wrecked fuselage. Behind him, a cyclopean wall of red rock rose over the landscape.

'What happened?', she asked weakly.

The pilot stretch out his arms. 'I don't know', he said, shaking his head; 'I can't understand it. All of a sudden the controls weren't responding, the craft lost altitude, and then we were in a tailspin. I managed to regain control by a miracle, but it was too late. Look at the skid we took before we banged up against this rock!'

Sophie pulled herself up, rubbing her bruised shoulder.

'Do you have any idea where we are?'

Mirko lowered his eyes.

'This is the Grand Canyon', he said. 'We're in one of the side chasms. This is one of the most inaccessible areas, but the Bright Angel Trail shouldn't be too far away...'

Sophie's eyes widened. 'The Grand Canyon?'

For a moment she was speechless. Then she burst out laughing.

'The Grand Canyon!', she repeated. 'That's very funny! In fact it's unbelievable.'

'What's unbelievable?'

'Don't play dumb, Mirko. The engine failure, the forced landing, here, right in the middle of the Grand Canyon ... Just like the film I made last year, *Ecstasy*. You do remember it, don't you?'

Suddenly a suspicion crossed her mind.

'Tell me something', she said, frowning. 'You didn't by any chance do it on purpose, did you! I mean, there are an awful lot of coincidences here. You're a real pilot, and I may not be a Persian princess but on the other hand I am Sophie Barlow. You wanted to get marooned out here with me, didn't you? You planned it to happen just like the film.'

Mirko puffed up indignantly. He turned his back on her and went over to the aircraft. Shifting aside the twisted pieces of fuselage, he managed to crawl into the cabin. He tossed out a pile of equipment, two blankets, two back-packs, a plastic canteen, a tin of synthetic food, a flashlight. He emerged from the wreck with the bottle of brandy in one hand and a heavy piece of equipment in the other.

'Let's go', he said. 'Carry as much of this as you can.'

'Go where?'

'Surely you don't want to rot out here among the rocks. We have to get to the main canyon. Phantom Ranch must be more than fifty miles east of here, but there's always some stupid sentimental tourist who will come west to take a picture of the pretty view.'

'Did you try radioing?'

'The radio's broken. Get a move on. Take what you need and let's get out of here.'

He moved fast, his stride long and springy. He had tucked the brandy bottle into his hip pocket, and he marched along stooping slightly under the burden of his pack, in which he had placed a battery and the heavy electronic device.

Sophie stumbled along behind him, carrying the food and water containers.

Half an hour later, they came to a halt. Sophie was out of breath, her eyes were pleading. Mirko stared straight ahead. It was clear that the woman was a hindrance to him, the classical ball and chain which he could not get rid of.

'Walk slower, Mirko.'

The man looked at the sky, which was filling up with menacing clouds.

'Let's go', he said. 'In a couple of hours it's going to be pitch black.'

When they reached the main canyon, they could hardly see anything. Mirko pointed up at a place in the rocky wall, red and brown as a piece of burning paper.

'The cave', he said reverently.

'The cave', Sophie repeated. 'Just like in the film. Everything is just like in the film, Mirko.'

He helped her up the cliff, and lowered his pack to the floor of the black hole that opened into the rock.

She watched him as he clambered down the sandstone and granite crags, rooting out the dried-up shrubs, making big bundles of them and dragging them up to the cave entrance. 'It'll be cold in a while', he said. 'We'll have to start a fire.'

He lit the flashlight and inspected the cave. It was about fifteen yards deep, and bent at right angles in the middle. He set the bundle of kindling right in the elbow of the cave, and lit the fire with savage delight.

They ate in silence, in the dark and glowing cave, under an enormous fluttering bat's wing.

'I opened your pack', Sophie said. 'While you were down gathering kindling. I saw what you have inside there. An Amplex! What did you need to bring that along for?'

'It's worth 120 coupons', Mirko said. 'For an actress like you, that's a pittance. But it takes me three months to earn that much, you see?'

He picked up the metal box and the reel case.

'Well?', Sophie asked, curious. 'What are you up to now?'

'I'm going to the rear of the cave. I have a right to my privacy, don't I?'

Yes, but what do you need the Amplex for? What are you up to, Mirko?'

The man snorted. When Sophie grabbed the reel case, he didn't put up a fight. Passive, he let the woman go through his reels at her leisure, let her read the descriptions printed on the plastic boxes.

'But these are all my films, Mirko? My heavens, you have every single one of them! *Blue Skies, Seduction, Adventure in Ceylon*. There's even a matrix, the matrix for *Ecstasy*. Is that your favourite Oneirofilm, Mirko?'

Mirko lowered his eyes without answering. Sophie closed the reel box. A matrix was a luxury relatively few people could permit themselves. The ordinary Oneirofilm, once viewed, was useless, because the Amplex demagnetized the tape as it ran through. But a matrix lasted forever, it was practically indestructible. For that reason, it cost a small fortune.

'When did you buy it?', Sophie asked.

The man shrugged, annoyed. 'Oh, quit it', he snapped. 'You're too curious. What do you want me to say? Your films sell millions of copies to millions and millions of consumers. I'm just one of them. I bought a matrix of *Ecstasy*. So what? What's so strange about that? There was something about it that I liked. I—'

'Go on', Sophie urged, squeezing his arm.

'A day doesn't pass that I don't watch it', the pilot said tartly. 'So now why don't you leave me alone, go to sleep, because in a little while it will be daylight and we have to cover quite a few miles. I'm going to the back of the cave.'

'With the Amplex?'

'Yes, for God's sake. What's it to you? I want to enjoy my film in peace.'

Sophie gulped. A sudden feeling a frustration passed through her, as if all desire to live had left her. This is impossible, she thought. This can't be happening to me. What do I want, anyway, from this man who has a thousand reasons not to care a hoot about me?

She felt a desire to hurt him, to heap abuse on his head, to slap his face. But the image of Mirko embracing her broke through her inhibitions and spread through her mind.

'I'm here', she was surprised to hear herself say in a seductive tone.

Mirko wheeled round.

'What did you say?'

'I said, I'm here, Mirko. Tonight you don't need that reel.'

'I don't need it?'

'No. You can have me, just like in the dream. Even better than in the dream ...'

Mirko started to snicker. 'It's not the same thing', he said. 'And don't be ridiculous with this Anti-Dream League propaganda of yours. Who are you trying to kid, anyway?'

'I'll say it again: Mirko, you can have *me*.'

'And I still say it's not the same thing.'

'Mirko!', the woman pleaded, beside herself. 'You need me, every day you run through that matrix, and you dream, dream, you keep on dreaming of this cave, the firelight, my kisses, this body of mine which I've just offered you. This is exactly like the film, you stupid fool. What are you waiting for? I can do everything that's in that film, even more, and it will be for real ...'

For a moment Mirko wavered, then he shook his head. He turned and moved off toward the back of the cave.

'Mirko!', she cried, exasperated. 'I am Sophie Barlow! Sophie Barlow, don't you understand?'

She pulled down the zipper of her overalls. Her shoulders shrugged out of the cloth shell, and she quickly pulled off the suit and threw it on the ground.

'Look at me!', she shouted. And as he turned around, she uncovered her breasts.

The fire burned brightly, red and green tongues lapping upward, emitting a penetrating odour of the primeval jungle. She watched the man's hands clench into fists, his lips trembling, as if in a long, wearisome struggle.

Mirko hesitated a moment longer, then threw the matrix in the fire and ran toward her.

*     *     *     *     *

First the blue light came and then the red. Then blue again. When the reel came to an end, the set turned off automatically.

Sophie lifted off the Amplex helmet. Her temples were perspiring, her heart pounding in spasms. All her extremities were trembling, particularly her hands. She couldn't keep them still. Never in her life had he lived a 'dream' with such intensity, an Oneirofilm that forced her to be herself. She must thank Bradley right way.

She rang him up on the videophone. But faced with the image of the supervisor, the words stuck in her throat; she stammered, truly moved. Finally she started to cry.

Bradley waited patiently.

'A little present, Sophie. Just a trinket. When an actress reaches the peak of her career she deserves far greater rewards. And you will have them, Sophie. You will have all the recognition that's due you. Because the system is perfect. There's no going back.'

'Yes, Bradley. I—'

'It will go away, Sophie. It happens to all actresses sooner or later. The last obstacle to overcome is always vanity. Even you felt that a man ought to prefer you to a dream. You fell into the most dangerous of all heresies, but we caught it in time and rushed to correct it. With a little gift. That matrix will help you to get over this crisis.'

'Yes, Bradley. Please thank everybody for me, the machinist, the technicians, the director, everybody who was involved in making this Oneirofilm. Above all, thank the actor who played the pilot.'

'He's a new fellow. A real live wire, no?'

'Well, thank him for me. I had some beautiful moments. And thank you too, Bradley. I can imagine how much time and money this film cost you. It's perfect. I'll keep it in the slot of honour in my Oneirofilm collection.'

'Nonsense, Sophie. You belong to the ruling class. You can allow yourself a personal Oneirofilm from time to time. We have always helped each other out, haven't we? —But there's one thing I want you to bear in mind.'

'What's that, Bradley?'

'That matrix. That's more than a gift. It's meant to be a warning.'

'Okay, Bradley. I get your point.'

'Don't forget it. Nothing is better than dreaming. And only in dreams can you deceive yourself to the contrary. I'm sure that after five or six viewings you will get the point and toss that matrix in the wastebasket.'

She nodded, in tears.

'I'll see you tomorrow at nine in the screening room.'

'Yes, Bradley, tomorrow at nine in the screening room. Good night, Bradley.'

'Good night, Sophie.'

translated by L. K. CONRAD

# The Proving Ground
## SEVER GANSOVSKY

## 1

The first men came on a small cutter.

The water at the shore was muddy and motionless and smelled of rotting seaweed. Green waves boiled up over the reefs and beyond these stretched the warm surface of the blue sea; from it the wind blew day and night without ceasing. Above the beach stood spear-tipped bamboos and, behind them, towering palms. Spirited crabs dashed out from under stones and threw themselves on the tiny fish that were stranded by the waves.

The three men from the cutter conducted a leisurely examination of the near part of the island. They were watched by the disturbed and suspicious Indians who lived here with their families in a small village.

'It looks like the kind of thing we want', said one of the strangers. 'The nearest island is three miles away; there are no sea lanes or air lanes nearby, and the area is generally rather quiet. It will probably please the brass; but you never know how they'll react.'

'We won't find anything better', said the second. He turned to the third man, who was an interpreter: 'Tell the Indians to leave the island. Explain that they can come back in about a week.'

The interpreter, a thin man with tinted glasses, nodded and stumped off across the resisting sand to the village.

The first man opened a map case and took out an aerial photograph of the island, along with pencil and ruler; he studied the photograph for a while. 'We can put the billets here, and the canteen next to them. The firing trenches go over there, and the dugout in that direction. They can set up their installation on that hill; it's about 550 yards from the dugout.'

'What's the whole thing supposed to be?', the second man asked.

The first shrugged and kept his eyes on the photograph. 'How should I know? I'm supposed to reconnoitre the island. Somebody else brings in the equipment. That's none of our business, right?' He sighed and tore open a package of chewing gum. 'What heat! Where's that interpreter?'

The interpreter returned half an hour later. 'I can't do anything with them. They refuse to leave. They say they've always lived here.'

'Did you tell them there would be military manoeuvres on the island?'

'Do you think they can understand that? They have no words in their language for such ideas. They can't even get the idea of a "forbidden area".'

'Okay', said the second man, 'let's go. We've found the island and warned the natives. They'll clear out soon enough when the equipment starts landing.'

They trudged down to the cutter and shoved off with the boatman's help. Ten minutes later they had disappeared over the horizon.

For a while the waves breaking on the shore tossed the chewing gum wrapper back and forth. The Indians came and gazed after the departing cutter for a long time. A child ran after the bit of silvery gum wrapper, but the chief of the tribe, a man with wind-carved face and powerfully muscled body, scolded him.

Strange people, these white men! None of them ever does a complete job. They had said: 'Go away'. But why? The tall thin man who hid his eyes behind spectacles had explained that he himself didn't know why. Each individual performs only a little piece of a whole job, but how the little pieces would fit together later on doesn't interest them.

Two days later a small fleet approached the island. A shallow-draught barge landed a bulldozer and a dredger. A crane with its muscular claw transferred bags of cement, pipes, beams and window frames to the beach. Then it summoned all its strength and carefully set a great tarpaulin-covered object on the sand, an object so heavy that it immediately sank several inches into the ground. Two motorized anti-tank guns rolled down a runway and came ashore under their own power.

Soldiers with machines quickly dug trenches. The bulldozer toppled a grove of palms; the palms tilted and their thick fronds intermingled as they collapsed on the sand. Within ten hours the palms had been replaced by a barracks with a double roof, and a dugout with concrete walls was concealed in the sand.

The Indians did not watch to the end. At midday the chief went down to the beach and looked at the heavens for a long time; to the south the sky had become a peculiar red. Then he returned to the huts and spoke to two men. The villagers quickly loaded their possessions into two boats and sailed away to another island.

In the evening a tall, thick-set man with a commander's insignia on his collar spent a long time checking crates, which were piled near the barracks, against a list. Everything had to be ready before the next group came.

The construction boss flicked the lights in the barracks on and off, and tested the water spigots. The dredger dug a final hole and, with the bulldozer, shoved all the debris from the building operation into it. Then the soldiers drove both machines to the water's edge and the cranes lifted them aboard the lighter. The soldiers themselves boarded an armoured carrier and the whole flotilla sailed away.

On the island there remained only a corporal with an automatic pistol, and a grey-haired civilian with sharp features and hollow cheeks. The corporal strolled around the tarpaulin-covered colossus. There seemed to be no one around who might be dangerous. He went down to the beach and flipped a stone over with his toe; a small crab sprang out.

Then the corporal took his evening meal with the civilian. The civilian asked the corporal's name, the corporal told him. The civilian asked where the corporal came from; again; the corporal told him. The civilian asked whether the corporal knew what he was guarding; the corporal said he didn't know and wasn't interested.

After sunset the civilian strolled around for a while, then crossed the island and sat down on the sand near a dense, overgrown bamboo thicket. The sky was now filled with vivid blue and green patches, the colours mingling and never still; on the horizon there was an even brighter band of colour, but above the island itself if was already dark. In the northwest a storm was raging over the sea: lightning tore through clearly-defined areas of rain; behind the rain a gigantic blue cloud suddenly appeared, rising to cover a third of the sky and perhaps signalling a typhoon. In the south a chain of clouds, crimson below, violet above, filled the air down to the surface of the water.

Strange, that only one man should be witness to such an extraordinary, immense, almost overpowering spectacle of light, colour and darkness! And it was to be seen only here in this one chosen spot in the universe, only once in the endless eternity of time!

The civilian pulled a notebook from his pocket, thought for a while, and began to write. 'Dear Miriam, I'm tired. I've been sleeping poorly these days, dozing for ten minutes, then waking with my mind full of what I had been thinking of when I went to sleep. I carry on an endless dialogue with myself, as though my consciousness were split in two and the halves couldn't agree. It's painful. Victory for one side would mean defeat for the other, but I am the other, too. So defeat is inevitable, either way.

'Let me take events in order. The general has now joined the group (not any general, but the one I was counting on). For a long time he was off somewhere, but everybody was so aware of his absence that it became a kind of presence. I waited for him as I would for a missing element in the periodic table, and now he's here. He hasn't aged since our last meeting, but he looks weathered, harder, and plays the part of the old warrior who still has more courage and energy than ten younger men. He didn't recognize me, but I'm not surprised at that. People of his type remember only the people on whom their promotion depends; his promotion didn't depend on me when we first met. In any case, he's here. I should, of course, be glad of it, but I feel nothing.

'Why? It's a long story. A man lives and works and accomplishes something important (as I did from 1943 to 1945). He has a family: they need him and he needs them. But time passes and the situation slowly changes. He stops serving the cause that he still accepts intellectually. Then destiny begins to play with him. He finds that his wife is a stranger and wants no part of him. Even worse: his children are choosing the wrong path. The path had once been the right one, when he himself had deliberately travelled it. Now it leads to destruction, and the children will travel it to the end. Then the man is brought up short: who is responsible for all this? He finds them and wants to bring them to judgement.

'All that is a first stage. Now the second. He's involved in a great undertaking which he regards as reasonable and necessary. Men, materials and the necessary documents are gathered, and the avalanche he started rolls on by its own power. Then a moment comes when he begins to see that the whole business is false and unreal. But now he's no longer master of what he started. The enterprise runs its course, even after he has realized how senseless it is.

'You don't understand what I'm talking about, dear Miriam? I realize that. Moreover, I'm convinced that my sons do not want me to avenge them: revenge changes nothing, for it doesn't change the causes of further crimes. My sons look for something else: deeds. Of course—but I have no strength left. I'm building a house that's already condemned; and the most terrible moment for me will be when the last beam is in place, when I have no further goal in life and am filled with dull, anguished emptiness. Of course, you don't understand. But even if you did, it would make no difference.

'All this has come to me fairly late. The tragedy of life is that you become aware of a good many things when it's too late to change them.'

The pen ran across the page. The corridors of the War Office, the countless 'secret', 'strictly classified' and 'top secret' council sessions, the private conversations, the semi-official meetings with 'important people', the official meetings with unimportant people, and, most of all, the things the civilian had busied himself with in these last years— it all flowed out into hasty lines on the paper.

'Now everything is ready and the commission arrives tomorrow. Everything is so top secret that we're not even allowed to use each other's name. No single individual is master of the whole project, and if we were all suddenly swallowed up by an earthquake, no one could ever figure out completely what had been going on.

'I wonder how the commission members would feel it they knew what awaited them here?'

The grey-haired civilian folded the pages neatly together and stuck them in his pocket. He couldn't send them anywhere. Miriam didn't exist. He had written down his thoughts simply in order to come to grips with what was going on inside him. For some time now he had believed that nothing in his life was as important as that.

He smoked, gazing upward. The sky was now dark, but not black. The darkness was not a solid wall, but transparent and yielding, and drew the onlooker's eyes into the distance.

The civilian got up, went to the barracks, undressed in the room assigned to him, and took fins and diving gear from his suitcase. He wanted to see what the currents were like on the southern shore of the island.

He returned to the beach. The wind had died down and there were few waves now. He could hear the sea splashing on the distant reef and smell the strong night scent of the flowers. He went down into the water: it was bitter cold at first but his body soon adapted to it. He put on his diving mask and opened the valve on the oxygen tank.

A few more steps and he ducked his head under the water. Darkness closed about him: a living, transparent darkness, broken here and there by points of light which were constellations and galaxies of luminescent living things. The swimmer turned on his lamp; something iridescent flamed up near him and he shrank back. Then he had to laugh under his mask: it was only a sardine, dull grey on land and in the shop window, but gleaming and sparkling here in its natural element. A second and third visitor were drawn by the light, and soon they were all whirling about him like festive fireworks, now blue, now green or brilliant red.

Gradually the swimmer could distinguish swaying tendrils of solid matter. Long red worms came, then other fish, and soon the water around him was teeming with life. He drew aside and turned the golden beam of light downward to the uneven bottom. The sand moved under his feet, molluscs sat in their funnels and drew in oxygen, and two round mysterious eyes suddenly gazed at him from a small hole. He forgot for a moment why he was on the island.

The next morning the cutter returned with the commission members and the gunners.

## 2

'Interesting', remarked the general. He left the trench wall and smilingly brushed the damp sand from his uniform. 'If this sort of thing goes much further, we soldiers will be out of a job, won't we?'

The colonel with the jutting jaw looked him in the eye and laughed loudly: 'Probably before we even reach retirement age. Too bad!'

Everybody in the trench began to move. Men brushed sand from their equipment and straightened their uniforms. The fat major took off his cap and wiped his perspiring neck and forehead. Then he asked the inventor: 'How does the tank actually work? What's the main principle of the thing?'

The inventor looked at the major and began to answer, but the captain, who was ashamed of the slow-thinking major, broke in: 'Oh, that's been explained clearly enough. The principle behind it, if I understand it correctly, is that the real battle takes place in the mind before it breaks out in action. If one of us wants to destroy a tank, he thinks about it first, doesn't he? Let's suppose I'm a gunner sitting at my weapon like the corporal there. Before I shoot, I have to aim the gun; only then can I fire it. At this moment my brain sends out a special E-wave or "action wave". The instrument panel in the tank reacts to this wave, opens the necessary relays, and gives the tank the order to move.'

'Maybe so', insisted the major, 'but then why doesn't the tank move in reaction to any thought whatever? For example, I'm thinking right now that it would be good if the tank took a direct hit on the turret. There's my thought; but the tank doesn't move! Yet they tell us that all of us, the whole island, will be within the machine's range of action.'

The inventor shrugged almost imperceptibly. 'In that case the tank would be constantly receiving orders and constantly moving. I told you, however, that the mechanism reacts only to E-waves, not to normal alpha rhythms. The E-waves arises in the brain only at the moment when we are passing into action. In more scientific terms, the machine reacts to the charge which arises in the brain once the conditional stimulus is received and continues until the unconditional stimulus is formed.'

'What the devil! I still don't understand', interrupted the colonel with the jutting jaw. 'Why does the tank leave the exact spot the shell will hit? After all, I may think of the shell hitting one spot, but it may actually hit another. So, what serves as signal for the mechanism in the tank: the actual flight of the shell or my wish?'

'The tank has a computer for that', the inventor answered. 'Before the gunner beings to fire, he reads the necessary information off his instruments: distance to target, speed of the target, direction. He reads it, it remains for a moment in his head, then he transmits it to the computer of his gun. But my mechanism in the tank also receives all these figures, determines the trajectory of the shell, and moves accordingly from the spot where it would be destroyed.'

The general cleared his throat. He felt the conversation had been going on too long with no word from him. 'But I still don't think it's the perfect weapon yet.'

'When the perfect weapon is invented', said the inventor coldly, 'no one will need the professional soldier's opinion of it.'

There was silence for a moment, then the colonel laughed. 'It looks as though we're reaching that point!' He looked at his superior: 'What do you think, General? Machines will do everything. We'll simply draw our pay.'

The general smiled and nodded. Then his face grew serious. 'Well, let's get on with it. Major, give the order to fire.'

He spoke in a formal tone, but with the throaty hoarseness of the supreme commander and father of his troops. As he did, he reflected that no machine could reproduce these fine distinctions with such precision.

The tests went on. The target, a tank with reinforced armour and a short-barrelled gun, stood still until a shot was fired. But the flame of the shot had hardly appeared at the trench when the tank's treads were moving, the tank sped aside, the shell exploded, shrapnel rattled like peas against the armour, and the target was motionless again like a gigantic grey rock. At the general's order the gunners began to fire two guns simultaneously at the tank. Clouds of dust mushroomed up and the tank disappeared into them, but when dust and sand had settled, the tank was still unharmed and waiting calmly and indifferently for the next shots.

By 2:00 p.m., everyone was weary from the heat and the cramped quarters of the dugout.

'Splendid!', said the general. 'So much for defence. What about attack? Command the tank to shoot at the dugout.'

'Of course', answered the civilian. 'Just a moment.'

He was the only non-soldier there, set apart by his rumpled street-clothes and unsuitably coloured shirt as well as by polite verbal flourishes like 'gladly', 'immediately' and so on. He went over to an instrument that resembled a small radio set, lifted the cover, looked in, and touched a knob.

'But I can't give the order to shoot. The tank wastes no shots and does not fire as long as people are unafraid. It goes into action when it receives a signal of fear. That signal is its guide. Shall I switch on?'

He looked at the general with a gleam in his blue eyes.

'Yes, switch on', said the general. He looked at his watch. 'Let the tank fire for a while, then we'll break for lunch.'

The inventor turned the knob. The instrument squeaked and then was quiet again.

'Ready.'

Everyone looked at the tank. There was no sound from it.

'Something wrong?', asked the colonel with the jutting jaw.

The inventor spun around to him. 'Not at all. Nothing is wrong. The tank needs a signal. It doesn't shoot now because to shoot would be pointless. It never wastes ammunition as even your expert gunners do. The soldiers are under cover and the shells wouldn't reach them. If the tank is to destroy them, they must feel unprotected and become frightened. In short, E-waves are necessary again, but this time they signal fear. As soon as anyone becomes afraid of the tank, it opens fire. The principle here, if I may so put it, is that the victim must summon the executioner.'

The major sighed. 'Perhaps we ought to eat lunch first?' He was the heaviest man there and suffered more than the others from hunger.

'Good', agreed the general. 'First, lunch; then more tests. We've got something to think about here.'

It was a good distance to the barracks with the double roof. The members of the commission were strung out along the path, with the inventor, the general and the colonel bringing up the rear.

'By the way', said the general, as the inventor stopped to tie his shoelace, 'you've turned off the tank, haven't you?'

'It can't be turned off; there's no mechanism for that.'

'Why not?', asked the colonel with the jutting jaw.

'Simple: I didn't think of it.'

'Then when does it stop operating?'

'Never. It's a self-loading machine and is powered by the rays of the sun. If it runs out of ammunition, it crushes the enemy with its treads. But it has a good deal of ammunition.'

'Pleasant thought', said the general. 'And how do we take the tank away from here if it keeps on firing? How do we get near it?'

'We don't take it away', said the inventor, who was still tying his shoelace. 'It will destroy us all.'

The two officers looked down at him and said nothing.

'Come, colonel', said the general at last.

They went a few steps ahead. The general shrugged and said: 'Damned if I can understand these civilians. "It will destroy us all" A learned fool's remark? Too bad; but we can't get along without them at the moment.'

'It is too bad', sighed the colonel.

### 3

They drank fruit juice provided by the general's orderly and chatted about golf and the weather. The general defended tennis. Despite his fifty-two years he had an excellent digestion and first-rate health. In almost every situation, even during highly important sessions at the War Office, he was aware of his rugged, taut body with its constant eagerness for movement and nourishment.

They drank potato soup and chatted about mountain climbing. The general lamented the fact that today's young officers had so little interest in the noble sport of horseback riding. Even now as he was speaking, he was continuously aware of his body. He remembered how three months earlier he had occasionally suffered from lumbago:

at his doctor's suggestion he had added some exercises to his morning workout and the pains had disappeared.

They ate the main course and reminisced about how they had been boarded and lodged on various long-distance journeys, service trips and campaigns. The general told how difficult it had been for a while to get supplies in the Congo; a quite different situation from Vietnam. He was the only man present who had taken part in military operations in both countries, and, though war was being considered primarily from a gastronomic viewpoint, everyone listened attentively to him.

The inventor took no part in the conversation during the meal but sat there making bread pellets on the table cloth. When the commission members had finished their coffee and were beginning to smoke, he took a spoon and tapped it against his cup.

Everyone turned to him.

'I ask your attention for a moment.' He leaned forward. 'I'd like to tell you that along with the tests on the self-defending tank, I've determined to conduct another little test. I intend to study the reactions of men who are certainly doomed to death. But I also want to tell you briefly why I've undertaken this modest bit of research. The point is that all of you here are soldiers and, if I may so put it, professional dealers in death. You, General, for example, worked out the plans for Operation Murder and Operation Noose in that "banana republic" down there (as you call it), and similar operations as well. Incidentally, my second son fell in the part of the world where we now are.'

'You have my sympathy', said the general.

The civilian made a gesture of refusal.

'No, thank you. You plan wars, but they involve you only indirectly, don't they? On maps, in plans, orders, cost estimates: so many missing in action, so many wounded, so many killed. In short, it's all quite abstract. So I've made it my business to make you feel what it's like to lie in a trench with a bullet in your belly or to feel burning napalm on your back. It will complete your education and allow you, at least this once, to carry a task through to its logical conclusion.'

He stood up and shoved his chair back.

'Remember that the tank is not turned off. Try not to be afraid. Keep in mind that the tank reacts to E-waves of fear.'

He quickly left the dining room.

The telephone rang. The curly-crested, blond captain, lowest ranking officer present, automatically lifted the receiver.

'The captain here.'

Everyone could hear the gunnery sergeant's voice quite clearly. 'Can we leave now, sir? We're ready to leave, but is that thing turned off?'

'You can leave', said the Captain. 'Eat your lunch and be back in position in half an hour.'

He hung up the receiver and stared at it. Then his lips began to move, fright filled his eyes, and he seized the receiver again.

'Sergeant! Who's there?' He spoke so loudly that the veins in his neck swelled. 'Hello, Sergeant!'

He let the receiver drop and looked in confusion at the others.

'Perhaps you'd better not go outside, under the circumstances.' But he himself sprang up and hurried out of the barracks. The others also stood up.

The sun bathed the island in a glowing white light. It was as though everything were afloat in a veil of mist that was tinted blue by reflection from the ocean. Two figures emerged from the dugout and started across the sand. 'Sergeant! Danger!', shouted the captain. He waved in the vain hope that the gunners might take the signal as an order to return to the dugout.

'Just a moment!', said the colonel. His jaw dropped: 'What about us?'

The general, napkin still in hand, looked at him in terror. He grew pale, and his pallor communicated itself to the others. Suddenly the colonel sprang from his place and with unbelievable quickness threw himself under a bamboo bush.

In the next instant there was a sharp whistle. A flash of flame, the crack of a shot and the thunder of an explosion all merged together. The bitter smell of powder hung in the air: the signal of war, suffering and misfortune.

## 4

The colonel had been wounded by shrapnel. He now crouched, curled up, in the trench and listened to the drone of the nearby tank. He shivered and swallowed. Tears ran down his thin face with its manly chin. They were not tears of pain: both wounds were slight and had quickly stopped bleeding. They were tears of grief and raging hatred. At the age of forty he had never in his life done anything despicable; he had always obeyed his superiors' orders and never even thought of introducing any novelty of his own into the world. From his point of view he was perfect: yet suddenly his superiors had turned him into a victim. The tank that was meant to kill others was hunting for him.

He shook with bitter grief. As the first of the commission members to reach the entrance to the barracks, he had become aware of the situation and rushed blindly, like an animal, into the bamboo thicket. Behind him he had heard the explosions and heard two shells strike among the gunners who obviously had taken fright. From the thicket he had seen how a single shell knocked the cutter to pieces at the shore and sank it along with the boatmen who, at the first disturbance, had quickly started the motors.

Then the tank began to hunt for him.

Leaping from trench to trench, the colonel moved steadily forward and several times avoided a direct hit. Then he saw that he must reach the blind angle of the tank, where it could not hit him. He manoeuvred closer to it and leaped into a trench. The tank was now about thirty yards away and had stopped firing.

The colonel knew that the only reason the tank was holding its fire was that it could not hit him. Here, precisely, was the demonic power of the machine: the victim must summon his executioner. He chewed his lip and then peered over the breastworks. The tank was standing nearby, peaceful and indifferent. The hatch for the crew was welded shut and the usual searchlights on either side under the turret were missing. This lifeless creature did not need them in order to see before it; it was directed by the anxious thoughts of those it hunted.

The tank waited, squat and grey.

The colonel swallowed several times. He was comparatively safe here, and he reflected, spitefully, that he alone had thought of running toward the tank instead of away from it. Then it came to him, sluggishly, that the others hadn't been in a position to realize where they should flee to. The first shell had bowled them over.

He looked toward the ruined barracks, then back to the tank; he suddenly became aware of its treads. The inventor had said, hadn't he, that the tank could use these too for destruction?

Immediately the tank roared into action, obediently moving its treads and surging forward. The colonel sank to the bottom of the trench. The tank came screeching up, the treads appeared over the breastworks, descended—and rested on the opposite edge of the trench. The bottom of the tank was directly over the colonel's head. He curled up, to make himself as small as possible, and then thought, with a sense of relief: it can't catch me. Immediately the motor switched off.

Supposing the tank were to turn? the colonel asked himself.

The motor roared again, the treads moved, and the tank began to turn above the trench in an effort to reach him. But the walls of the trench were shored up with heavy beams and the relieved colonel told himself the manoeuvre wouldn't work. The thought was still in his mind when the motor shut off again and the tank stood motionless.

Damn! The colonel ground his teeth.

All was still, as if the whole island had died. He touched his shoulder; the bleeding had stopped and the wound wasn't even painful. But the heat was getting worse. The air was close, sweat was running down his brow, and his back was soaking wet. He lay there and saw how the sky was changing colour and becoming strangely overcast: bluer and a bit reddish.

The colonel tried to think, as uncontrollable sobs racked him from time to time. Here he lay. How long would that last? After a while, the party's absence would surely rouse concern back at the supply point from which they had sailed. But not very soon. The whole operation was so secret that no one knew exactly where they were and when they should be returning. The commission was not under the command of the supply base officer. He would first have to get in touch with the War Office back in the capital, initiate a discussion, seek out the proper authorities, send cables; and then, perhaps two weeks from now, other cutters would arrive at the island. Two weeks. He could not last two days without food and water.

And even if he did hold out, what then? If help came and men landed and searched the island, they were safe as long as they did not know what was up and begin to fear the tank. But if someone came near him, he, the colonel, would call out that the tank had him pinned down in the trench. That someone would immediately grow fearful and the tank would open fire and kill the whole landing party.

But he could handle it differently: say nothing of the tank and have a radio transmitter brought to him in the trench. Then he could establish contact with the supply base and explain the situation. But the landing party would surely sense that something was wrong: they would leave him there and beat a retreat.

No. No escape that way—especially since he wouldn't be alive when the cutter arrived.

Once again, his hatred of the general flared up. It was surely all up with him already, and he deserved it. How could anyone be such a fool?

The colonel stared at the belly of the tank. *If only I had a handgrenade!* — The tank came suddenly alive, as the motor switched on.—But he had no handgrenade.—The motor shut off.

*Suppose I crawl out of the trench behind the tank and climb on to the turret.* He got up on all fours and raised his head cautiously. *If only the tank doesn't move off now and turn around!*

Immediately the motor roared, and the tank rumbled off and turned around to face the trench. The colonel groaned and sat down again. No escape! He looked up. Suppose the tank now moved further off and shot at him from a sufficient distance? The trench wouldn't save him then. He thought this, and immediately another thought came: he shouldn't let such thoughts in! The tank would shudder, its motor would roar, and it would roll off in reverse. That was the terrible thing about it: the tank did exactly what you feared and didn't want.

Pressing a hand to his shoulder, he sprang up. He knew he couldn't stay here it he wanted to live any longer. As soon as he would see the tank in a position to fire at him, he would be terrified at the thought and the tank would indeed fire.

The tank moved more quickly, and the colonel hurried after it. The years of comfortable living would now exact their toll. The tank moved faster and faster, because the colonel was afraid it would.

\* \* \* \* \*

The fat major and the general's orderly were blown to pieces by the first shell.

The captain, all of twenty-nine years old, was severely wounded. But he had felt no fear and this protected him from further fire. He lay bleeding in the sand, pinned beneath the collapsed roof of the barracks, and thought only of his wife and two daughters. With a clarity of mind that surprised him he calculated how much of a pension his family would receive; this involved his years of duty, his rank, his branch of service and even the circumstances of his death (whether fallen in battle or not). The pension would be large enough, and the thought left him peaceful. Then it struck him what a good thing it was that this exercise had miscarried. If such a weapon came into use, even his own daughters would not be spared.

Better I than they, he thought with relief, and in his last faint glimmerings of consciousness he told himself that back at the beginning he would never have chosen such an end to his life.

Rainbow-coloured circles moved before his eyes, his brain reeled under the lack of oxygen, and the captain slept forever.

The general died slowly. His first feeling after the shell blast was of pain. He didn't know where he was wounded, for the pain bathed his whole body. Like the colonel, he felt sharply the injustice of what had happened. He didn't belong to the type of people who could and must be killed!

Then the pain abated and was replaced by weakness and an upsetting disquiet. It became ever stronger, and the general even tried to raise his head a bit to order it stopped.

He raised his head—and saw the inventor crouching near him. The man's face was as calm and indifferent as ever. He extended his arm and laid something on the general's chest.

'That's the medal for outstanding service that was posthumously conferred on my son in 1965. You gave it to me yourself.'

The medal felt as heavy as a mountain on the general's chest. He didn't understand the inventor's words, but only felt that the end was near, for his disquiet was growing by the second and had become almost unbearable. He had never been wounded in his life, had never had to have an operation. He didn't know that the same anxiety and suffering had marked the passing of those thousands of men whose death he had planned and that in his most recent project millions of people were schedule for the same experience.

The inventor watched the dying general for a while, then rose and searched the rubble of the barracks for his suitcase. He took his fins and walked slowly to the shore. The tank droned in the distance: he did not turn around, for his own life was a matter of indifference to him. Within himself he felt only a terrible emptiness—the kind of emptiness a man can feel only when he has done everything in life that he wanted to.

\*    \*    \*    \*    \*

The colonel was chasing the tank. The tank increased its speed, and now the colonel realized it was all up: he was winded, his lungs were on fire, his heart was racing so madly that the tremors shook his whole body. He staggered ten yards further, then stopped, exhausted.

The tank also stopped. It was like a miracle.

Immediately the desire to live flamed up again in the colonel's consciousness and gave him new strength. He reeled forward a bit, then stopped again, for he realized that here where there was no cover, the tank could crush him with its treads. He groaned in despair, tried to dispel the thought, to force it from his brain. He shook his head, squeezed his eyes closed, and heard the motor of the steel colossus roar once more.

\*    \*    \*    \*    \*

The inventor swam with even strokes, intending to reach the next island. He gave no thought to what might happen after that. His mind was still filled with the endless arguments in smoke-filled workrooms, the opinions of every possible authority, directions, cost estimates, plans. In his ears he could still hear shell bursts and the groans of the dying. But gradually all that receded.

Murmuring billows flowed over him. He lowered his head and saw stripes of sunlight, moving with the movement of the swell that was bright at the surface but darker down below. Schools of mackerel passed effortlessly beneath him, turned suddenly as if on command, and disappeared into the pearl-green glimmer that suffused the upper reaches of the water.

Pompous and slow, jellyfish swam by like brightly coloured parasols adorned with old-fashioned fringes. Then a stream, like a strange silver ribbon with all its parts moving simultaneously, suddenly showed amid the water. The swimmer drew near and stopped. The stream was made up of a vast number of some kind of large fish which he didn't recognize. There were thousands, perhaps hundreds of thousands of them. They appeared out of the blue darkness, gleaming and twinkling with unusual purples and reds, numberless, silent, in dense swarms, turned at the identical spot, and disappeared again into the bottomless depths.

How many thousands of miles lay behind them? Perhaps they had come from the forested shores of Africa or perhaps from amid the weeds of the Sargasso Sea and through the old pirate waters past the Antilles, Haiti and Puerto Rico? Where were they heading now, and why had they chosen just this spot in the ocean as their turning point? Why were they so beautiful in the immensity of their luminescent train?

The inventor was reminded that his own children were dead; but there were other children. Eager eyes would feast on the marvels of ocean, forests and cities. Perhaps there was something worth living for after all?

Suddenly he wondered whether he had swum far enough away

from the island. Could his own tank still reach him with a shell? The inventor raised his head above the water, and instantaneously a penetrating whistle rent the air.


## 5


At night, ants and crabs went to work on the corpses. They disappeared when the day grew hot, but the next night they were back, working so swiftly that on the second morning only white bones were left on the sand. A typhoon began to blow and reached full strength on the third day after the destruction of the commission. The first blasts of wind whipped away the remnants of the barracks; the builders had erected them in the open, not in a hollow as the Indians did their huts. The palms were bent double; the frenzied storm levelled the dunes. Then the storm shifted to the shore of the mainland; the palms straightened up once more and, of all that the soldiers had brought, only the tank was left, half covered with sand.

The villagers returned. The children climbed over the strange colossus until they grew tired of the sport. Inside the tank the hidden mechanical brain waited to be awakened again by the impulses of hate and fear.

translated by MATTHEW J. O'CONNELL

# Sisyphus, the Son of Aeolus
## VSEVOLOD IVANOV

The soldier recognized his native mountains the moment he caught sight of them.

In the midday light they were a gloomy, brimstone grey, cut here and there by deep, orange-coloured ravines. From where he was standing, he could even see the Sciron red running along the steep southern face of the mountain range. It was curved at one end like a shepherd's crook—at least that's what it had looked like to Polyander the soldier when he was a boy, and that's what it still looked like to him. The Sciron was a road with a terrible reputation, people travelling on it were always coming across pools of blood and other omens of impending trouble.

More trouble was the last thing Polyander wanted. Worn out prematurely, his complexion yellowish and wasted, he'd had his fill of trouble.

He had sworn an oath to serve King Alexander of Macedon—more commonly known at Alexander the Great—and he had served him. And then he had served King Cassander, a cruel, brutal, ambitious man who seized power and soon as Alexander was dead, imprisoning the widow and son of the conqueror to whom the gods and arms of the whole world had paid homage. Despite this Polyander had loyally turned his silver-studded shield against Cassander's enemies. What a fool he was! He'd wanted to win Cassander's favour. They say faith can move mountains. As things turned out, though, even the biggest mountain would have been easier to move than Cassander. Of all his men Cassander most distrusted Polyander—he was terrified by the mighty shield, the ruddy, muscular neck, the powerful voice so admired by the other soldiers. When Polyander was barely forty years old, Cassander declared him a supernumerary, unfit for further service in the light infantry, and sent him home without pension or mustering-out pay.

And now the mountains stood before him—and behind them his home, the prosperous city of Corinth. The soldier gazed up at the mountains, wondering how his native city would greet him and which of his relatives he would find alive. It was years since he'd been home. He'd been young and strong then, but now his wounds and battle scars were considered a liability and he'd been discharged from King Cassander's army—now all his strength was gone.

'For whom are my wounds a liability? By the gods, for you, my king, I swear it. One day little Alexander will grow up to be as warlike as his father, and you're afraid of that, aren't you? Veterans like me are just what he'll need. All you can think about, my king, is keeping Alexander the Great's conquests for yourself, but you'll never be able to keep his son down, Cassander.'

While muttering to himself like this he was keeping a wary eye on the Sciron road. He really didn't want to climb it. He'd had enough trouble as a soldier. He'd had enough of omens. All he wanted now was to lead the peaceful life of a solid citizen—the life of a cloth-dryer, for instance.

Suddenly, from the old days, he remembered a short-cut to Corinth: a side path, more difficult walking, perhaps, but at least there weren't any omens and portents of doom along the way.

'Hey, you!'

Some peasants from a nearby village, working in a field beside the road, were watching him respectfully. Because of the heat he had taken off his armour, but his chest was so broad that it looked as if he were still wearing it. His arms were spread wide, for he was accustomed to carrying a shield and spear and to wearing armour that was a little too big for him, so much so that he had even got into the habit of sleeping flat on his back with his mouth hanging open. His eyes, like those of all seasoned travellers, had a quizzical expression: they were greenish, about the same shade as mowed grass about to turn into hay—dry and mature, but retaining something of the colour and aroma of youth.

He stood there like a statue, posed majestically as befitted a soldier of Alexander the Great, who had marched with his king from the borders of Thrace to icy Lake Mesta, where it is always winter; to the Caucasus Mountains, the end of the world, where the Kingdom of Darkness begins; to Memphis, Damascus, Suez and Ectabana and the rockbound hill fortresses of Persia; and to the banks of the Hydaspes and the Indus marshes, where he had held his ground against the narrow-eyed, strong-tusked fighting elephants of King Porus of India.

Wishing the peasants a good harvest, and expressing his hope that Zeus and Athene would help them, he asked for a drink. An alert-looking fourteen-year-old girl, with thick, badly cut brown hair, brought him a pitcher of warm water. There was a smell of grain in the air from the nearby threshing floor. A mule, puffing quietly, stood twitching his tail. A well-fed village girl, whose round, full thighs were a testimonial to the nearness of the rich commercial city of Corinth, bent over and resumed her work, quickly and skilfully separating the full, shiny ears of grain and putting them into baskets. Another girl was stacking the baskets, notched sides southwards, on the deep-violet beaten-earth threshing floor. A light dust rose above them, kicked up by some approaching pack mules and a couple of heavy, solid-wheeled threshing carts pulled by oxen.

Returning the pitcher, Polyander spoke again:

'By the gods, the girls of Corinth are as hospitable and good-looking as ever. The artists are right to show them off so often on vases, in bronze and on columns adorned with acanthus leaves.'

The peasants smiled at this; the girl who had given him the water, struck dumb with amazement, began to suck her thumb.

'I want to get to Corinth as quickly as possible', he told them. 'I've had enough of fame and fortune—now it's the peaceful life for me. I have some genuine purple dye—it comes from shellfish. I saw them myself from a boat, I swear it by the gods, and the Phoenicians themselves taught me how to dye fabrics purple. I learned from the best dye-masters of Tyre, Cos and Byzantium.'

He showed them his sinewy fingers, the long hairs of which were dyed the colour of blood. The villagers shuddered and backed away in fright, while an old man with a thick, bulbous nose spoke to him:

'You asked about the Sciron road. There it is in front of you.'

'Is it safe?', asked Polyander.

'Safer than a lot of other roads.'

'In my time', the soldier spoke reticently, 'strong walkers in a hurry used a short-cut. They turned off onto a side path called the Alma. Mules and oxen couldn't manage it, but my feet still remember the way.'

The peasants glanced at each other. The soldier read the fear in their faces.

'Has there been a rockslide?', he asked. 'Has some new cliff been discovered since my time, or have the gods blocked off the path with a waterfall?'

His question was answered by the old man with the big nose.

'It's a bad place.'

'Robbers?', asked the soldier with a laugh, showing the peasants his short throwing spear and his long, narrow sword with its silver-studded ivory hilt. 'Ha! Are there many of them? Ha-ha!'

The old man scratched himself between his shoulders with a hooked staff and somewhat reluctantly spoke again:

'It's a bad place. Take the Sciron road—it's been years since anyone has used the Alma path.'

'Where are there more omens?', the soldier asked with an air of determination.

'On the Sciron.'

'Then what am I supposed to be afraid of?'

'The son of Aeolus', the old man answered, looking around nervously.

The soldier began to laugh.

'The son of Aeolus? The son of the god of the winds? What is he? A breeze?'

'You'll see', the old man answered, walking away. The other peasants, afraid to listen in on a conversation about such a dangerous subject, had already deserted the two men.

Purposely laughing out loud again, Polyander picked up his helmet with its split horsehair plumes and his battered cuirass and backplate, which were joined together by dented metal shoulder-pieces. He noted sadly that moths had eaten away the felt lining. 'But I can still get a good price for my armour in Corinth. I'll fix it up with a nice piece of Greek felt; it won't be too hard to manage, although the truth is that Greek felt isn't worth a damn and all the thick, beautiful Persian felt is gone. What if the moths are an omen?'

Grumbling, he hoisted his sun-warmed harness and weapons onto his shoulders, and taking big strides, as if he were eager to come face to face with the danger, he headed for the Alma path.

As he walked along, his feet comfortably clad in cork-soled leather sandals, the clanking of his weapons and armour reminded him of marches and friends from the past, all long since swallowed up by time as completely as a drowned sailor by the bottomless sea.

Leaving the village behind, he came upon a dried-up stream hidden by some shrubbery. A few scrawny goats, standing on their hind legs, were nibbling the leaves. The stream bed was strewn with dark greyish-blue stones. Hanging motionlessly just overhead, a barely perceptible mist exuded an evil, deathlike gloom. Some sand, streaming down the steep banks of the stream, made a sound something like someone using a knife to shave the bark off a tree. The soldier began to feel uneasy. He stood watching the goats for a while; before very long he started to get hungry.

He took a flat piece of bread from his knapsack. Nibbling at it with his front teeth the way goats do, both to prolong the pleasure and to give himself time to think things over, he shifted his gaze across the bare, stony ground to the place where he should have been. 'Why didn't I take the Sciron road?', he asked himself. 'Maybe I should turn back. But as a soldier how can I, especially after bragging about storming the hill fortresses of Persia? It would be dishonourable for a soldier of Alexander the Great to do such a thing!'

He began reminiscing about the Alma path, which he had first climbed some thirty years before—maybe even more. His uncle, then young and powerful, had carried him on his shoulders. Uncle's long, thick hair had smelled of butter, his tunic had been wet, and the young boy had leaned carefully on his sloping shoulders. Every once in a while Uncle would turn around, glaring at the child with mock seriousness, then shoving him a flat chunk of bread that smelled of smoke and olive oil. In those days you never heard a bad word about the Alma path, much less about the merciless son of Aeolus.

'Why merciless? Since when? By the gods, who stuck him with a tag like that—it's such a damned painful word, it makes you sit up and pay attention, like a tight collar on a dog!'

He stopped, rested his equipment on a rock, and looked downward in annoyance.

He had already come quite a distance along the Alma, he realized, recognizing the path even though it was now so overgrown with thickets that it required intense concentration to keep on the trail.

Far below the villages merged with the olive trees and vineyards and the whole valley took on the colour of rough-hewn stone. He began to feel a strong desire to climb as high as possible. He was alone among the indestructible, eternal stones, and there was an indestructible, eternal silence all around him.

But not inside him! He still felt the same foreboding and was beginning to sense an impending evil that it would be impossible to evade—or to endure.

Like a horse nervously drumming his hoofs, the soldier kicked the ground several times, brushing his foot against the stone on which he had placed his weapons. The sword clanked. He fastened it to his waistband, repacked the rest of his equipment, and put his knapsack on his back.

The walking was easier now, and as he strode along he reflected that impatience, as wise men so truly say, is closely related to rashness. If only he had taken the Sciron road! He would have joined up with some caravan or other and told the merchants how he had dyed garments for all the monarchs of the East. They would have welcomed him eagerly, glad to have the protection of a soldier on their journey, and in the evenings they would have regaled him with big, thick slices of juicy mutton. At night, warmed by the campfire, he would have felt as relaxed as if he'd just spent a day in the marketplace.

But here, even though it was daytime, he felt anxiety, as if the dome of the night sky were hanging overhead. Suddenly remembering the dyestuff, he asked himself a question: 'Are you really such a skilled dyer?' Now that he was so close to Corinth he wasn't sorry he had spent the last of his money on a tiny flask containing three grains of the precious purple powder. He opened the flask and began to tint a bit of cloth torn from the four-cornered cloak slung over his left shoulder. The hair on his arms ended up the colour of blood and the cloak, to his surprise, turned a pumice grey. What the—Wasn't this the tinting compound the dye-masters at Tyre had sold him? Had he paid them so many drachmas for nothing?

In his mind's eye he saw the cellar with the wide, low vats of steaming purple; the glassy-eyed, dissipated-looking master dyers circling around the vats; the two slaves swaying rhythmically at the door, the clay squealing between their toes as they kneaded it with their feet ... Damn it, the Tyrian dyers had cheated him, all right! Down in that dingy little cellar they had succeeded in tricking a man who had been to Cassander's court and to the four corners of the earth.

And here he was on his way to Corinth—Corinth, the cruel city of hucksters and seamen—so near and yet so far away. What awaited him there?

Both to keep his hopes up and to overcome more quickly his unexplainable sense of fear, he speeded up his pace. In the end, it seemed to him, all memory of his journey would be lost in oblivion. Cheered by this thought, he looked upwards and noticed a huge grey rock, tinged violet at its base and shaped like a tree stump. Quickly skirting around it, he found himself in a shady glen overgrown with oak trees. Far below, where the oaks came to an end, there was an open field, and in the stony area below that, a roaring torrent hurtled downward, its green waters churning up an angry white foam. The oaks, the field, the stones, the green waters were all baking in the heat of the sun.

The path finally disappeared, swallowed up by the oaks. The trees were close to each other, offering a dense shade, and as the soldier walked through it he felt as uncomfortable as he would have at the bottom of a constricted, foul-smelling ravine. The roaring of the torrent was relentless and deafening. Overhead, the solid, unmoving oaks stretched upward as far as the eye could see, while the short, dried-up branches on the lower part of their trunks caught at the soldier's cloak, sword, knapsack and water bottle.

Stooped over so that his knapsack began slipping off his shoulder, neither willing nor able to stop long enough to adjust it, the soldier whispered a prayer and ran out of the grove into the field, beyond which still more rocks could be seen.

No longer even trying to find the path, he leaped over the stones in his way, stumbled and fell. Some of the stones tore loose and crashed downward. As soon as the stones came to rest he braced his foot in a hole, but the sides of the hole began to give and he jumped out of it in desperation. His hands and legs were covered with scratches and cuts. Letting his feet do the thinking—the feet that had crossed the Euphrates at Zevgem and endured the march from the Euxine Sea to the farthest boundary of Fergana—he was soon completely lost.

He began sweating profusely, a pungent, burning sweat. He couldn't think. His normally keen powers of observation were gone and he was barely able to see more than ten spear-lengths ahead. The only thing that kept him moving forward was the training he had received as a soldier of Alexander the Great, for he had been taught to advance in all circumstances and against any odds, a virtue that every human being should strive to attain—even the gods envy it.

The sun, admiring the submissiveness of the rocks, the fields, and the oak trees, as well as the soldier's singular nobility of spirit and perseverance, withdrew its deadening, vicious heat, which eats away human strength as persistently as water undermines a wall, leaving soft, moist, violet shadows behind. Refreshed by a drink of water, the soldier took heart. 'By the gods', he exclaimed; 'I'll find that path yet.'

All of a sudden, from just behind the very rock he was about to step past, he heard a sound—a weird, peculiar sound that was completely out of place in the mountains. It was something like the whirring, humming noise of a discus flying through the air—a sound the soldier knew well, for he had been taught discus throwing, not only for the games, but also to build up strength for hurling missiles at the enemy.

He leaned against the rock and listened.

The sound became louder, came closer, and suddenly, with a tremendous crash as if it had smashed through something solid, it stopped completely—disappeared.

A teasing silence enveloped the rocks—a piercing, burning silence that was even more alarming than the sound.

The soldier felt a sudden need to hear his own voice, to shout out loud the way he and all the other soldiers had shouted when they were hauling a siege engine or charging the enemy.

Finally coming to a decision, he circled around to the other side of the rock. There was nothing there but a field, much the same as all the others he had passed. All at once it seemed as if he had been enveloped by a wind. He shuddered, remembering what the old man had said about the son of Aeolus. The very thought thundered around him like a blast from a huge trumpet. He sat down on a stone, gasping hoarsely.

After a while he climbed past still another rock and crossed still another field. His sword drawn, and calling on all the gods, including Aeolus, he made his way up to the rocks at the opposite end of the field and rounded them cautiously, pausing, just before he emerged from the cover they gave him, to sharpen his sword against the side of a stone.

Suddenly the noise began again. Only this time it wasn't anything like the sound of a metal discus hurtling through the air. It was more like the roaring of ocean waves, which begin far out at sea, then break on the beach, and end up playing gently with the pebbles they find there. The noise was coming from somewhere up above him, although the sky seemed as serene as before. Intensifying with such speed and strength that the soldier had to jump out of its way, the noise swept past the rock, then bounced back off some stones like a handle flying off a knife that has been brandished too forcefully.

Polyander was frightened, but having been a soldier he resolved to meet his enemy face to face, deriving a certain amount of comfort from this decision, even though he was staggering from fear and barely able to move his rubbery legs when he began working his way around to the other side of the rock.

There was no field behind this one. Instead, a small valley came into view, and in the valley, moving swiftly away from the mountains, a cheerful little brook with oak and fruit trees growing along its banks. Off in the distance the brook abruptly ran into a river, whose sound was barely audible to him.

Alongside the brook, Polyander noticed, there was a road, shaded by a lane of oak trees. It was like no road he had ever seen before. Its surface was the colour of wet cork, and it was worn into the stony ground like a gutter or an infinitely long, narrow grooved channel, beginning somewhere high in the mountains and ending up far below at the edge of a glen, in a small marsh that looked as if it had been trampled up by the hooves of a gigantic horse.

In among the oaks that lined this grooved channel, the shadows of their branches darkening his broad, muscular back, there appeared a hairy giant with huge, powerful shoulders, an animal hide wrapped around his waist. He was pushing a round black boulder the size of three full-grown men—it was worn smooth and polished as brilliantly as a pebble from the sea. The giant was breathing deeply and his huge, sagging belly, looking something like a wine cask, now rammed against the stone, then pulled itself away from it. His toes dug into the bed of the stream and Polyander noted that they had worn out footholds for themselves.

'By the gods', he said to himself in amazement, 'I've seen a lot of strange things, but I've never seen anything like this before. This giant, whoever he is, shoves that boulder around as easily as a storm at sea tosses a ship.'

Meanwhile, the giant heard Polyander approaching. He turned his huge, red-bearded face towards the soldier and spoke, though clearly it was something of an effort for him to do so.

'Praise the gods, a traveller. G-g-glad! Go into the hut. G-g-glad! See to the fire. Serve the beans. Mix the wine. G-g-glad!' Setting the beat with the word 'glad' each time he braced his foot in one of the depressions his toes had worn into the rocky ground, the giant kept pushing the stone forward.

'Who are you, mighty one?', Polyander asked.

'I'll be back soon', the giant answered, then growled, 'G-g-glad! Behind the hut—the well. Go down into it. On one side—a hole. G-g-glad! In the hole—snow. Mix some with the wine. Oh, I'm g-g-glad.'

He glanced back at Polyander again, and the soldier took this opportunity to study his face. It was old and wrinkled, but possessed that rarely seen confidence that comes from fullness of years and suggests, more than anything, extraordinary strength used skilfully and with patience.

Backing away, Polyander moved towards the hut; the giant kept pushing the stone, which, as if on a pivot, rolled quickly upwards, diminishing in size as it did so and increasing in brilliance, so that it seemed afterwards as if the giant had flung an ingot of burning orange-yellow metal at the bright blue sky.

Inside the hut Polyander found a big pot filled with beans—they were already tender. He rekindled the charred embers in the hearth and put in some firewood. Next he found the well near the hut and went down into it, walking with care on the cold, wet steps.

Slightly above the level of the water he found two recesses in the wall. There were some earthenware jars of wine in the first; the second was solidly packed with compressed snow. Polyander tried to lift the nearest wine jar onto his shoulder, getting it up with some difficulty and in the process tipping it sideways. Soon the whole area began to smell of wine.

'By the gods, I think I'll stick with him for a while', Polyander said to himself.

It was hard work, but he managed to carry the smallest wine jar up to the hut, then went back for the snow. In it he found some wild goat meat wrapped in the leaves of various aromatic herbs. He put the meat into the pot with the beans and mixed the wine with some water, seasoning it a bit with some spices from the precious handful he'd brought back from the East.

He had barely finished preparing the wine when he again heard that terrible noise—the combined whistling and droning that sounded like a metal discus hurled by a giant—only this time it was much closer. Polyander rushed out of the hut. The branches of an over-hanging oak cast quivering shadows across the threshold. Far away, bobbing up and down in a cloud of iridescent dust, a round boulder was rushing downwards in its grooved channel. The massive stone sphere ran to the end of its appointed course and slammed into the marsh, splattering grassygreen mud in all directions.

Shading his eyes with one of his big hands, the giant glanced at the sun, then waddled down the mountain. As he drew near the hut he wiped his hands on the goat skin wrapped around his hips and smiled awkwardly.

'Are you glad, traveller?', he asked in a hoarse bass voice. 'I'm g-g-glad! G-glad. Where you from? Where?'

Polyander felt a tenseness in the air, so he responded cautiously.

'By the gods, isn't this the way to Corinth?'

'To Corinth?', the giant asked with some effort. 'G-g-glad. To Corinth.'

He passed his guest some water and watched as the soldier washed his feet and hands. The giant's broad, square face was furrowed with wrinkles from a life of peasant troubles and hard work, and he appeared to be deep in thought, as if wondering what a Corinth might be. And seeing this, the soldier realized that it might not be as easy as he'd expected to come to a friendly understanding with the giant.

'To Corinth! I'm going to see my family!', the soldier said in a loud voice, as if talking to a deaf man.

'To Corinth? G-glad! Sit down. Eat.'

They ate the beans in silence. Then the host, apparently indifferent to the heat, scooped the goat meat out of the pot with his bare hands and placed it on a board. He salted it liberally and pointed to the wine.

'Salt? G-glad! We'll drink plenty.'

Clasping his stomach with his hands he began laughing. It was clear that talking did not come easy to him and that the words he had just uttered had given him a great deal of pleasure—he was intoxicated by them just as if he had been drinking strong wine.

After they had wiped their hands clean with some rolled-up soft bread, the host pulled himself over to the jar of wine and melted snow. His obvious delight with the aroma of the spices was another sign that he hadn't been in human company for quite a while. Noting this, the soldier finished the meat, greedily crunching the bones with his strong teeth. He was pleased with himself for having brought the giant's long period of solitude to an end, and this gave his spirits a lift.

'By the gods', he said, raising his cup, 'we'll have a good time together!'

From the old days he knew all the best wines—Phasian, Lesbian, Naxian, even the famous Chian—and this was the best he had ever tasted. He was effusive in expressing his delight.

'Glad!', said his host, giving him some more wine from the pitcher. 'G-glad. Drink. G-glad!'

He himself drank little, however. For him it was pleasure enough just to see a human being. The wine soon made the soldier garrulous, and he wanted to tell the giant about all that he had won and lost and squandered in his time.

'Is it really so long since anyone else has passed by here?'

'Long time', his host answered, smiling broadly. 'I'm glad.'

'And have you been here very long?'

'Long time', his host answered. 'Today is the last day—yes, last day!'

'Why the last?', the soldier asked. 'Have you sold your hut, garden, and field? Who bought them? Did you get a good price?'

'Zeus be praised for setting me free', replied the host, his dark-blue eyes shining. 'Glad! The last day.'

'Zeus be praised', the soldier said without much enthusiasm. 'But don't try to tell me it was Zeus who bought your hut and land.'

His host, gesticulating excitedly and trying as hard as he could to make the soldier understand, began to speak more distinctly:

'Zeus put me here. Zeus will set me free.'

'Oh, the priest', said the soldier, lifting his cup to his lips. 'They want to build a temple here. I don't blame them—it's a beautiful spot.'

'Not priests! Zeus', the giant persisted. 'Zeus put me here. Zeus himself.

'Zeus?', the soldier said in a mocking voice. 'Who are you that Zeus should go to the trouble of putting you here?'

'I am Sisyphus, the son of Aeolus.'

A blank expression came over the soldier's face and his wine spilled in a thick stream onto his cold knees.

'By the gods...', he stammered, 'You are... Sisyphus?'

His host responded with an affirmative nod of his shaggy head, taking a sip of wine, and the soldier continued:

'Of course I've heard of Sisyphus, the son of Aeolus the wind god. He was once the king of Corinth, but that was a long time ago—long before Homer even.'

'I'm him', answered the host, speaking with such dignified simplicity that the soldier downed the contents of his cup in one gulp and began to feel as if the heavy oak beams supporting the roof of the hut were swaying before his eyes.

'By the gods, you're him.'

'I'm him—I'm Sisyphus', his host replied, taking another sip of wine. 'Drink!'

But the soldier couldn't drink, and his host had to enter upon a long, obviously rather painful explanation.

'I was a sinner. I committed murder. I robbed. Zeus punished me. He sentenced me to roll that boulder up the mountain forever. When it reaches the top a mysterious force throws it down again. You saw it. And today you saw the last day. I obeyed. Yesterday Zeus came to me. He said, "Last day". G-glad!'

The giant began to laugh.

A frightening thought occurred to the soldier and he began to shiver.

'Tell me, honourable Sisyphus, son of Aeolus. They say you were punished by being taken down to the land of the dead, to the underground kingdom of Hades. Is that where I am now?'

Sisyphus replied: 'In Hades, for untold days, I rolled the stone up the mountain. I obeyed. I didn't anger the gods by complaining. Zeus pardoned me—I didn't even know he had done it—by transferring me from Hades to the world of the sun. That's why I'm so glad to see you, traveller.'

'Since you're able to express yourself so well, Sisyphus, son of Aeolus', the soldier continued, 'tell me what Hades is like.'

'Mire. Rain. Dampness. All the time.'

'By the gods', the soldier exclaimed, 'you'll never be able to thank the gods enough for the sun and this wine!'

'Drink', Sisyphus laughed. 'G-glad!'

'Zeus be praised', the soldier said, lifting his cup, which was filled with the murky red wine. 'How long have you been up here on this mountain!'

'A long time', his host answered. 'Sunrise to sunset, I pushed the stone. I obeyed.'

'And at night you worked in your garden, trapped wild animals, gathered fruit?'

The giant nodded his head, and the soldier continued to enumerate the many hardships he had endured. In the hot weather it was bad enough; in the winter, when the rains came, it was even worse, for the water made everything more difficult...

'Floods', said the giant. 'In my way—a river! Up to the chest. Stone in the water. Slippery. Hands slip off. Wet. I must push against current. But I obeyed the gods. Now Zeus has pardoned me.'

'Zeus be praised for his wisdom', said the soldier. 'Please be so good as to pour me some more wine. It's wonderful wine—I haven't had anything so good since I was in Persia.'

'Were you a prisoner?'

'Me—a prisoner? Do you think those no-good Persian cowards could have captured me?', the soldier asked contemptuously. 'Don't you know that Alexander the Great marched across Persia from one end to the other?'

'I didn't know', Sisyphus answered. 'I was pushing the stone. Who is Alexander?'

'Ye gods', Polyander shouted. 'He doesn't know who Alexander of Macedon is. You mean you don't know about all the battles he won— how he defeated King Darius and crushed the army of King Porus of India, how he married the beautiful Princess Roxana and captured treasures beyond belief?'

'I don't know anything', Sisyphus answered. 'The stone was so heavy I couldn't even turn around.'

'By the gods', the soldier said, 'I'll tell you the whole story from beginning to end, I swear it. Pour me some wine.'

The host filled his cup again and the soldier began talking.

Night fell. The stars gazed down through the overhanging foliage of the oaks. All was still—the branches of the trees, the mountains behind them; from inside the hut it even seemed as if the rippling of the brook had stopped. Sisyphus sat with his arms clasping his knees, his dark-blue eyes lit up by the reddish light from the hearth.

The soldier told him about the great cities of the East—cities built of sun-dried bricks cemented together with the sticky black slime produced by the fertile Babylonian soil. He told about the desert oases with their tall palm trees, and how there are as many uses for the trunks, branches, leaves, sap and fruits of the palms as there are days in the year. He told how they make boats from inflated leather bladders and use them on the deep-flowing rivers; he told about the great man-made dams and canals and the rich gifts the land offered: horses, spices, women. Ah, what places—Persia, Egypt, India...

'And what happened to them?', asked the giant.

'Praise the gods', the soldier replied. 'We crossed the Hellespont, we sacrificed to our ancestor Achilles on the ruins of Ilium, which you've probably already heard of, and we made our way to the river Granicus, where we defeated the Persians. And then we marched across their country from end to end, burning their cities, destroying the dams and canals, chopping down the trees in the oases. We marched along roads lined by palms groves, and we cut down every tree and burned them all. We even went as far as the sweltering tropics, never before visited by a civilized human being.'

Inflamed by his story and by the wine, Polyander spoke with more and more passion. 'There, in that torrid, desolate place, we encountered purple-horned satyrs with cloven hoofs of solid gold, wild, unruly hair, flat noses, and cheeks swollen from over-indulgence in wine, women and song. We killed them. We even killed the sirens—those fiery women who lure men to destruction—we killed them as they sat in their flowery vale, surrounded on all sides by the bones of men who perished out of love for them. We killed the centaurs of India and the pygmies of Ethiopia. With my own sword—you saw it, Sisyphus—I wiped out a whole phalanx of pygmy cavalry. Every spring, mounted on sheep and goats, they go out in battle formation to gather crane eggs ... Ha-ha-ha!'

'I'm g-g-glad!', shouted the giant, lifting his cup and emitting a pained roar that echoed back from the unseen, miserable mountains outside.

The soldier went on with his story.

'We destroyed and burned everything in the name of Achilles and his glorious descendant, Alexander of Macedon. Thanks to us, even Corinth was enriched. Even Cassander, who treated me so shabbily, was enriched. . .'

Now quite drunk, the soldier was shaking with anger. His thoughts began to wander. He studied the giant, who still hadn't moved from his place next to the hearth.

'Sisyphus, son of Aeolus! Aren't you the king of Corinth?'

'I was the king of Corinth', Sisyphus answered.

'And you'll be the king of Corinth again', the soldier exclaimed. 'You'll be the king of all Greece. You'll kill that no-good, money-grubbing, pompous Cassander, and then you'll wear the crown!'

The soldier really meant that young Alexander, the son of Alexander the Great, would become king, but how could he say that? Sisyphus' eyes were sparkling. Clearly he liked the idea, but there was no way of knowing whether he'd let young Alexander ascend the throne on his shoulders. Eager to win Sisyphus over to his scheme, the soldier began shouting:

'Yes, you'll wear the purple and sit on the throne. Don't you . . . don't you see, Sisyphus, the gods have sent me to you?'

'G-g-glad!'

'You'll leave here and come with me, won't you?'

'G-g-glad!'

'We'll plunder, kill, rape—we'll be rich!'

'G-g-glad!', the giant roared. From deep in the ultramarine darkness beyond the oaks the mountains roared back at him.

Sisyphus laughed and laughed and rocked back and forth happily, the light playing now on his huge, powerful shoulders, now on his knees, which were as round as haystacks. Still shouting, the soldier babbled nonsensically: there's nothing more beautiful than a besieged city on fire; to tell the truth, though, storming a city is a horrible experience; Persians and Indians shooting arrows at you from every corner; the best of the booty going up in flames; your eyes smarting in the hot, acrid smoke; the prettiest girls flinging themselves into the fires; no one but old people for prey and killing them is no fun at all—their tough old bones and tendons dull the edge on your sword; and more such nonsense that even he didn't seem to take very seriously. Staring into the reddish flames on the hearth, he remembered his promise to dress Sisyphus in royal purple.

'Those dirty brown goat skins you're wearing, Sisyphus, give them to me.'

'Why?', Sisyphus asked.

'Give them to me and I'll turn them purple.'

He found another pot, filled it with water, which he quickly brought to the boil, and spilled in all his dye powder. Spots of purple began swirling and whirling in the bubbling water. Polyander dipped the shaggy goat's fleece into the mixture, then carefully stretched it between two sticks near the hearth to make sure it wouldn't shrink. Then, admiring his handiwork, he sat back and began mooning about noisy, bustling Corinth; about great banquets in honour of King Sisyphus; about Cassander lying dead at his feet, and he, Polyander, the commander in chief of the royal army, standing side by side with Sisyphus.

'Yes, Sisyphus, fame is just around the corner for both of us', he shouted. 'This lousy valley doesn't mean anything to you. You can't even get a good night's sleep here, you're so busy tilling the garden, weeding, watering, fishing and trapping. From now on you're going to have a featherbed, with beautiful girls to sing lullabies to you, and you can sleep late in the morning—till noon if you want.'

'I'm g-g-glad—to sleep', roared Sisyphus, his strong, even mouth gaping open in a yawn. 'G-g-glad.'

'You—are the king of Greece, and I'm your chief adviser—' Having said this, Polyander lay down on a pallet. From force of habit he slid his cuirass and backplate under his head and covered his feet with his oval shield, placing it so that the hooks and clasps were easily accessible. He put his short Argive sword at his side and, having completed these arrangements, immediately fell asleep.

The soldier was awakened by the sound of fighting. As always at such moments, he felt a cold, trembling fear in his ankles, but as befitted one of Alexander's soldiers, he overcame it at once and jumped up, holding his sword at the ready.

It was quite early and the morning was cold and crisp. The battle noises had come to a stop. Squinting at the narrow band of light, the soldier stepped over to the door and pushed it open.

Looking across the threshold of the hut, Polyander saw that it was dawn—a reddish sun, slightly tinted with yellow, was rising over the scarlet mountains; below in the glen, illuminated by the morning light, a huge, black basaltic ball was being rolled up the mountain along its grooved channel.

And Sisyphus was rolling it.

Polyander began to shout, his voice shaking from a combination of consternation and the effects of a hangover.

'By the gods, I don't believe it. Is that really you, Sisyphus? I thought Zeus the all-wise had pardoned you? Didn't you say you would go to Corinth with me, and beyond, if necessary—we were going to make our fortunes together.'

Pushing his shoulder against the stone as he spoke, Sisyphus answered:

'My legs, my skin, my feet are old. This younger generation of Greeks is too fast for me. I'd fall behind somewhere in the East and wither away in the hot desert sands. But here—I'm used to it here. I have all the beans I can eat—traps to catch wild goats—wine, cheese every once in a while. I don't need anything else. I'm used to it. You go to your Corinth, traveller, and I'll go to my mountain.

Taking slow, heavy steps, he began rolling the stone.

But before he disappeared from the soldier's view, he growled something out loud to himself:

'I'm g-g-glad to move—towards the wind—useless stones, better to sow now than to reap evil.'

He didn't usually make such long statements, and as a result his speech wasn't very distinct. The soldier didn't catch what he said, but even if he had, it's doubtful whether he would have understood.

As Sisyphus moved farther and farther away, his appearance seemed to change—he looked small and fragile where before he had been solid and muscular, and his stone again became an ingot of burning metal. They quickly drew closer to the top of the mountain, where an invisible force was waiting to throw the stone back down. The soldier was in no mood to again hear the sickening screech and earth-shaking rumble of the stone's downward career, so he quickly grabbed up his armour and ran off on a path which suddenly appeared before him.

As he walked along the path he began to feel heartsick, anguished by a premonition that everything was turned upside down, that Corinth wasn't very friendly nowadays and wouldn't give him much of a welcome. Maybe it would be better not to go there at all. But what then? Was there a home for him anywhere? He was like an arrow shot into the air but without a kindly wind to keep it on course. Now who would turn all those rags and old clothes a glorious regal purple?

He looked back.

Sisyphus was high up now, at the top of the mountainous ridge. The goatskins he was wearing, which Polyander had stupidly tried to dye for him the day before, were shot through with flecks of purple. Alas—he had wasted what was left of his precious purple dye.

Polyander spoke out loud, his voice hot and feverish:

'By the gods, Sisyphus, Homer was right to call you selfish, evil and crafty. Son of Aeolus, you took advantage of me. Could this be an omen? Will I always be a dupe?'

translated by ADELE L. MILCH

# A Modest Genius
## VADIM SHEFNER

1

Sergei Kladesev was born on Vasilyevski Island, Leningrad. He was a strange boy. While other children were making sand pies and building castles, he was drawing sections of odd-looking machines on the sand. In the second grade he built a portable machine, powered by a pocket flashlight battery, which told each pupil how many good marks he would receive during the coming week. Grown-ups considered the machine uneducational and took it away from him.

After leaving grammar school Sergei attended the Technical School for Electrochemistry. He paid no attention to the many pretty girls he met there—perhaps because he saw them every day.

One fine June day he rented a boat and sailed down the Little Neva to the Gulf of Finland. Near Volny Island he came upon a skiff with two girls in it, strangers to him. They had run on to a sandbar and, in attempting to float their boat, had broken the rudder. Sergei introduced himself and helped them back to the dock where they had rented the boat. After that he visited them frequently; the two friends lived, like Sergei, on Vasilyevski Island, Svetlana on Sixth Street, Liussia on Eleventh.

Liussia was attending a course in typewriting at the time, but Svetlana was resting up from school; secondary school had provided all the education she wanted. Besides, her well-off parents were trying to persuade her that it was time to marry; she agreed in principle, but had no intention of taking the first acceptable fellow that came along.

In the beginning Sergei preferred Liussia, but he knew how to behave toward her. She was so pretty, modest and easily embarrassed that in her presence he too became embarrassed. Svetlana was quite different: gay and quick-witted; in short, a daredevil. Though naturally timid, Sergei felt happy when he was with her.

A year later, Sergei was visiting a friend in Roshdestwenka and there met Svetlana, who was staying with relatives. A coincidence, of course, but Sergei took it as providential. Day after day he walked in the woods and by the sea with her and was soon convinced that he could not live without her.

Svetlana did not find him especially attractive. To her he was an average fellow, and she dreamt of finding somebody unusual for her partner through life. She went walking with Sergei in the woods and by the sea only because she had to pass the time with someone.

One evening they were standing on the shore. On the smooth surface of the water there lay, like a carpet woven by nymphs, a strip of silvery moonlight. Everything was still, except for the nightingales singing in the wild elders on the opposite shore.

'How beautiful and quiet!'

'Yes, it's pretty', answered Svetlana. 'If only we could gather some elder branches! But it's too far for walking around on the shore. We have no boat and we can't walk on the water!'

They returned to the village and their respective lodgings. Sergei didn't go to bed that night. He took pencil and paper and filled page after page with formulas and drawings. In the morning he went back to the city and stayed there two days. When he returned he had a bundle under his arm.

Late that evening he took his bundle with him on their walk to the sea. At the water's edge he opened it and took out two pairs of skates for travelling on the water.

'Here, put these water skates on', he said. 'I made them just for you.'

They both put them on and skated easily over the water to the other shore. The skates slid very nicely on the surface on the sea.

On the other shore Svetlana and Sergei broke off elder branches and then, each with a bundle, went slowly over the sea in the moonlight.

From then on they went skating every evening over the mirror-smooth surface of the water, the skates leaving behind them only a narrow, hardly visible trace, which immediately disappeared.

One day Sergei stopped out on the sea. Svetlana slowly approached him.

'Do you know something?', asked Sergei.

'No. What's wrong?'

'Do you know, Svetlana, that I love you?'

'Of course not!', she answered ironically.

'Then you like me a little, too?'

'I can't say that. You're a fine fellow, but I have a different ideal of a husband. I can only love a really extraordinary man, but to tell you the truth, you're just a good average fellow.'

'Well, you're honest, anyway', said a downcast Sergei.

They skated back to the shore in silence, and the next day Sergei returned to the city. For a time he felt wretched. He lost weight and wandered aimlessly through the streets. He often left the city to stroll about. In the evenings he went home to his little workroom.

One day he met Liussia walking along the river. She was glad to see him, and he noticed it immediately.

'What are you doing here, Sergei?'

'Nothing. Just walking. I'm on vacation.'

'I'm just walking too. If you'd like, perhaps we could go over to Cultural Park.' She blushed as she made the suggestion.

They rode over to Yelagin Island and slowly walked along its avenues. Later they met several more times to stroll around the city and found that they were happy to be together.

One day Liussia came to Sergei's house to take him off for a trip to Pavlovsk.

'What a disorganized room!', she exclaimed. 'All these machines and flasks! What are they for?'

'I go in for various little inventions in my free time.'

'And I never suspected!', said Liussia in amazement. 'Could you repair my typewriter? I bought it in a discount store; it's old and the ribbon keeps getting stuck.'

'Sure, I'll take a look at it.'

'What's this?', she asked. 'What an odd camera! I've never seen one like it.'

'It's a very ordinary FED camera but it has an accessory that I built just recently. With it you can photograph the future. You aim the camera at a place whose future appearance you'd like to know, and take the picture. But my machine isn't perfected yet. You can photograph things only three years ahead, no more than that as yet.'

'Three years! That's a lot. What a wonderful invention!'

'Wonderful? Not at all', said Sergei with a disdainful gesture. 'It's very imperfect.'

'Have you taken any pictures?'

'Yes. A short time ago I went out to the suburbs and shot some film there.' He took several prints from his desk.

'Here I photographed a birch in a meadow, without using the accessory. Then here is the same tree in two years' time.'

'It's grown a bit and has more branches.'

'And here it is three years from now.'

'But there's nothing there!', cried the astonished Liussia. 'Just a stump and next to it a pit, like a shell hole. And over there are a pair of soldiers running along stooped. What strange uniforms they're wearing! I can't understand the picture at all.'

'Yes, I was surprised too, when I developed the picture. It looks to me as though there are some kind of manoeuvres going on there.'

'Sergei, you'd better burn that photo. It looks too much like a military secret. That picture might fall into the hands of a foreign spy!'

'You're right, Liussia. I never thought of that.' He tore up the picture and threw it into the stove with a pile of other rubbish; then he set fire to it.

'Now I feel better', said Liussia, obviously relieved. 'But now take my picture as I'll be a year from now. In this chair over by the window.'

'But the accessory will only photograph a certain sector of space and whatever is in it. So, if you're not sitting in that chair a year from now, you won't be in the picture.'

'Take me anyway. Who knows, maybe I will be sitting in this chair this day and hour next year!'

'All right', Sergei agreed. 'I still have one picture left on this roll.' He took the picture. 'Come on, I'll develop the film immediately and make some prints. The bathroom is free today; no one is doing any wash.'

He went into the bathroom and developed the film, then brought it back to his room and hung it up near the window to dry.

Liussia took the film by the edges and peered at the last exposure. It seemed to her that someone else was in the chair. At the same time she was secretly wishing that she might be sitting there in a year's time. It's probably me, she concluded, only I didn't come out too well.

Once the film was dry, they went into the bathroom where the red light was still on. Sergei put the strip of film into the enlarger, turned the machine on, and projected the image on to photographic paper. He then quickly put the picture into the developer. On the paper the features of a woman appeared. She sat in the chair and was embroidering a large cat on a piece of cloth. The cat was almost finished, all but the tail.

'That's not me sitting there!' Liussia was disillusioned. 'It's a different woman entirely.'

'No, it's not you', Sergei agreed. 'I don't know who it is; I never saw the woman before.'

'Sergei, I think I'd better be going', said Liussia. 'You needn't stop by; I can have the typewriter repaired at the store.'

'But at least let me bring you home!'

'No, Sergei, there's no need. I don't want to get mixed up in this business.' She left.

My inventions bring me no luck, thought Sergei to himself. He took a hammer and smashed the accessory.

## 2

About two months later, as Sergei was walking along Bolshoi Avenue, he saw a young woman sitting on a bench and recognized her as the unknown woman of the fateful photograph.

She turned to him: 'Can you tell me the time?'

Sergei told her and sat down next to her. They chatted about the weather and got acquainted. Sergei learned that her name was Tamara. He saw her often and soon married her. They had a son, whom Tamara named Alfred.

Tamara proved to be a very boring wife. Nothing roused much interest from her. Day in and day out she sat in the chair by the window and embroidered cats, swans and stags on little strips of cloth which she then hung proudly on the wall. She didn't love Sergei; she had married him only because he had a room of his own and because after her examinations at the Horse Trainers' Institute she didn't want to work in the provinces. No one had authority to send a married woman away.

Herself a boring person, she regarded Sergei too as boring, un-interesting and insignificant. He was always spending his leisure time inventing something; she didn't approve, and thought it a senseless waste of time. She was constantly scolding him for filling the room with his machines and apparatuses.

To get more freedom of movement in the room, Sergei built his LEAG or Local Effect Anti-Gravitation machine. With the aid of this machine he could do his work on the ceiling of the room. He laid flooring on the ceiling, set his desk on it, and brought up his instruments and tools. In order not to dirty the wall on which he walked up to the ceiling, he glued a narrow strip of linoleum on it. From now on the lower part of the room belonged to his wife, and the upper became his workroom.

Tamara was still dissatisfied: she was now afraid that the superintendent might find out about the expansion of the room space and demand double rent. Furthermore, it displeased her that Sergei should walk so nonchalantly along the ceiling. It just didn't seem right.

'At least have respect for my superior education and don't walk around that way with your head hanging down', she cried up to him from her chair. 'Other women have normal husbands, but here I am, stuck with a bird of ill omen.'

When Sergei came home from work (he worked at the Transenergy Authority as a technical control officer), he ate quickly and went off up the wall to his preserve. He frequently went for walks through the city and its environs so as not to have to listen to Tamara's constant nagging. He became so used to hiking that he could have walked to Pavlovsk with no difficulty.

One day he met Svetlana at the corner of Eighth Street and Sredni Avenue.

'I've married an extraordinary man since we last met', were her opening words. 'My Petya is a real inventor. He's working just now as a beginning inventor at the Everything Everyday Research Institute, but he'll soon be promoted to the intermediate class. Petya has already invented something all by himself: *Don't Steal* soap.'

'What kind of soap is that?', asked Sergei.

'The idea behind it is quite simple—but then every work of genius is simple, of course. *Don't Steal* is an ordinary toilet soap, but its core is a piece of solidified, water-resistant, black India ink. If someone, let's say your neighbour in the community house, steals the soap and washes with it, he dirties himself physically as well as morally.'

'And if the soap isn't stolen?'

'Don't ask silly questions!', Svetlana flashed back angrily at him. 'You're just jealous of Petya!'

'Do you ever see Liussia? How is she getting along?'

'Oh, she's the same as ever. I keep telling her to look for a suitable extraordinary man and marry him, but she says nothing. She seems bent on becoming an old maid.'

Soon afterwards the war began. Tamara and Alfred were evacuated; Sergei went to the front. He began the war as a second lieutenant of infantry and ended as a first lieutenant. He returned to Leningrad, exchanged his uniform for civilian clothes and went back to his old work at the Transenergy Authority. Shortly afterward, Tamara and Alfred also returned, and life went on as before.

**3**

Years passed.

Alfred grew up, finished school, and went through the minimal course requirements for the training of hotel personnel. Then he went south and got a job in a hotel.

Tamara continued to embroider cats, swans and stags on wall hangings. She had grown duller and more quarrelsome with the years. She had also made the acquaintance of a retired director, a bachelor, and was constantly threatening Sergei that, if he didn't finally come to his senses and give up inventing things, she would leave him and go off with the director.

Svetlana was still quite satisfied with her Petya. Yes, he was going places. He'd been promoted to intermediate inventor and had now invented four-sided wheel spokes to replace the old-fashioned round ones! She could really be proud of him.

Liussia still lived on Vasilyevski Island and worked as a secretary in the office of Klavers, which designed and built replacement parts for pianos. She hadn't married and often thought of Sergei. She'd seen him once from a distance but hadn't approached him. He was walking with his wife along Seventh Street on his way to the Baltika Cinema; Liussia immediately recognized his wife as the woman in the photograph.

Sergei thought often of Liussia, too; he tried to distract himself by concentrating on new inventions. The things he made never seemed to him quite perfect and therefore he thought he had no right to get involved with more difficult ones. Recently he had invented a Quarrel Measurer And Ender and installed it in the kitchen of the community house where he lived. The apparatus had a scale with twenty divisions, which measured the mood of the lodger and the intensity of a quarrel that might be going on. The needle trembled at the first unfriendly word and slowly approached the red line. If it reached the line, the Quarrel Ender went into action. Soft, soothing music filled the room; an automatic atomizer emitted a cloud of valerian and *White Night* perfume; and on the screen of the machine appeared a fellow who leaped about in a comical way, bowed low to the viewers and kept repeating: 'Bet at peace with one another, citizens!'

Due to the machine people would make up in the early stages of a quarrel, and all the lodgers in the house were quite grateful to Sergei for his modest invention.

Sergei had also invented a telescope by making a windowpane with the properties of a gigantic magnifying glass. Through this window of his room he could see the canals of Mars, the craters of the Moon and the storms of Venus. When Tamara got on his nerves too much, he distracted and soothed himself by gazing out into distant worlds.

Most of his inventions had no practical value. But one did save him the expense of buying matches. He had succeeded in extracting benzine from water, and, since he smoked a good deal, he now lit his cigarettes from a lighter filled with his own benzine. Otherwise he led a rather joyless life. Neither Tamara nor Alfred brought him any happiness. When Alfred visited Leningrad, he talked mainly with Tamara.

'How are you getting along?', he asked her.

'What do you expect?', she answered him with a question. 'My only pleasure is my art. Look at this stag that I'm embroidering!'

'What a splendid animal!', cried Alfred. 'It's so lifelike! And the antlers! If I had antlers like that, I'd really get somewhere!'

'Your father has no feeling for art. He's only interested in inventing things. But there's hardly any use to what he makes.'

'Well, at least he doesn't drink; you ought to be grateful for that', was her son's encouraging answer. 'He's a slow comer, but maybe he'll wise up a bit. When I look at the people who stop at the hotel, I'm ashamed of Father. One guest is a head buyer, another is a foreigner, another a scientific correspondent. A short time ago a lecturer who wrote Pushkin's autobiography was living in one of our luxury apartments. He owns a country cottage and an automobile.'

'How can I dream of a country cottage with a husband like mine?', Tamara asked dejectedly. 'I've had enough of him. I'd like to get a divorce.'

'Have you hooked anyone else yet?'

'I know a retired director, a bachelor. He has an eye for art! I made him a gift of an embroidered swan, and he was as happy as a child over it. With someone like that you come out on top.'

'What was he director of? A hotel?'

'He was a cemetery director, and he's a serious, sensitive man.'

'He'd have to be, in that job', agreed her son.

## 4

One June evening Sergei was up on the ceiling working on a new invention. He didn't notice the time passing, and it grew quite late. He went to bed but forgot to set the alarm, and overslept the next morning, so that he couldn't get to work on time. He decided not to go in at all that day: it was the first and last time that he stayed away from work.

'You're going to the dogs with your inventions', said Tamara. 'At least you could have missed work for something worthwhile! But this stuff! Clever people earn a bit extra on the side, but you produce nothing, no more than a he-goat gives milk.'

'Don't be angry, Tamara', Sergei tried to calm her. 'Everything will turn out all right. It'll soon be vacation and we'll take a boat ride on the Volga.'

'I don't need your cheap boat rides', Tamara screamed. 'You ought to take a ride behind your own back and listen to what people say about you. They all consider you a perfect fool and laugh at you.'

She snatched an unfinished wall hanging from its hook and stormed out in a rage.

Sergei was thoughtful. He reflected for a long time and then decided to take a ride behind his own back as his wife had suggested. Some time earlier, he had invented an Invisible Presence Machine (IPM), which was effective up to a distance of thirty-five miles. But he had never used the IPM to observe life in the city, thinking it unethical to look into other people's homes or to pry into their private lives. Instead, he often set the machine for the woods on the city's outskirts and watched the birds building their nests or listened to their songs.

Now, however, he decided to test the IPM within the city. He turned it on, set the knob at a very close range and turned the directional antenna towards the kitchen of the community house. Two women were standing at the gas stove, gossiping about this and that. Finally, one of them said: 'Tamara's off to the director's again— and not the least bit embarrassed!'

'I'm sorry for Sergei Vladimirovich', answered the other. 'What a good and clever man—and this woman is destroying him!'

'I have to agree with you', he could hear the first woman say. 'He really does seem to be a good and clever man, but he has no luck.'

Sergei next spied on his fellow workers, and they too had nothing but good to say about him. He turned off the IPM and thought for a while. Then Liussia came to mind and he felt a strong desire to see her again, if only for a moment. He turned the machine on and searched for Liussia's room on the fifth floor of a house on Eleventh Street. Perhaps she no longer lived there? Perhaps she had got married and moved away? Or just changed to another floor in the same building?

Unfamiliar rooms and unknown people flashed on the screen. Finally he found Liussia's place. She wasn't there but it was certainly her room. The furniture was the same, and the same picture hung on the wall as before. On a small table stood her typewriter. Liussia was probably at work.

He next aimed the IPM at Svetlana's house, wondering how she was getting along. He found her rather easily in a house stuffed full of all sorts of brand-new things; she herself had aged a bit but seemed cheerful and content.

Suddenly her bell rang and she went to open the door. 'Hello, Liussia! I haven't seen you for a long time!', she exclaimed in a welcoming tone.

'I just happened by; it's our midday break', said Liussia, and Sergei too could now see her. Over the years she hadn't grown any younger, but she was just as attractive as ever.

The two friends went into the house and chatted about all sorts of things.

'Aren't you ever going to get married?', Svetlana suddenly asked. 'You can still get some worthwhile man in his prime.'

'I don't want one', said Liussia dejectedly. 'The man I like is long since married.'

'Are you still in love with Sergei?', Svetlana persisted. 'What do you see in him? What's so great about him? He's the kind that never amounts to much. He was a nice young fellow, of course. Once he gave me water skates, and we used to skate together across the water. The nightingales were singing on the shore and the people were snoring in their cottages, but we flew across the sea and showed our skill.'

'I never knew he invented anything like that', Liussia said thoughtfully. 'Did you keep them?'

'Of course not! Petya took them to the junk dealer long ago. He said the whole idea was nonsense. Petya is a real inventor and knows what's what with inventions!'

'Is Petya's job going well?'

'Excellent! A short time ago he invented MUCO-1.'

'What's a MUCO?'

'A Mechanical Universal Can Opener. Now housewives and bachelors will be spared all the trouble they used to go to in opening cans.'

'Have you got one?', Liussia wanted to pursue the matter. 'I'd like to see it.'

'No, I haven't and never will. It's to weigh five tons and will require a cement platform. Besides, it will cost four hundred thousand roubles.'

'What housewife can afford one, then?', Liussia was amazed.

'My, you're slow!', said Svetlana impatiently. 'Every housewife won't be buying one. One will be enough for a whole city. It'll be set up in the centre of town—on Nevski Prospekt, for example. There they'll build the UCCOC—United City Can-Opening Centre. It will be very handy. Suppose you have visitors and want to open some sardines for them; you don't need a tool for opening the can and you don't have to do a lot of work. You just take your can to UCCOC, hand it in at the reception desk, pay five kopeks and get a receipt. At the desk they paste a ticket on the can and put it on a conveyor belt. You go to the waiting room, settle down in an easy chair and watch a short film on preserves. Soon you're called to the counter. You present your receipt and get your opened can. Then you return contentedly to Vasilyevski Island.'

'And they're really going ahead with this project?'

'Petya very much hopes so. But recently some jealous people have shown up and are trying to keep his inventions from being used. They're envious. Petya's not jealous of anyone: he knows he's an extraordinary man. And he's objective, too. For example, he has the highest regard for another inventor—the one who invented the *Drink to the Bottom* bottle cap and saw it through production.'

'What's a *Drink to the Bottom* cap?'

'You know how vodka bottles are sealed? With a little metal cap. You pull the tab on the cap, the metal tears and the bottle is open. But you can't use that cap to close it again, so you have to finish the bottle, whether you want to or not.'

'I prefer the water skates', Liussia reflected. 'I'd love to glide across the bay on skates on a white night.'

'The skates have really caught your fancy, haven't they?', Svetlana laughed. 'Petya and I wouldn't want them back if you paid us.'

Sergei shut off his IPM and thought for a while. Then he came to a decision.

## 5

That same evening Sergei got his pair of water skates from an old suitcase. He filled the bath with water and tested them: they didn't sink but slid across the surface just as well as they had done years before. Then he went to his retreat and worked late into the night making a second pair of skates for Liussia.

The next day, a Sunday, Sergei put on his good grey suit and wrapped the two pairs of skates in a newspaper. He put an atomizer and a bottle of MSST (Multiple Strengthener of Surface Tension) in his pocket; if a person covered his clothing with this preparation, it would keep him afloat.

Finally, he opened the large closet in which he kept his most significant inventions and took out his SPOSEM (Special Purpose Optical Solar Energy Machine). He had worked very hard on this and considered it the most important of all his inventions. It had been finished for two years but had never been tested. Its purpose was to restore a person's youth to him, and Sergei had never wanted his youth back again. If he made himself young again, he would have to make Tamara young too and begin life with her all over again—but one life with her was quite enough. In addition, he was frightened at the extraordinarily high energy consumption of the machine; if he were to turn it on, there would be cosmic consequences, and Sergei had never regarded himself as important enough to warrant those consequences.

But now, after thinking things out carefully and weighing all considerations, he decided to use the machine. He put it in with the skates and left the house.

It was a short walk to Sredni Avenue. In a store on the corner of Fifth Street he bought a bottle of champagne and a box of chocolates before continuing on his way. At Eleventh Street he turned off Sredni Avenue and was soon as Liussia's house; he climbed the steps and rang two long and one short on the bell. Liussia answered the door.

'Hello, Liussia! It's been a long time since we met last.'

'Very long. But I've always been expecting you to come, and here you are.'

They entered Liussia's room, drank champagne, and reminisced about things that had happened years before.

'Oh!', cried Liussia suddenly, 'if I were only young again and life could begin all over!'

'That's in our power', said Sergei and showed her his SPOSEM, which was the size of a portable radio and had a rather thick cord attached to it.

'Do you plug it into the electrical system? Won't it burn out? The house was recently switched to 220 volts.'

'No, it doesn't get plugged into the electrical system. A thousand Dnieper powerhouses wouldn't be enough to supply it. It gets its energy directly from the sun. Would you open the window, please?'

She opened it, and Sergei led the cord over to it. The cord had a small concave mirror attached to the end, and Sergei laid this on the window sill so that it was turned directly to the sun. Then he switched the machine on. A crackling could be heard from inside the apparatus, and soon the sun began to look weaker, the way an incandescent bulb does when the current drops. The room grew dusky.

Liussia went to the window and looked out. 'Sergei, what's going on?', she asked in astonishment. 'It looks as though an eclipse is beginning. The whole island is in dusk, and it's getting dark in the distance, too.'

'It's now dark over the whole earth and even on Mars and Venus. The machine uses a great deal of energy.'

'That kind of machine should never be mass-produced, then! Otherwise, everyone would become young again but there'd be darkness from then on.'

'Yes', Sergei agreed. 'The machine should be used only once. I gave it extra capacity for your sake. Now let's sit down and remain quiet.'

They sat down on an old plush sofa, held hands, and waited. Meanwhile it had become dark as night. Throughout the city light sprang out of windows and streetlamps were turned on. Liussia's room was now completely black, except for a bluish light along the cord of the SPOSEM. The cord twisted and turned like a tube through which some liquid was being forced at great speed.

Suddenly the machine gave a loud crack and a square window opened in the front; from it leaped a ray of green light, which seemed to be chopped off at the end. The ray was like a solid object, yet it was only light. It became longer and longer and finally reached the wall with the picture of the pig and the oak tree. The pig in the picture suddenly changed into a piglet, and the oak with its huge branches into a tiny sapling.

The ray moved slowly and uncertainly across the room as if blindly seeking out Liussia and Sergei. Where it touched the wall, the old, faded hangings took on their original colours and became new again. The elderly grey tomcat who was dozing on the chest of drawers changed into a young kitten and immediately began to play with its tail. A fly, accidentally touched by the ray, changed into a larva and fell to the floor.

Finally the ray approached Sergei and Liussia. It ranged over their heads, faces, legs and arms. Above their heads two shimmering half-circles formed, like haloes.

'Something's tickling my head', Liussia giggled.

'Don't move, stay quiet', said Sergei. 'That's because the grey hairs are changing back to their original colour. My head feels funny, too.'

'Oh!', cried Liussia, 'there's something hot in my mouth!'

'You have some gold caps on your teeth, haven't you?'

'Only two.'

'Young teeth don't need caps, so the caps are being pulverized. Just breathe the dust out.'

Liussia pursed her lips like an inexperienced smoker and blew out some gold dust.

'It feels as though the sofa were swelling under me', she said suddenly.

'The springs are expanding because we're getting lighter. We did put on some weight over the years!'

'You're right, Sergei! I feel wonderfully light, the way I did at twenty.'

'You are twenty now. We've returned to our youth.'

At this moment the SPOSEM shivered, rumbled and burst into flame. Then it was gone and only a little blue ash showed where it had been. All around them, everything was suddenly bright again. Motorists turned their headlights off, the street lamps went out and the artificial light disappeared from the windows.

Liussia stood up and laughed as she looked at herself in the mirror. 'Come on, Sergei, let's go for a walk—maybe to Yelagin Island.'

Sergei picked up his bundle of skates, took Liussia's arm, and went down the stairs into the street with her. They rode the streetcar to Cultural Park where they strolled about for a long time, rode the merry-go-round, and ate two meals in a restaurant.

When the still white night had descended and the park was deserted, they went to the sea shore. The sea was completely calm, without even the smallest wave, and in the distance, near Volny Island, the sails of the yachts hung motionless in the moonlight.

'Just the right kind of weather', said Sergei as he unwrapped the water skates. He helped Liussia tie hers and then put his own on.

Liussia ran on to the water and skated lightly across it; Sergei followed. They came to the yachts, whose owners were waiting for a breeze, waved to them, and skated on past Volny Island to the open sea. They glided over the water for a long time, then Sergei suddenly slowed down; Liussia stopped and skated back to him.

'Liussia, do you know what I'd like to say to you?', Sergei began, somewhat unsure of himself.

'I know', Liussia replied, 'and I love you too. From now on we'll stay together for good.'

They embraced and kissed, then turned back to the shore. Meanwhile the wind had risen and was forming waves. It was becoming difficult to skate.

'Suppose I stumble and fall down into the water?', said Liussia.

'I'll take precautions right now so that we won't drown', answered Sergei with a laugh. He took the atomizer and bottle of MSST from his pocket and sprayed his and Liussia's clothing with the liquid.

'Now we can even ride the waves', he said to her.

They sat down, close together, on a wave, as though it were a crystal bench, and the wave carried them back to the shore.

translated by MATTHEW J. O'CONNELL

# Notes on the Authors

## LINO ALDANI

Lino Aldani (born 1926), is best known as the author of the urban dystopia *Quando le Radici* (1977). His short stories have been collected in the volume *Quarta Dimensione* (1964). A professor of mathematics by profession, Aldani was one of the editors of the short-lived SF magazine *Futuro* (1963–1964) and the *Interplanet* anthologies. His short stories have been translated into French, German, Japanese, Spanish and Russian; the story 'Buonanotte Sofia' was adapted for French television (Théâtre de l'étrange, Paris, 1966). The TV version of his story 'L'Altra River' won first prize at the Festival of the Fantastic Film in Trieste in 1970. Aldani has also written some fantasy and is the author of a book on SF, *La Fantascienza* (1962).

## JEAN-PIERRE ANDREVON

Andrevon was born on 19 September 1937. Educated at the École des Arts Décoratifs de Grenoble, he received the Diplôme National des Beaux-Arts in 1965. From 1961 to 1969 he was a professor of art, and he has had a number of exhibitions of his paintings. Andrevon has published fiction and SF criticism in many French periodicals, including *Fiction, Horizon du fantastique* and *L'Écran fantastique*. His many books include the novels *Les Hommes-machines contre Gandahar* (1969), *Le Désert du monde* (1977), and *Le Travail du Furet à l'intérieur du Poulailler* (1984), and the short story collections *Aujourd'hui, demain et après* (1970), *Cela se produira bientôt* (1971) and *Le Livre d'or de Jean-Pierre Andrevon* (1983). Andrevon is considered one of the most innovative French SF writers.

## HERBERT W. FRANKE

Herbert W. Franke, born 14 May 1927 in Vienna, studied physics, mathematics, chemistry, psychology, and philosophy at the University of Vienna from 1945 to 1950. He holds a PhD in theoretical physics. Franke worked for a time as an assistant college professor and later for the Siemens company in Germany. Since 1957 he has been a freelance writer, with many books of a scientific or popular scientific nature to his credit. He has done pioneering work in the field of computer art and is an enthusiastic spelunker. Books on both subjects have been translated into English. As an SF writer, Franke has developed a laconic, unadorned style that is in keeping with his bleak subjects of anti-utopian manipulation and rule. Long before cyperpunk, virtual worlds were a prominent feature of his fiction. Three of Franke's SF novels have been translated into English: *The Mind Net* (New York: DAW Books, 1974, translation by Christine Priest of *Das Gedankennetz*, 1961), *The Orchid Cage* (New York: DAW Books, 1973, translation by Christine Priest of *Der Orchideenkäfig*, 1961), and *Zone Null* (New York: The Seabury Press, 1974, translation by Chris Herriman of *Zone Null*, 1970). Franke's other science fiction includes the novels *Die Glasfalle* (1962), *Die Stahlwüste* (1962), *Der Elfenbeinturm* (1965), *Ypsilon minus* (1976), *Sirius Transit* (1979), *Schule für Übermenschen* (1980), *Tod eines Unsterblichen* (1982), *Transpluto* (1982), *Die Kälte des Weltraums* (1984), *Endzeit* (1985), *Zentrum der Milchstraße* (1990), and the short story collections *Der grüne Komet* (1960), *Einsteins Erben* (1972), *Zarathustra kehrt zurück* (1977), *Paradies 3000* (1981), *Keine Spur von Leben* (1982, radio dramas), *Der Atem der Sonne* (1986) and *Spiegel der Gedanken* (1990), most of them Suhrkamp. Franke was also scientific consultant with Goldmann SF (since 1960), co-editor of Heyne SF (1974–1979), and 1979–1982 again a Goldmann consultant.

### SEVER FELIKSOVICH GANSOVSKY

Gansovsky was born in Kiev in 1918, and worked as a sailor, a stoker and electrical engineer in Leningrad. He died in 1990. In the Second World War he was severely wounded when he volunteered for service in the Red Army to fight against the Germans. Later he worked in Kasakhstan on a horse-farm. When still a student, Gansovsky started publishing stories in newspapers and periodicals and wrote several volumes for children before he turned in the 1960s to science fiction. His time-travel novella *Vinsent Van-Gog* (1971), was filmed in the German Democratic Republic. Gansovsky's SF stories have been collected in the volumes *Shagi v neizvestnoe* (1963), *Shest' geniev* (1965), *Tri shaga k opasnosti* (1969), *Idyot chelovek* (1971), and *Chelovek, kotoryi sdelal Baltiskoie More* (1981). A collection of tales in English translation was published in Russia: *The Day of Wrath* (1989, translated by Alexander Repyev). The title story of that collection was also included in the anthology of Soviet SF *Path Into the Unknown* (London: MacGibbon and Kee, 1966; New York: Delacorte Press, 1968, paperback, Dell, 1968). Further stories were translated in the anthologies *World's Spring*, ed. Vladimir Gakov (New York: Macmillan, 1981) and *Earth and Elsewhere*, ed. Roger DeGaris (New York: Macmillan, 1985, 'A Part of the World').

## VSEVOLOD VIACHESLAVOVICH IVANOV

Ivanov (1895–1963) was no genre writer but an important figure of Russian literature. After an adventurous life in Siberia as a clerk, fakir, clown, member of the Red Guards, political agitator and school director he moved to Leningrad where he became a member of the 'Serapion's Brothers' circle of writers which fought for the independence of art. His first story, published in 1916, caught the attention of Gorky who sponsored him. Many of his stories, beginning with *Partizanskie povesti* (1921–1922) told of the fight of the Communist partisans against the Kolchak Army. His stories and dramas are remarkable for their imagery and unusual situations and motifs; his early work combines realism with romanticism. The story 'Sisyphus, the Son of Aeolus' first appeared posthumously in the periodical *Nash sovremnik* No. 12 (1964).

## WOLFGANG JESCHKE

Wolfgang Jeschke (born 1936) was first a tool-maker and mechanical engineer; later he studied German and English literature and philosophy and worked as an editor for a German reference work publisher. He is best known as an editor of SF. In 1969–1971 he edited an SF series of quality paperbacks for Lichtenberg, in 1973 he became co-editor (with Herbert W. Franke) of Heyne SF, the most successful SF line in Germany, which he has edited as sole editor since 1977. He has put together more than 100 SF anthologies. His own work is small but of excellent quality, remarkable foremost for its stylistic quality. Both of his SF novels have appeared in English translation: *The Last Day of Creation* (London: Century, 1982; New York: St Martin's Press, 1984, translation by Gertrud Mander of *Der letzte Tag der Schöpfung*, 1981), and *Midas* (Sevenoaks, Kent: New English Library, 1990, translation of *Midas*, 1987). His long post-doomsday novella 'The Land of Osiris', translated by Sally Schiller, first appeared in English in *Isaac Asimov's SF Magazine*, March 1985. Jeschke's stories were collected in *Der Zeiter* (1970, greatly expanded paperback 1978) and *Schlechte Nachrichten aus dem Vatikan* (1993, includes also many radio dramas). The best of Jeschke's early stories is a baroque tale of time travel paradox, 'Der König und der Puppenmacher', translated as 'The King and the Dollmaker' in *The Best from the Rest of the World: European Science Fiction*, ed. Donald A. Wollheim (New York: Doubleday, 1976). Jeschke's latest work is a picturesque cosmic tale of genetic manipulation, 'Meamones Auge' (1994). Another story in English is 'A Little

More than Twelve Minutes' in *New Writings in SF*, ed. Kenneth Bulmer (1975).

## GÉRARD KLEIN

Born 27 May 1937, Gérard Klein has studied economics and psychology, in which he holds advanced degrees, and has written books; by profession he is an economic consultant. He started writing at the age of ten and broke into print with 'Une place au balcon' (1955) in *Galaxie*, the French edition of *Galaxy*. Between 1956 and 1962 he wrote some 40 elegant, carefully crafted and poetic stories that often show the influence of Ray Bradbury, and some 200 eloquent critical essays on SF ranging in length from a few pages to one hundred. For his space operas he used a number of pseudonyms: Marc Starr, François Pagery, R. Garance and Gilles d'Argyre. Of the five novels written under the Gilles D'Argyre pseudonym for the Fleuve Noir series, one, *Les tueurs du temps* (1965) was translated by C. J. Richards as *The Mote in Time's Eye* (New York: DAW Books, 1975) and published under Klein's name. The others were *Chirurgiens d'une planète* (1960), *Les voiliers du soleil* (1961), *Le long voyage* (1964), and *Le sceptre du hasard* (1966). The first book under Klein's own name was the collection *Les perles du temps* (1958). Other short story collections are *Un chant de pierre* (1966), *La loi du talion* (1973), *Histoires comme si* (1975) and *Le livre d'or du Gérard Klein* (1979). Klein's first SF novel was *Gambit des étoiles* (1958) in Hachette's SF series 'Le rayon fantastique', translated by C. J. Richards as *Starmaster's Gambit* (New York: DAW Books, 1973). The novel *Le Temps n'a pas d'odeur* (1963) appeared in English as *The Day Before Tomorrow*, translated by P. J. Sokolowski (New York: DAW Books, 1972). Klein's best SF novel *Les seigneurs de la guerre* (1971) was translated by John Brunner as *The Overlords of War* (New York: Doubleday, 1973). In the last decades Gérard Klein has written very little, but he shaped the French SF field as an editor. Since 1969 he has edited the SF series 'Ailleurs et Demain' for publisher Robert Laffont, in which he not only published the crop of Anglo-Saxon SF writers (Philip José Farmer, Philip K. Dick, Frank Herbert, Robert A. Heinlein, Ursula K. Le Guin, Samuel R. Delany, Norman Spinrad, Gregory Benford and many more), but also encouraged French SF writers (Stefan Wul, Michel Jeury, André Ruellan, Philippe Curval). Klein also edited a representative three-volume set of the best of French SF, *Anthologie de la science-fiction française* (1975, 1976, 1977).

## STANISLAW LEM

Born 12 September 1921 in Lvow (now Ukraina), Lem is without doubt the leading SF writer on the continent of Europe. He studied medicine in Lvov (1939–1941, and again 1944–1946), and Cracow (1946–1948), without taking a degree. After the German attack on the Soviet Union he worked as a mechanic for the German Wehrmacht. His first story was written during that time purely as a diversion and published in 1946 in the dime novel series *Nowy świat przygód* ('New World of Adventure'): 'Człowiek z Marsa' (The Man from Mars). His first SF books were *Astronauci* (1951) and *Obłok Magellana* (1955) in which he envisioned a bright socialist future, but his first novel was the contemporary *Szpital przemienienia*, published as part 1 of the trilogy *Czas nieutracony* (1955, 'Time Not Lost'; only the first novel was translated by William Brand as *Hospital of the Transfiguration* (San Diego: Harcourt Brace Jovanovich, 1988). Lem also wrote philosophical discourses on cybernetics (*Dialogi*, 1957) and futurology (*Summa technologiae*, 1964), a meandering tome on the theory of literature (*Filozofia przypadku*, 1968), a highly theoretical tome on SF (*Fantaskyka i futurologia*, 1970), and an autobiographical novel on his youth in Lvov (*Wysoki Zamek*, 1968, translated by Michael Kandel as *Highcastle*, New York: Harcourt Brace, 1995). With translations into some 36 languages and a world circulation of more than 20 million copies, Lem is the most successful author in modern Polish fiction; nevertheless his commercial success in the world is limited, and the bulk of his large editions was due to the special publishing conditions in the Communist countries: Poland, the Soviet Union and the German Democratic Republic. Only in West Germany was Lem really a critical and a commercial success, but in all other countries his sales are very modest, and in recent years interest in him has waned. But he is the only writer of European SF of whom most books have been translated into English, and, despite poor sales, been kept in print in the USA. Lem's critical success in English is due mostly to the excellent translations of Michael Kandel, who, even when he was not named as a translator, re-wrote most of Lem's translations from scratch, except those of Louis Iribarne. Lem's SF novels in English are, all published by Harcourt Brace, except the earliest: *The Chain of Chance* (1978, translation by Louis Iribarne of *Katar*, 1976); *Eden* (1989, translation by Marc E. Heine of *Eden*, 1959), *Fiasco* (1987, translation by Michael Kandel of *Fiasko*, Poland, 1987, first published in German translation 1986); *The Futurological Congress* (New York: The Seabury Press, 1974, translation by Michael Kandel of

*Kongres futurologiczny*, 1971—published as part of *Bezsenność*), *His Master's Voice* (1983, translation by Michael Kandel of *Głos Pana*, 1968), *The Investigation* (New York: The Seabury Press, 1974, translation by Adele Milch of *Śledztwo*, 1959), *The Invincible* (New York: The Seabury Press, 1973, translation by Wendayne Ackerman of the German edition of *Niezwyciężony*, 1964), *Memoirs Found in a Bathtub* (New York: The Seabury Press, 1973, translation by Michael Kandel (only the introduction) and Christine Rose of *Pamiętnik znaleziony w wannie*, 1961), *Peace on Earth* (1994, translation by Michael Kandel and Elinor Ford of *Pokój na ziemi*, Poland, 1987, but published in Swedish, French and German 1986), *Return from the Stars* (1980, translation by Barbara Marszal and Frank Simpson of *Powrót z gwiazd*, 1961), *Solaris* (New York, Walker & Co., 1970; London: Faber and Faber, 1970, translation by Joanna Kilmartin and Steve Cox of the French translation of *Solaris*, Poland, 1961)—filmed by Andrei Tarkovsky in a masterful author's film.

Short story collections, mostly cycles of stories, are: *The Cosmic Carnival of Stanisław Lem* (New York: A Continuum Book, 1981), a reader selected by Michael Kandel; *The Cyberiad: Fables for the Cybernetic Age* (New York: The Seabury Press, 1974, translation by Michael Kandel of *Cyberiada*, 1965); *The Star Diaries* (New York: The Seabury Press, 1976, translated by Michael Kandel) and *Memoirs of a Space Traveler* (1982, translated by Joel Stern and Maria Swiecicka-Ziemianek)—these two volumes comprise the *Dzienniki gwiazdowe* (1957, many later enlarged editions); *Tales of Pirx the Pilot* (1979, translated by Louis Iribarne) and *More Tales of Pirx the Pilot* (1982, translated by Louis Iribarne, Magdalena Majcherczyk and Michael Kandel)—*Opowieści o pilocie o Pirxie*, 1968, individual stories published previously in many different collections; and *Mortal Engines* (New York: The Seabury Press, 1977, translated and selected by Michael Kandel, contains the *Bajki robotów*, 1964, a forerunner of *The Cyberiad*). A hybrid form between story and essay, often in the form of reviews or of introductions to non-existent books, is offered in the collections *A Perfect Vacuum* (1979, translation by Michael Kandel of *Doskonała próznia*, 1971), *Imaginary Magnitude* (1984, translation by Marc E. Heine of *Wielkość urojona*, 1973) and *One Human Minute* (1986, translated by Catherine S. Leach of *Biblioteka XXI wieku*, 1986, but first published in German translation 1983). Excerpts from Lem's criticism of SF are offered in *Microworlds: Writings on Science Fiction and Fantasy*, ed. Franz Rottensteiner (1984). Untranslated remain the early SF novels, a huge sprawling novel *Wizja Lokalna* (1982), the non-serial SF short stories, and most of Lem's non-fiction writings. Lem has hardly written any fiction since *Peace on Earth*, and his latest Polish books are collections of journalistic ephemera: *Lube czasy* (1995), *Sex Wars* (1996), *Tajemnica chińskiego pokoju* (1996) and *Dziury w całym* (1997).

## SVEND ÅGE MADSEN

Born on 2 November, 1938 in Åarhus, Madsen studied mathematics but is a full-time writer of plays, radio dramas, stories and novels that are often of an experimental nature and cross genre borders, containing elements of myth, mystery, the fantastic and science fiction. He has been much influenced by the fairy tales of Hans Christian Andersen, the stories of Tania Blixen and the existentialist philosophy of Søren Kierkegaard (1813–1855). ' "Truth" ', he writes, 'is no longer something handed down to us by the gods, and it is not something which can be arrived at by means of scientific calculation or deduction. "Truth" for me, is determined by those stories for which I can sincerely vouch, those stories which hold meaning for me.' Two of his complex novels are annotated in the third edition of Neil Barron's *Anatomy of Wonder* (1987): *Tugt og utugt i mellemtiden* (1976, translated by James M. Ogier as *Virtue and Vice in the Middle Time*, New York and London: Garland Publishing, 1992), a look at the 1970s in Åarhus from the future, and *Se dagens lys* (1980), an anti-utopian novel. Newer novels in the SF vein are *Edens gave* (1993), *Den usynlige myre* (1995, a juvenile), while *Den største gåde* (1986) and *Kvinden uden krop* (1996) are long SF tales. Some of Madsen's short stories have been translated into English, notably 'The Judge' (in *New Writers 11*, Calder and Boyars, 1974; also in *The Devil's Instrument*, Peter Owen, 1971) and 'On the Way to the Cemetery' (in *Double Danish*, Cormorant Books, 1991), and others. Madsen's books include: *Besøget* (1963, 'The Visit'), *Otte gange Orphan* (1965, 'Orphan Times Eight), *Sæt verden er til* (1971, 'Suppose the World Exists'), *At fortælle menneskene* (1989, 'To Invent Humanity') and *Mellem himmel og jord* (1990, 'Between Heaven and Earth').

## JOSEF NESVADBA

Born in 1926 in Prague, Dr Nesvadba studied medicine, specializing in psychiatry. After writing dramatic sketches he turned to mysteries and the satirical SF stories that were widely translated and made him the best-known Czech SF writer abroad since Karel Čapek. His best work is to be found in his subtly ironic early stories that often take up common themes from earlier SF or refer to it (from H. G. Wells to Fredric Brown). These are to be found in his collections *Tarzanova smrt* (1958), *Einsteinův mozek* (1960), *Výprava opačným směrem* (1962) and *Vynález proti sobě* (1964) which were assembled later in many different editions. His later work of psychological stories and novels, beginning with *Řidičský prukaz rodičů* (1979), *Minehava podruhé* (1981) and the novel *Hledám za manzela muže* (1986) has found less attention in the West. A mystery novel with fantasy elements based on the ideas of Erich von Däniken is *Bludy Erika N.* (1974), while *Dialog s doktorem Dongem* (1964) is a contemporary novel based on Nesvadba's experiences in Vietnam. Many of Nesvadba's stories have been filmed in Czechoslovakia, including 'Death of an Apeman', 'The Idiot of Xeenemünde', 'The Lost Face' and 'Vampires Ltd.' Nesvadba's complexly absurd stories have been widely translated and anthologized. English-language collections of Nesvadba's stories are *Vampires Ltd.* (Prague: Artia 1964, translated by Iris Urwin) and *In the Footsteps of the Abominable Snowman* (London: Victor Gollancz, 1970, US edition as *The Lost Face*, New York: Taplinger, 1971).

## ADRIAN ROGOZ

Born in 1921, Adrian Rogoz studied philosophy and then became a journalist, but also wrote plays and translated poetry (Hölderlin, Rilke, Rimbaud, Poe). His first publication was a poem in the manner of Mallarmé, 'The Nymphaunesque'. He was editor-in-chief of the 466 issues of the Romanian SF magazine *Colectia Povestiri Stiintifico-Fantastice* (1955–1974),a bi-weekly magazine that appeared as a supplement to the popular science magazine *Stiinta si Tehnica*. He is married to the writer Georgina-Viorica Huber-Rogoz. They have been living in Germany for many years. Rogoz's work in the SF field includes a number of stories and short novels and a huge poetic novel written in a synthetic Joycean language that took ten years to write: *Omul și Naluca* (1965). His best stories were collected in the volume *Pretul secant al genuii* (1975).

## VADIM SERGEIEVICH SHEFNER

Born on 12 January 1913, Shefner is a poet and mainstream writer who made only a few excursions into SF. Two short novels 'The Unman' and 'Kovrigin's Chronicles' were published by Macmillan in their 'Best of Soviet SF' series (1980, translated by Alice Stone Nakhimovsky and Alexander Nakhimovsky, and Antonia W. Bouis). His delightfully ironic and poetic urban fairy tales that are told in a charmingly naive manner have been collected in various volumes like *Skromny Genii* (1974), *Imia dlia ptitsy* (1976), *Kruglaia Taina* (1977) and *Skazki dlia Unmykh* (1985).